The First Kiss . . .

At the sight of her, it felt like a fist slammed into Michael's gut, and he remembered Cloe's lips moving on his twelve years ago. She'd been like that the day she'd hurled the ball at him, splitting his lip, all filled with fire and heat and ready to take on the world. The real Cloe, the woman ready to defend herself and what was hers, had that same expression as in the past. She stood now in the March sunlight, powerful, lethal and curved, unvarnished by sweet, feminine wiles, the ones she'd just begun using on him so long ago.

Three Kisses

Cait London

AVON BOOKS
An Imprint of HarperCollins*Publishers*

This is a work of fiction. Names, characters, places, and incidents are
products of the author's imagination or are used fictitiously and are not
to be construed as real. Any resemblance to actual events, locales,
organizations, or persons, living or dead, is entirely coincidental.

HarperCollins*Publishers*
77-85 Fulham Palace Road
Hammersmith
London W6 8JB

ISBN: 0 00 775069 2
www.avonbooks.com

This edition published 2005
First Avon Books printing: November 1998

Avon Trademark Reg. U.S. Pat. Off. and in Other Countries, Marca
Registrada, Hecho en U.S.A.
HarperCollins® is a trademark of HarperCollins Publishers Inc.

Printed and bound in Great Britain by Clays Ltd, St Ives plc

To Lucia Macro, my editor, for her inspiration and confidence in my new career adventure with Avon Books. To all my faithful Cait London readers, who have for years put my series books on their keeper shelves and asked for more. Finally, this book is dedicated to my own personal Wild Willows Club—to my childhood girlfriends, the invincible This 'N Thaters Club, who have remained lifelong friends.

Then there is my mother, Stella, whose loving influence will always be with me.

Prologue

❦

"MY DAD DID not kill stinky old Gus Ballas!" ten-year-old Cloe Matthews exclaimed, as her bicycle sailed toward the Wild Willows' clubhouse. Hidden in a stand of Wyoming cottonwoods, The rickety shelter, made of wooden apple boxes and weathered boards, provided the feeling of safety she needed after seeing her father taken away in handcuffs. Before her prized bicycle skidded to a full stop, Cloe jumped off and ran toward the clubhouse near the stream.

Josy and Angelica, the same age as Cloe, had been riding behind her. They both skidded their bicycles to a stop, too. They glanced uneasily at Cloe's beloved bike, lying in the dust, the kickstand unused. Dropping their bikes beside hers, they scampered inside. Cloe huddled in a corner, knees folded and arms wrapped protectively around herself. She dashed tears from her eyes and glared at her friends, the other two members of the Wild Willows all-girl club. "My dad was good and mad after that man hurt Mom. But he's always said that killing was wrong, and he wouldn't have! He wouldn't have!"

1

"The sheriff comes to our house all the time to talk with my old man. I'll find out what I can," Angelica stated. The daughter of Lolo, Wyoming's most elite family, was harder than her years, and she narrowed her eyes over Cloe's bent head to Josy. "We always take care of each other, don't we, Josy?"

The daughter of a recovering alcoholic, Josy nodded. Then she did what she knew how to do best—comfort. "Angel is smart. Remember how she signed those excuses for us and no one knew they weren't our parents' signatures? Remember how she put a note on poor Mrs. Barnes's garden shed, and Mrs. Barnes went to find the money we left her in that can?"

Josy wrapped her arms tightly around Cloe and rocked her. "Nothing can stop the Wild Willows, and we'll get your dad out of jail, won't we, Angel?"

"Your dad is the best dad there is, Cloe. He's not like my dad—"

Josy looked at Angelica's white face; Angelica kept dark scary secrets and never wanted to return to her big fancy house. She slept under her bed, barricading herself with a thick layer of books and toys.

"My Dad was good and mad, but he didn't kill Gus Ballas," Cloe repeated. She shivered, terrified by the tears that had streamed down her mother's bruised and devastated face, the rage in her father's expression as he had torn from the house to find the man who had raped her mother. "My dad said a man takes care of his own, and he was going to teach Gus a goddamn lesson he wouldn't forget. He never says 'goddamn.' Mom won't give any of us pie if we cuss, and he minds her . . . *he minds her*, just like she does him, unless they're playing and kissing and stuff. He promised her that he wouldn't kill Gus, and my Dad always keeps his promises. He said he was just going to teach Gus manners and that's all he was going to do, not kill Gus!"

Cloe swiped tears from her cheeks. Why wasn't this yesterday, when her laughing father was lifting her onto a horse? When her brothers, Dan and Gabe, were tormenting her and stealing pieces of her mother's best apple pie, cooling on the windowsill? Why wasn't it yesterday, when Michael Bearclaw, her brothers' friend, was teasing her, his gold eyes dancing with mischief?

Fear crawled into Cloe, causing her to shiver. She'd never been afraid, not really. She'd always been safe with her family and at the ranch. But now she knew how Josy and Angelica felt, each uncertain in her own life, strong and happy only when they were together. Cloe had always had what the other Wild Willows craved: a safe, warm, well-fed, well-loved childhood, and for the first time, uncertainty tore at her.

Then, despite the Wild Willows and her mother and brothers, the safety of her childhood tore apart.

Chapter 1

ॐ

"SMALL TOWN GIRL returns—older, wiser, and without a penny to her name. I hate crawling back to Lolo. I really do not want to do this," Cloe muttered to herself as she pushed the brake pedal of the battered, rusted van. On her left hand she wore Bennie, the hand puppet she'd created for an advertising blitz. The van squeaked, easing to the side of the highway overlooking Lolo, and Cloe prayed the brakes would hold on the steep descent into the small Wyoming town.

Her heart was as bitter, bleak, and cold as the February night, and the old, scarred cobblestones that ran, wet and gleaming, through Lolo's main street.

Cloe scanned the moonlit, snow-covered Rocky Mountains in the distance, the recent chinook—a warm wind—had melted most of the valley's snow. She longed for the luxurious purr of her BMW, but her beautiful champagne model had been repossessed. The boxes in the back of the van represented what was left of her twelve-year marriage and career. Cloe inhaled; she'd left Lolo when she was nineteen with only a suitcase and had created the successful, rippleless, glossy life she'd craved.

She'd left behind the 1880s stores—picturesque red brick buildings with their windows that overlooked the historical western town—the cobblestone streets, and the porch posts layered with paint until they were smooth.

She had thought she'd had it all; that she could make her marriage work—but she couldn't.

The rearview mirror of the van, catching her reflection, wasn't kind. The past three months of struggling to survive, the separation severed by her divorce, finalized last week, had left shadows beneath her eyes. Her recent weight loss honed her cheekbones and edged her jaw. A crooked trickle of rain water ran down the windshield, resembling the tear in her perfect life.

One day not long ago, she'd had all her dreams come true. A baby she wanted was nestling inside her. She'd floated down to Ross's office, confident that the baby would repair their marriage and then—well, there was that little problem of his secretary's head in his lap.

Cloe lifted Bennie, her only "companion" on her trip from Chicago. Bennie's round plastic eyes stared at her as she spoke, "My teenage beauty queen days are definitely over."

Bennie's big cloth mouth opened and closed several times. The silence mocked Cloe and she said, "Yeah, right. Life's good. I'm really on top. That's why I'm here, now, with you, broke and facing a town I never wanted to see again."

Cloe frowned and winced, the bruise around her

left eye fading, but still painful. She touched it gingerly with Bennie's hand-thumb. The first and last time Ross hit her was a monument to her ingenuity— Cloe had methodically destroyed his credit and simultaneously his prized image as a hardworking rising executive.

"Amazing. No wonder he needed all those vitamins." After their college graduation, she'd run full blast into the life of an up-and-coming executive power couple, hosting and smiling at Ross's business associates when she ached from doing the work of two people. Before Cloe had discovered Ross's infidelities, she had developed his new sales campaign for Abra Advertising. As his wife and corporate subordinate, she'd put her own career on hold while developing Ross's dynamic presentations. Looking back, she saw how much time she'd given him to play. "He's on his own now, that no-talent—"

Cloe's free hand rested briefly on her stomach. She'd lost the baby just after their separation, which had been cool and smooth; between feeding creditors, she'd crafted it that way. No tears, just the mechanics of tearing her dreams—and Ross—apart. She'd pasted herself together somehow and moved quickly, destroying their lives together with the keen, precise dissection of a surgeon's scalpel and had given him a wedding gift he'd never forget.

After building Ross's career, brick by brick, she knew its weaknesses well. Ross could skim along, wearing the protective cloak of the boss's daughter's new husband, for just so long before Abra Advertising's sympathy crumbled and they'd want honest work from him.

She jammed the van's gear into park and surveyed Lolo, nestling in the Wyoming night like a worn and dirtied book she never wanted to open again.

Her gaze skimmed the valley before it settled on Bearclaw Ridge, its red rocks jutting from the mountain junipers and aspens overlooking Lolo Valley. Over a century and a half ago, a half-blood mountainman, Xavier S. Bear Claw, had stepped from the Rocky Mountain forests and discovered the lush, grassy valley. The bear claw tied to his throat had been ripped from the territorial grizzly he'd just killed. Xavier was painted in rivers of his blood and the bear's, his flesh torn in clawed furrows. But he'd stood on that red jutting rock and with a roar had claimed the land; later he'd charged the passing drovers for use of the grass, and when civilization had moved in, Xavier had taken a mail-order bride from Boston, a lady, and he had founded Bearclaw Ranch. Now Wade Bearclaw's high priced registered Hereford cattle and quarter horses grazed on the lush grass.

Big horn sheep favored the bold, jutting red rock that had been named Bearclaw Ridge, and the Bearclaw men had passed down that huge, ugly claw from father to son, a symbol of keeping what they claimed.

The valley was wrapped in relationships through the years, mostly good. But it was also enveloped in the secrets of The Club, men who sprang from the same roots, but who had chosen a different path.

When spring came, the fields surrounding Lolo would begin to turn emerald green in the sunlight, rich grazing for cattle, and lush crops springing from the black soil. While the good citizens of Lolo slept in their beds and the secrets whispered around the town, Cloe—who never cried—fought back tears. Lolo's night lights twinkled through her tears, and Cloe dashed them away, impatient with herself. The street lamps on the single main street looked like a ribbon heading to nowhere. At thirty-one Cloe suddenly felt old and brittle, as if one more slice of bad luck would crush her.

She leaned back in the van's torn vinyl seat, a spring threatening her bottom. She nudged at it, pushed it back to its correct position, and sat firmly over it. She'd always been strong and talented, and she didn't want anyone seeing her weak and defenseless. Before she drove to The Pinto Bean, the one asset she and her mother owned, Cloe would be back to herself—smart, flip, smooth, glossy, invincible.

She used Bennie to brush away the tears on her cheek. Twenty-one years ago, her life had been torn apart, and now she felt just as shattered.

The western night twinkled overhead and her father rested on a slope of the mountain cutting into the night sky, his grave separated from those of the "good people."

Cloe gripped the stained steering wheel, then reached for the suckers in the Cat in the Hat mug sitting on the littered dashboard. She propped a Gucci boot upon the dash. Her favorite peach flavor did little to stop her urge to turn and run. Or at the least, crawl into the van's back and wrap herself in the comforter where she'd spent the last two nights. Martha Stewart's lush quilted roses hadn't helped then and didn't offer solutions now.

Cloe idly picked up Bennie and cuddled him

against her cheek. She stuck another boot up on the dashboard, the steering wheel between her knees. She studied the boot's leather shine; she refused to start life in the divorce-and-broke pits wearing battered running shoes. She settled back with her thoughts. "Cloe Matthews, up-and-coming advertising executive. At least I'm not wearing the Ross Bennett name anymore, thanks to the legal decree. New packaging, new woman—one who can't afford a motel."

While Ross was getting married again, she'd managed to buy The Pinto Bean, her mother's formerly leased deli and coffee shop. Angelica, now a bank executive in Lolo, had ramrodded the deal through in a matter of an hour. Though Stella had rented the coffee shop for years, now it was hers and Cloe's. It wouldn't have done for Cloe's mother to be evicted for nonpayment twice in her lifetime; the first eviction—from the Matthews ranch—had almost destroyed Stella.

Cloe had no choice but to use the one asset she had to protect her mother and get herself out of Lolo, no strings to the past.

Cloe rolled down the window, leaned her head back against the Turkish towel–covered seat, and inhaled the cold pine-scented air, fighting the tears that rolled down her cheeks.

The sound of footsteps on gravel startled her before Michael Bearclaw loomed beside her van. He leaned down to peer at her as the night wind lifted his sleek black hair. There was nothing sweet or welcoming in his expression—he had the same hard dark eyes, angular face and eyebrows too thick and evil to be tamed that she remembered. A raw-boned, broadshouldered six-foot-three package of arrogant male, Michael Bearclaw was too tough looking and rangy for an advertising campaign. His unrelenting stare speared her, slashing like steel, cutting, seeing what ran beneath skin and control.

When she'd last seen him, he'd been twenty-four to her nineteen, and the years had hardened his face, lined the broad, harsh angles. While coyotes yipped in the night, the moonlight skimmed over his deep-set eyes, gifting him with the alert, predatory look she remembered. His arrogance had remained and the tiny scar she'd given him; the black leather jacket turned up at the collar only enhanced his bad-boy looks.

She almost laughed at herself, at her mind searching for concepts to package a product: Michael fitted the image of a western warlock—soaring black eyebrows, piercing eyes, a nose that angled slightly at the bridge, cutting through the breadth of his wide, blunt cheekbones, followed by a sensuous mouth that curved slowly as he watched her. Dark skinned, a heritage of his Sioux ancestors, Michael was bred of the same western steel as she, as most of the people in Lolo. The fingers resting on her door were blunt, tough, and capable, the big hands of a working cowboy rather than a shoe design expert and world-class footmark examiner, forensic expert, Dr. Michael Jedidiah Bearclaw.

She slapped a mental label on him, "Past Mistake. Do not reopen."

His hand brushed away Cloe's smooth blond hair and was gone before she could slap it away. "You're back and you're a blond. Too bad. I liked that red fire in your brown hair and those wild curls, too."

"I'm not Mopsy any more," she shot back, her tone flat, giving him nothing.

Packaging was everything, Cloe decided darkly, and Michael's looks had nothing to do with the way he attracted women; it was more the cocky tilt of his head, that slow drawl and simmering, challenging male look, that made a woman want him. His eyes were almost gold in sunlight, slashing steel in the shadows now, unreadable.

Cloe had gotten rid of him years ago, when she'd hurled that softball at him and left Lolo.

"At least my hair isn't gray," she swiped at him, noting the moonlit silver at his temples.

Michael's father, Wade, had turned silver almost overnight, after the loss of his wife and Cloe's mother's rape.

When she had last seen her own father in prison, his hair was gray, too. He'd aged centuries in two years, and in another year he was dead.

For a moment Cloe slid into the flowing images of the faces that waited for her in Lolo, all familiar, some of them loving, others dark with hatred—

She'd had enough hatred inside her for the last three months; another drop and she'd shatter into nothing. Her needs were simple now—to survive and to protect her mother. She didn't need Michael's smirking reminder that her hair had once been unruly curls, the shade of curly reddish-brown shared by all the Matthewses, with a spray of freckles that an hour of Rocky Mountain sun could bring back.

She turned away, focusing on Lolo's lights. Michael, in the flesh, was a solid reminder of the mistakes she'd made. "Go away. Go find another road. This one is taken."

"You're pouting. You always used to snarl and hiss and then settle in for a good pout. Then you'd usually come out swinging," he said pleasantly, and the wolfish grin widened as he spotted Bennie snuggled against her cheek.

"You're intruding on my quiet moment, Michael. You may leave anytime."

Michael leaned his hip against the van and crossed his arms. He wasn't going anywhere. Cloe Matthews— what was that jerk's name she married? Michael mentally searched through the newspaper clippings his father had sent him of Cloe—the name "Bennett" slapped him.

Michael had seen pictures of the Bennetts—smooth, glossy socialites, an up-and-coming business team. Bennett wore Cloe like an accessory, and from her expression, she had adored him.

He studied Cloe's smooth profile, her bitter expression. Interesting. Cloe, an upscale Chicago advertising executive, married, and alone on a deserted road, returning to Lolo in a rusty van with her hand in a puppet. She looked as if she'd lost her best doll.

Michael tossed away his current tenderness for her. He steeled himself with the old rage, the old hurt, that Cloe had gone to another man, when all Michael's life, he'd known she was his.

There was nothing sweet about Cloe; there never had been, but at one time he had understood what drove her, the gritty need to succeed, to grasp money and power, and to equal The Club. He didn't blame her; the Matthews family had suffered after Sam had gone to prison."So you're pretty happy about coming back to Lolo, huh?" he tossed at her, just to get her fired up.

If there was one thing Michael appreciated, it was Cloe's temper. He always knew how to nettle and set her off.

Cloe firmed her lips and refused to rise to his bait. How like Michael, to slap her when she was down. Here she was, crawling back into a town she never wanted to see again, and Michael was reading her too easily. An expert at shielding her emotions, Cloe hated people reading her, especially Michael Bearclaw. Typical. Arrogant, confident male.

Cloe started to roll up the window, to close him out of her thoughts and life. The window promptly stuck; she refused to tug at it. She followed Michael's smirk to the lacy bra she'd hung on the rearview mirror to dry. She snatched it away, stuffing it in her large thousand-dollar leather status purse. The final cherry on her ruined-life sundae had been washing her underclothes in an quick food/gas bathroom sink, while waiting for the van's rusted exhaust pipe to be wired onto the dented back bumper.

Well, fine, Michael thought. Cloe wasn't happy, and neither was he. He sure as hell didn't want to ask her for a ride back into town, and he wasn't happy that the sight of Cloe rattled him, that he was sniffing the night air for the tiniest scent of her.

"I need a ride back to Lolo," he stated, straightening. Maybe Lopez, his father's prize quarter horse stud, had done Michael a favor by tossing him into the sagebrush and the mud. He stood there beside her battered van, legs braced apart, his hands in his jeans pockets and his leather coat collar hunched up around his jaw. The cold night wind whipped at his sleek black hair, riffling it.

She eyed him, weighing her chances of taking him down. He hadn't asked, she noted, and that meant he hadn't learned manners since the last time she saw him.

The confident western male image might sell on billboards, but right now she wanted to rip it off him. As if anything ... anyone ... could take something from Michael.

She glanced at him again. The lock of his jaw said that he wasn't exactly happy. The night breeze toyed with a sprig of weathered sagebrush in his hair and he shot a big hand up to dust it impatiently away.

"You look like hell," she told him. Michael wasn't a wimp, but he'd been delivered to her on a moonlit platter at ten-thirty in the evening—a perfect time for revenge. She did what she did best—that long, slow look taking him in and coolly tossing him out like yesterday's newspaper. "For some reason, you're stuck out here—I don't want to know why. You're not getting in my van. I am not giving you a ride."

"Okay. Tomorrow I'll tell everyone I see that I saw you crying and you had a beaut of a shiner." Michael's smirk—a slight lifting of one corner of his mouth—was just as she remembered all those years ago—arrogant, evil, exalted male. The moonlit scar on his bottom lip added to his sinister, rawly masculine look and Cloe hated him just as much as when she had hurled a softball at him.

She knew him as well as her brothers, who had grown up in the same athletic western boys' club as Michael. He was no gentleman when he wanted something; he would carry out his threat. "Get in and don't talk," she said tightly. "I don't want to know anything about you—why you're out here walking, and where you're going, or why. I don't want to know why you're in Lolo, rather than feeling up some model's toes."

"I am a footwear expert, after all, darlin'—forensic footmarks, toss in sole prints, and a consultant for Italian designs. And the models I know haven't complained."

She shot him a searing look that had sent other men scurrying. Michael stared back, his expression unreadable.

She smelled the same. If Michael lived to be two hundred, he'd never forget Cloe's scent. In the van's heated enclosure, the soft touch of heady musk with a hint of lemony wildflowers and tantalizing woman circled him. Thin, tired, and taut, Cloe slashed him a smoky, bitter resenting look that he thoroughly enjoyed. He eased his new custom-made boots away from the clutter of fast food sacks and cups on the van's floorboard. Whoever had given her the black eye had probably paid for it, one way or another.

The black and white coroner's photos of a woman who had been abused by her husband-killer and yet had gone back to him every time slid through Michael's mind. He had been the expert witness who had nailed the husband, an upper-class executive who no one would suspect of beating his wife. Hell, he was doing his daughters, too. The images came at Michael; it was the reason he'd been riding Lopez through the night, matching the great beast's evil temper.

Michael closed his eyes briefly, locking out the brutal sight of the woman's bloody body on the pristine snow. Michael had known, even as he coated the snow with a wax spray, preparing to take plaster casts, that a big man had left Sarah there like rotten garbage. Michael had sensed immediately that the footprint casts matched the size of the husband's shoes. From the weight on the ball of the print and the spray of blood toward the footprints, the husband had probably kicked her, too.

Michael sucked in the cold night air and with it scents of Cloe. She wouldn't be like Sarah—defenseless, mild-mannered, so abused that she felt as if she deserved every kick.

Cloe could always be counted on to finish what she began . . . except the desire she had triggered in him years ago.

Back then, desire was one thread of what he had felt for Cloe. Michael had wanted the whole picture—kids, family get-togethers, neighbors helping each other, safety for his family. If he had stayed in Lolo, he would have faced The Club. That had frightened his father.

He frowned, remembering his father's fear when he had told him. "Michael, don't even think about it. You have no idea what they are capable of," Wade had warned shakily. "Go on, get out of here. Make a life away from here. When it's time, when I'm gone, I want you to sell this place. Take what you want and make certain your sister, Rose, gets everything she wants, then sell the rest. Don't come back. Don't let Rose think for a minute that she's bringing her family back. Promise me you'll stop her if she wants to settle in Lolo."

The plea had nagged at Michael for years, and he'd been too busy to return. While he was back temporarily, he wanted to know why his father was so desperate. Before his death, his father sent the huge bear claw on the thong, a family inheritance from father to son, to Michael. Why?

And now Cloe was back in Lolo, too. As a teenager, she'd glossed over the fire inside her, hidden it. He'd always preferred the real Cloe—hot, steaming, and ready to claw.

Moonlight passing through the window caught the smooth sweep of her hair, tendrils escaping to frame the bones that would keep her young. He'd once wanted to feast upon that too generous, too mobile mouth, now locked into a taut line. The same smooth skin . . . a mix of honey and cream without makeup. Michael doubted that anyone had seen Cloe without cosmetics since she was old enough to buy them with her babysitting money.

He almost thanked Lopez for pitching him. Cloe Matthews had lurked in the back of his mind for years, and now he had caught her creeping back into Lolo, no makeup, no money, and riding on nerves.

An image of twelve-year-old Cloe flashed in his mind—the wind pressing her T-shirt against her budding chest while she rode a bicycle toward him. He'd just finished rolling in the hay with Brenda, and the sight of Cloe, her smooth legs gleaming in the sunlight, muscles surging, had poleaxed him, low in the belly. Even then, she always knew what she wanted, where she was going, and how she was going to get what she needed. She'd shot him a fierce, hot look that had said she knew what he wanted, what he would want from her, and that she'd know how to give it to him, and how to take. Though Cloe was careful her parents didn't know, her lips had been glossy with a sinful red-hot shade, and her long, light brown lashes coated too heavily in black mascara. Her legs had been long and slender-strong, her cutoff shorts too skimpy, just showing the rise of her bottom.

Even then Cloe Matthews could draw lust out of him like a hungry trout after a juicy fly. Later, as a teenager and beauty queen, she'd learned how to blend cosmetics and entice with a slow, secret smile— as if she knew exactly what men wanted and she had it all—her clothes clinging to that long, willowy body, jeans too tight to be decent and a wildly curling long mane of reddish brown hair that a man wanted to grab with both fists. Lust had punched Michael every time he thought of her, and somehow back then he knew that one taste of her would lead to a dangerous addiction.

He was the only boy she didn't have dancing to her call, and that had made her wild enough to go after him. She'd never forgiven him for turning her down in the barn and had beaned him with a softball.

That memory was old trash, but Michael found himself sifting through it. He should have gone after her, told her that he wanted to wait for her, that she needed a chance to see what life was about—and that had been his mistake. Michael hated mistakes.

As a small girl, Cloe had adored him like an older brother. As a young woman, she had always been too systematic, too cool, too controlled. Whatever rode her now was not sweet. Her slender fingers gripped the steering wheel as she turned on the ignition and jammed the shift into gear and the van lurched, hesitated, and speared onto the road leading to Lolo. Despite the battered, rusted van, the woman still looked expensive and classy.

Years ago, a news photo had caught the big diamond on her left hand, and now her artistic long fingers were bare.

"You still drive like hell," Michael murmured, as she sailed over a melting snowdrift; he wanted to hear her speak. He fought the rage within him; he'd like just one punch at whoever had given her the black eye. Michael eased a broken plastic spoon from beneath him and dropped it to the clutter on the floor. The upscale, relax-from-stress cassette tapes that littered the dash board obviously weren't helping her. He pushed the Chuck Berry tape into action and the solid beat of a guitar throbbed in the van. "You used to play rock and roll when you were revved up and ready to take someone out. Who is it now?"

Cloe's jaw locked in silence. He plucked a pill bottle from the dashboard clutter, grabbed the flashlight rolling on the floorboard, and read the prescription label. Cloe snatched the bottle from him and sailed it into the back of her van. Michael recognized the tranquilizers; whatever disturbed Cloe was enough to override her dislike of drugs. Her other hand was white in the moonlight, locked hard to the steering wheel. Her look slapped at him, then back at the winding road taking them down to Lolo.

"Moving back?" he asked mildly, hoping the screeching brakes would hold on the sharp grade. He appreciated the long line of her jeans down to her black Gucci boots—still a size seven, narrow with a high arch, according to his trained eye. He allowed his gaze to stroll back up to the slender curves beneath her black sweater. He wanted to hear that husky purr wrap around him just once more.

Cloe, as though she had just realized she was still wearing the puppet, swiped it off her hand and tossed it onto the back.

He didn't expect her answer. Michael settled back into the seat and closed his eyes; he'd lost enough sleep over Cloe in the past years and his instant desire for her nettled. "Let me off at The Long Horn," he said, indicating the local bar owned by Quinn Lightfeather.

She skidded the van to a stop like a kamikaze fighter coming in for the kill. The clutter in the van rattled and slid, a back tire jumped up on the curb, and after a long look at her, Michael took his time easing out of the cab. She'd tantalized his dreams for years and probably ruined the few attempts he'd made at serious relationships. When a man's morning wake-up call was a hard, pounding ache ready to spurt from him, and he dreamed he had Cloe hot and hungry, naked flesh steaming, in his arms, he deserved a small revenge.

Whatever ran between them, he intended to get Cloe out of his system. He bent down and locked his eyes with hers. "See you."

"Bastard."

"You know, my folks were married," Michael returned easily, and knew that nothing had pleased him in years like the hot look Cloe had just shafted at him.

Chapter 2
∽

CLOE'S HEART KICKED into overdrive as she pulled the van into the tiny alley behind The Pinto Bean. Her mother's battered red Volkswagen bug gleamed in the shadows, water beaded upon it. Lolo was quiet, dogs barking in the distance, rap music coming from the window of a passing car. Snow melted and ran from the roof tops lining the alley, pounding a steady silvery stream into the puddles below.

Her mother's upstairs apartment lights were on at eleven o'clock, long after Stella's usual early bedtime. The 1880s square brick building loomed with the rest of the structures its age, like a two-story monument to a bad investment. Still, The Pinto Bean was her mother's dream, and Cloe now had a half interest.

Her mother would not lose a dream a second time.

Cloe's fingers locked to the steering wheel. "I really do not want to come back here. I'll get Mom to sell out, then leave with me," she muttered, before steeling herself and jerking open the van door.

Her feet touched the wet 1880s cobblestones in the alley; she tightened her lips and shivered with the icy,

21

bald truth. *She couldn't tear her mother from Lolo with a crowbar.*

"Cloe!" Her mother, dressed in a tattered robe, hurled down the outer stairway, her long hair silvery in the moonlight. She hurried to Cloe and hugged her.

The same height at five foot ten, and with a slender build, Cloe's mother held her tight. She'd always been safe in her mother's arms, always loved and warm, even in the bad times.

Cloe hugged Stella tightly, wishing she could have protected her all those years ago when Stella was raped and Gus Ballas was brutally killed. There in the alley, snow water dripping steadily onto the old bricks, the buildings lined like monuments, Cloe's protective walls crumbled softly into the shadows.

Stella leaned back, the years and hard times kind to her face in the dim light. She brushed Cloe's hair back and touched the cool tears upon her cheek. "You're home now, honey. You're safe."

Safe. Cloe almost let out a wild, crazy laugh. When had the Matthews family ever been safe?

"Ross, I suppose." Stella studied Cloe's face and angled it to the light, studying her bruised flesh. She had never liked Ross, but had managed to be civil when she visited them in Chicago. "That man—if you can call him that—has no soul at all. He should have waited a decent time after the divorce before he re-married, not done it the next day."

"Mom, don't—"

"Tell me." A mother who protected her children through years of hardships and gossip, pushed them to keep their pride, Stella stepped back and crossed her arms over her chest.

Cloe plowed through her hurried, thorough revenge. The image of herself, driven by pain and hatred, wasn't pretty. It was as if another woman hadn't slept, working feverishly, obsessed with destroying Ross. She'd torn off the smooth, glossy image of a successful businesswoman and had gone for Ross with her claws. "I sent a penile implant company Ross's picture and endorsement to be used for magazine advertising all over the world. I've screwed his projects as best I could, and I've got most of any work we've done together—rather, my work, for which he took credit—in the computer disks in my bag. He has no records at all or any of the marketing concepts that he is obligated to fulfill. They are gone, deleted, zapped, except for those disks. He'll have to use his own brain—not mine—to get out of this mess, and chances are he'll sink. Eventually they will want an idea out of him, and his new wife isn't going to be happy when she discovers that he hasn't a clue how to create anything past a good spin on a tennis ball."

"He owed you. I suppose once he discovers the extent of how you've ruined him, Ross will be out for revenge."

Revenge. It hadn't given Cloe satisfaction. For three months she'd been coldly dissecting Ross's career, and now, her goal achieved, Cloe was hollow, drained, and more than a little frightened by the future and by herself.

Why didn't she see Ross for what he was?

"He can't admit that most of his career was built on my ideas. He'd be ruined in business. Don't think that this," she lightly touched her bruised eye, "was the usual. He wouldn't have dared, and it cost him."

Cloe skipped wrestling with Michael Bearclaw, his image still stark in her mind—that fresh sage, Wyoming wind, and the scent of memories clinging to him as he filled the van's seat opposite her. "My aim was good. Ross was rolling on the floor, holding his crotch, and I was still standing. He probably couldn't perform on his wedding night."

Cloe swung her overnight bag and her leather purse onto her shoulders, locking the van. *Oh, God. I never wanted to come back here. I wanted money, a lifestyle that meant I'd have a bankroll and a name that caused heads to turn. . . . I'll take care of you, Mom. I'm good, really good at what I do, and no one is taking anything from the Matthewses again.*

The memory of Ross's verbal slap snapped Cloe's head back, her fist locking on the door handle. *"You think I'd want you? Someone who can't carry a baby full term? My family name requires a son, Cloe. The odds are you won't ever be a mother."*

Cloe stiffened, braced herself against the memories ripping through her. Her body felt as though it were a shell of ice covering aching, brittle bones, and one more blow would shatter her. She gripped the stairs' weathered railing, using it as an anchor to hold her in this place, in this time . . . here with her mother. She shot a look down the alley, glistening eerily with clumps of snow and water. She forced away the hungry need for a tranquilizer; she'd taken enough of them in the past months. If she was going to survive, put The Pinto Bean on a paying basis, she'd need her wits.

I'm good at what I do. I can do this. Mom won't be evicted again. . . . She clung to the litany, swinging away from the fear of failure, as she had trained herself to do. She looked up at The Pinto Bean, her mother's dream, a stark monument to the Matthewses' ability to survive—placed smack in front of The Club's noses.

"Your brothers want to buy back the old place, the ranch we had, and set up a partnership, raising cattle and farming. You know Dan was just fifteen and Gabe fourteen when Sam was sent away, but they were already helping your father like men," Stella said, moving up the stairway with Cloe to the second-story apartment's back door. "They want to raise their kids on the old homestead. The new owner's price is reasonable, but—"

Kids. An icy spear shot through Cloe's body and she forced herself not to place her hand over the place where her baby had rested. Only a few weeks of life had nestled within her—then a quick wrench of hellish pain, blood surging down her legs, and a taxi to the hospital. Already separated from her, Ross had been too busy to call, or visit, or express any sympathies. But how could he? He needed them for himself. The pain sliced through her as Cloe forced her body up the stairs, following her mother.

Dumb. Dumb. Dumb. Cloe Matthews Bennett, creative advertising wonder, had actually thought a child would cement a crumbling marriage—she'd gone to tell Ross that day, and found his secretary hard at work—over his open zipper.

"Maybe we can work something out, and my brothers can have their dreams," Cloe murmured. Uh-huh, and she believed in Jack and the Magic Beanstalk.

Cloe glanced at the moonlit back patio, filled with

a clutter of lawn chairs, a table, and rows of clay pots, waiting to be planted with Stella's herbs. *They'd once had a ranch house, cows and horses and crops in the field, and now her mother lived in an apartment over a deli.*

Stella led her into a spotless kitchen with gleaming linoleum, the familiar, enticing scent of Italian bean soup. "The Pinto Bean is my dream, Cloe. Leasing it for all those years was nice, but then you bought it, and now it's all truly mine—and yours, my partner. Thank you for making it come true. I told you that I haven't done a good job managing the books, but I do have faithful customers, and Quinn Lightfeather at The Long Horn Bar has a standing daily order for my soup and breads. He opens late in the day, so he isn't competition. I don't even have to deliver. He always sends someone over to collect the stock pot and breads."

"It's still beans, hmm?" Cloe studied the huge jars lining the counter, filled with lentils, garbanzos, pintos, and others. Her mother's respect and fascination with legumes came from raising a household of hungry kids on a skimpy budget.

"Beans and legumes and grains, the healthiest food in the world. I've got nice Italian mixed bean with zucchini and tomato soup waiting for you. You always liked that—I can't wait until I have fresh herbs. But let me show you what I've done to the apartment since you visited here three years ago. You know, this is the old café where the cowboys—drovers—used to come. It still has great vibrations. Some of my regulars remember their parents talking about coming in here with their families back in the 1880s."

Cloe recognized Stella's uneven tone; Stella wanted

her children safe and well fed—the need would never end, though they were adults, Dan and Gabe with families. *Oh, Mom. I'm glad you don't know everything. I'm glad you're happy. You're always here when I need you . . . I'm sorry I can't stay. . . .*

"*You've forgotten how to be a woman . . . you're a machine. . . .*" Ross had said, smirking at her. Cloe steeled herself against the old taunt; Ross wasn't a part of her life anymore.

Compact and decorated in soft beiges and two matching sofas with floor cushions, plants, and an entertainment center, the living room was comfortable and welcoming. A row of small framed family pictures danced across an old mantel, the tiny ancient fireplace filled with potted plants. Against the wall rested layers of Stella's paintings. Cloe prowled through the delicate landscapes of pastel yellow and pink, an old log building covered with brush. "You're really good. Are you showing them anywhere?"

"I started by ordering an artist's kit from a television program." Stella blushed and brushed her long hair, usually in a neat chignon, back from her cheek. "I enjoy it, but the first time someone told me how awful I am, I'd probably quit. My paintings are like my children, somehow. I . . . they are just too personal, bits and pieces of my life—see that garden with the white picket fence and the marigolds fighting with the garlic by the green beans? The winter onions in the corner? You used to like separating those onion buds—"

Stella swallowed unevenly and pain briefly shadowed her face. She paused, smiling softly at a painting of a topaz cat, lying belly up on a sunlit shelf, eyes sleepy in the window's warm sunlight. "That's your old Topaz. Remember? She used to sleep with you. Remember how Michael climbed that tree after his dog had chased Lucy up? Topaz clawed Michael, the ungrateful hussy. I never could tell what was going on in Michael's mind when he looked at you . . . most other times, he was just like Dan and Gabe, but—"

Stella took Cloe's hand. "I was frightened you'd reconcile with Ross during those three months. So I painted Topaz."

Cloe studied the large, mysterious yellow eyes looking back at her from the canvas. She'd needed Topaz in the past months, warm and cuddly against her empty, aching body.

Stella hurried on, filling the silence. "It's not your penthouse, but it's home. Dan and Gabe remodeled it for me in their spare time. Gabe is so busy at Livingston's Farm Machinery. They couldn't run it without him. I don't know how Dan finds time to do anything other than run his body shop—you really should have the boys look at your van, honey. It sounds awful."

"I'm used to taking care of myself . . . I'm okay."

" 'Okay.' " Anger flashed in Stella's eyes, quickly hidden. "Dan and Gabe bring vegetables from their family gardens. Mickey, Gabe's seven-year-old, is so cute when he brings his red wagon to the door. I pay him a few pennies, nothing like the vegetables are worth, and off he goes . . . Karen, Gabe's ten-year-old, doesn't have time. She wants to be a detective, and you should hear how she talks. Be prepared for 'perps'—perpetrators—and 'M.O.'s and having your fingerprints lifted with her new crime set."

Stella smiled softly. "Karen watches Michael like you used to. She follows him around like you used to do, too. He's a top forensic expert now, and Karen adores him."

Michael Jedidiah Bearclaw. As a teenager, Cloe had wanted him more than air—she pushed away the image of an older, harder Michael, looking as savage in the night as his ancestors.

Stella motioned down the hallway. "The three bedrooms are down the hallway and the office downstairs."

She inhaled, her blue eyes brilliant with tears. "Oh, I'm so glad you've come home, Cloe."

Would everything ever be all right? Cloe hesitated, then wrapped her arms around Stella, holding tight. She feared if she gave herself too much to the softness, she could never leave—and she had to leave Lolo, to make a life somehow . . . to survive—after her mother was safe. She eased away from Stella. "I suppose The Club is still here . . . Bradley Gilchrist, Orson Smith, and the rest."

"Yes." Stella's tight expression said there were still deadly rules and hidden power in Lolo that could crush dreams easily. She drew Cloe into a room, clicked on a light, and kissed her cheek. "You need to rest. Go ahead and settle in, and I'll fix you something to eat."

Cloe entered the big, comfortable bedroom, which looked like home and heaven, comfortably furnished with a handstitched quilt on the Jenny Lind bed. An antique dresser and a full-length mirror completed the furniture; the walls were lined with framed family pictures.

Cloe ran her fingers over the one of Josy, Angelica, and herself, all gangly, nine years old, and full of wicked energy, enough to keep them in trouble for years. "The Wild Willow Girls" had been written across the bottom of the photo in her father's scrawl. They were ready to ride their bicycles down any road, under any bridge, and along the way they'd seen too much—Angelica's father parked, the windows of his gray Cadillac steamed on a lonely shaded lane with a woman who wasn't his wife. A mother of their classmate, a family struggling against the harsh land, had been writhing beneath Bradley Gilchrist. Angelica had paled and then ridden off, never to speak of the incident. Months later, the woman had committed suicide and her family had moved away.

The girls had collected incriminating paper trash, followed the plans of The Club, and sent notes to warn the victims and to threaten the men who ruled Lolo. Angelica had skills—forgery and blackmail—that would have made her father proud, if his friends hadn't been on the wrong end of her efforts. Angelica's mother, Susan, had all the warmth of an Arctic winter; she wanted power, position, and money, and she'd sacrifice everything—even Angelica.

Cloe's fingertips smoothed Josy's wide grin. Josy was the sweet one, fighting to survive with an alcoholic father she loved desperately. Just after Sam Matthews had been sent to prison, Max Small Bird had been drunk, setting a fire that almost ate Lolo and devoured the crops and cattle on thousands of acres. Josy had borne the brunt of Lolo's anger; her father had been too drunk to notice. Angelica and Cloe had protected Josy against the cruelty of other children. For her part, Josy gave absolute loyalty and understanding.

Angelica . . . Josy . . . Cloe. The Wild Willows lived on dreams and schemes and excitement, sisters beneath the skin.

Cloe's fingers strolled to an old gilt frame containing a tattered black-and-white of her mother and father, her brothers, and herself as a gangly ten-year-old. She turned to find her mother at the doorway, her hand over her heart. "That was taken just the year—the year it happened. That was in the spring—see your knee? That mark on it? You'd just scraped it . . . a fall from your new bike. We had just bought that used spreader for the tractor."

"Dad's trial was in the fall. October twenty-second. They worked fast."

Stella inhaled sharply, straightening her shoulders as if ready to battle. "The Club, you mean? That gang of bankers and lawmen and city fathers, more corrupt than any criminal—?"

"You should have moved, and Dan and Gabe. Life here isn't easy for a Matthews. I was making enough at one time to help all of you. Instead, you wanted this place and you wanted to stay."

"I never considered moving away. I wanted to remind them of what they'd done to us—taken away our lives, my husband and your father . . . taken away our ranch. Every day, they see The Pinto Bean and they know. Lolo is a good town, despite The Club. I have friends here, and so do your brothers. I'm not going anywhere."

Stella's head lifted and her eyes burned bright with pride. "They tried to break Sam and they couldn't. The police are still weak and The Club rules through the sheriff. I don't allow any of them into my coffee shop and they know it. Judge Lang has tried. He's retired now, but he's still controlling decisions, playing people. He has to send someone after my soup . . . I won't let him eat it here. He actually sent his cook after my recipe."

Cloe laughed outright, the quick, hard ripping sound, rather like a release of pain, startling her. She glanced out onto Lolo's wet glittering streets below the apartment. Circles of gold lamplight patterned the street, the street lamps old and ornate. "I bet that galls them—to be persona non grata in a deli."

Stella's eyes, as blue as Cloe's, hardened. "So what? The only thing I feel bad about is not managing your investment." The fierce expression settled into a worried one. "You bought into a mountain of bills, honey."

"Mom, you've raised all of us and you've never failed anything in your life," Cloe said, and hugged her mother. "Now feed me some of your fabulous Italian soup."

"You're just skin and bones." Stella turned too quickly, shielding the tears. Her hand shook as she ladled soup into a bowl. "I'm sorry, Cloe. I didn't feel right about letting an outsider, an accountant, tend our family business. And I couldn't worry the boys. But the bills just piled up, and now it is a mountain."

Cloe remembered the hours Stella had spent after her husband had left, toiling over yellow pads and checkbooks to feed and clothe her family, then more hours spent mending and turning Dan and Gabe's collars and cuffs and patching jeans. Cloe moved close, wrapped her arms around her mother, and rocked gently. "We'll be fine, Mom. I'm good, very good, and this could be just what I need right now."

She intended to keep busy; she wouldn't think about the pain slamming into her, dropping her to the floor amid her own blood, and about the lost baby. She wouldn't think about those lost years with Ross; she wouldn't think about anything but surviving.

She wouldn't think about how much she still loved him.

"Cloe Matthews, mad as a wet hen, without that flashy diamond and from the looks of the van, broke. This could get interesting." Michael cradled a glass of his father's favorite smooth Kentucky bourbon. Used to traveling out of a suitcase, Michael hadn't felt the need of a home, and now he wished he'd returned sooner. . . .

He pulled open a deep drawer and studied his father's western Colt revolver, wrapped in the gleaming, bullet-studded gunbelt. A contrast to Michael's sleek Baretta automatic, lying in the bedroom, the revolver had been used in gunfights, protecting the land, and the symbol for the Bearclaw family rested upon it.

He put the gun down, then lifted a leather thong bordered by tiny red trading beads and knots. The huge bear claw dangling from it gleamed in the firelight. Why had Wade Bearclaw sent Michael the sign that Bearclaw men held the land, that they kept what was rightfully theirs?

Michael had grown up in this house. Cowboy spurs and barbed wire hung from the old square nails pounded into logs hewn from the mountain behind Bearclaw Ridge. The original log cabin had been kept safe, serving as the main living room with other rooms added around it. In one corner, plastic sheets gleamed like ghostly reminders of his mother; they covered her sewing corner, where she had slowly, quietly slid into death. Her quilting rack was still hung from the ceiling, a glass Dazey butter churn stood next to the rocker that had soothed children from across the valley. His grandmother's huge wooden bread bowl lay on the shelf near the window, heaped with wool cards and bobbins filled with Bearclaw sheep's wool. The big handmade split oak basket still sat on the floor, filled with balls of dyed wool.

Michael's sister, Rose, had refused to take anything, saying that when it was time, she would sit down over a cup of tea and discuss the matter with a new Bearclaw bride—Michael's bride.

Michael dropped the gleaming bear claw onto the desk. Rose was a romantic, and Michael had lost that inconvenience years ago.

The house echoed with the click-click of his mother's knitting needles, with the whirling of her spinning wheel, walnut glowing richly in the firelight. How many shirts and dresses had his mother made on that old black sewing machine, scrolled in gilt? Too fragile for farm work, she'd spent her hours here, in the shadows and squares of filtered sunlight. There would be scraps in the covered basket, waiting after all these years to be cut and pieced into a quilt. The neighbor women should be coming, gossiping and quilting while their husbands talked of crops and—

The old hoot owl up in the canyon had settled near,

the eerie sound welcome. Michael propped his old work boots up on his father's scarred desk. The boots had been his father's, battered and comfortable, like almost everything else in the spacious log home but the massive hand-hewn bed in the master bedroom. It had been lovingly crafted by a man who had waited and planned for a special woman.

Wade had gotten that woman. Michael didn't resent his father's relationship with Stella Matthews. All those years of nursing Michael's mother were gone now, and if the hefty supply of condoms in the bedside table drawer was any gauge, Stella had put the zing back in Wade's life. Stella was an appealing, generous woman, a sensual woman, who had weathered bad times. Cloe would look like her as she aged—

Cloe. The name whispered around Michael, like her unique scent. In the flames of the fireplace, Michael saw her approaching womanhood, her blue eyes devouring him, hungry—Michael pushed away the heated stirring of his body; he wasn't in the market to start down that old trail with Cloe. *Damn her.* She hadn't waited. Damn her for making his noble effort to wait until she'd gotten a few years older and wiser, to level it into a cowpile.

Back then, he didn't want to make any mistakes with Cloe.

Then, she'd jumped him, wanted everything—right there in the barn—and Michael had turned down her offer.

Cloe wasn't a woman to turn down, not when she came calling like she did that day.

Michael fingered the scar cutting his lip. He could almost see her hurling that softball toward him, with hatred in her eyes. Before impact, he'd moved just that fraction of an inch, protecting himself—and late enough to see the horror on her face. She'd always had spirit and heat, but he'd stood, boots pinned to the ground, locked with the image of the woman pitting herself against him. She'd been beautiful, alive, fiery.

Wade had told Michael that Cloe was ripe and that a female like her was, at nineteen, already fully matured and ready to start life.

But Michael, with one college degree and headed for another, thought he knew better. He'd thought to give her time to cool off, and instead—

Wade's new scanner crackled on the police band, the digital lights jumping, as Lolo's finest spotted Cloe's van parked behind The Pinto Bean and ran a radio check on it. The high-powered scanner was out of place in his father's rustic home; the hidden ultra-sensitive antenna system puzzled Michael, at odds with his father's taste. Wade had sworn that modern electronics were killing family relations and making kids "bug-eyed." When settling into the ranch, Michael had changed Wade's old black rotary dial telephone for a modern connection, allowing his laptop's modem to receive and send information.

Michael's eyes cut back to the scanner; it nagged him. Why had it been hidden? The gleaming black box with leaping, colored digital lights didn't fit in Wade's home or life. Michael had found it beneath a piece of tooled leather, bearing old Wyoming ranch brands. The scanner had been set to the Lolo Police Department frequency. The on/off button had been worn and was not dusty when Michael arrived for the funeral.

While the police dispatcher ran an identification check on Cloe's van, Michael studied his work boots, their leather laces repaired by knots. Michael's high-priced dress shoes weren't suited for manure, but his father's were. The sheriff's deputies picked up the police dispatcher's report, and Michael frowned—Lolo's city police were just as ineffective as ever, taking orders from the Sheriff's Department.

He scanned the framed pictures over the desk, the old logs rich and dark behind it. The six pictures in new walnut frames were lined in an exact row over the desk.

A woman would have used picture matting, a decorator touch, but the photographs were just stuck into the frames. Michael had never known his father to care for pictures, much less frame them.

He studied the pictures, one by one—there were Sam and Wade as teenagers, grinning, with their arms looped around each other's shoulders. Sam and Stella Matthews stood next to Michael's parents with their children tucked up against them. Next, a picture of the Bearclaw family—his sister, Rose, married now and living in Vermont, raising a houseful of kids; his mother, always frail; Michael, in his football uniform at just seventeen and high on a touchdown. The next picture was of Rose, a glowing bride on the arm of her groom, the Bearclaw family around them.

The next picture was of Wade and Michael, a man now, just setting off on his career—his first assignment in Italy to help a leading manufacturer of high-priced shoes scale down the design, modifying it for an average consumer's pocketbook. After that he'd been requested by the New York Police Department to testify on footprints around a maliciously slain woman in the park. The sacrificial cult—just teens, for God's sake—shouldn't have gotten their shoes from the same supplier, an odd brand, retailed to two outlet centers.

Michael narrowed his eyes and studied the last picture—Wade standing with his arm around Stella. A crumbling rose had been pressed beneath the glass. Michael remembered that rose from a Bible that Wade had kept hidden in the barn; he'd discovered it one day while playing and his father had made him promise not to tell. Michael scanned his father's expression in all the pictures, then zeroed back to the last picture. Wade loved his family and his wife, but with Stella, he seemed almost boyishly happy and proud.

Michael smiled. Life had twisted, and Wade was happy to die in her bed.

A detailist, Michael scanned the other pictures in the large living room. Stella's touch remained in the kitchen, though her clothing was neatly placed in Wade's bureau drawer. A woman would have placed the herbal prints in the kitchen, and added The Life's Rules to the bathroom. Those frames had matting. The rest of the house bore pictures of Wade's champion quarter horses, favorite western Remington prints, a collage of family pictures. Michael and Rose's rooms were the same, filled with high school mementos.

The fire crackled in the huge rock fireplace, the house filled with shadows. Michael studied the fat file of newspaper clippings his father had kept, all concerning the Matthews family, beginning with Stella's rape. Inside the plastic holders, the clippings were carefully dated, the ordering precise.

The hair on the back of Michael's hair shifted, his senses prickling. The neatness and order of the clippings was at odds with Wade's usual haphazard filing system. Michael's father had wanted him to come home. Michael flipped open the note from his father, addressed to his mailing service in New York. "It's time I made things right, son. Come home. Dad."

Why? Michael sloshed bourbon into his glass. *What was it his father wanted to make right?*

The six pictures haunted him, his gaze coming back to the one of Cloe, a four-year-old girl riding her father's hip, the wind tossing her short cap of reddish brown curls and her rag dolly tucked under her arm, her knees skinned. Michael wiped the back of his hand across his mouth, the memories bittersweet. The one thing that wasn't right about Michael's life was Cloe Matthews.

He hadn't expected the need to hold her rip into his guts. The need to pick her up as he had when she was a small girl battling tears.

Or lay her back in the van and bury himself so deep and hot in her that she'd forget the man who'd been her husband.

Michael lifted a gold chain that glittered in the firelight, mocking his dreams of long ago. He slid a finger into the chain and lifted it to study the locket, given to him by his mother. The gold locket was old, rich, and gleaming, an inheritance from the Boston woman who had married Xavier S. Bear Claw, reformed mountainman. The oval locket, sheltered by gleaming old gold and a link necklace, matched pearl eardrops, and were handed down from Bearclaw bride to—

Michael crushed the locket in his fist, the rich patina of the old gold gleaming against his dark skin. Before Cloe had jumped him in the barn all those years ago, Michael had been working up the courage to ask her to wear the locket. Back then, he had the need to have Cloe wear his mark, but instead, she—

"It seems I've got a little grudge against Cloe, Dad," Michael muttered, and lifted his glass to Wade's pictures. "You see, she didn't wait for me. Instead, she reached out and took what she wanted. Now, that wasn't nice, was it? Not when I'd been waiting for her all my life. So much for giving her time to mature, to be certain—"

Michael smoothed the scar Cloe had given him, the softball splitting his lip. He should have had stitches, but he treasured that memento of Cloe's passion. He didn't want to think about Cloe at nineteen, thrusting her hips against him, her big blue eyes pleading with him to take her. She'd looked as if one touch would send her up in flames, as if she were opening for him already. He could have done anything but taunt her— hell, he was battling not pushing her flat on her back in the hay, battling his conscience, battling what he wanted for the both of them—what he thought was right, keeping Cloe a virgin until she wore his wedding ring. He'd wanted to see her dressed in white and standing beside him in the old church, with all their families—

Michael abruptly tipped up the glass, drained it, and pushed away the thick manila envelope the Seattle Police Department had sent him about a case. He had enough loose ends to straighten out right here in Lolo, especially with Cloe back in town.

He rubbed his fingers across the hair on his chest and tore open the snaps of his western shirt. He wanted his life straightened. He didn't want to be dreaming about Cloe begging him to make love to her, looking for Cloe in every woman he bedded.

He snorted, deriding himself. In the past ten years, he'd had as many women, but none of the affairs had lasted past the slaking of his need for sex. Slaking? The term was too rich for the methodical coupling of his body to a woman's, the pleasure hurried and gone before he'd rolled away. He'd been fastidious about his relationships, dissecting them, making certain that his partners knew his base rules.

"Damn it," Michael exploded and reached for another glass of bourbon. He didn't allow himself to drink, to block off memories, but tonight, jolted by the sight and scent of Cloe—he'd caught that sweet mountain violet scent and it had hurled him back—

He grabbed the locket and necklace in his fist again, pivoted on the old chair, studied the old fireplace and hurled his glass into the flames.

The locket escaped his hand, the chain slithering free as Cloe had done, years ago. On the desk, tangled with the primitive bear claw necklace his father had sent, the locket gleamed as rich and perfect as Cloe's skin, the bear claw dark and poised to rip into secrets of the past.

Chapter 3

∽

THREE O'CLOCK IN the morning was Cloe's usual prowling time, when the world was safe and dark and quiet. She roamed downstairs—

The Pinto Bean. In her restless, creative mind, she was already packaging, advertising, pushing the name, the products. She had connections, favors to call in, and she knew how to sell. She'd been Ross's tool for years, and now all that experience was going to pay off in keeping The Pinto Bean. From the wooden louvers on the big wide windows to the menu over the coffee bar, she was half owner, for better or worse, in her mother's dream. The Pinto Bean was her first investment without Ross's name on the mortgage, though part of the payment came from the money from her two-carat engagement ring—a status symbol she'd bought herself at Ross's insistence.

Cloe, dressed in men's briefs and her brother's old long black Harley T-shirt, glanced at the quiet streets outside. Dark secrets whispered through the howling night wind—an image of Gus Ballas, a huge, coarse man bending over her, crooning, wanting to touch her hair, slid by; Cloe shivered, slamming the mental door shut on the man who had raped her mother while Cloe played in the barn with the new calf.

Cloe moved through the neat coffee shop. Stella had salvaged the small round tables surrounded by arched wooden chairs from a soda shop that had gone bankrupt; The Club hadn't liked the Armenian family in their midst. The scrolling gilt letters across the window shadowed the shelves lining the wall, running over the huge glass canisters of beans with scoops and a scale and sacks nearby. Behind the counter, lined with stools, were various coffee pots, marked with different flavors—vanilla, raspberry, chocolate, Colombian, and house blend.

Cloe picked up the canister marked "House Blend," opened it, and sniffed. The aromatic blend was just as enticing as any food her mother prepared. Stella had a knack of catering to the senses, visually and in taste. The glass cabinets framed cinnamon rolls and breads and pies, and her mother's homemade crackers were lined in another glass case. There were shakers of Parmesan cheese, pepper grinders, and salt shakers and soup spoons placed upright in pottery mugs across the counter and on each table.

The old drovers who had once filled the old café seemed to linger in the shadows, Bull Durham tobacco tags dangling from their pockets and tall stories on their lips.

I can't bear to see your father like this, Cloe, her mother had cried, after returning from a prison visit. *He really believes he killed Gus . . . he said so and told me to stop trying to get him out and making trouble for us all. How can I stop? How can I?*

Cloe wandered into the tiny, spotless kitchen. She passed the gleaming big steel stove, the huge polished soup pots, and a variety of ladles hanging from the ceiling racks. Wire vegetable bins of potatoes and onions filled a counter, and a huge standing chopping block lined with knives dominated the kitchen.

She ran her fingers over the smooth frame circling her father's picture, which hung on the wall. At twenty-five, he had looked just like her brothers—a rangy westerner, long jean-clad legs, feet firmly locked to the land, the wind whipping his reddish brown curls, and enough arrogance in his grin to stop any woman in her tracks. Dan and Gabe had those same high cheekbones, deep-set eyes, and straight eyebrows . . . that same chin.

She had been only ten when Samuel Matthews had last held her, his hands cuffed as he'd picked her up, his silvery eyes softening. He had held her like a baby on his hip, her long legs dangling beside his. "Pretty girl, you be good for Mama, hear?"

She'd been so angry with him, jerking her face away from his kiss. . . . *How could he leave her?* she remembered thinking angrily, a child faced with an enormous loss, the father she adored.

She braced herself against the fresh wave of tears. She had no time to wallow in the past; she steeled herself for the job ahead of her, getting a good picture of The Pinto Bean, her mother's and her own financial bog. She checked the lock on the back door, which led out to the alley, and bracing herself, clicked on the light to the tiny room just off the kitchen.

The hanging lightbulb exposed Cloe's worst expectations and turned them into a real-life nightmare of unbalanced checkbooks and uncollected tabs from the regulars. Baskets of envelopes and papers loomed on top of stacks of other papers. Another picture of Sam Matthews, this time as a teenager dressed in a high school baseball uniform, hung on the thin boards of the wall.

A soft cry of pain slithered through her. She missed him; he should have been holding his grandchildren and laughing with Stella. Instead, a burst appendix and poor medical treatment had killed him in prison.

Cloe rubbed a mixture of fatigue and tears from her eyes and turned her attention to the bills cluttering the old desk. Joe Issaks had scrawled his name on several scraps of paper, which accounted for "day olds and rest of soups." Stella had marked "paid in full" on Joe's IOUs. Cloe inhaled and remembered Joe at his height, a rodeo rider busting broncs with Friday night hangovers and turning up on Saturday mornings to help at the Matthews ranch. Time ran out for Joe when his legs were crushed beneath a two-ton bull, and while he was recovering, Stella had made a room for him on the back porch.

There were other people who owed her mother. Stella never could turn down a hungry-looking face, a woman fallen upon hard times, or children drooling over her cookies.

Cloe lifted a clutter of old cookbooks and dirty aprons from the battered desk's wooden chair, placing them aside. The movement disturbed the desk's stacked papers, which promptly slid onto the floor. Cloe hefted the papers back onto the desk and noted that a blob of dried blackberry jam stuck the restaurant supply bill to the grocer's. She scanned the disconnect notice from the electric company. Beneath it, other overdue notices scattered everywhere, mixed with recipes clipped from newspapers. The butcher couldn't extend more credit, the bean suppliers demanded a payment of any kind, and a stack of credit card notices had been clipped together with a clothespin.

Cloe ran her finger down the credit card purchases. In the last two months her mother's television home shopping habits had leaped into compulsion. Cloe shrugged; she knew about stress and its outlets.

To Cloe, who had faced a paper war of her own in the last three months, a second war looked as appealing as sharks in a swimming pool. She glanced in the mirror and found her hollow, drained eyes, her hair tousled and beginning to curl; the roots had a good inch margin of natural color and she was lucky it wasn't gray. The skin over her cheekbones gleamed, taut with her loss of weight. Cloe ran her trembling fingertips over the pale face of a tired, burdened woman.

Did she love Ross? Maybe. She'd never asked for love, rather a partner to her needs; they'd worked well together, lived well together—she'd loved the image, the picture of their perfect lives. . . . Why hadn't she seen Ross for what he was, a user and a betrayer? Where was the passion that should have been between them?

"Because I didn't look. Because I was too busy to see what was happening in my own life. Because I wanted success and money and I didn't see that it wasn't real." Cloe inhaled shakily and refused to give in to tears. Once she'd fought her battles, packed herself into the old van with her disks and dead dreams, tears never seemed far away, as if they'd been dammed for years, waiting.

She should have known that Ross had been unfaithful— she'd thought that he was just as tired as she was and she'd been too busy, working for the both of them, building his career and hers, maintaining the lifestyle that suited a young executive couple—seeing that they met the right people, attended the right functions, wore the right brand names, traveled right—

She'd wanted the success picture as badly as Ross, the up-and-coming executives, the power images, exclusive brand names dripping from them. The bright, unshakable couple. . . . She wanted to scream, to let it rip from her into the quiet night—

She glanced at the paperwork waiting for her. She always did the job she was expected to do, and for her mother's financial security—and her own—Cloe gathered herself together, scraping the pieces into herself into the same body and brain. This is what she knew how to do, she thought, pushing away the panic that came when she didn't know why those years existed, why she hadn't seen reality. She shakily eased into the battered wooden chair, forcing her mind to the task at hand. She knew how to organize and plan and this time she'd have to be even better, wiser, because her mother depended on her and because Lolo wasn't watching the Matthewses family lose anything again. Losing the ranch was enough.

Michael listened to dawn crawling upon the mountain, the birds coming to life. Nimo, his father's dog, should have been sleeping by the fire.

Since Michael had come back to stay, none of the

pieces fit, and he wasn't leaving Lolo until he had
finished the puzzle of what his father wanted to finish. He picked up the heavy hunting knife from his
Sioux ancestor, studied the honed, gleaming surface,
and saw Cloe's blue eyes, hard and shimmering with
unshed tears.

Cloe. Michael wanted to kill his fascination with her,
the soft memories of when she had tagged along after
him and her brothers, the time he'd cuddled her when
her favorite cat had died. He hurled the knife expertly
into the board his father had hung on the log wall for
that purpose. The point stuck, the blade and grip
quivering, reminding him of the tension that had run
through him since seeing her once more.

Michael frowned and ran his finger over the scanner. A trained professional, he focused on the missing
pieces at the ranch, not on Cloe, not down that
damned heartless trail again.

His father always kept barn cats for mousing, but
now there wasn't a cat on Bearclaw Ranch. There was
nothing, except for the tracks of the utility vehicle up
on the knoll, where someone had been watching him.

He was an outsider now, after years of traveling,
and they were watching him, waiting for him to leave.

They could wait. Michael flipped open his laptop
computer. He'd worked through the night, disturbed
by Cloe. He brought up his latest case on the screen,
studying the pictures, magnifying details. He needed
to finish his case load, making way for a leave of absence, and he wasn't leaving Lolo. Not just yet.

At five-thirty, Stella came down the stairs. Cloe's
edges were brittle and painful, a fine tension hum-

ming in her that was almost frightening. She was in the tiny office now, punching calculator buttons and stacking papers and muttering.

Her daughter was home and safe. Stella added water to the soup stock and turned it to simmer on the deli's big cookstove. She settled into the everyday rhythm of work, bracing herself for what Cloe would unravel. "They are not taking this away from me, Sam. Not after taking you," Stella whispered furiously.

Sam, something is wrong with me . . . I just can't keep my mind on numbers. Things keep coming back at me—Gus Ballas hurting me, the leers and what the kids went through. I'm scared, Sam. I don't have Wade any more. Has time run out for me?

Then a stronger message came from what ran inside her heart—*You didn't kill Gus, Sam, even if they made you think you did. I know you couldn't have—*

Stella shaped biscuits automatically, sinking into her thoughts just as the rim of the glass sank into the biscuit dough, cutting it. From her shattering rape, Stella knew that Cloe needed routine to keep her plodding in a single line, on track, and then Cloe would slowly make sense of her life.

Stella knew how her day would go. By coffee hour, around ten, the scent of Stella's plate-sized cinnamon rolls and fresh-brewed coffees would bring a crowd to replace the early-morning breakfast crowd. The soup-and-sandwich crowd arrived at noon. By four o'clock, the afternoon coffee-break-and-pie bunch had cleared out, and by five, she would have had all those empty hours to fill.

Taking a cup of coffee to her daughter, Stella leaned against the doorway. Cloe tossed down the pen and stretched, sniffing at the coffee. She cradled the cup in her hands. "Mmm," she murmured appreciatively.

"How bad is it?"

Cloe sipped her coffee and reached out with one hand to tap the calculator, scowling at it. "Not good. But numbers are soldiers. All we have to do is make them line up and play for us."

Stella smiled; Cloe had a smooth way of understating—Sam's way. *Don't worry, honey. This is just a little rough spot. I'll be back home plowing that north field before you know.* "I'm so sorry."

"Mom, look at the pluses. You've done what you set out to do. You've got a huge customer base that keeps returning. You've got Quinn Lightfeather's steady account, and several of the gas stations carry your deli sandwiches and sweet rolls. So you have a good product."

"People like good food. And the bad news?"

Cloe stood, rolled her shoulders. Her weight loss caused pain to whisper through Stella. She remembered her daughter, the sleek, smart advertising executive, shielded by her expensive business suit, prowling through her offices, fishing for ideas, tossing them out, concentrating on packaging, delivering, success. Cloe fed upon success and pride, and now, with a failed marriage behind her, she was hiding her emotions. *Oh, honey . . . I'm so sorry.*

Cloe tugged the string on the lightbulb, darkening the office cubby hole before walking out to the kitchen. She slathered butter and blackberry jam onto a freshly baked biscuit and munched it as she leaned back against a counter. Her long bare legs extended in front of her, as she studied the spotless black-and-white tile. Stella waited; Cloe had inherited Sam's trait of doing what she had to do, doing the job in front of her.

Sam. Stella remembered his expression when he'd found her, those twenty-one years ago, her clothing in shreds, her face swollen and bruised—*Oh, Sam, Cloe needs you now. I'm not cut from the same "do it the way it should be done" cloth. I'm not that strong.*

Bracing herself for what she had to do, Stella checked the biscuits browning in the oven. "Cloe, there's something you should know. I'd rather you heard it from me."

Cloe's eyebrows lifted, and she licked a buttery crumb from her lips. "Gee, Mom, how much better can it get?" she asked, with a touch of humor Stella had not expected.

"You remember Wade, Michael Bearclaw's father, the Bearclaws that own Bearclaw Ranch at the base of the mountains, near our old place?" Stella sipped her coffee and prayed Cloe was up to her news.

Cloe yawned and stretched, her arms over her head. "Dad's friend? How is he?"

Numbers, bills, and a statement of resources plowed through Cloe's head. A good clientele meant a good product. A good product meant that it could be marketed. Her mind was already clicking, fastening on to pluses, packaging them, marketing them. Cloe knew how to sell high-tech products, multimillion-dollar industry, how to make bad products look good, how to— She glanced at her mother, who was too quiet. "Mom? How is Wade?"

Stella pushed her hands down her apron, her fingers spread open. "When things were bad, Wade helped us. His wife was my best friend. You remember Tina, how pretty she was? You remember she died of cancer? Remember before that, how you kids and Michael and Rose all used to play while your father and Tina and Wade and I played cards? They were good friends—"

Cloe frowned, and waited. Her mother never hurriedly relayed harsh news, her words tumbling out into the kitchen sunlight. In the bright light, Stella's cheeks were flushed.

"I want you to hear this from me. Wade Bearclaw died two months ago, Cloe. A heart attack. I lost a good friend—"

"Mom, I'm sorry about Wade. That must be why Michael is back. I gave him a ride into town last night. I didn't want to know why he was out walking at ten-thirty at night."

"Lopez probably threw him. Wade's stallion hasn't been ridden for a while. When Michael heard about Wade two months ago, he left a case in England— you remember those clippings I sent you? Michael came home for the funeral, went back to finish the case, and returned about a month ago. Michael is like his father—he always finishes what he starts."

Stella's face softened. "Michael reminds me of Wade—all tough, invincible male on the outside, and sweet and tender, rather fragile, on the inside. Michael has the same way of tilting his head, an angle that reminds me of Wade."

She glanced at Sam's picture. "And Wade reminded me of Sam, I guess. But we were friends, too, with a history between us."

Stella drew out a huge stainless steel mixing bowl,

dumped in dry yeast, and added warm water, stirring it thoughtfully. "Wade wanted to marry me, but I couldn't let go of Sam, and it wouldn't have been fair to Wade. I was too locked in the past and what might have been if Sam had—"

Her eyes locked with her daughter's. She placed aside the wooden spoon she'd been using and folded her arms over her chest. "Cloe, you should know what the whole town knows . . . Wade Matthews died in my bed."

Cloe's eyes softened, luminous in the harsh light, shadows bruising them. "You always took care of those who needed you, Mom. No one is going to gossip about you taking care of an ill man, taking him into your home to take care of him while you ran your business."

Stella shook her head, her expression amused. She settled her hips against the counter. She'd given Cloe that impetuous, fiery streak. Her daughter always raced on with her own conclusions, lining up reasons and making sense of them to suit her and absolutely confident that she understood everything. Stella wanted to enjoy Cloe's expression.

"Cloe, honey, Wade didn't have a clue that his heart was ailing. Neither did I. He was in good shape, unbelievably good shape—aging beautifully, just as Michael will, with all those strong bones—just a drop of that wild, fierce Indian blood, mixed with pioneer stock. . . . Cloe, Wade died just after we'd had really good sex. He died with a smile on his face."

Cloe's eyebrows shot up. She studied her mother's expression and after a long moment said, "You're enjoying this, aren't you?"

Stella laughed outright. "Would you rather I didn't tell you, and you heard it from someone else? I loved Wade in my way; we took comfort in each other. He knew I would always be married to one man, and that was Sam."

Cloe reached out to take her mother's hand. "Mom, come with me. We can go anywhere we want . . . to San Francisco . . . to Seattle . . . Denver," she said urgently. "I can call in favors. I know people. I'll have a job in no time and you won't have to worry after that. The title to The Pinto Bean should more than pay the bills you owe, and we can start—"

Stella's head went back, pride filling her. "Why would I run now? This is my home, where I belong, where my grandchildren and friends are. The day The Club gets the best of me, that's the day I'll go with you. I don't think for one minute that putting The Pinto Bean on a paying basis is enough of a challenge for you to stay here forever. And when it's time for you to go, I'll understand that, too. You're my daughter, and whatever you choose to do—even if you choose to leave now—I understand."

"I'm not going anywhere, Mom." Cloe sounded older than her years, and deathly tired. Stella fingered the curls like Sam's dark ones. She could almost hear him say, "There, there, baby girl. You'll be fine, Cloe-honey. Do your squalling and then go do what makes it right. You're a fighter. You'll come through."

Everything was always so right . . . and then, suddenly it wasn't.

"Go on up to sleep, honey," Stella urged, aching for her daughter. She lightly touched Cloe's bruised cheek, studying it intently. "We'll talk when you're rested. Ross tried to isolate you from us. That's a sickness . . . not love, honey."

"I know. I'll get it figured out, Mom. Right now—" Cloe wouldn't give way to the tears burning at her lids.

Stella hugged her, turned her, and shoved her toward the stairs leading up to the apartment. "Right now, you'll get some sleep."

"I've tried sleeping. It doesn't work. I'll be down to help you, right after my shower."

Recognizing that her daughter needed her pride, her independence, Stella nodded.

Cloe wiped off the deli counter, picked up the coffee pot, and circled the tables. At ten o'clock in the morning, ideas layered her mind, working, churning—The Pinto Bean needed a recognizable logo which could be used on T-shirts and mugs. The idea wasn't spectacular, but it provided a good building block. Labels needed to be added to the rolls and sandwiches that were packaged for the gas station and quick-stop stores. Images moved through her mind, forms taking shape, the design of a logo. She needed a computer—

Byron Lang, dressed in an expensive western-style suit and a pearl-shaded Stetson, walked by the deli's front window. He stooped to stare under the scrolled gilt sign, scanning the customers and scowling. Cloe knew that Byron's scowls were meant to threaten. She moved closer to the window, poured Jake Willis more coffee, and blandly met Byron's stare through the glass.

The judge's expression went blank. He glanced at Stella, who was visiting with a couple nearby, then back at Cloe. His lips formed "Hell!," his scowl deepening.

"That's right, you old coot, there are two of us now." Cloe smiled slowly, coolly. She reached for the window blind, tugged the cord, and it dropped down, sealing Byron from her.

Dan jerked open the door, the tiny bell ringing over it. Her brother grinned at her and stepped inside, nudged by her other brother, Gabe. The two tall men, dressed in checkered western shirts, denim jackets, and worn jeans, looked so much like her father that Cloe shivered. She carefully placed aside the coffee pot, wiped her trembling hands on the apron covering her jeans, and tried not to cry as she hurried to them.

"Welcome back, sis," Dan drawled with a grin when she stood in front of him. Unable to stop herself, Cloe flung her arms around her two brothers. They looked like anchors, safety she had to have; they looked like love. They were her family and her strength, and she realized in a heartbeat how much she needed them.

"Glad you're home, Trouble," Gabe added. He reached to take Cloe's chin and ease her face into the light. "Who gave you the shiner?"

The words came out as a threatening, protective growl. Gabe released her. "I should have plowed that uppity city boy the first time you dragged him home from college. It cost Mom not to go to you these past three months, but you wanted to handle your life alone. She understood your pride. She would have closed down The Pinto Bean and come to you."

"I managed." Cloe knew exactly what it would

have cost her mother to leave The Pinto Bean. She would have lost everything.

Stella came to hug her children and handed Cloe a flannel lined denim jacket, too large for her. She whipped off Cloe's apron and tossed it to the counter. "You boys take Cloe outside. She's been working since three o'clock this morning. And don't pester her for details. Ross didn't come away walking."

Gabe nodded curtly and stuffed Cloe's arms into the jacket as though she were still a child. "Good enough."

"Button up, tag-along. It's cold outside. Your roots are showing. Bet you have freckles inside of two weeks." Dan flipped her hair, teasing her. Her brothers had rights and used them, asking direct questions and sometimes shoving aside good manners.

"Take me outside to play," Cloe tossed at them. "Leave me at home and I'll tell what you've done."

"Man, I hate tag-alongs," Gabe stated with a big grin. "We used to have to take you everywhere. Carrying extra panties in a guy's jeans while his little sister was potty training was embarrassing."

She elbowed him lightly and linked her arms between her brothers'. "Mother said to take me outside and play," she singsonged, righteously reminding them of their dreaded childhood task.

Sunlight swept down Lolo's main street, danced over the rooftops of the old brick buildings. Cloe inhaled the fresh cold morning. "Lolo looks the same."

A hundred and twenty years ago, drovers had pushed cattle down the dusty streets, and their cattle calls whispered around the shadows of the old brick buildings. Civilization and power came in the form of the old Cattlemen's Club, their descendants still holding power as "The Club."

She avoided the intense expressions of Dan and Gabe as they scanned her face. "You're tired. Bone tired, sis," Dan stated baldly. "You've got shadows under your eyes."

"You're such a gentleman."

Gabe's eyes ripped down her and back up. "Nothing but skin and bones. You're pale as a sheet."

"Thanks. I knew I could count on my brothers to let me have the painful truth, whether I wanted it or not." Cloe closed her eyes against the bright sunshine. When was the last time she'd stood in daylight, breathing fresh air?

The February air ripped through her, freezing but with the sense that soon spring would come, making the earth fragrant, and the valley would come alive. . . .

When was the last time she'd taken time to stand still and listen to the birds?

"Do you want to go to the old place?" Dan asked softly.

Chapter 4

❧

Josy Livingston replaced the telephone to the receiver and punched the button on MKIZ Radio's audio panel. She ran her hand through the practical short, sleek boy cut of her raven hair and smiled. Quinn Lightfeather's call had just given her the best news she'd had in years. Cloe was back in town, and anything could happen once the Wild Willows were reunited. The husky, invitingly sensual voice that was her paycheck's trademark purred out of Josy, smooth as silk despite her excitement. "Now let's listen to the Wild Willows' favorite rock and roll—"

While Chuck Berry's guitar pounded over MKIZ air waves, Lolo's small radio station, Josy leaned back in her chair. Angelica had pushed through another loan on Josy's run-down ranch, but even the vice president of Lolo's First Bank couldn't keep the Small Bird Ranch afloat if she missed another payment.

Cloe. A creative thinker, Cloe had a way of making impossible tasks seem only right. Josy smiled, sipped her coffee, and dialed Angelica's office number. Angelica answered, her tone clipped and businesslike.

Beneath Angelica's steel was a loyal, fighting heart, and a healthy hatred for Quinn Lightfeather. In ways, Josy's childhood life with an alcoholic father was easier than Angelica's high-class cruel one.

"Angel, Cloe is back," Josy stated. "Stella said Cloe has finally divorced that mutt and that she's okay, just tired."

The fire-woman was back, battle weary and scarred. Quinn Lightfeather paused as he washed the Long Horn's front window. Through the dark glass, his view of Lolo's Main Street allowed him to see Cloe ride between Dan and Gabe, her face pale in the shadows of the four-wheeler. Quinn trusted his instincts; he'd depended upon them to survive. *When she is ready, the fire-woman will bring a fresh, clean wind to those around her, and many will fear her.*

Angelica Gilchrist settled back into her bank executive's chair. The Club was entrenched behind the solid walnut doors of the bank's meeting room. A rusty van and Cloe working at The Pinto Bean was enough to stir The Club into a froth. According to Moses Xavier, a regular at The Pinto Bean, Cloe wasn't wearing that status rock on her left hand, third finger, and she was sporting a shiner. "Well, well, well. Interesting. I'll bet hotshot calendar boy didn't walk away from that one," Angelica mused.

Angelica smiled, stood in a fluid motion, and ran her hand over her smooth chestnut-brown chignon. She straightened her collar and the expensive gray designer suit.

"The Wild Willows Girls just could be back in business," she murmured, as she wound her way around the desks to the bank's conference room. Cloe always had a way of making things happen, of stirring a pot until it boiled. As a perfect counterbalance to Angelica's well-plotted style, Cloe moved fast and instinctively. The Club had gotten too confident, and now Angelica wasn't alone any longer. If there was anything Cloe knew how to do, it was to fight, and Josy needed them both now.

Josy was in danger of losing the small ranch where she trained horses, an inheritance from Max Small Bird. Josy was also in danger of losing Cody, her son. Edward Livingston, her ex-husband, had remarried and wanted his son taken from Josy.

Angelica smiled tightly. Cloe knew how to reach Josy, how to give her emotional support that did not come easy to Angelica. Thanks to her family, Angelica knew little about warmth. Stella had been more of a mother than her own, and Dan and Gabe were more caring than her own brother, Jeffrey.

Angelica released the pleased smirk within her; she felt like purring. Add Michael Bearclaw—a controlled, thorough, and dangerous man who would not be pushed—to the mix, and The Club was in for trouble.

"Miss Gilchrist, you can't go in there—" Maxine Stephens, the bank's secretary, began as Angelica strode past her desk.

"My father will want me in the meeting," Angelica stated, as she turned the ornate knob on the solid walnut doors and stepped into the room filled with men. She smiled. "I know you probably just forgot to invite me, so I'm saving you the trouble."

She allowed herself to enjoy The Club's closed expressions, and the disapproving scowl from her father. Angelica did not fit the mold that The Club expected from women; however, if The Club respected anything, it was power. And for the moment, Angelica held a few aces and hefty insights to their shady lives.

She wondered distantly if Jeffrey, her brother, had recently beaten his wife; Ann always had far too many bruises and accidents. Angelica glanced at Edward Livingston; he'd once tried to rape her at one of her parents' elegant soirees. Edward had cheated on Josy from the start of their marriage.

Angelica smiled slightly, coolly. She'd teethed on these games, and the knowledge that she had an edge over her father—he hid his drinking and his lack of power—but not from his daughter. In The Club, where men ruled supreme, Bradley Gilchrist, the head of the powerful clan, could lose face if his secrets came out.

"Gentlemen, is there anything I should know?" she asked lightly, and then eased into a conference chair to enjoy The Club's discomfort.

"The fields will look like the squares of a quilt." The Matthews family quilt, Cloe thought, as she braced her legs apart on the land that had once been Matthews land. She stood between her brothers, the cold wind stirring memories as they stood on the knoll overlooking the ranch. Fields nestled beneath the towering Rocky Mountains, pine and fir and aspens covering the foothills up to the ragged, jutting red rock cliffs and higher to the rugged snow-capped mountains.

To the north stood a cliff that marked Bearclaw Ridge, which marked Bearclaw land, and up on the hill lay her father, overlooking the valley which held Lolo.

"The ranch is up for sale. Two thousand acres of prime land going to waste, and not a cow on it and no working horses. There's the old creek where we went skinny-dipping in the summer. The new owners can't take the lack of social life and a foreign film theater," Dan stated quietly, as he traced the path of antelope moving across the fields. "City folks have grand ideas when they buy a place like this and not a drop of sense on how to feel the land moving beneath their feet."

"They're just people. They wanted a better life for their kids, fresh air, and lots of pets. Looks like the fields need fertilizer. It's a shame they aren't running cattle. There's been cattle on Matthews land since it was homesteaded by our great-great-grandfather Luke. Land ought to stay with the families that loved it and died on it," Gabe murmured, reverence ringing in his deep voice.

Cloe took her brothers' hands and lifted her head, the wind stirring her curls. "There was nothing we could do to keep the ranch. It was mortgaged to the hilt and drought took the crops."

"Before Mom's . . ." Dan swallowed the bitter memory and continued, his head high, "Before Mom was raped, The Club didn't like how Dad told them off, how they shouldn't allow contaminated waste to be buried, despite the profit the corporation offered. He had the Environmental Protection Agency watching them. They would have contaminated the ground-water, the idiots." Fury burned in his tone. "The river would have taken it right to town and the whole valley would have been contaminated. No telling how many people would have suffered—"

"The Club hated that Dad had stepped outside their little circle of arrangements and contacted the EPA. I've always wondered how it would have been if the town had done something to stand with Dad, rather than outsiders doing the job." Rage curled through Cloe. "Someone should have helped."

"They were afraid of losing their own spreads and homes. The Club's roots are deep . . . deeper after they ruined Dad. Remember the day they auctioned everything, that old tractor, the bailer, that trailer? Mom kept her back straight, her chin up as her favorite piano went up for auction. I don't know how she managed, getting that little place in town. She cleaned houses and waitressed at the café and never complained," Dan murmured.

Gabe nodded. "She cried at night behind closed doors. I wanted to bash something, someone—namely, The Club."

"The newspaper wouldn't carry the story. They said they didn't have the space. And worse, they cut off other reporters from other newspapers. What kind of a goddamn newspaper doesn't cover the news?" Gabe asked roughly. "Thank God for Muriel Perkins. The minute she received her inheritance last year, she bought the *Lolo Star*. She must have taught English to everyone in Lolo, and she's never married. She's made the *Star* her baby, and she runs the stories she wants."

Cloe leaned her head on Gabe's familiar shoulder. She was ten when her father was arrested for Gus Ballas's murder, just eleven when her father was put in prison, and twelve when the ranch was auctioned. She remembered her brothers' unreadable expressions when they had moved the Matthewses' few belongings into the old house in a back street. Dan had graduated from high school that year, and had a football scholarship for college. But he had stayed, helping support the family, and at their mother's insistence had taken correspondence courses. When Gabe had graduated the next year, their mother had pushed them both into taking Saturday classes at a junior college a hundred miles away and they continued their correspondence courses.

"What's Mom's situation now?" Dan asked, leaning back against the old Jeep. "When she called me this morning, she said you'd been going over her accounts. You should have seen her face when your money arrived to buy The Pinto Bean. Angelica Gilchrist handled the deal in one hour and brought down the price. Man, she's slick. And tough."

Cloe inhaled the clean air she'd missed. "Angelica didn't want anything to happen to Mom, who's been there for her."

"The Wild Willow bunch sticks together, right?" Gabe asked, grinning as he ruffled his sister's hair. "Ouch!" He jerked away, escaping Cloe's pinch to his butt.

She settled into her thoughts, folded her arms across her chest, and studied the ranch below them.

"She's got that look," Dan stated in the voice of experience.

"Looks like she did when she beaned Michael with that softball, as if nothing could stop her."

Dan grinned. "The guy was lucky it wasn't his family jewels. She fired that ball like a bullet."

"He shouldn't have smirked," Cloe returned, concentrating on the plans swirling around her head. She had no time for Michael Bearclaw's smirk years ago or in the future; she had a job to do and a life to create. She had to push Ross from her mind, and strangle any dreams she had of loving a man, having children. If she *was* a machine, as Ross had said, then she would function just fine.

"Mom won't move," Dan murmured, as he folded his arms over his chest and locked his western boots to the lush, dark soil that had once been Matthews soil. "None of us will."

Cloe lifted an eyebrow. "To answer your question, Mom is charged up to her eyeballs. She's got to do something, and fast."

"Since you're partners now, that means your credit is tied to hers." Gabe crossed his arms, widened his legs, locking them at the knee, and studied the ranch. He kicked a stand of wild gama grass, used by cattlemen before the cultivation of alfalfa. The wild grass had been used by the pioneers when they'd arrived in the valley, their milk cows producing milk to feed and nourish families. "I can barely keep up with expenses, let alone get enough capital saved to set up in business. Matthews land should have cattle and kids running on it. Our kids should be planning to skinny-dip in that creek this summer."

"The mortgage on the body shop isn't freeing up any of my cash," Dan added. "But I dream about cattle and farming the old place, my kids running free on it."

They stood apart, bracing their feet on Matthews land wrapped in sunlight and wind and memories. "We don't expect you to stay, Cloe," Dan said finally. "But we appreciate what you're doing for Mom."

Cloe laughed shakily. "It's not as if I had anywhere to go. I'm broke, and don't you tell Michael one thing about my life."

Dan lifted an eloquent, thick eyebrow. "He hasn't asked."

His smirk earned him a sharp elbow jab in the ribs. "I won't have my brothers and Michael ganging up on me like when we were kids."

"Michael always *protected* you, if you remember. I've got to get back," Gabe stated, checking his watch. "Eddie Livingston may not know his head from his butt, but with my wife and two kids, I don't want to give him any logical reason to dock my pay or fire me. Elaine wants you to come over when you can, Cloe. Mickey and Karen want to see their aunt."

After a last look at the ranch, Cloe and her brothers slid into the old Jeep. Dan didn't turn the key. "This isn't how it should be," he said quietly. "You ought to be coming home . . . really home . . . to the ranch."

Cloe placed her hand on his shoulder. She recognized his deep ache as her own. "Mom seems happy enough," she said, in an effort to turn the sad tide of memories.

"Yeah. Right. I guess you know where Wade Bearclaw died, huh?" Gabe asked with a slow grin that reminded her of her father.

From the back seat, she leaned forward to kiss each brother's cheek and they made a show of rubbing it away, with the prescribed "Yuck. Sister kisses."

The taut frustration inside Cloe eased. She grinned, familiar with their teasing. "I love you guys."

When Cloe entered the kitchen, Joe Issaks was washing dishes, nodding to the beat of the music coming from his earphones. His sagging jeans slipped a little lower with each tap of his foot, and the perpetual cigarette dangled from his lips, a small, thin line of smoke spiraling upward. Periodically, he reached a hand behind him and hitched up his tooled belt. Stella looked up from starting the next day's soup stock. "Ross called for you . . . and Elaine wants us to come over tonight for a family get-together, but only if you're up to it."

Cloe picked up a cinnamon roll, plucked a nut from the top, and munched on it. At two o'clock Wyoming time and three o'clock Chicago time, Ross would probably already have his hand wrapped around a highball glass. Cloe didn't want to think about where his other hand might be, or who might be with him. "I'd like to go to dinner, to see Elaine and the kids. What time?"

Stella chopped onions and tossed them into the pot, the kitchen filling with the scent of beef stock. "Six. Everyone eats dinner at six here in Lolo; even the filling stations close then unless it's hay baling time. Remember when you sewed Dan's jeans closed with baling wire? I was impressed . . . your first sewing attempt to hide your brother's rear end."

Cloe picked another nut from the top of the roll as Joe turned, lifted the headphone, and said, "Hi, Cloe. You're still prettier than the dew on the daisies."

"Oh, you old sweet-talker." She smiled as Joe went back to work, suds flying onto the floor beside him. She studied the angle of his bowed legs. "He still favors that right leg, Mom."

Stella turned slightly, studying Joe. "That leg was the worst. They wanted to take it, but Joe wouldn't let them. Quinn helps him, rubbing oil on it and massaging the muscles."

She glanced at Cloe. "Cloe, Ross said you 'accidentally' removed some of his personal belongings, and he wants them back. He'll pay shipping. He wants them delivered overnight, so there will be less possibility of anything happening to them. Or he'll send a personal messenger to pick them up."

"When hell freezes over, or The Club gets a conscience," Cloe muttered, as Ross's furious face slid through her mind. "He wants the disks. That was *my* work on them. *I* took them."

"Send him back empty disks. Keep your work."

Cloe gave way to her fatigue and the frustration that she'd hidden from her friends in Chicago. Were they her friends? Or were they part of the facade, glossy, revolving, unfeeling window dressings of the up-and-coming popular executive couple?

How could she have loved him? Or did she now?

Stella continued to look at her daughter and suddenly Cloe dashed away the tears burning her eyes. "*Me*—" She thrust her thumb against her chest, making no attempt to hide her bitterness as it poured out of her for the first time. "Me, I made Ross a success . . . I worked my job and did his, lived on no sleep, and got up every day to help him do just that much more . . . that much more—oh, Mom, I rarely saw you and the family."

"You feel used, honey. You're bitter. Those are normal reactions."

"Yes, damn it, I am bitter. If you want to know how I feel, I feel disgust." Cloe fought the rage inside her. Was it for Ross? Or directed toward her own stupidity? "I loved him, Mom. I knew we had some differences, some rough edges, but I thought I could make it work—make it work, isn't that a laugh?"

Cloe tore apart the cinnamon roll and tossed it into the garbage. She'd never opened her emotions to anyone, and now they came pouring out. "I *was* used. Ross hasn't had two ideas to scrape together since he graduated. You're right, I did work two jobs to put him through school, and I did my classes as well, and his homework. Do you know that he graduated in the top five percent of his class? While I was in the middle? When it came to my studies, I was just too tired. Those average grades haunted me when I was first starting out. On the other hand, he was a prime candidate for employment. I was just his tag-along, duhwife."

"I don't believe anyone who ever saw your work would think that. Cloe, you're a believer, and when you believe in someone, something, you support them all the way. That takes heart and strength, and I've always been proud of you."

"Mom, what if I'm not proud of *myself*?" Cloe

asked hollowly, feeling her anger pool out of her, leaving her limp and exhausted. "I let him take advantage of me. I *let* this happen to me. I've always been so in control of my life, knew exactly where I was going, and how to get there. And I couldn't see what was happening in my own marriage. Twelve years. . . . How can that be?"

Stella wiped her hands on her apron and came to put her arms around her daughter, rocking her. Cloe inhaled and held tight to her mother, a woman who had already walked too many painful roads. "Maybe I loved the dream—success, money in the bank, power . . . I probably gave him too much of myself. Then, looking back, I see how much I wanted my marriage to be like yours—perfect."

"There's nothing wrong with loving, honey, or being loyal, or wanting to help your husband succeed." Stella kissed her damp cheek and rocked her in her arms. "But that was then and this is now. You've got to make a life for yourself, Cloe. You've got your family around you now, and you've got to love yourself."

Lopez, reins dragging across the hard-packed reins of the corral, backed from Michael's outstretched hand. "I could sell you," Michael threatened.

Lopez's nostrils flared as he lifted his head to sniff the wind coming from the mares in the pasture. Michael rubbed his bruised backside and refused to give the stud that pleasure.

He backed Lopez into a corner and while the stud eyed him warily, Michael swept out one hand, gathering the reins. "Let's just ride this one out, shall we?"

Lopez was just what he needed after seeing Cloe

standing with her brothers in the valley. Legs spread, hands resting on her waist, body taut against the valley's icy spring wind, Cloe still had more power than any woman Michael had known. The thought burned and nettled as though those twelve years had never spread between them. *They'd never finished that kiss—*

Cloe's bruised, swollen eye nagged at Michael, angered him. He shouldn't feel anything for Cloe, but he did. His hunger was riding him, the need to see Cloe, to torment her.

That bastard hit her, and hurt her some other, deeper way.

Furious with her, with himself for caring, Michael swore.

*All those years, and he still wanted her. Still thought of her wrapped around him, soft and sweet—*Cloe had tossed those years away, and he should have been over her long ago.

Michael snorted and pushed his shoulder against the stud, muscling him into position. He swung up on the saddle in one motion. *Damn. He hated seeing her hurt.* "You're not her older brother anymore, Michael. Get over it. Cloe is a big girl."

That's just the problem. This time, if and when you two come together, the gloves will be off.

Michael swiped his arm across his sweating face. *Gloves off was just the problem. His hands ached to touch that silky, honey-cream skin. He still wanted Cloe, hot and furious, soft and silky skin, battling him, making love—the memory of her lips just brushing his slammed into him. . . .*

Michael reached down to unlatch the corral gate. Lopez barreled through it and Michael pitted himself against the stallion, forcing Cloe from his mind.

Chapter 5

ॐ

"Oh, Josephine?" Angelica crooned, as she tapped her perfectly manicured nails on her leather desk pad. She waited while Josy finished her radio announcement of the local 4-H Club's bake sale, and eased into Mantovani.

"What's up?" Josy, her glossy short-cut hair covered by a ball cap, adjusted her headset while doing paperwork. After a click, her smoky, lilting voice purred, "Now folks, take time from planting that spring lettuce, from playing with your baby chicks, and get out and support Lolo's 4-H kids. This is Coffee Time at MKIZ, and you're listening to Josy Livingston, Lolo's favorite deejay of the year, award courtesy of our one and only Lolo Chamber of Commerce. Eddie Rabbit is on the road now. I can hear those windshield wipers clacking—"

Another click preceded music, paper rattled, and Angelica noted the scratch-scratch. "Josy, are you listening to me?"

"Make it quick, and don't ever call me Josephine again or I'll break those perfect nails you glue on

73

every Sunday," Josy ordered, impatient because Angelica had always taunted her with the feminine name. "I want to push that 4-H bake sale a little more. Then I've got to bake a million brownies for Cody's contribution. He's with Edward tonight—required visitation. Edward wants to 'integrate' him into 'a family environment' with his new wife."

Angelica smiled at the edges that only turned up in Josy when her son was endangered. Josy's life was all hurry-hurry, until it came to her son. Angelica couldn't change Edward's legal visitation rights, but she could distract Josy. "Gosh. Gee. A million brownies. Is that a one oven and a microwave deal, or solar-powered baking pans the size of Texas? I'm impressed. Can I help?"

Click. "This is MKIZ Radio, folks, 590 AM on your radio dial, Lolo's one and only prize-taking radio station. This hour is brought to you by Livingston Farm Machinery, best new and used farm machinery around."

Click. "I hate promoting my ex-husband's business. . . . Stella said Cloe took back the Matthews name. I can really see not wanting to wear some jerk's name tag for the rest of your life. If it weren't for Cody, I'd—bake brownies, Angelica? Get real. You'd break a nail. Then we'd all have to wonder where it was." Josy's normally low, husky tone sharpened. "Is something wrong with my loan papers? With the mortgage?"

Angelica narrowed her eyes. "Nothing is going to happen to the Small Bird ranch, Josy. I'm good at what I do, trust me."

She sensed that Josy's tension eased as she asked, "What's up?"

"Cloe. She's sporting a black eye and she hasn't called me yet. Has she called you?"

"No. What does that say to you?"

Angelica tapped her three-hundred-dollar fountain pen on a stack of paperwork. "It says that Cloe is ashamed to face the two best friends she ever had. I know about being ashamed. I've been there."

"I have, too. When are we cornering her?" Josy sounded firm, enthused, and not afraid that her son would be jerked away from her.

"She's got that black eye, so we'll keep in the shadows. That way it won't be obvious, and she won't be ashamed," Josy stated. "She keeps things to herself, locks them up, like you do. She's not likely to say too much."

"Okay, I get the message. I'm not going to push her into telling her secrets, as if Cloe could be pushed. I detest men like Ross. I knew what he was the minute I met him. We were bridesmaids at her wedding and yet he actually made a pass at me."

"Did you tell Cloe?" Josy asked, after a moment's silence.

Angelica glanced at her father across the bank; if he'd been faithful for an hour, it was a record for him. He'd encouraged her to become more socially experienced, drawing in big money. "How could I tell her she had picked a prime class-A bastard? I hate that feeling of being exposed, when dreams die and everyone knows your business. Cloe's a fighter and all heart, but she's probably devastated about her divorce. She hates failure. We'll have to wear her down, get the details, and convince her that Ross was a real creep and the failure of her marriage wasn't her fault."

"Mmm. It's not like Cloe to take the fall for something that isn't her problem. She told me she thought it would last forever, like her folks' marriage should have done. Got to get back to work, kid. Check with you later," Josy said, clicking off the telephone.

At nine that night, Stella, wearing her battered robe pulled tightly around her legs, said, "While you were in the shower, Angelica and Josy called. They'll be cruising by in a few minutes. Turn on the back porch light if you want to talk with them."

"I don't." How could she face her best friends? She'd left town, married shortly after, so arrogant that she would succeed, that she'd have her perfect world and enough money to buy what she wanted. Now here she was, hating her uncertainty, and her failure. Worst of all, everyone knew exactly how she'd left, filled with dreams, and how she had returned.

Stella lifted her eyebrows. "Too bad. What was that pledge, years ago, about the Wild Willows never refusing to see each other? They love you, Cloe. You're a part of them. I said you'd like to get together tonight, and invited them in. I don't like how Josy is looking lately, and Angelica's too hard and crisp, as if she were all steel and no heart. The three of you were invincible back then. You'd be good for each other now. Don't forget to send leftovers home with Josy, and tell Angelica that I need to hug her, okay?" Stella asked, as she stood, stretched, and bent to kiss Cloe's cheek. " 'Night. Sleep tight, honey."

Alone, the lights turned down, Cloe clicked off the

television set and finger-combed her hair. In the back, a car honked, and she knew it was—"The Wild Willows."

Another honk and she smiled. Josy and Angelica weren't going away. Many years ago, Angelica's girlish voice stated, *"We're here, and you're ours, me and Josy's. I know that The Club had a lot to do with your Dad going to prison, but I can't find out anything. I will, Cloe. Don't you cry. When I grow up, I'm making everything right in this town, and I'm taking that damn Club down. Isn't that right, Josephine?"*

"Angel! Don't use words like that or call me Josephine. Angel is right, Cloe. You're ours. Your mom is just exhausted now, that's why she doesn't have time for you. She's hurting, too, 'cause your Dad is away, and she loves him so much. My dad drinks bad because he misses my mother, but I understand. You haven't lost us, Cloe. Me and Angel are right here. The Wild Willows take care of each other. Did you know that Angel found a mushy note from her dad to Mrs. Wilkins? You should see how good she can copy handwriting—"

In the van, Josy and Angelica moved aside, making room for Cloe between them.

"The last time we did this was after Cloe told us she'd gotten that scholarship to go to Chicago. What a blast! She just picks up the telephone, calls the dean of the school, and does a number on him. She makes herself sound like a genius. He overnights a form, she fills out papers, and *violà*! Our little Cloe is on her way and we settled down to celebrate." Angelica reached into the ice chest, screwed the cap off another wine cooler bottle, and tilted it up to drink. The van creaked beneath the movement. Bennie, the puppet on Angelica's other hand, toyed with Cloe's hair. "I had to sleep on your mother's floor that night."

"You puked up your guts and moo-goo-gai-pan on Stella's carpet. You never should have tried to drink fuzzy navels, mai-tais, and screwdrivers all in the same night. Stella held your head while you worshipped the porcelain god. She knew you had no one to help you at home. I had my own problems, with no sympathy to spare," Josy added with a grin, as she balanced her bottle on her knee. She glanced around the back of Cloe's van, lit by the flashlight on the floor, and hefted a crushed Advil box into a paper sack as though she were shooting a basketball through a hoop. "Nice interior decor. Early hippie? I like the jumbo sunflowers."

Josy glanced at Cloe, her expression concerned, but shielded. "Tough times, huh?"

Cloe drank her wine cooler, barely tasting the peach flavor. They'd come to pry her secrets out of her and make things better. Things weren't getting better; she had an idea, locked onto it like a pit bull, and it would make money. After that, after her mother was safe, she was leaving Lolo. "I don't like you ganging up on me."

"Tsk, tsk. I do apologize . . . well, not," Angelica murmured with a grin, and after digging in the iced cooler, tossed Cloe another bottle. "I've missed picking on you. Josy doesn't know how to throw it back."

Cloe plumped up the pillow behind her. These were her best friends, with the best of intentions, and all she wanted to do was to lick her wounds in private. She fired a look at Angelica. "You want everything, don't you? Here, pick a vein."

"You love us and you know it," Angelica returned,

unbothered as she opened her throat and drained the bottle.

Josy glanced uneasily at Angelica. "Angel, lay off the booze. That's your fifth one."

The soft reminder of Josy's alcoholic father, the problems she'd had as a child, caused Cloe to stop focusing on her own dark life. Angelica shrugged elegantly and held Bennie up to speak very properly. "Josephine, I'm Bennie. Mind your own business. Everyone loves and cares about Angelica. She's perfect."

"We do love you," Josy shot back furiously, pushing the puppet aside and glaring at Angelica. "You know it. You just like being difficult. I've seen an alcoholic's life, and I'm not losing you to that pit." Tears came to Josy's eyes. "You and Cloe are all I have, and Cody. I'm not losing one of you, period, so swallow that, Angel."

Cloe inhaled roughly. Josy's stops were open; she had a gentle heart and was protecting those she loved. Angelica hid her scars well, but the other Wild Willows had always known that at times, Josy and Cloe and—Stella—were all she had. Angelica settled down to sulk, but she returned the bottle to the cooler.

"So, how do we kill him? The old, reliable peel-the-bastard method, or burning toothpicks beneath his nails, or something more inventive?" Josy asked, nudging her worn boot against Cloe's Guccis. Sweet, gentle Josy had the ability to draw both high-powered personalities with her into easier moods.

"It's over." Cloe settled back into her thoughts, barely realizing she was speaking aloud.

"You've always been a ray of sunshine," Angelica

murmured, smoothing back a coppery tendril from her cheek into the smooth chignon. "I thought you were a fighter. Wasn't that in our pact when we were kids?"

"Guilt won't work, Angelica. There's nothing here for me."

"Your family. They needed to see you."

"I'm divorced, Josy," Cloe shot at her, surprised that she had given anyone an insight to her secrets. After months of fighting to survive, to clean up her debts, Cloe wanted to rip into someone, something.

"So what? So is Josy," Angelica said, moving in to protect Josy. "So your big expectations are in the toilet . . . the perfect marriage is in a coffin and you're mad at the world. You always fought much better when you were really mad, revved up, and in a corner. I liked you best then—all flashing steel. I could just see you wear those Wonder Woman bracelets—and that neat, pointed steel bra," Angelica said, stretching out her legs and studying the slender shape in the designer jeans. "I have no doubt that you took care of the bastard in your own way. But remember that Josy hasn't had an easy time, either, and she's got a kid."

Cloe noticed Josy's stiff expression and couldn't bear to think what her friend had suffered. "How is Cody?"

"Worried that he's going to be taken away from me . . . thrilled with each gift Edward gives him. Why do kids have to get caught in between? I hope it's okay that I'm out tonight—"

Angelica glared at her. "If Cody isn't with you, why shouldn't you have a drink with friends? You've got to stop watching your back and let me do it for you."

Temper flashed in Josy's usually soft brown eyes. "I've managed."

"You're too easy on Edward, Josy. By now, I'd have his—"

"Is that why I'm out here, lying between you guys, is to talk about Edward? Hey, is this my pity party, or what?" Cloe interrupted, protecting Josy from Angelica's sometimes too-hard jabs.

"You should have married Michael. I could have been a godmother to more rug rats. You two looked like breeding stock if ever I saw it. You could be riding that stud right now, all sweaty palpitations and midnight screams of lust," Angelica winked at Cloe.

Cloe eyed her coolly. "Ride him yourself, darling."

"Mmm, nice comeback. I've missed that. All those dark, mysterious corners, that rawboned, broadshouldered, hot studly body. And in all this time, El Yummy never married. What do you know about that?"

Angelica snorted delicately, and lifted her head to glance out the van's window. She rubbed the steam from it and peered closer. "Hmm. Here come Lolo's finest. Always sticking their noses into places where they think they can get a payoff."

She scooted to the back of the van just as the doors jerked open. "Hi, Leland," she singsonged as she sat cross-legged in front of the high-powered flashlights.

The lights lasered into the van, finding Josy and swinging to Cloe, then clicking off. Two of Lolo's deputies stood in the moonlight. "Don't you ladies have somewhere else you can go to get drunk?" Leland Jerkins asked.

"We're parked in a private area, behind a business that Cloe owns—"

"Cloe Matthews?" the deputy jerked out, the light clicking on and pinning Cloe.

"You're on private property, Deputy," Cloe said, shading her eyes.

"Leland, I wouldn't want any problems," Angelica stated smoothly. "There won't be any, will there? And get that damn light out of my friend's face." The hard edge of her voice lashed at the deputies, who straightened.

"No, ma'am. Just wanted to check to see that there wasn't any mischief going on in this back alley," Leland murmured. "Come on, Fred."

Angelica grabbed the van's doors and slammed them shut. "Toads."

Cloe couldn't help smiling, then giggling, then laughing until her sides hurt. She realized distantly that the unexpected release was hysterical, bred of keeping her emotions intact, willing herself to survive. Then she began to cry, grabbing a pillow and clutching it to her.

"Move over," Josy ordered softly, lying beside Cloe, and taking her in her arms.

"Make room for me." Angelica settled on the other side of Cloe and drew the opened sleeping bag over them. "Man, this is like old times. The Wild Willows packed into a sleeping bag, talking about boys and planning to raid the world."

Cloe sniffed, her emotions shredding after she'd kept them shielded for years. She tried to stop the tears while Josy and Angelica soothed her. "Why is that? Why did I try so hard? Why didn't I see what was happening?"

"Because you're a hardhead," Angelica answered flatly. "Stubborn. You thought you could make it work. You grew up poor, scraping for every dime, and you wanted money, security. You would have woke up sooner or later. Some things just don't work, no matter how hard you try. You tried. You lost. You'll be okay. The ball game of life goes on."

"So much for a sympathetic shoulder," Josy muttered. "Cloe loved him or she wouldn't have married him."

"I did my teething on reality, chum, and we both know that she was on the rebound from Michael Bearclaw. She wanted to prove something to everyone. That sap she married came from the life she wanted," Angelica snapped back. "I care, Cloe. I don't know the right words. But I'm here, and I care. Got it?"

Josy rocked her on one side and Angelica on the other. "Those cops probably think we're lesbians à trois," Josy whispered after a time, her voice deep and sexy as the steady stream of melting snow water plopped onto the roof of the van.

Angelica giggled wildly and Cloe wiped her eyes, gritty with dried tears. "Lolo's finest must be wondering what's happening in here with the van creaking and rocking."

"Imagine, the finest family in Lolo could have a daughter who isn't straight."

"Oh, you're straight, all right," Josy threw at Angelica. "You have an orgasm just looking at Quinn Lightfeather. The drool on your chin is hard to ignore. You embarrass me and I breed horses for customers."

"It's still Quinn, huh?" Cloe asked.

"I wouldn't waste a single, tiny one of my very many, frequent ecstatic orgasms on Quinn," Angelica said in very elegant tones.

"Oh, sure. You drag Liam McKensie out when you need to have a date, but if Quinn touched you, you'd have more than one itty bitty little orgasm, and you know it. I am going to wet my pants if we laugh any more," Josy said finally, after another round of giggling.

"Don't make me laugh once more." Angelica knelt beside Cloe, looking down at her tenderly. "Better?"

Here they were, her friends, Josy holding her hand on one side and Angelica on the other side, just as they had on the day her father had died. She studied their faces, women now, with hardships behind and in front of them.

They were hers; she gave them the piece of her heart that had not been savaged, a bit of reclaimed pride. "I changed my name back to Matthews."

"Way better." Josy slapped her on the backside. "Let's go see what your mom has in the fridge."

"Trouble, and it's only Cloe's second night home. You come storming in here the first night, and now— guess what? You're back again. Cloe is good for business." Quinn Lightfeather expertly slid a mug of foamy beer down the gleaming bar into Michael's waiting hand. "I had to toss Eddie Livingston's butt out earlier. I liked it . . . that gold-plated, soft office-butt hitting Lolo's dirty snow and mud pavement. I had to wait, though, while he got primed to take a swing at me."

He whipped the bar towel around his shoulders, crossed his arms, and glanced at Michael. "Cloe always *could* stir things up without half trying. She's gotten to you, hasn't she?"

Michael dipped his finger into the suds, then circled the thick, cold mug. He didn't like the storms brewing inside him, the need to finish his ache for Cloe. That unfinished kiss in the barn had haunted him for years. "Let's just say that I put in a hard day at the ranch. It's been years since I dug post holes by hand."

"Uh-huh. The ground is frozen solid and you were battling Cloe. You know it as well as I do. If Cloe stays any time at all, something is going to happen. I heard on the police scanner that the three of them—the Wild Willows—were found in the back of her van."

Michael focused on that thought, turned it. "Dad always listened to the police band. His equipment is pretty sophisticated."

"Wade didn't seem the type. Something was bothering him, though. He found ease with Stella."

Michael thought of Quinn's laughing raven-haired wife, buried long ago. "I'm sorry about your wife, Quinn. I can understand why you jumped Richard Thomsen. The Club protected him—a drunk driver who kills should have been—"

"I know. Thank you for speaking up for me at the parole hearing. Someone with say-so sent a letter, too. The loan for the bar was easier than I expected, too. Someone who wanted to remain anonymous cosigned. I never found out who." Quinn stared into the shadows. His wife, Lomasi, lingered in his mind, the memories soft and sweet; unfortunately, his desire for Angelica's white body and fiery hair still burned him.

Angelica wouldn't have signed for his loan; she didn't want him in Lolo. She hated him now, and he fed upon that thought, nourishing it. Perversity made him step into her path at every chance. The daughter of The Club and the reservation Indian—now, wasn't that a laugh? He briskly polished a brandy glass, disgusted that his thoughts had turned to Angelica.

Michael glanced at him. "You're looking grim."

"Yeah." Quinn had taken nineteen-year-old Angelica's virginity, prized it, and now she hated him.

Though she would never know it, his heart still leaped softly inside him, like a quivering rabbit's, when he saw her. A slant of her meadow green eyes could stop the blood running through his body . . . or warm it.

"You know, if Cloe stays long and the Wild Willows get together, there will be hell to pay," Michael noted.

Quinn nodded. He'd already paid in hell, in prison, in the Navy, and with his wife's death.

"Josephine? What do you think?" Angelica asked the next morning, as MKIZ's award-winning deejay finished the first segment of Coffee Time.

"I think you got raked over the coals this morning and your voice has knives in it," Josy answered over the phone. "Your father didn't like reports of us in the back of the van, did he?"

Angelica pressed her lips together and met her father's glare across the office with a smooth, professional smile. He resented her now because she was becoming stronger, a young lioness challenging him. "You got it."

Touch Daddy this way, Angelica-honey, he'd crooned, years ago. Angelica gracefully smoothed the instant terrifying rise of the hair at her nape.

This morning his office attack had happened before she had finished the luxury of the cappucino Stella made especially for her each day. A small thing, but one that showed just how much Stella cared; when Angelica had told Stella that she loved the coffee, Stella had instantly gotten a tiny cappuccino machine and learned how to make it. Now a cup waited for Angelica every morning before she went to work.

Angelica shifted luxuriously in her contoured modern chair, the cut of her expensive French designer suit adjusting, flowing around her body. She knew how to dress, how to act, how to keep the fences up. *My shield,* she thought, *my image. Everything I do is like a shell to protect myself, like an armadillo wears his armor.* The exchange with her father was the same as it had always been—cold, slashing knives, threats, all without heart. She knew how to slash now, but she hadn't as a child. Maybe she'd inherited his perversity, the need to threaten. She shrugged elegantly within the expensive suit. "Josy, tell me what you think about Cloe. You've got a heart. You can read her better."

"I hate it when you start picking on yourself. But okay, there's a big piece of her missing. Her ex-husband hurt her in a way she doesn't want to talk about."

"Should we leave it alone? Or dig it out of her?" Angelica depended on Josy on a level where she trusted no one else, because Josy was all heart and feelings and totally selfless, her strength and her weakness. Angelica did not trust her feelings; she might hurt Cloe.

"Leave her alone. All we can do is be here for her. I'm on the air now. Got to go." Click.

This is my family, my real family, Angelica thought, warming, as she always did, to the idea that families were good, like the Matthewses, and people like her— ones who were too damaged by life to enjoy it— should take care of those families. *Treasures, like pearls to be protected*, she thought.

Her eyes narrowed and she realized she had just snapped the pencil in two.

Chapter 6
ᔕ

THE NEXT WEEK, as March winds blew down Lolo's main street, Cloe used Muriel's computer to design The Pinto Bean's new logo. She'd decided to start small, with personalized mugs, hopefully making enough money to then produce a country boutique catalog. A friend of Stella's, Lorene Nelson, was a cottage potter and agreed to produce exclusive hand-thrown mugs, designed by Cloe with The Pinto Bean's design etched into the side. The logo, The Pinto Bean elegantly scrawled across a small burlap bag over-flowing with a variety of cooking beans, was simple enough to be used in ads. Muriel had traded ad space in the *Lolo Star* for mugs for her staff.

Excited about the prospect of having her work handled exclusively by a top Chicago ad executive, Lorene signed a contract and agreed to subsidize the first mugs if Cloe would design a personal logo for her pottery which could be used as a potter's stamp.

"I had no idea," Stella said the next week as her regular customers began signing up to have personalized Pinto Bean mugs to be made, stored, and used at the deli. "Lorene is going to have her hands full just with these orders. Nels Flores wants small ones made for his three- and four-year-old grandsons for when he brings them in here for treats. The gas station crowd showed up this morning and said they wanted personalized mugs, and that they'd be taking their coffee breaks over here. It was as if they were asking me for an honor. I just can't believe it!"

Stella shook her head. "I would never have thought to triple the price of the mugs and then sell them as if they were a gift for my customers, and not something they had actually already bought for themselves. Joe will make pegs to hang them on—"

Cloe followed her mother's suddenly impassive stare out the window to Orson Smith. "That man," Stella snapped. "He took everything we had and wanted to . . . he wanted me in the bargain. It wasn't enough he had already taken over Maggie Ten Feathers' life. Oh, don't look so shocked, Cloe. You're old enough to know that now—we did not have money to find a lawyer outside of Lolo, or to make calls for help. I wrote letters, but cheap justice wasn't on the menu for the attorneys I contacted. I felt so inadequate, helpless, and—"

Stella's voice broke. She maintained the hard stare as Orson lowered his head to avoid The Pinto Bean's window lettering. He quickly scanned the crowd inside and Stella frowned. "I see you and Angelica and Josy, and I *know* I should have been different. If I had been more intelligent, experienced with business, instead of making do and raising a family, I would have known how to present Sam's case to a good attorney, how to make them take interest. Sam knew what to do when he fought The Club—but then, in prison, he didn't want to fight. He said he'd had enough. I will never forgive myself for not knowing more and being there for Sam when I should have."

Cloe took her mother's hand, aching for her. "You were there, Mom."

"No, I wasn't. I knew I wanted to marry Sam from the time I was ten. I planned my whole life around making a home and a family. But I didn't know I'd have to defend them with letters and fine words, or I would have—"

Stella picked up the ringing telephone and her expression darkened. "It's Ross. I forgot to tell you that he had called again when you were collecting Lorene's first batch of mugs. Do you want to talk with him now?"

"I'll take it in the office," Cloe said, already moving toward the kitchen and the cubbyhole she had arranged into a neat office. She inhaled and closed the door, preparing herself for the sound of his voice. At one time she had found it sexy, enchanting, not anymore. Ross came from a different world, fine expensive things and the manners to go with them; inexperienced with the world, she had been enchanted by him. She stared at the telephone, suddenly aware of how naive she had been, how protected within Lolo. "Cloe," she answered simply, not willing to give him more.

"Hi, gorgeous," Ross crooned, and she heard the sound of his office music, used to keep his conversations from being overheard. Cloe waited, aware of how much Ross hated that trait, how much it nettled him. She'd learned how to wait, how to let him unravel.

After a tense moment, his breathing sharpened. "You're going to make this very difficult, aren't you? It's not a very good trait for a woman, or a wife."

She waited, listening, recognizing the sound of creaking leather upholstery as Ross shifted several times in his office chair. She heard a pen tapping on Ross's desk and then he spoke. "I want my work back. I know you always have copies . . . I'm coming down to pick up the disks."

Cloe leaned back into the chair. Ross's aggressive in-command tone only meant he was uncertain and was pushing his bluff. She could picture him huffing up, trying to make himself more imposing, more authoritative.

"You're not getting *my* work back, Ross. Those ideas were mine and I'm keeping them."

"I'll sue the panties right off you. We were married and created those ideas together. They are marital property—"

Cloe hung up and ignored the next furious rings. She exhaled slowly, fought her rising temper, and in the next ring tossed it away. She jerked the receiver to her ear and snapped, "Take what's in your pants, stuff it in your ear, send me a picture, and then maybe . . . just maybe I'll consider giving you what you want."

Silence. It stretched on, and Cloe shifted uneasily. By this time, Ross would have had a threat flying at her—court hearings, lengthy legalities, a biting, ugly remark about her not being a woman.

"Hello, Cloe," Michael Bearclaw's deep, whiskey-smooth, amused voice curled around her. "I didn't know you were interested in my manhood or where I put it."

"Michael," she said shakily, stunned that he had once more seen emotions she wanted to be kept private.

He chuckled, the sound causing electricity to skitter over her skin. "Is that all you have to say? 'Michael?' As if it's the end of the world and—"

"You *are* the last person on the planet and I still won't have anything to do with you." Who had he loved? Who had he put that beautiful mouth on and— Cloe inhaled sharply and shoved the thought into the cluttered paper trash basket.

Silence. Then, Michael's dark, deep, raspy voice curled around her, locking in her bones. "Anytime you're ready to call it, darlin', come ahead. I'm not wearing any more of your scars, and this time I won't be nice," Michael murmured smoothly, and tipped her into uncertainty. The steel in his voice sliced through the old, good-natured Michael she had known at nineteen. Then he asked, "Is your mother there?"

Jealousy, fury, hatred all slammed into Cloe. Heat rushed into her cheeks, startling, unbalancing her. She hadn't been that angry before, not even with Ross. With Ross, her anger came from hurt and pride and she reacted in a cold, carefully plotted retaliation. With Michael, her instincts ruled her, shocked her. She didn't think; she just reacted, flying at him. "Because my mother liked Wade does not mean she will have anything to do with you."

"Stella adores me, Cloe. What are you going to do about it?"

She hated the amusement purring in his voice. Michael had always been able to laugh at her, draw her fury from her. "You're a perfect example of why I left here."

"You came back," he reminded her. "Your mother still has some things up here. I wondered if she wanted them."

Cloe couldn't bear for a piece of her life, of her mother's life, to be in Michael's keeping. "If it's kitchenware, box it up and bring it in here."

He chuckled, a rich, dark sound that set the hair on her nape rising. "You wish it was forks and spoons, don't you? It's nightgowns, Cloe. Sexy ones."

She fought the heat pulsing through her. Only Michael knew how to scrape her nerves raw. "You're enjoying this, aren't you?"

"I'm glad they had each other," he stated, the amusement gone from his tone. "I'll see you around, Cloe. Try to be sweet, will you?"

"I don't like it at all. Too many outsiders in Lolo." From Bradley's office in Gilchrist House, Orson Smith wrung his hands as he watched Cloe's van soaring out of town.

Byron Lang settled back against the posh chair, chewing on a fat Cuban cigar. "First that Liam McKensie comes back—he's only a sheepherder's son. Went away to get some fancy degree in finance and came back with that six-year-old daughter. He's been here a year now, and that finance business of his has taken away some of the bank's good customers. He

does business right in his own home so that he can
watch his daughter . . . now, what kind of a businessman doesn't set up a separate office away from home?
He's real competition for us, Bradley."

"McKensie won't last much longer. I have that on
good authority," Jeffrey muttered.

"He's beating our financial advisor all to hell and
back with his investment calls." Bradley stared at Jeffrey, who served as the bank's financial advisor, and
the younger man shrunk in his chair.

Bradley tapped his pen on specially watermarked
paper. "Orson, how is Maggie Ten Feather doing?
Still in that sanatorium?"

"She's no danger and you know it, Bradley. She
won't be telling the outsiders anything." Orson
looked out the window. Maggie's vacant stare, after
years of drugs and shock therapy, haunted him. Once
she had been so alive, hair black as a raven's, her eyes
gleaming, all that coppery skin. She'd given him love
when his wife had denied him; Maggie had given him
a son.

Orson fought the familiar ache. He'd loved a
woman who didn't fit into his powerful, wealthy family. They were all gone now, even his frail wife, and
he was alone—except for the nights he went to
Quinn's Long Horn to drink.

He closed his eyes and saw Maggie running to him
when she was only sixteen. The lush meadow grass
brushed her coppery thighs, and they had fallen into
the sunflowers and each other, making savage, hungry love.

At least he had saved her life, and his son's, by
putting Maggie in the sanatorium. She knew too

much, they said, and could destroy what The Club had built. Orson glanced at Bradley, hating him and the others. It had all been so easy, just a scrawl of Byron Lang's judicial pen and Maggie had been sent into that hellish vacuum.

She didn't know him now and maybe that was better. *But she had given him a fine, strong son who bore his grandfather's name.*

"Outsiders. I don't like it at all," Orson repeated.

"Michael Bearclaw could be real trouble. He's not making any move to leave, or to sell that property. I never liked that Matthews girl. She's too full of herself and always was unpredictable, except when it came to her family. They're clannish, those Matthewses, Dan and Gabe, and Stella—damn it, it's not right for a woman to live alone all those years and then take Wade Bearclaw to her bed. For God's sake, he died there," Lyle Davenport snapped.

"Cloe is trouble. There's real interest in The Pinto Bean now that she's advertising. There's some talk that she's been visiting locals, calling them, seeing what they'd like to handcraft and put in a catalog she could market. She and Angelica have always stirred up Josy," Edward Livingston noted. "I don't like it."

Bradley leaned back in his leather chair, studying the Remington statues lining one wall. He steepled his fingers and looked at Edward Livingston, who hadn't inherited the hellfire and damnation backbone of his father. Old Freemont Benjamin Livingston would have whipped Eddie's backside if he hadn't married Josy Small Bird after getting her pregnant.

The recognized head of The Club, Bradley had little use for Edward, but their lives were tied together. Ed-

ward's fatal mistake was to think that he suited Angelica. Bradley's daughter had too much spirit and
steel to let Edward claim her; she was a Gilchrist, after
all. And she was Bradley's. "I can take care of my
daughter, but that Matthews woman could stir up
real trouble if she gets rolling good. Jeffrey, why don't
you punch some numbers and see what our little
friendly group can do to buy out Bearclaw and The
Pinto Bean. Put together a nice little package, will
you?"

"Still the same whirlwind and hot temper . . . that's
nice to know. Cloe never had patience. Not a drop."
Through the barn's open window, Michael studied
the battered van barreling up the winding road to
Bearclaw's Ridge, the mid-March sunlight dancing on
the rusted metal and water spraying from the puddles
as she passed. The road from Lolo was a fast half-
hour drive, and Cloe must have started as soon as she
hung up the phone. Michael grinned slightly, remembering her shocked silence when he spoke instead of
whomever she'd expected. Upsetting Cloe Matthews
could be interesting, if she was back up to fighting
power. He ripped away another rotted board from the
stall and tossed it to a growing stack.

Lopez nickered at the window, angling his head to
peer into the barn, finding Michael instantly. The stallion was as contrary as Cloe Matthews had been, until
she started looking at Michael as a potential first
lover. Then she had become all silk and cream.

A sometime and forgotten lover hadn't suited her,
not when Michael had wanted her for a wife. Now he
wanted something else; he wanted Cloe hungry be-

neath him, fighting him on a primitive level where words didn't clutter what ran beneath them. Michael swore he should be long past thinking about Cloe.

He tore off another board; it cracked with the force of his anger, and Michael used the claws of his hammer to pry out the old square nails, neatly dropping them into a coffee can. He glanced out the window to the van skidding to a stop on the gravel in front of the house. Michael studied the sway of Cloe's jean-clad hips as her long legs ate up the distance to the house and knew that no other woman had ever fascinated him as she did. She knocked furiously on the door, planted her hands on her waist, and turned to scan the ranch yard.

At the sight of her, something like a fist slammed into Michael's gut as he remembered Cloe's lips moving on his twelve years ago. She'd been like that the day she'd hurled the ball at him, splitting his lip, all filled with fire and heat and ready to take on the world. The real Cloe, the unpolished raw female ready to defend herself and what was hers, had that same expression as in the past. She stood now in the March sunlight, powerful, lethal, and curved, unvarnished by sweet, feminine wiles, the ones she'd begun using on him so long ago.

Alive. Sunlight and wind, tossing her hair, dancing in it, and blue fire in her eyes, Cloe had enough life in her to kill those images that plagued Michael—bloody wounds, open, blank stares of the dead, mouths opened to cry out and stilled by death, children—He slammed a rotted board onto a pile of rubble. How could humanity kill itself and still produce to kill again?

He wanted life and energy and the red-hot desire slamming into his gut as he studied the woman who had haunted him for years. The sunlight glinted off her blond hair, the wind tossing her curls up and away from her furious expression. She had the poised look of a hunter, eyes narrowed, not missing a detail in the ranch yard.

She scanned Bearclaw Ridge, up to the bighorn sheep leaping over the red rocks, and then down to the gama grass field, preserved in its natural state by Bearclaws through time. She slowly traced the small Hereford herd and Lopez and his five mares, as though Michael might be hiding among them.

Years had honed her face, sharpening the angular features and reminding Michael of how much Cloe looked like her mother; Dan and Gabe's features were cut from Sam Matthews's rawboned mold.

Years ago, Michael had been a part of that family, as close to her as one of Cloe's brothers, and now— now he wanted the woman striding across the ranch-yard as if she owned it. Smooth strides, supple body adjusting from the hips, shoulders straight and tense with anger. From her neck on down, Cloe was all lean curves and stalking female, the few new pounds added to define her breasts, taut against her T-shirt, her thighs long and flexing with the tap of her toe. The oversized flannel-lined jacket—probably one of Dan or Gabe's—only enhanced her feminine feline look. . . .

Michael intended to come close enough to wipe her out of his mind, leaving him to go on with his life. Hell, after coming back, he'd discovered he still wanted that home, those kids—

He could have killed her then for taking that away from him, hating her. She tapped her Gucci boots on the porch, placed her hands on her hips, and continued to search the ranch yard. There was nothing sweet about her voice, caught by the wind. "Michael! Michael, you come here right now!"

Surprised at the fine trembling of his hand, Michael wanted to jerk her up close, tell her that she was nothing—had never been—but that would be a lie. Until she fired that ball at him, he'd been hearing wedding bells and thinking of how he would gently take Cloe's virginity and make her his—*that unfinished kiss had taunted him for years.*

"The lady calls, Lopez, my man." Michael tossed aside another board. He took his time walking out of the barn into the sunlight, controlling the fury riding him. He didn't bother to put on his shirt; Cloe had come to call on his land and he wasn't treating her like a lady.

Her arms folded over her chest as she spotted him leaving the barn and watched him approach. An expert witness, Michael recognized the defensive body language. He took his time studying her, from her size seven Guccis to her long taut legs, to the T-shirt she wore pasted to her lithe body. The thin leather belt was Armani.

"Your freckles are coming back," he noted, coming up the steps to the wide porch. He stripped off his leather gloves and tucked them in his belt. She smelled like heat and wildflowers and Stella's cinnamon rolls. To set her off, because he was already simmering nicely, Michael studied her narrow hips. "You used to fill jeans out real nice."

Cloe angled her chin, her eyes narrowing as her lips pressed firmly closed. He reached past her to turn the doorknob, and Cloe eased away. He could feel her retreating, drawing back. From his experience with abused women, Michael recognized the look. Now, behind that look he sensed that despite her loss of weight, Cloe was up to fighting him, and that was good.

"Afraid?" he taunted, noting the tired circles beneath her eyes, her pale complexion. Was she dreaming about her ex-husband? Craving him? Michael's stomach turned sour despite his smirk.

Her glance at him was amused and too practiced. Michael cursed mentally; Cloe's intricate feminine reactions had fascinated him. Someone had taught Cloe to protect her fleeting wild emotions, her expressions almost automatic. "Give me my mother's things, Michael."

For an instant, he hated whoever had taught Cloe to hide her high-wide, blazing emotions. He pushed open the door and walked past her into the spacious living room, the cabin Xavier Bear Claw had built for his mail-order bride. Michael realized his fingers were still trembling as they wrapped around the cool refrigerator door handle. "Drink?"

He turned to her and noted her uncertain stance in the middle of the room, the door still open, as if at any minute she'd make her escape. She looked like a doe backed against a fence as the dogs moved in to tear her apart. She looked like she had the day her father was taken to prison and teenage Michael had lifted her up into his arms, unashamed that his friends were watching. That tenderness went sliding through him now. *Oh, Cloe . . . come here, let me hold you. . . .*

She'd escaped him once and had wrecked their lives. The bitter knife turned slowly in Michael, infuriating him, and the sympathy he'd been feeling for her slid into the trash. "So, I hear you're divorced," he managed lightly, as he reached into the refrigerator for a beer. *Keep it civilized,* he promised himself, *and maybe she won't see how much you're hurting.*

"Look, you're obviously busy. So am I. Where are they?" Cloe glanced around the sprawling living room. Her gaze lingered on the plastic sheets covering his mother's sewing corner, then snagged on the six new pictures lined up over the scarred desk.

Another time, and in a gentler mood, Michael might have asked her what she thought about them, the way they were lined up, the dried rose tucked into one. At the moment, all he could deal with was keeping his boots locked to the floor, a distance away from her. He'd had only a taste of her as a woman back then and the taste of her had haunted him for years. Would she still taste hungry, wild and sweet?

Michael dropped the "sweet" back into all those aching nights and slammed the door on it. *Damn. He wanted to sink into her and take what he could get.*

Michael popped the lid off the bottle of beer and drank deeply. "Just what is it that you don't like about me, Cloe?"

"You're a meathead. You're arrogant. And you're you. Any more questions?" she shot at him.

Michael placed the beer on the counter, and took his time walking to her. The rules had changed. He'd given her two full weeks of riding her temper while he worked on the ranch and on a serial murder in

Denver, and now he was done waiting. "You're worked up, Cloe, and I'm not the reason. I won't take any temper you may have left over from whoever gave you that black eye. Got it?"

Cloe arched a sleek eyebrow. "You're going to be difficult, aren't you? You're probably going to try . . . try to put me through some torturous, perverse Q-and-A. You haven't changed, Dr. Michael Jedidiah Bearclaw."

He smiled, noting her reference to the title used in the interview. "Your sister-in-law wrote a nice article for Muriel's paper. I didn't know you were so interested in my life."

Oh, fine. She hadn't thought about the consequences when she'd leaped into her van, her temper fired and ready to unload on Michael.

She'd forgotten that cool, deadly control, which had always unnerved her—yet had also drawn her to him. While Ross had huffed and puffed and threatened, Michael's dark gold eyes merely leveled a cool promise at her. She knew he would keep that promise. She knew what he was, cut from the same mold as her father and his father and her brothers and western men bred to keep promises.

She'd had two weeks to prepare herself to handle their next meeting. She was bone tired working on her new idea, talking to craftspeople, making contact with old friends, and spending every moment sketching and laying out designs to market.

Now here was Michael, all six-foot-three, part Sioux and the rest tough pioneer, wrapped in arrogance and challenge. She knew now that the gloves were off. This time they would rip and tear at each other, and

that was just what she wanted—someone to take the
anger, and give it back—an equal match. . . .

Oh, he'd give it back, all right. Cloe knew him
down to his bones. Without his shirt and wearing
only his jeans and workman's boots, Michael looked
like any other western rancher who had been caring
for his property. Bits of straw stuck to his shoulder,
corded with muscle and tendons. The gold stripes
against his tanned skin were almost white against the
glistening triangle of black hair on his chest. She
jerked her eyes away from the narrow line down to
his navel, enclosing it before continuing. . . .

His sleek black hair gleamed, striping the dark,
sweaty skin of his shoulders, and in the quiet, airy
room he looked more like his mountainman ancestors
than a modern day forensics expert. Sweat beaded his
skin, the scent of leather and male mingling with the
familiar smells of hay and wood smoke. The stubble
on his jaw only enhanced his primitive male look, a
look that had never failed to incite Cloe's temper, that
challenging come-get-me look. She was an adult now,
with a marriage behind her, faced with surviving financial disaster, and still Michael's lifted eyebrow, the
arrogant tilt of his head had set her off.

Cloe's heart raced, her hands curling into fists. If
there was anyone who knew how to test her impatience, it was Michael Bearclaw.

Michael had something that Cloe considered hers,
and she wanted it back. She wanted all the pieces of
her life in one neat, protected stack, and that included
her mother's affair with Wade.

"I'll deliver your mother's things tomorrow, when
I come into town for supplies," he murmured, watch-

ing her, that quick narrowing of his eyes, the light tipping his black lashes in a blue sheen.

"I want them now. Where are they?" She didn't want his hands on her mother's things. Or on her.

"Pushy woman," Michael drawled. "What can't you stand? That your mother and my dad had an affair? Or that I'm here and so are you and we're breathing the same air?"

Cloe sliced her hand out, cutting through any relationship with Michael Bearclaw. "You've got nothing to do with anything in my life. You never have."

"You're in a mood," he noted too pleasantly. "You're too busy demanding what you want, just as always. You've always been impatient, and now you're worked up, and you've got one damn thing on your mind—you. Your family spoiled you rotten—Cloe, the Matthews' Golden Girl," he murmured lightly, the sunlight hitting those high blunt and rugged cheekbones, his light honey-brown eyes glinting in the shadows like a mountain puma waiting for its prey to move.

This wasn't the sweet Michael who'd held her the day her father went to prison, or the twenty-four-year-old college man she'd hated for not giving her the sexual experience she'd wanted that spring day in the barn.

Years had honed Michael, lines across his broad forehead, a new scar marking those wide-set cheekbones, a tightness locked around those sensual lips, and the rest spread into tough corded muscles, an expanse of broad, gleaming shoulders.

"You need a shave," she shot at him, unwilling to trade the past with him. She forced her eyes not to wander down the wedge of black hair on his chest.

"Lay off," Michael returned easily, his eyes narrowing, taking in her T-shirt and long, jean-clad legs. He pushed away from the wall and walked to her with the movements of a man used to hunting, and now he was hunting her. "All grown up now," he said quietly, as if to himself, and traced the worn collar of her denim coat with one slow fingertip. "I guess that means you don't need me to protect you any longer."

"From what?" Cloe pushed back her hair from her cheek, her chin coming up. She felt herself gearing up, blood heating, pulse pounding, ready to finish her tangle with him. While her arguments with Ross were cool, cutting and painful, she had no doubt that fighting with Michael would be explosive. Maybe she wanted someone to rip into, someone who could take it and give it back.

His fingertip prowled along her jawline and she jerked her face away as he spoke softly, "I'm not about to cut off a part of my anatomy and stick it in my ear for you, but I admired the way you said that. Want to tell me about what caused that remark?"

She fought her stormy emotions and backed up a step, using her best, effective at cutting down to size, imperial queen tone. "You are sweaty, dirty, and standing much too close. Back off."

The word "cowboy" lingered in her mind and she dropped it. They both knew their roots; she was as western as he was, bred from pioneers, mountainmen, good sturdy Scots and German blood. But Michael's Sioux heritage, his glossy, straight black hair that clung damply to his throat, reminded her of another time when warriors simply took the white women they wanted. The flickering gold in his eyes spoke of another heritage, of men who claimed virgins and taught them fire.

"I guess you don't want to anwer my question." He shrugged and took another step toward her. "I've been working. It feels good to be back, working the land and the horses. Some things don't change."

The words were civilized. The look in Michael's eyes wasn't. Heat pushed at Cloe's skin, electricity skittering around her body, crackling on her nerves. "Get back," she ordered again, and knew he wouldn't.

Michael snagged her wrist and jerked her to him, her body slamming into his, knocking the breath from her. Or was it because she had forgotten to breathe?

She had forgotten how big Michael was, how his raw-boned, rangy frame had filled out to a man's body. Now he was harder, dangerous, and grimly determined to prove that he was bigger and stronger, that he could take control of her easily.

"What is this supposed to prove?" she asked, as his hands skimmed down her arms and settled on her waist, his thumbs caressing her stomach. The warmth of his hands seeped through her jeans, the heat unnerving her. She inhaled abruptly; she hadn't had a man's hands on her in months and her body was reacting normally, her mind explained, while big warning bells clanged.

Reacting normally? Had Ross ever tested her, challenged her, claimed her like this? Had her skin ever danced, heated with his touch?

She eyed Michael, the muscle contracting rhythmically beneath the dark skin of his jaw, the dark rim of black circling his eyes, catching her reflection in the center of the gold, and hated him more for making her feel . . . like a woman.

He studied her hair, the heat in her cheeks, and then her mouth. His purr was seductive, whiskey-smooth, and yet raw, trembling upon her skin. "You shouldn't come to a man in a froth, Cloe. Didn't any-one ever tell you that? Especially where you're alone and unprotected."

There wasn't anything nice in his expression; she hadn't expected tenderness. Anger simmered in him, steaming out of him, prickling her skin, and slamming into her heart, kicking up the beat.

Held overlong, her breath came out in a rush, her instincts telling her to let go, and let Michael take care of himself. "I can protect myself."

Michael studied her face, reading her. She hated it when Michael started prying beneath her practiced expressions. "My mother's things?" she reminded him, as his fingers smoothed her hips, splayed, and dug in slightly before releasing her.

"In the bedroom dresser. When was the last time you were on a horse?" Michael stepped back, his ex-pression closed to her. She hated that, too, when he closed himself away while she stood there, naked and exposed to his conclusions.

"I'm not here to chit-chat." Cloe pivoted, walked toward the large bedroom she remembered from the Matthewses' visits to the Bearclaws'. She pushed open the door, scanned the neatly made bed, the stack of magazines and files on the bedside table. She didn't want to think about riding with Michael, the way he used to hold her in front of him on the saddle when she was tiny and safe. With Michael now, here, that safety had fled and that unfinished kiss hovered in the shadows between them.

The windows' sheer panels had been drawn back, giving a full view of the mountain and Lolo in the valley. Sunlight poured into the room, splashing across the big handmade bed, covered with a floral comforter. Cloe braced herself. Wade wouldn't have chosen the feminine comforter, nor the matching ruffled curtains; her mother had.

She glanced at Michael, leaning against the door and watching her, then she ripped open the dresser drawer and grabbed the lingerie from it. She hesitated at the sight of the framed picture, her mother's arm around Wade, his around her, their beaming expressions as they held morning coffee cups.

"He kept their lives private," Michael murmured.

Cloe couldn't move. Wade, and the men she'd known and respected all her life, protected women from gossip. Michael's great-grandfather had gone into the Rocky Mountain high country in the dead of winter, crossed a dangerous snow-filled pass, killed a cougar with only a hunting knife, and skinned it. Using the hide for warmth, Jedidiah Bearclaw then went after his wife who had been kidnapped and claimed her from the outlaws. Honor ran high in the Bearclaw men, they'd staked their lives on it and family. Michael was born of that breed, proud men.

Cloe took in the silky robe. When at home her mother's robe was worn and comfortable. The silky robe made of no more than black satin and lace, was designed to entice.

She studied Michael over her shoulder, hugging the

lingerie scented of her mother close to her. "You're enjoying this, aren't you?"

"You're so outraged. What did you expect?" He grinned, and for a flash in time, she remembered how that sensuous curve—as if Michael knew something she didn't, all those years ago—had flip-flopped her stomach.

"Shut up." Cloe went to the closet, jerked the neatly folded jeans into her arms, ripped the blouse from the hanger. She stared at the elegant red satin bedroom slippers, standing next to highly polished western boots, an intimate contrast of male and female. *Her mother had slept with Wade. . . .*

"The boots are mine. I donated Dad's things to the church. Most of them were old and patched. I think he liked wearing your mother's patches, rather than buying new clothes. She's offered to sew a few of my buttons on—"

"Don't you dare bring your clothes to our house. I'm certain you've got a woman who can mend for you—probably several women," she corrected. Cloe hugged the clothing tighter, desperately trying to keep what was hers close and safe.

Michael forced his cool grin, mocking her despite his anger. "I imagine there would be someone who would patch my clothes."

"Figures," Cloe muttered darkly, and for a heartbeat Michael's anger eased. He'd gotten to her.

"You wouldn't expect me to wait all these years for you, would you?" he pressed, putting more tormenting power into his smirk.

Michael placed his finger on the fast-beating pulse on her throat and took one step that had her backing away. The dark fire in Michael's eyes, the stance of his body heating hers, the raw, primitive electricity prickling the air between them frightened Cloe. She turned away quickly, fearing her unsteady emotions— the need to take Michael into her and wipe away the years and the pain, losing herself momentarily in the heat and storms his eyes offered her.

Cloe clutched her arms, locking them protectively around her. Heat and storms. Where were they in her marriage? Where was one-tenth of the tension, the passion that was now in Michael's lashing eyes, his stiffened, corded body?

Time wrapped around her, memories snagging her heart. "I'm sorry about your father."

Michael breathed as though letting air held too long from his lungs. "He was a good man. Stella is a good woman. They suited each other."

Cloe turned to study Michael, the lines on his face deeper now. "You mean that?"

Michael laughed outright, his hand pushing back that glossy length of hair from his throat. "Cloe, you are a prude. My mother would have wanted Dad to be happy. Apparently he was. Look at the bed. He made it for Stella, it's a Bearclaw tradition. Those are their initials burned into that heart on the top."

Cloe whirled to look at the bed, pinpointing the dark burn in the light wood immediately. The sweet, romantic symbol of the shared bed seemed like a marriage certificate, shocking her. Wade would have done that, too, providing a new bed for Stella, cherishing her. Wade would have been faithful, because not a Bearclaw man had strayed from the woman he called his.

Bearclaw men traditionally handmade their brides new beds, cutting the proper trees by ax and saw, felling them. They treated and aged the wood, building the beds with their own hands—Wade Bearclaw had considered himself married to Stella.

The bed was a symbol of a relationship deep and lasting for Wade, a contrast to Cloe's own marriage, and pain shot through her again, twisting, hurting. She remembered her father's husky, low murmur behind the bedroom door, the silence, and the way her mother had glowed in the morning—how love had simmered between them, never cold, always ready to be fed.

Stunned, Cloe skimmed the sunlit room again—an intimate, romantic place where lovers shared their secrets, made love, and awoke in each other's arms. She fought tears—she should have known that Ross was unfaithful. *She should have known.* The thought echoed in her mind.

Michael shook his head and leaned back against the log wall and hooked his thumbs in his belt, watching her. "Let it go."

She rushed away from him, out into the sunlight, her heart pounding. She glanced at Michael, who followed, watching her quietly, waiting. "Where's Nimo? Your dad's German shepherd? Mom tried to get him to stay with her in town, but he wouldn't."

A ranch dog was to be prized, and according to Stella, Wade's dog—the son of the original Nimo that Cloe remembered—was faithful, loving, and fiercely protective of anything on Bearclaw land.

Michael turned to look out into the fields, the last of Bearclaw's finest quarter horses grazing in the thick, lush grass, their coats gleaming in the sun. "Nimo isn't here now."

"Why are you here?" she asked.

"I don't know. But I will," Michael answered too quietly, and the edge in his tone caused her to suspect that he did know.

Chapter 7

∽

QUINN LIGHTFEATHER FANNED the smoke toward him with the old eagle feather inherited from his ancestors. Quinn inhaled the sage scent deeply, slowly, methodically. Purification helped to clear his mind, and let him find his path through the dreams. The familiar call of the night owl, soaring past the open window in his apartment over the bar, the cold wind stirring through the windows, gave him the music he needed for his heart—the spirits were humming, wanting him to listen.

Taking care, Quinn slowly moved the feather across the bundled spear of sagebrush in the flat pottery bowl. When the tiny coals were bright, he crumpled a length of the dried sweetgrass braid into the bowl with the sage.

Quinn inhaled sharply, drawing the purification scents into his lungs, his body, forcing away the blackness of his mind, the need for pain and revenge.

In the back regions of his mind, a baby's cries haunted him. *Why did the baby cry?*

At the time of her death, his wife, Lomasi, had not

been pregnant; she could not conceive, and felt she had failed as his wife.

He let the cold, fresh air swirl around him, bringing him the visions. A woman of fire had walked back into his dreams. Quinn smiled lightly—dreams came to him though he had not studied the tradition. They bound his heart and body together. Within prison, dreams had saved him—Quinn pushed away the heavy bad thoughts streaked by vermilion, pulled in the good ones by inhaling deeply.

Inside the flow of his mind, the baby cried softly, beckoning to him. He loved the baby already, his heart tender, his arms aching to hold it.

Two more women joined the fire-woman: one a warrior—hard, cold, controlled, tearing at life; the other softer—the woman-heart aching for the others. Quinn slowly reached for the eagle feather, dropping more sage and sweetgrass onto the coals.

The women, arms linked around each other, walked into the fire, and then a young, strong wolf leaped into the smoke, tearing at an older, scarred wolf, tearing bits of flesh and fur away until nothing was left.

Why did the woman cry?

The rhythm of her sobs pounded in him, the pain in her heart and womb as the child was torn from her. The woman's cries were too soft for such pain, controlled, aching, hidden. . . . The woman and the baby's cries became one, a slow, pounding ache around Quinn's heart—

Thunder raged and lightning ripped through the black sky, then sunlight spread upon the river willows which swayed in the wind, rippling the water.

Quinn locked onto the rhythm of his heartbeat, his blood flowing through his body, and then the mountain primrose bloomed in his mind, growing over, through old roots, breaking the powerful tentacles, killing them. The old roots curled into skeletons and then a wind took them away. . . .

Quinn realized he was shivering, cold with sweat that poured from his body. Who was the baby he longed to hold in his arms, and why did the woman weep so softly, shielding her great pain?

He pushed back the sweaty, damp hair that clung to his throat, lying free upon his tense, naked shoulders. He crumbled sweetgrass into the bowl and smiled slightly. He knew the meaning of one of his visions: Cloe Matthews was that woman of fire, and with her the Wild Willows would have strength.

The Club would tremble.

Angelica Gilchrist wasn't sweet—the image of smooth, hard flint washed through his mind. She had been so ashamed of one night with him when he was home on Navy leave—ashamed of having shared her body, her first time with an Indian—that she had run to Europe.

Now, years later, Quinn made certain that she was the first to look away. She was still ashamed of taking him into her milk-white body. It pleased him that Angelica was ashamed, that she remembered back when she was nineteen and sighing in an Indian's arms.

It was the first of April now and Cloe had wasted no time. By June, The Pinto Bean's catalog would be mailed from Chicago, displaying the Lolo craftspeoples' goods. Sergei Cheslav, a world famous glamour magazine photographer and Cloe's friend, was scheduling time at Lolo to shoot the catalog. Sergei wanted to taste western life while he photographed the catalog's products. Calling in favors and bartering work with a color printers had gotten Cloe a nice production price.

On a hill overlooking Edward Livingston's house, Cloe and Angelica lay on a tarp to keep them dry. The night air was fragrant around them. "I need an investor, Angelica," Cloe said, focusing Gabe's field glasses on the house. "Do you think those skunks we lured under the house will work?"

"Ye old skunk trick is always good. I'd better be the first one on the investor list. I'm filthy rich and not enjoying it," Angelica stated, as she focused the night-camera on the Livingston house. "What's up?"

"A country boutique catalog. Marketing native crafts, The Pinto Bean logo on aprons, napkins, native teas, buffalo jerky, weaving, whatever, all under a neat country-looking package."

"I knew you'd come up with something fantastic, and then you leave town, right? You come in, make the hit, and leave."

The bitterness in Angelica's tone was usually reserved for others and slammed into Cloe. "You make me sound—"

"Well, anyway. Tonight we take care of Edward, right?"

"I hate to see Josy terrified of losing her son."

Angelica flashed her a dark look. "Yeah, well, stick around and we could make Edward pay plenty. I'm not as inventive as you. He'd better think twice before threatening to take Cody away from Josy, the mean bastard. I know how he got her pregnant on a stupid bet, and drugged her, to boot. She was in a fog for days."

Cloe focused on the house below them. Edward and his wife ran outside, yelling at each other; Angelica whistled low and began clicking shots. Dressed in a black bra and bikini panties, wearing a red satin garter belt with fishnet stockings and high red heels, Edward screamed profanities. His bride wore a tight black leather bustier and leather pants and carried a whip. "Hmm, now, *that* is interesting," Angelica murmured with delight. "Listen to that screeching—the man is a soprano."

Angelica turned to eye Cloe and tucked away the camera. "I keep a documentary on the powers-that-be in Lolo. You stay and we could get real good at this."

"As soon as I can, I'm leaving."

Angelica frowned and picked up a bottle of wine cooler, drinking it quickly. "I'm not ever leaving. I'm going to make them all pay. Tell me more about this country boutique catalog idea of yours."

Cloe inhaled the sweet night air and the satisfaction of knowing she had a good strong idea and the skill to pull it off. "We'll start small, taking orders and filling them as we go. Mom is working on a cookbook to put in the catalog. Right now, the main costs are printing and mailing. I can pull this off. I know it—"

Angelica whistled between her teeth. "You move fast. I know you can do it. Now, just how much money do you need to make a catalog and do it right?"

*   *   *

"Damn it, Cloe. I will not have a Wild Willow driving that tin can of a van. It's embarrassing," Angelica snapped a week later, cradling her morning cappuccino in her hand as she leaned against the kitchen counter. She returned Joe Issaks' sassy wink and leer, then grinned appreciatively as Stella dropped a dollop of whipped cream on her cappuccino and tucked two foil-wrapped chocolate biscotti into the pocket of Angelica's gray Armani suit.

"Stop tossing your weight around. I'm not taking the car." Cloe plucked the new T-shirts out of the box, studied The Pinto Bean's logo, and stepped into the tiny office to take off her blouse, replacing it with the T-shirt. She went back to the kitchen and turned around slowly. The kitchen was filled with April morning sunlight and the luscious scent of Stella's cinnamon rolls. "What do you think?"

"Moneymakers. Charge a mint for them. They'll sell like hotcakes." Angelica grabbed a T-shirt, stepped into the office and replaced her silk blouse with it, topping it with her Armani jacket. She glanced at her thin gold watch. "Got to go. Dan said that old BMW purrs like a kitten. I want you in it and I want you to shut up."

Angelica's green eyes met Cloe's stormy ones. "Double-dare you to drive it," Angelica purred with a smirk she'd used years ago to taunt Cloe.

"Snot."

"Toe crud."

Cloe grinned. Only Angelica could make a heated argument feel like friendship. In this familiar rite, they had always been an equal match, neither backing down. Angelica grinned back, "Rat poop."

"Lizard toes."

"Girls, be nice," Stella murmured as she swung past with a pan of cinnamon rolls in one hand and freshly ground coffee for the urns in the other.

"Give me one of those T-shirts for Josy. She was excited about the mugs—but wait 'til she sees these." Angelica snatched a T-shirt from the box on her way out of the shop.

"You owe me twenty times two, plus tax. Someone stop that woman, she's a thief!" Cloe shook her head as Angelica put a sedate but teasing wiggle in her Armani-clad hips as she hurried out the door. She stepped onto Lolo's Main Street, carrying the T-shirt for Josy high, as if it were a trophy. Framed by the front window, she jerked open her jacket, flashing her own T-shirt at Cloe and Stella.

"That's good advertising. People like to see what Angelica wears," Stella remarked with a smile.

"We're not in this for freebies, Mom. Josy is on radio, not television. No one will see that T-shirt. And nothing is going to make me take charity in the form of a BMW from Angelica." Then Cloe gave way to her pleasure and smiled back. "Maybe I *will* just take the old rust bucket for a spin. I'll park it in front of the bank. They'll have to pay for towing."

"This is no rust bucket," Cloe said appreciatively, as she ran her hand over the smooth champagne-beige BMW that sat in her brother's neat but cluttered garage.

Dan layered his greasy hands with a white soapy paste, washed, rinsed, and wiped them on his jeans. "Gabe helped me find the parts for it. Michael, too.

He brought back the distributor cap from Denver—he had to go finish work on the case of a serial killer. Got the creep charged too . . . he liked to murder in really expensive handmade shoes. Michael's specialty."

Cloe eyed Dan, weighing her dislike of Michael Bearclaw's contribution to her life against the marvelous car Dan had restored. "Does a car need a distributor cap to run?"

He laughed. " 'Fraid so."

Cloe pivoted to her brother. "Dan, I don't want anything from Michael. Can't you order one?"

"Sure. But you don't have any more diamond rings to hock, do you?" Dan grinned. "Take it easy, Sis. He's practically family. He's teaching Karen basic forensics and she's in love with him . . . she says she's going into forensics instead of having kids."

"He's not family." She hurled a greasy rag at Dan. "And do not say another word about Mom and Wade. Michael is not my friend and he's up to something. There is no reason for a world-famous forensic expert to be living here in Lolo."

"It's his home." Dan ran his hand through his hair and sent her another teasing nudge, "He would have been in the family, if you hadn't plowed him with that softball, run off, and got married. He's scarred for life because of you—"

Cloe faced him, her hands on her hips. She was nineteen again, tossing her head and battling her brothers over how she had injured Michael. "Don't give me that. He refused to have stitches. The hospital nurse told Mom. He's just as contrary now."

Dan dramatically placed his hand over his heart

and sighed. "Branded by the woman who loved him."

He caught the can of paste wax she lobbed at him and tossed her the keys. "Make me proud."

Bradley Gilchrist studied Main Street, his street, his empire. He'd built this town on his father's legacy; the Gilchrists owned the bank and Lolo depended on them. Bradley fostered those who deserved it and crushed those who didn't please him. Like his father and grandfather before him, Bradley was an emperor—and a king builder, if his new choice for senator proved right.

The Pinto Bean was only a slight thorn in his plans. Stella Matthews kept clinging to her pitiful little business, but her daughter would soon grow bored and take off. All the dust would settle.

A champagne-beige BMW, looking like a hot-house rose on a street layered with battered and new farm trucks, prowled past the bank window. Bradley peered through the windows, because he knew what everyone of distinction drove in Lolo. In the shadows of the plush BMW, Bradley recognized Cloe Matthews's clean-cut profile, a bandanna tied around her hair.

He turned to his daughter, innocently studying her manicured nails. "Angelica, exactly *what* is that woman doing with that car? She's been driving that rusty van. Where would Stella Matthews's divorced daughter get enough money for a car like that? I ran a check on her credit, and the only thing she has is that partnership in The Pinto Bean with her mother."

"I gave it to her. Well, I picked up the wrecked car

at an auction. Her brothers took care of the rest. Michael Bearclaw, too. You remember Michael, don't you? Dr. Michael Bearclaw, Wade's son?"

Bradley knew his daughter. She was hoarding secrets. She was becoming too confident for a woman in his domain, too confident by far. Used to controlling himself and others, he would merely wait, and when he needed, he would put Angelica in her place. When the time came, he would remind her that she was on *his* leash. Until then, he said, "I wouldn't get any ideas of kindling your friendship with Cloe or Josy. It wouldn't be wise."

Her eyebrows arched, her expression cool. He'd taught her that—that imperial bland, closed expression. She had his wife's elegant looks, but Susan did not have the steel that Angelica did—she had his blood, and therefore she was his. She had always been his.

Before Cloe and Josy had interfered as children, Angelica was sweet and trusting in her little bed . . . "Just don't get too close to that Matthews girl. Or Josy, who is nothing. I won't have my family contaminated by the likes of them."

"You won't?" Angelica asked too sweetly.

Bradley fought the rage her challenge evoked, sent her a sharp glance, and settled down to a list of priorities. He ran his priorities like his life and family— keeping them neat and under control. "You really should move back into the house, where your mother can take better care of you. You're looking far too thin."

"I am never coming back to Gilchrist House. Never," Angelica stated coolly, and Bradley almost admired her as she went on to the business before them. "And now that the interest rates are going down, we have to consider putting out a new brochure with new rates. Any recommendations?"

She has always been mine. Bradley glanced at Lyle Davenport, who had just entered his office with Jeffrey, the male heir to the Gilchrist name. Why couldn't Jeffrey have Angelica's cool, practical mind, her business flair? It should be a Gilchrist who stepped in to control The Club when he no longer could. Jeffrey did not show any qualities that would be necessary to take over the reins.

Bradley foraged for and found the morsel to wave in front of Jeffrey's nose, demonstrating that his sister was more capable than he. "Yes. Gentlemen, Angelica has suggested that we print a new brochure, perhaps put it in the next month's statements, about the interest rates. Angelica is always working long hours, trying to make The First State Bank the best that we can be. My grandfather and father, former owners of the bank, would have appreciated her clear, creative mind. Any suggestions?"

I've got a big suggestion, Angelica thought. *This town needs an industry, something outside The Club's reach, untouchable, something new and fresh and . . . untouchable . . . outside investors interfering with The Club's money and power. The catalog is a start, but it's not nearly enough.*

"Ross, you're not getting those disks," Cloe snapped, as she stepped out of her BMW and slammed the door. How like her ex-husband, to arrive in Lolo just as she was driving out on the single Main Street—to recognize her and follow her, motioning her over to the side of the dirt road. Ross's timing had always been unerring; he'd lived a charmed life—first his parents coddling him, and then Cloe . . . but now she wasn't doing him any favors.

She glared at the Hereford cows in the nearby field, red and white faces lined up against the fence, watching her and munching on their cuds. "You're invited to this party," she muttered to the cattle.

The mid-April morning was a time for sowing, calves dropping in the fields, frisking with the others, suckling their mothers. Angelica had put together an investor's package with people she trusted and wanted to help them make money; Sergei would arrive in another week, and in the next week, the layouts for the catalogs would be at the printer, who had agreed to push the project through quickly.

Cloe was exhausted, running on nerves and coffee and the success of a good project coming together. Maybe it was time to deal with a persistent ex-husband who had decided to squeeze her off the tiny farm road with a big, black shiny pickup truck. Cloe fought the leaping rage she had expected upon seeing Ross, and found it had dimmed. Ross removed his designer sunglasses as he stepped out of the black monster.

Cloe stopped in front of him. He'd pasted his most charming smile on his handsome, artificially tanned face. There was that practiced appealing little-boy sheepish look as he tucked his sunglasses in the vee of his buttoned chambray shirt. The dying sun caught his well-tended blond hair, glistened on his perfect tan, and stroked his athletic, toned body, dressed now in chambray and new designer jeans. The thick gold chain suited his outfit.

The price of his lizard western boots could finish off the last of the overdue grocery bill at The Pinto Bean. The extended cab pickup behind him had never hauled hay, but the roll bars and fog lights across the top were pretty, and the multiple antennas marked Ross's love of television and telephone while he drove.

"You're looking good, country girl," he drawled easily, his gaze drifting over her jeans, splattered with deli mustard and The Pinto Bean T-shirt with its coffee stains. He studied her Guccis, locked wide apart on the dusty country road, then his gaze strolled insinuatingly back up to the reddish brown tendrils framing her face and higher to the honey-hued practical ponytail.

She saw no reason to serve explanations about how she looked to Ross as he posed, bracing one hand against the hood of the new black rig, and angling his six-foot-four body to best advantage. He reached inside the pickup to retrieve a pearl white Stetson and ease it onto his head. Cloe began to laugh as he preened. "If that get-up is your idea of what a best-dressed western gent should wear, you're way off base. Most of the men here are planting now, fixing farm tractors and repairing fence. They might be up to their armpits in some cow's birth channel, pulling calves and wiping blood off their faces. Their jeans match their dirty shirts and battered hats, and French designer jeans don't cut it here."

Ross stiffened and frowned, probably still taking in the image of ranchers pulling calves that weren't turned right in the cows. She enjoyed the green tinge running beneath his artificial tan as he asked, "I think we should have dinner and talk, don't you, honey?"

"Sweat sometimes leaves marks in fake suntan lotions, Ross. Thanks for the laugh, but we don't have anything to talk about, and I'm due for an appointment." Had they ever really talked? Or was their dialogue necessary business—Ross had told her what he needed, the assignment, and she had completed the task, supplying him. They had mimed conversation, dealing with the business of keeping their images, their lifestyle, in the pretty picture. Was it all a picture? Hadn't she loved him? *Hadn't she?* Cloe asked herself desperately.

Ross lifted his head, scanning the lime green fields, the timeless mountains in the distance, the ravens gleaming coal-black and feeding along the roadside. Cloe settled her hip against his rig, letting him posture. "You know, I never really appreciated how much time and effort you put into your own packaging."

"What do you mean?" Ross removed his hat.

She shrugged. "All that posturing, the hours at the gym and sauna, selecting the right outfit and vehicle to suit the need. Applications of liquid tans. All that takes time. I just never realized how much dedication you have. Oh-oh, I think you're thinning a bit on top, Ross." She angled to look and anger flashed in his blue eyes, quickly banked.

Ross smoothed his receding hairline with an uneasy, reassuring touch that spoke volumes. He carefully replaced his hat. "We need to talk, Cloe. I realize now that my second marriage was a mistake. I realize now how much I love you. I'd like us to work this out."

Darn. She should have used that hair removal cream on his scalp while he slept—

Cloe pursed her lips and watched mule deer cross the wild meadow to water at the creek. "You're years late, Ross."

How could she ever have loved him? Did she? Or was it the image, the picture of success, she'd needed so desperately?

He tilted his head toward hers, a practiced act designed to be appealing. "We could make it work. I could divorce Linda . . . we could start with a new company, a couple again. A marriage counselor—"

"I'm late for my appointment." Cloe turned and began walking back to her car. If she had had regrets and fears that she hadn't tried harder in her marriage, she did not have them now. She glanced out to where cows were grazing, and in the far field, Ben Adams was driving his big John Deere tractor and sowing for winter silage. That's how real life should be led, not like the caricature of her past existence.

"This is more important than any appointment you could have in this hick community." Ross caught her shoulder, spinning her back against his pickup; the sleek gym muscles had enough power to knock the breath from her. He quickly masked his desperation with a forced smile and a drop of sweat trailed down the cosmetics he'd used on his fading tan, leaving a white trail. When she looked pointedly at his fingers, biting into her shoulder, Ross forced them into a caress. "I don't think you understand, Cloe. I'm ready to leave Linda for you."

Anger, despite her promise to keep calm, surged into her. "I was pregnant, Ross, coming to tell you, and there you were being sucked brainless by your secretary. Then I find out that you're doing them both. You weren't interested then in keeping me, and I doubt now if you ever were."

"We can start all over. We'll go to counseling. You can see a doctor about your conception problem."

Cloe tossed back the curl the evening breeze had loosened. There was a good three inches of natural color at her roots, and Ross hadn't mentioned it as he once would have. "You're really straining at this, aren't you? Do those disks mean that much to you?"

Had she ever loved him? How could she have been so blind?

"I am trying to make you see how good we are together." Ross ran his hand through his well-groomed, treasured hair.

"Together? I built you. You're not getting—"

Ross jerked her to him, his fingers biting into her upper arms. He shoved her back against the pickup hard, his scowl menacing. "You're not knifing your knee into me this time. Now, I want those disks. You are going to get in your car—better, I'll drive you back to town, or wherever you've hidden my property, and then—"

He glanced at the dark green worn work pickup that had purred to a stop beside the road. Michael slowly unfolded himself from the dusty cab, stood and stretched leisurely, slapped his battered black Stetson on the back of his head, and slammed the door behind him.

Cloe noted the extra force he'd used and the narrowed smoking-gun look in his darkened eyes. "Michael, stay out of this."

"Who is this hayseed?" Ross snapped. Cloe ignored him.

Cloe shook her head; how like him to arrive now, looking just like the western man she had just described, right down to the manure bits clinging to his worn, dusty boots. She almost groaned. The packaging was all long-legged tough, western territorial male, coming to her rescue.

Ross didn't release her, jerking her to him. "This is none of your concern. Move along. We're married."

"Not anymore," Cloe said between her teeth. She made a shielded attempt to draw her arm away and Ross jerked her back. Before Michael closed his expression, something primitive and grim flashed in his eyes, his mouth tightening.

Cloe didn't need him stepping into her life. She pushed back her hair with one hand. "Michael, I can handle this."

Ross nodded. "This is a family matter. You can be on your way now—" Ross glanced uneasily at Michael's rangy broad-shouldered, hard-muscled frame as though suddenly aware of raw power pitted against pretty, gym-molded muscles.

Michael took his time, ripping off his leather gloves and tucking them in his worn Levis back pocket. He tugged down his hat, a muscle running along his cheekbone and clenching his jaw. He leisurely flicked a piece of straw from his shirt. "The name is Michael. I've been like a big brother to Cloe . . . changed her diapers one or twice, let her cry all over me when her best doll got run over by a tractor, and gave her pet cat a real nice funeral."

"Michael, will you please leave?" Cloe demanded desperately and knew that Michael wasn't going anywhere until he was ready.

"When I'm ready. So this is what you married, hmm?"

What, not who.... Cloe sucked in air. Michael was speaking too softly, a sign, she remembered that concealed a heated temper. When she was eighteen, she'd tried out her powers with slow dancing. The dance was meant to attract Michael, who wasn't paying attention. Later, an older married man had caught her outside, shoving her against a wall. Michael had used that same slow soft drawl, before he'd stepped up close and dangerous. He had moved fast—short, powerful jabs—and Frank Whitley had crawled away, while Michael breathed easily.

Ross moved restlessly. "Cloe, get rid of this hayseed. We need to talk—"

"Looks like you're shoving her around to me. I'd say you outweigh her, or I'd let her have at you. She's pretty good when her temper is riding her."

Cloe rolled her eyes; she'd lost control the moment Michael had arrived. "I can handle this."

"Sorry." Michael slowly took in Ross's grip on Cloe's arm, her tense body and clenched fists. There on the dusty road, dressed in a torn checked shirt, just as dirty as his faded jeans and worn boots, Michael's tall body seemed to coil. He reached out to grip the T-shirt covering Cloe's chest and slowly drew her away from Ross. Ross tightened his grip on her arm instantly, until one long, dangerous look from

Michael caused Ross to release her. Michael pushed her gently aside without taking his eyes from Ross's uncertain expression. "Stay put, Cloe. You shouldn't have given her that black eye, Bennett. Because if her brothers don't get to plow you before the night is over, I will."

Ross bristled, huffing in air. "I can't be responsible if you're hurt. I am trained in karate and tai chi."

Michael smiled coldly. "Well, then. The hell with waiting."

"Dr. Michael Jedidiah Bearclaw. Those degrees didn't mean a thing to you, did they? You're still—" Michael rubbed the spot where Cloe's fist had sunk into his stomach. She eyed him, furious with him, and with her back hand, knocked his hat from his head. He bent easily, retrieving it, and slapping it against his thigh as Cloe rounded on him.

Michael studied her curves, appreciating her lean, taut body. There with the calves playing behind her and Ben Adams's John Deere tractor prowling back and forth across the field, Cloe looked as if she belonged. He touched the dark border of hair at her roots and she brushed his hand away.

Cloe jabbed a finger into his chest. "I told you I could handle Ross. If you think this macho display proves anything, but that you are still Michael Bearclaw—rude, cocky butt-in-ski."

She glanced at Ross's black pickup tearing around the dirt road's corners, barreling toward the highway leading out of Lolo. "You probably broke his nose."

Michael shrugged. The bastard needed more than his nose broken. "It got in my way." He grinned, that slow, easy, I've-got-you grin that he knew would send her rage even higher.

"In another minute you're going to explode. Why don't you just come on and get it?" Michael invited in a slow, soft drawl.

The light wind riffled the tendrils around her flushed face and Michael fought to get his heartbeat back to normal.

Cloe tossed her head, shaking with the need to tackle Michael and make him pay for interfering with her life—for seeing what she had spent her life upon, for stepping into her pain. She wouldn't let him get to her, she wouldn't. "Get lost."

"You're putting on a few pounds from this angle . . . filling out those jeans pretty good," he murmured, as she walked away from him toward her car.

She hesitated, curled her hands into fists, and walked back to Michael. She jabbed his chest with her finger. "Stay out of my business from now on, and if you need to take an edge off your . . . needs, I'm certain you can call someone."

He stood there, thumbs hooked in his belt, long legs braced apart, his gold-brown eyes narrowing on her. Then he smiled, that same slow, sensuous, knowing curve of his lips that he had given her when he was twenty-four and she was nineteen.

Cloe launched herself at him, hands hitting his chest, intending to knock him off her road, out of her sight. Off balance, reeling backward, Michael snagged her wrist in one hand, wrapped his arm around her waist, and took her with him, tumbling off the slight embankment.

She fought him; she fought herself, pounding at Michael's rangy, hard body, kicking, until he pinned her beneath him, his hands locking her wrists in the grass by her face. "Get off me," she snapped, fighting for breath and glaring up at the hard, blunt masculine face above her.

They slid down two inches on the embankment before he answered. "The hell I will." Michael's husky deep voice stroked the hairs on her nape, lifted them in warning.

She saw his eyes darken, watched his head lower to hers there in the new lush grass. As if in slow motion, his mouth brushed her lips, back . . . to the corners, his breath sweeping her skin. He had that raw, unforgettable scent of a man, who had been working outside, of leather and sweat, and of hand soap, and the boy that had placed her on his saddle, and held her safely. She was terrified of her answering need to step into the flames.

"Damn you, Cloe. It's about time we finished that kiss." Michael fused his mouth to hers and raw hunger sprang to curl around her, shocking her, devouring her. He pressed his hips hard down on hers, his body aroused.

Before she could inhale, force her heart to stop leaping, Michael jerked his head back, his eyes lashing at her. They stared at each other and while Cloe trembled, awakened, softened, Michael slowly looked down the length of their tangled bodies, locking on the sight of her breasts rising and falling against his chest as if he wanted to devour her.

Her heart flip-flopped when he looked at her again, hunger brilliant and hot in his eyes as he found her mouth.

This time his kiss was soft, enchanting, more devastating than the first, tasting, brushing, running over hers like feathers, stirring her. He breathed unevenly, as if holding himself in check, reining in his body to reach beyond the heat and test another emotion.

She arched beneath him, needing more, aching for the sweet taste, the gentle brush of his lips, never stopping, never letting her feed, fuse hungrily upon him. Michael's breath was harsh, his body taut above hers as she heard herself groan, arching up into him as his big hand covered her breast gently as if it belonged there.

She cried out, taut and shaking, shocked by the need rising in her.

Michael took her mouth again and this time, released, her fingers splayed into his hair, angling his mouth, slanting it to hers. She dived into the taste of him, the scents and textures, the hard muscles sliding over hers, easing her from the damp, fragrant earth and onto his body.

Cloe fought to draw back, her body shivering as Michael's big hands caressed her hips, her bottom, and a faraway sense told her that she was alone in the kiss, that Michael had withdrawn—

She warily lifted her head, forced her lids to open, and found his hard stare. "That was some kiss," Michael murmured unevenly.

Cloe reacted instantly. She rolled to one side, leaped to her feet, and stared down at Michael, while he folded his arms behind his head, looking up at her with undisguised appreciation. She shook with the need to—she dragged air into her lungs, curling her hands into fists. There was no mistaking the hard aroused contours of his body . . . or the melting, damp, quivering reaction of hers.

"Are you all done?" he asked in a conversational tone, gold eyes flicking over her warmly, seductively. "Or would you like a second round?"

"You're still not my prince," she shot back at him, furious with her lack of control and the rumpled grass where they had just lain, evidence of her passion for Michael.

"Ouch. Now *that* hurts." Michael's laughter followed her scramble up the slight embankment.

Chapter 8

❧

THE MID-APRIL AIR wasn't sweet anymore as Cloe prowled across Angelica's sleek, contemporary living room.

Angelica glanced at her. "So the catalog just needs Cheslav's photographs and then goes to press. I like reports, but I trust you on this one, kid, and I've got my hands full at the bank. My brother has made another mess and the auditors are prowling."

She adjusted the cotton balls between her toes, then briskly shook her bottle of burgundy polish. She tugged up the strap of her short, leopard-print satin nightie. "This place needs a health spa and a good beauty salon. I'm not about to let Minnie Paycheck touch my hair or ruin my nails. The things a self-righteous girl has to learn when she prefers to live in the sticks."

She glanced at Cloe, who was stalking the sleek glass-and-chrome living room. Angelica had designed, contracted, and built her angular, contemporary redwood home with sprawling decks that overlooked Lolo and Gilchrist House. "Cloe, surely the encounter among Michael and Ross and you couldn't have been that bad. My gosh, neither of you is a teenager. You should have expected Michael to finish that kiss you started years ago."

Cloe tensed, her back to Angelica. "How do you know?"

"Gee, duh, I don't know. Try this . . . city slicker arrives—a dude with designer jeans and lizard boots, driving a new custom pickup that has never run over a cowpile or hauled hay. Michael's beat-up pickup stops. Next scenario—the dude gets a ticket barreling out to the interstate. Someone smashes his nose. Then Sid Odell drives by while you and Michael are discussing crops, all tangled up and steamy on the side of the road. You've got grass stains on your backside, like you were mashed beneath something heavy and hot."

Angelica studied Cloe's expression for a moment and then painted her toenails, studying her work. "Oh, yeah, my Wild Willow friend . . . you went to the post office with grass stains on your back and murder on your face. All afternoon you waited on customers, mauled Stella's meatball submarine sandwiches, and sloshed her adzuki bean soup on Clayton Frei's best Stetson. You almost threw her black bean and vegetable tortilla rollups at Lily Waters . . . poor Lily, she really needs an exercise program. Lily had to eat three more of them to recover from your brutality."

Cloe glared at Angelica while she continued, "Then you come here, barreling down the road, on the warpath, and gee, I'd say those red marks on your cheek are a pretty good imitation of whisker burns. Then there's that sassy, pouting hot look on your lips. Add

that to the fire in your eyes and I get the feeling that
dealing with Ross isn't a priority anymore."

Cloe glanced at her face in the mirror, noting the
red marks Michael's stubble had left. Michael had actually placed his hand over her breast—covering it,
claiming her. It wasn't a caress, a movement of his
fingers in a caress, molding her—it was a claiming.
Worse—she wanted him to caress her, to—"Michael
is just as irritating as I remember. And I do not want
to hear any frog-prince humor."

Angelica studied her polished toes. "Hmm. He
never irritated me. In fact, I'm glad he's staying a bit.
I like the guy, always have. Toss Liam McKensie into
the mix, and you, and things could get interesting in
this town. You three are already tagged as 'those outsiders.' I like shifting the percentages against The
Club, and you're definitely stirring them up. Tsk. Tsk.
Imagine. Trying to market outside of Lolo. What can
you be thinking?"

She shot Cloe a grim look. "Josy has that scared
look. Let's visit her. You're mad as a wet hen and
wanting to brood. Josy has always been able to calm
you down. You won't sleep—Michael has got you all
stirred up—and I never sleep, haven't for years. I'll
just put on my robe."

Over the rim of her champagne glass, Cloe studied
Angelica. "You're mad, aren't you? You've got that
icy nip in your tone."

Angelica lifted an expressive auburn eyebrow. "Me,
darling? Now, why would I be in a snit?"

"You are. You tear off your words like you were
tearing flesh from bone—"

Angelica ripped the cotton balls from between her

toes and slammed them onto the glamour magazines on the glass table top. "All right, you asked for it, princess. You've been so tied up with yourself that you've forgotten a few things . . . like Josy. Edward-the-creep, her ex-husband, is after Cody. That kid is my godson, damn it, and I care. The words are all inside me and won't come out when Josy needs them, but I care. Edward doesn't care for Cody. He's just being—controlling, power-hungry, an ineffectual man tossing his weight around on someone weaker, and you haven't had the time to go out to Small Bird ranch, help her, listen to her. Josy does not know how to fight and you do. *Do* something for her."

Cloe knew she'd failed Josy, but she wasn't letting Angelica run over her. "You *did*, I suppose?"

In an athletic, feminine movement, Angelica stood. "Damn straight, I did . . . in my own way. But Josy clammed up the minute I told her my opinion of Edward. I've never learned how to hold back with you or her. You're the only ones I've trusted. I'm not built to feel, to say the right things. You are, but you're hoarding yourself for you—I call that selfish."

"Why don't you let it all out, Angelica? You've been wanting to," Cloe invited, lifting her champagne glass in a toast. They were evenly matched, Angelica and herself, and Angelica's methodical mind served Cloe's more creative one. Angelica's storms had been building for weeks, and now it was time to unleash them.

Angelica lifted the champagne flute to her lips and drained it. "All right. You asked for it. Josy never complains. I doubt if you'd have taken time to contact her, taken time to come back, that any of this would have happened. Eddie was just on the point of loaning her out to his friends—doping her up because she trusted him. I went to see his father. The old man made Edward marry her. I didn't want *that*, but at least she had a little respectability and protection with a baby coming."

She glanced at Cloe and poured more champagne. "I see you winding up, getting nasty. I did not say it was your fault, but I'm lousy at emotions and you know it. I'm slow and methodical, but you . . . you had the heat and the verve—swashbuckling verve, may I add—to make a difference."

" 'Verve'?"

"Style. Don't fight me on this—I'm on a roll. You never were afraid of a good fight, leaping right into the middle of it, while I was still circling and making plans and weighing the losses. Josy needed you, not me. Remember, I wrote you and at the time you had just miscarried—you just paled."

Cloe fought the nausea dampening her palms, the sudden empty aching pain in her womb. "Twice, Angelica. I miscarried twice, and the last time was three months before my divorce to Ross was final. He made a point to let me know exactly how I had failed as a woman to reproduce his required offspring."

Angelica stiffened as if taking a slap. "Leave it to me. I'm sorry. Really sorry."

She inhaled sharply, narrowing her gaze on the neat business arrangement in one corner—the spacious desk, her computer and stock market reports, before continuing, "You remember Josy's father, Max Small Bird? He was an alcoholic, but he had standards. Not even the Livingston dollars could force him to make Josy have an abortion, and old man Livingston finally made Edward marry her. She was so sweet—she thought she could make it work. I am sick to death of being a bridesmaid to friends who are thick headed and think they can make nowhere marriages work."

Angelica too carefully placed the glass on the neat bar, studying it. She licked her fingertip and ran it around the rim, the whine eerie, dipping into the shadows. She glanced warily at Cloe. "Okay, so I believe in romance. It's got to be out there somewhere. Your folks had it—okay. The kid is sweet. Cody thinks I'm a goddess. He gives me flowers. He's going to marry me when he grows up. What can I say?"

Angelica wouldn't want to hear that she loved Cody, just out and out loved anyone; she was too wary, too scared. Cloe met her wary glare. "So you're mad at me, right? What would happen if I gave you flowers?"

"People would talk." Angelica moved on, mulling Josy's problems as if they were her own. "Josy has to have something more than she does, sometimes training and boarding a few horses, working for peanuts as a small town deejay. She could lose that job at any minute if The Club puts pressure on the station. Every job in town is controlled by them in some way—except at The Pinto Bean, and Stella doesn't have enough work. Anyway, Josy can't leave town because of Edward. He'd have Cody in a minute. Josy needs something so damned strong that—this town has got to have something big and tough and lean, something outside of agriculture, something to bring in investors and—" She lifted and wickedly wiggled her eyebrows, mocking The Club. "Those damn outsiders. The town is going downhill."

"Angelica, what you're talking about is really big."

Angelica glanced at her computer. She'd been very discreet, investing away from the bank, using her computer, and her investments were enough to rattle The Club if the right business came along. Rattle them? That was timid. She intended to take them apart.

She wanted to bring in new people and give new work to the ones already living in the valley. These were her people and she wanted them out from under the thumb of The Club, where they could make choices about their lives.

Liam McKensie was making a difference; she had an ally, and Liam had tossed good investment leads her way.

She tensed, recognizing her father's ability to plot clearly without sentiment. Maybe she had inherited her father's need to rule, engineering lives. She had the capital, and one chance to prove herself—with Cloe, that was possible. She studied Cloe under her lashes. "Tell you what, Cloe. You're tough, smart, creative. If you come up with a concept that will bring new life into Lolo and take care of Josy, I'll back you. I have a little capital tucked away. Whatever you come up with, I want it big and flashy, with hefty profits, and there can't be any backing up once we step into the ring. I'm not about to let my father put *me* in the sanatorium."

There. Angelica relaxed slightly after dropping her plan into Cloe's talented backyard. Cloe had just exactly what Angelica needed—she knew Lolo's inroads and most of all she wouldn't back down from a good fight. This was Angelica's first sharing of an idea that she'd coddled for years, pushing The Club into a corner where all the nasty edges showed. At the moment, Cloe was too shaken by the encounter with her ex-husband and whatever Michael Bearclaw had taken from her on that embankment. Angelica would let Cloe circle the idea, getting used to it—

"I'm not exactly concerned about remaking Lolo, right now. And I'd rather not tie our friendship to a bankroll and payments. You're not talking about the catalog, but something that would take time to build . . . big money." Cloe sipped her champagne. Angelica was right; in her hurry to survive, to wrench The Pinto Bean out of debt, she'd forgotten Josy. Josy. Always there, always sweet and kind and understanding. "You're right. Josy does need something else."

"I know. But tonight we can do her hair and give her a pedicure. I will not bikini wax another woman, but I can try to salvage those rough cowboy hands of hers. How are you on hair? Not that she's got enough to style. By the way, did you know your roots are making a definite three-inch statement?"

Michael listened to the police scanner and smiled grimly. The police were outside the city limits, chatting with the sheriff's deputies. Cloe's BMW was spotted going toward the Small Bird ranch.

The Wild Willows were having a meeting. Fresh from his shower, his hair wet and a towel draped around his waist, Michael propped his bare feet on the desk. He let his instincts take him prowling.

Roy Meadowlark had worked on Bearclaw Ranch

for years; an expert horseman, he treated the Bearclaw registered quarter horses like children. Though Roy was friendly enough now, he was edgy and wary. His weathered, lined face had closed when Michael had asked him if Wade had been troubled. Roy had shaken his craggy head, plopped on his battered hat, and walked out of the Lickety-Split Café as fast as his bowed legs would take him. Roy, like most of the people in Lolo, was keeping secrets.

Michael scanned the six pictures over the desk— ordinary pictures measuring the lives of a family. The dusty, crumbling rose had special meaning, and the newly discovered camera, which his father had said was lost.

Michael picked up the camera, focusing it. He remembered the day his father had purchased the used bag of camera and gadgets. Wade had taken the camera with him, the day Stella Matthews had been raped. He'd read about proving rape, how to do it, and photography of bruises would make a case. He'd been white and shaken when he returned; his big, rope-scarred hands had trembled when he'd emptied the film roll from the camera.

That day, Michael had seen hell in his father's eyes. And pain, the gut-ripping, gaping wound kind that never heals. Later, when Wade was called to take pictures of Gus Ballas's body, he'd been silent for days— his friend Sam Matthews had been taken to jail for murder.

Maybe the evidence that had led to Sam's conviction was the reason Michael had decided to go into forensics. Sam Matthews was big enough, strong enough, to beat a man to death, but honor and the love of his family would have prevented that. Wade had been shaken by the guilty verdict. "Sam wouldn't have killed Gus. We grew up together . . . brawled a bit when we were young. Sam knew when to pull his punches and hold his temper. He wouldn't have beaten Gus to death," Wade had repeated.

Later, he'd been more distracted, especially after the sheriff had visited, and he had called young Michael aside. "If anything happens to me, you take your mother and sister and get the hell out of here. They'll yammer and cry, but you do it. You take what you can for the stock and the land and you git."

The coyotes on the mountain howled as Michael tapped the lens cover thoughtfully. The eye of the camera stared at Michael. What had it seen? What did Wade Bearclaw want to settle now, after all these years? What had happened to Nimo, the barn cat, and why had someone wearing Nike joggers with untied laces—approximately over two hundred pounds and walking on the balls of his feet, a little heavy on his right side, like a man wearing a holstered pistol—circled every building on Bearclaw Ranch? Why had he broken into the old milk barn, which contained nothing but airy shadows and concrete block bound by cobwebs and dirt?

Several high caliber rifle bullets had been dug out of the house's wood exterior; the number, size, and penetration force matched the flattened slugs in Wade's desk, a knife groove running down them where they had been dug out. Two windows had been newly replaced and new locks had been added to the doors. The front and back doors had been forced open, the deadbolts shattered.

Wade's Colt .45 had been waiting, oiled and cleaned, jammed into the gunbelt that had been worn to protect the land. Bullets waited in the chambers.

Michael opened the black velvet cloth on the desk. He dangled the gleaming, huge bear claw in the light. Wade had stirred someone enough to make threats. Michael glanced at the new alarm system he had installed, minute wires hidden and sensitive, motion sensing cameras that required codes to activate and disable them.

The wind carried the old owl's hoot to Michael. There were secrets in Lolo and Michael intended to finish his father's business.

Michael ran his fingertip across the old locket, nestled in the black satin with the bear claw. *After all those years, Cloe could still make his head spin.*

Cloe. Michael tensed as he remembered his surprise, the way Cloe opened up to him, pouring into him, her temper turned to heat and hunger, matching his.

For a moment, she'd taken his breath away, that sweet demanding mouth searching for his, tasting him. Beneath his hand, the quivering soft curve of her breast had startled him, because all of his instincts had told him to claim her.

Michael ran the back of his hand across his scarred lip. He crushed the locket in his fist and closed his eyes, forcing the rage away, back into the past.

He carefully replaced the old camera to its bag of gadgets, his instincts telling him that the old camera held a clue he needed. Right now, his mind filled with Cloe as she had been this afternoon, all flushed and soft and hungry, her eyes drowsy with need, her lips burning beneath his, searching for his mouth, slanting against it.

The towel covering his lap shifted and Michael hit the desk with the flat of his hand. He pushed himself to his feet and walked toward his second cold shower of the night. Cloe's hot, open reaction to him may have come from the tension of seeing her ex-husband and Michael didn't intend to act as a substitute.

He wanted nothing but the raw emotions flying between them—no rules, no kindness, just clearing away all those haunting memories of dreams Cloe had smashed the day she'd walked out of his life.

Michael studied the collection of antique spurs, gleaming on the logs above the long wood-and-cushion couch. In drover days, he would have taken his needs to town, spending his paycheck on a pretty woman and waking up with a hangover in the morning, his body slaked. Unfortunately he knew his needs now, after a misspent youth trying to get over Cloe, and they still sang with the need to sink into her, claiming her.

So much for honor and not taking what she'd offered in that barn when she was nineteen. The need to have her still burned in his gut, and this time he'd walk away, freed of his addiction.

Michael grimly ripped away the towel, turned on the shower, and stepped into the icy, pelting water.

The third week in April, Cloe Matthews was busy, tearing around the countryside in her BMW and serving soup and sandwiches at The Pinto Bean. She stirred life into the community, to Angelica, to Josy, and most of all to Stella, which Liam appreciated.

Liam McKensie wiped the raspberry-nut ice cream blob from his daughter's chin. He adjusted his six foot-two-body on the bar stool his daughter favored when in The Pinto Bean; six-year-old Tracey loved to spin on the stools, but legs as long as Liam's had to fold tightly, fitting behind the bar. While he enjoyed The Pinto Bean's house coffee and Stella's famed apple pie at two o'clock on a Saturday afternoon, Tracey had dived into the bowl of ice cream. Later, Tracey would stay overnight with her friend Cherry and would go to church with her in the morning.

At the other end of the counter, ten-year-old Karen Matthews was lifting fingerprints from a "perp"'s coffee cup and had just stealthily placed a Beanery spoon in a plastic bag for later forensic work. She lifted her head, caught Liam's smile, and blinked innocently.

Stella moved by him, on her way to serve hot apple pie à la mode to Orley Johnson. Liam caught her fragrance, swirled in cinnamon, and automatically his gaze locked to her curved, jean-clad hips, swaying beneath the tantalizing confines of her apron.

A lonely Saturday night stretched before Liam; he took another shielded look at Stella's ripe body and sighed silently. There were other women in Lolo; unfortunately, his hormonal temperature rose near a woman who thought of him as a pseudo-son.

The Pinto Bean's quiet, familiar afternoon chatter soothed Liam. Lolo was much quieter than Seattle, where Liam had developed his skills. The son of a sheepherder whom The Club had ruined, Liam had decided to return to Lolo to raise his daughter. Tracey would have been just as happy somewhere else, but he liked planting himself in The Club's midst, twisting financial screws.

He used a napkin to wipe the ice cream from Cherry's cheek and then from his daughter's. His family had come to this same café long ago, as a Saturday treat, amid cowboys and their "good old days." The McKensies had a small, warm dry house, crops, plenty of grass, and lambing had been good; the high-powered ram had done his work with the ewes. The mortgage was due, and the flock was ready to market. Then, in one violent spring storm, six hundred sheep bolted, running off a cliff. In the morning, their bodies were piled like a bloodied white, soft mountain, and Bradley Gilchrist had come to call, flanked by Monroe Tibbs, Sr. The sheriff had slapped an eviction notice into Liam's father's hand.

Then, in the middle of the night, his father had bundled the family in a broken down pickup—all five of them, Liam, his brother and sister, and his mother. His mother's face had been silvery with rain and tears, her shoulders slumped, hunching with muffled sobs. Despite the pain tearing through him, twelve-year-old Liam did not cry; instead, he swore to repay The Club for his family's heartbreak.

Liam studied the picturesque storefronts beyond The Pinto Bean's window, tombstones of the past. A sheepman in cattle country didn't last in those days, but things were looking good for the McKensie family, thanks to the Matthews and the Bearclaws.

Stella spoke softly to an elderly woman and Liam's attention swung to her. The primitive need to make love to Stella shocked Liam, who had always been able to methodically control his life and his body.

He'd been celibate since Tracey was a year old and his wife, Sue Ellen, had died in an auto accident.

He glanced at Stella, who would turn any man's head. Her husky laughter spread over The Pinto Bean, and she lifted her head in an angle that brought all that beautiful, arched throat to the light, gleaming smooth skin, waiting for a kiss. Classic bones, he thought, admiring the sweep of her cheek, the soft curve of her mouth.

Liam's heart quietly slid into his throat as the Saturday afternoon sunlight outlined Stella's tall, voluptuous body, the flaring curve of her hips. His thumb moved over the warm smooth surface of his coffee cup, emblazoned with The Pinto Bean's logo.

Stella passed, refilling his coffee. Her scent, that of cinnamon, coffee, and fine, prime woman curled around him. "How's it going, Liam?" Then, without missing a beat, Stella leaned down to kiss Tracey's cheek. "Hi, honey. When Cloe was just your age, she and Angelica Gilchrist and Josy Small Bird . . . Livingston, now, used to call themselves the Wild Willows. They were demons, really, terrorizing the countryside, and always, always in trouble."

Liam tapped his fingers on the smooth counter. So much for Stella's interest in him; he was jealous of his own daughter.

"Really? The Wild Willows?" Tracey asked, her ice cream spoon dripping into her almost empty bowl.

"Really. They got that name from Cloe's dad." Stella turned, replaced the coffee pot on the burner, and bent down to forage on a low shelf. Liam tensed, sitting straighter, angling subtly, focusing on the tight press of her jeans across a lush backside. Someone nudged him, and Liam nodded a curt acknowledgment.

At the second nudge, he turned abruptly, frowning at the intrusion. He met Michael's lifted eyebrows, his too bland gaze. Michael slid onto the stool beside Liam and grinned knowingly. "Muriel and I have a Saturday night date at the newspaper later. What are you doing tonight? A late-night poker game at Quinn's?"

Liam glanced down at the gauze layering Michael's palm. His attraction to Stella wasn't a smirking matter. "Did you hurt that sticking it into someone else's business?"

At the other end of the bar, Karen caught Michael's glance. She lifted the plastic bag for his view and when he nodded, Karen beamed. She began to whistle casually, slung her big bag across one shoulder and strolled out the door. Once outside the door, she ran, eager to fingerprint the perp's spoon.

Michael's laughter lines deepened when he turned to Liam. "I wouldn't want some hot pants Romeo putting the moves on Stella. After all, she was almost my stepmother."

"I'm aware of the relationship. How did you hurt your hand?"

Michael frowned as he studied the gauze on his hand. "I've been asking questions no one wants to answer. Someone just doctored Lopez's watering trough with loco weed. He wasn't sweet. The vet confirmed what I had suspected."

"You've probably stepped on The Club's toes. Be careful." The Club had been too pleasant to Liam and he knew then that they were at their most dangerous.

Though Michael's father had been a cattleman and acceptable to them, Michael could be a threat. He wasn't going to be dislodged without a fight though. He was a hunter, a tracker, bred of mountainmen and Sioux, and he'd take care of himself.

"Right. The Club is still here," Michael agreed grimly. "Stella says that she and Cloe have been getting telephone hangups."

"Mmm, predictable. I'm disappointed in their old-fashioned methods," Liam noted. "They won't like Cloe's catalog business. They think they are just dealing with mugs and T-shirts, but once they discover she's started an small industry under their noses, all hell will break loose."

Michael flashed Liam a wry grin. "All hell will break loose when she finds out I'm an investor."

Cloe swept by, her arms filled with a cardboard box marked "Mugs." She glared at Michael, and he nodded, a slow smile replacing his frown. "Why, hello, Cloe," he drawled. "Miss me?"

"Get out of here," she snapped, coming back to push the box into his shoulder. Liam admired how Cloe dived right into the heart of what bothered her, focused on Michael like a hawk, and was careless of pretense. Slow-moving, casual, dark-skinned Michael was a perfect foil for Cloe's golden skin, her hurry-hurry attitude.

Michael pushed the box back with an easy shrug that took Cloe back several steps. "I'll leave when I'm ready." Michael's hand swept out, his thumb wiping the ink on Cloe's cheek and her head jerked back. "You need to wash your face, little girl."

"Don't you push me, Michael Jedidiah Bearclaw," she shot back tightly.

"Oh, you know I'm going to," he returned easily, and smiled at Stella as she slid her peach pie onto the counter in front of him. She took his personalized mug from the rack, pouring coffee into it.

When Stella braced her arms on the counter and smiled warmly at Michael, Liam's throat tightened. The gap in her blouse exposed a deep crevice and the curve of a soft mound—and Liam almost drooled—

Stella glanced at him, did a double take, and placed her hand against his cheek. "Why, Liam, you look a little flushed. You're not coming down with something, are you?"

Oh, he'd like to come down on her, Liam thought darkly, as she patted his head and swept back into the kitchen, her hips swaying elegantly. Liam's usual easy temper hiked up a notch. He was a boy to her, like her sons. "Excuse me, Michael. Cloe, would you mind keeping the girls company for a minute? I have something to discuss with Stella."

Liam followed Stella into the kitchen, his height causing him to angle his head away from the hanging pots. She smiled at him absently, her hands working eggs into flour for tomorrow's egg noodles. Liam watched those elegant, strong woman's hands massage the dough and realized he'd just shuddered. He might as well humiliate himself, and asked aloud, "Stella, are you busy tonight?"

Dumb. Double dumb. He should have called . . . invited her to dinner . . . given her days to think about it. He should have polished some line, added some astrology bunk, and slid his invitation out smoothly.

He swallowed as she put her weight into rolling the dough into a thin circle, her T-shirt taut against her full breasts. "Mmm? Busy? Yes, I am—I'm watching the shopping program tonight. They're featuring small kitchen appliances. Then there's a Gary Cooper movie I want to see—*High Noon*."

Great. He couldn't compete with kitchen appliances, could he? Here he was, almost forty and feeling like a boy next to a woman who didn't see him as the potential lover he wanted to be.

He's cute, Stella thought—that oh, gee shucks, rangy look like Gary Cooper—and he was sweet, adoring his daughter. Today he wore a dress shirt rolled back at the cuffs and gray slacks, for Liam was never casual about anything, always so serious. Shadows rode him, except when he looked at his daughter. "You should find someone," Stella offered softly. "You're too young to be alone. You're interesting, polite, and sweet, and there is no reason you should be alone on a Saturday night."

"That's just the problem—" he began.

"I know." She patted his cheek, leaving a flour imprint, which she patted off with a towel. She hadn't realized that Liam was quite so tall, or so tense, almost vibrating to her touch. "Sorry."

Those Gary Cooper eyes flashed; Liam was angry. Stella smiled at him. She'd known men; she'd raised boys. The need for feminine attention usually ran high on a Saturday night. "You really should think about dating now and then, Liam."

"I'm working on a relationship," he stated grimly, glaring at her.

"That's good. Don't be shy when you see the right

girl," Stella urged, in the motherly tone she would use for Dan or Gabe or Michael.

"I'm only ten years younger than you, Stella," Liam stated, bracing his hands on the chopping table. He stared at the flour on her chest and wanted to hold that full soft body against his just once, to tuck her head beneath his chin, hold her close, and keep her safe.

Stella briskly dusted away the flour spot on her breast; the unconsciously feminine movement caused Liam's entire body to jolt to attention as she continued, "I know. That's exactly why you should be out there dating someone and not wasting yourself. If you want, I'll see what I can do. You know Karen Watkins is pretty lonely these days. She's sweet as could be. Here. Take this piece of pie home with you for later. You're just as lanky as my boys, Dan and Gabe, and they're always hungry."

She pushed a plastic-wrapped plate of peach pie into his hands. Liam breathed unevenly, a muscle leaping along his jaw and throat as his fingers tightened on the plate. "I think I've found someone, Stella," he said tightly, then stalked out of her kitchen.

Stella rinsed her hands beneath running water. Liam McKensie really needed to be held by a woman, loved by her, stretched out and devoured, until whatever anger filled those beautiful Gary Cooper eyes was gone. Lately, Liam's moods were like Dan and Gabe's before they were married—edgy, contrary, and hot.

Chapter 9

❧

"THANKS FOR BRINGING my supper from the deli—I sometimes forget to eat," Muriel Perkins said, as she placed the cartons of food and soup on the counter. "Michael, I've copied all the articles I could find about the Sam Matthews case onto disks for your computer. The strange thing is that there aren't photographs of Gus Ballas's body, or the crime scene. The county coroner lists multiple bruises, cracked and broken ribs, a perforated lung, et cetera. But the cause of death was a bashed skull. Old Al knew his business."

Muriel Perkins clucked to the parakeet sitting on her shoulder. She studied Michael. "Your father was very interested in the Sam Matthews case, too. In fact, he was pretty troubled by it these last few months—"

"As if he wanted to finish something before his heart gave out," Michael supplied slowly.

Muriel handed him the envelope with the disks on it and peered up at Michael from beneath her green visor. "You've got all those fine degrees. Are you going to use them?"

"Why, Ms. Perkins. Are you challenging me? You used to do that in school."

"You had a keen mind that needed challenges." Muriel tucked a wisp of white hair beneath her visor and straightened her thin shoulders. "This newspaper will print the news, whether it offends The Club or not. The Matthewses were destroyed because Sam prevented that contaminated waste from being buried near our valley. You want something from me, Michael Jedidiah Bearclaw, you just ask for it."

"Thanks." Michael leaned down to kiss Muriel's velvety, lined cheek, then plucked birdseed from her hair and handed it to her. "Still have all those parakeets?"

"After my mother finally passed, they're what family I have, outside of all you children, who grew up and left me," Muriel muttered, wiping a tear from her eye.

She stood on tiptoe and peered out into the street, sundown glowing on the old brick buildings. "The deputies are out there, wondering why your pickup is parked in front of the paper. They run the town more than David Williams's policemen do. I see Leland and Fred. They were always sneaky like that, even in kindergarten, and they were bullies to boot. Still are."

"They might think you and I are smooching," Michael drawled, enjoying the blush creeping up Muriel's wrinkled cheeks.

"Shoo. You just remember that I want to help." Muriel's bony hand pressed Michael's arm. "I heard you were down at the police station, asking questions about Sam Matthews's files. Did they help you?"

"Not much, though they admitted that Stan Collins was the first officer at the site. I'd like to know more about that." Michael tucked the disks into his shirt pocket. "I know Dad took those photos. I want them."

Muriel patted his arm. "That's a good boy. You've decided to unwrap this from the inside right? Rather than calling in outsiders?"

"Muriel, haven't you heard? I *am* an outsider. Even Roy Meadowlark won't talk with me." Michael gently touched the bouquet of flowers on Muriel's desk; the texture reminded him of Cloe's skin. He circled a delicate fuschia petal with his fingertip; after seeing Cloe's ex-husband push her around, Michael realized the volatile strength of Sam Matthews's rage.

"It's fitting that The Club be brought down by the people who survived their sick rule. Roy is scared. He wasn't talking to Wade, either . . . in fact, they had a lollapalooza of a fight and wouldn't tell anyone what it was about. But I like the idea of us taking care of our own. Somehow it doesn't seem right that we should let outsiders clean up something that we should have stopped years ago."

"I agree, Muriel, and revenge is just that much sweeter when you do it yourself, right? That hands-on feeling?"

"Such a smart boy, Michael. I knew you'd understand."

Monroe Tibbs, Jr., who had succeeded his father as sheriff, eased into the side door of Bradley Gilchrist's home office. Bradley's gaze lingered at his daughter's photograph, placed on his desk, before he glanced meaningfully at Monroe. Monroe removed his western hat and caught the scent of expensive bourbon.

The sheriff looked uneasily at a chair and decided

against sitting. "We're got trouble, Mr. Gilchrist. That Michael Bearclaw is nosing around. He came down to the police station and told David to show him the file on Sam Matthews, or he'd pick up the telephone that minute and do some real damage. Got a call from the county coroner's office that said both he and Miz Muriel had called about the Sam Matthews's trial. They both asked about pictures. The coroner wanted to know what's up. Like usual, I said I'd find out. I don't want no trouble with the county coroner, Mr. Gilchrist."

"Michael Bearclaw isn't staying. He'll be gone before you know it. He's only settling his father's estate."

"His old man, Wade Bearclaw, wasn't no easy chore, either. Michael could get it into his mind to stay. Outsiders make things difficult, Mr. Gilchrist. There's that Cloe Matthews over to The Pinto Bean, that Liam-money fellow, and your daughter is right in the middle of the mess."

The banker slid Monroe a too quiet, knifing look. "Leave my daughter out of this."

The sheriff sulked, but knew better than to challenge Gilchrist when his high-nose daughter was involved. "All that I'm sayin', Mr. Gilchrist, is that it's a bad pot brewing. That Michael fellow could be trouble. I grew up with him and he's no easy ride."

"Michael Bearclaw is born and bred to this valley. The Bearclaws and the other old-time families of this valley like to handle their own business. He's got contacts that could make trouble, but he won't use them. He's just like Wade, and that gives us the advantage, because I know him down to his bones. I'm certain

you can take care of Michael Bearclaw, Monroe,"
Bradley murmured smoothly. "You've been taking
care of us since your father passed on, and haven't I
always backed you?"

Monroe preened and stuck the toothpick resting
over his ear into his mouth, chewing on it. With
Gilchrist behind him, Monroe might make state sen-
ate, maybe U.S. senator. Monroe wasn't a drunk like
his father; he'd use The Club to get what he wanted.
The president of The Club had just given him a hunting license on Michael Bearclaw. Monroe remembered
how Michael had knocked him around for drinking
and having fun with that whining Morris girl. "Yes,
sir. You have. Don't you worry none. I'll take care of
Michael. By the way, I think Orson has a problem.
He's been up to visit Maggie Ten Feather twice this
last week, and he's been drinking."

"Orson was always weak but controllable with
Maggie in our grasp. Don't worry about him."

Side by side, arms wrapped around waists, Josy and
Cloe two-stepped country western style. Hours spent
over her drawing board with a telephone propped between her shoulder and ear had caused her to stiffen.
Josy had taken one look at Cloe and turned on the
radio. "You need exercise," she'd said, grabbing Cloe
and moving her in tune to the country music.

When the song was over, they sprawled on Josy's
worn couch. "We're good," Josy said, panting heavily. "I wish Cody weren't at Edward's for the weekend. He'd have liked showing off how good he is at
dancing."

Cloe lifted her iced glass of genuine, homemade

lemonade and placed it along her hot cheek. "I missed you," she said, meaning it. When had she really had this much fun? The years stretched behind her, bleak and dreary.

Josy took her hand and held it. "I missed you."

"All we need is Angelica and no telling what the Wild Willows could do tonight. She said she was busy. Now, how busy could she be in Lolo? Isn't Saturday night her big spa night, when she crushes cucumbers for facials and gives herself a buttermilk bath? I hear the grocery store orders extra buttermilk for the weekends, just for her."

Josy's husky laughter spread over the country western music. "She's got a plan for tonight. I saw her stop by the dry-goods store for bib overalls ... designer bib overalls. She came by the radio station and asked what I knew about smoking cigars—Dad loved a good rum-soaked Cuban cigar. She asked which one—the thin dark kind, or a fat stogey—suited a cream Armani silk blouse and denim. I don't think she worried about the Tiffany brooch. She had that closed in, furious go-for-Quinn Lightfeather look—and tonight is his usual Saturday night poker game that lasts until dawn. Since an all-boys' club is one thing our girl can't stand, I'd say Angelica is going to crash that party."

Josy sipped her lemonade. "I've been too worried lately and that just upsets Angelica. She seems to get mad just looking at me. She said she didn't think you were up to another encounter with Michael—he's at the poker game—so soon after that lip-locking with him in the grass, so she decided to fly on her own."

" 'Lip-locking.' That isn't exactly what happened."

Cloe settled into dissecting that earth-shattering Michael-kiss. Sprawled over her in the grass, Michael had known just how to touch her, how to tantalize her with a brush of his hard, warm lips. He had her arching, searching for more, hungry—

His tongue had pushed between her lips, ignoring her resistance, taking, soothing, entrancing her own— the invitation was too sexual and primitive, and it had shaken her.

The wild hunger had surged out of her, surprising her, and she'd latched onto the textures, the solid weight of Michael against her.

Compared to Michael's kiss, making love with Ross seemed clinical, dispatched, bodies moving against bodies, the quick shower to cleanse, the unfinished ache, the sleepless night.

She stirred restlessly, remembering the slow, easy fit of Michael's large hand over her breast as if he meant to keep her—

"I'm not going to make it," Josy was saying. "I don't have enough money to play Edward's ball game. He'll keep a custody suit going until he takes everything, and then he'll take Cody. Cody loves me, but he loves Edward, and the idea of a father in his life, too."

"Why did you marry Edward, Josy? I know you were pregnant, but you could have gone away. We grew up with him. You knew what he was."

Josy smiled softly. "I thought I could make him love me. I even wore dresses, frilly ones, but I couldn't make him love me. You grew up with Michael. You knew what he was, what he would be— honorable like his folks, with a feel for what's right and for the land—but you *didn't* marry him."

"Michael wasn't what I wanted." Wanted him? Cloe mocked herself. At nineteen, she'd wanted that fine, hard body locked to hers, discovering what sex was with the man she had chosen—Michael Bearclaw. He'd been top on her list of priorities and he had turned her down that day in the barn.

Josy snorted delicately. "I think he got that idea when you beaned him with that ball. You should have never attacked him in that barn. Michael Bearclaw was always a guy who calls his own shots, especially when it concerns a woman."

"I shouldn't have told you that I approached Michael. I was upset and just nineteen."

"Approached? When you were nineteen, you strolled up to him and told him you wanted him to take your virginity right there, right then in that barn. Let's see . . . you wanted to schedule Michael between washing your hair that morning and cruising town with Angelica and me that night. That's right, you told Angelica and me everything while you were packing your suitcase and your mother was trying not to cry, her baby flying from the nest. You put the moves on a guy who was almost like your brother."

Josy pulled Cloe's ponytail. "You know what they say about those Bearclaw men—they get what they want. Then there's that romantic bed-thing—where they cut the trees by hand and make beds for their brides—good sturdy ones."

"Mind your own business," Cloe ordered mildly, and knew Josy wouldn't. Cloe didn't want to think of Michael's hot honey-brown eyes flickering over her mouth while his hand lay heavy and possessive on her breast. He'd captured the softness of her as if he had that right, as if nothing would take her away from him. Not once did Ross put his hand on her like that, a firm, gentle claiming.

"Did he use his tongue—you know, when he kissed you?" Josy pressed, as if on cue, grinning wickedly. "Did you melt? Did you push your hungry, throbbing body next to his magnificent, studly one and invite him to . . . you know? Did you . . . touch *that*? Was it big? Tell me everything. Details. Did your heart pound? Has he got that thing right about undoing a bra without looking? While he's kissing you? Angelica tells me everything, and so should you. Of course, Angelica hasn't been rolled in the grass at all. She's too careful of her Versaces," Josy teased, then pursed her lips dramatically and made kissy-kissy noises.

Cloe nudged Josy with her elbow and couldn't help returning the grin. "Lay off. I've already told you about Ross, only because you tortured me. Tell me about you. Anyone you're interested in?"

"Would I be sitting here on a Saturday night with you, if there were someone?" Josy shook her head, her short boy haircut spraying out, gleaming blue-black in the lamplight. She studied her sock-clad feet. "Anyway, there isn't a man around here who would be interested, not with my background. I've got to survive this, for Cody. I've got to get more money to fight Edward. I can't go on borrowing from Angelica, though she insists. She just wrote a personal check for the new roof and plumbing, and she's been fighting those mortgage papers for Small Bird Ranch for years. I'm barely keeping afloat."

Josy stared at the wall as though seeing her past. "I

can't see Michael trying to strip you of your pride and make you into something you're not . . . I can't see him living off you, using you, running you until you couldn't think straight."

Josy turned to Cloe. "You're scared right now, of what you're feeling for him. You're working too hard to prove that you can save your mother from a second eviction. You're fighting yourself, too. Trust me. Everything will work out."

"Trust you . . . 'Everything will work out.' How many times have you said that to me through the years?" Cloe leaned back against the couch and closed her eyes. She was too tired to deal with Michael's raw hunger, or his tenderness.

Sleeping with Michael's kiss haunting her hadn't been possible; she was running on coffee and nerves and his kiss wouldn't let her rest. No matter how hard she tried, how tired she was, that kiss branded her thoughts—it was a claiming, an old-fashioned, raw, I've-got-you-staked-out kiss.

"When are you leaving, Cloe?" The shadows under Josy's eyes reminded Cloe of her friend's hardships.

"As soon as I can. If the catalog idea takes off, I'll need someone to manage it when I do leave. That could be you."

"Like I'm sure. Marketing is a foreign language to me. I know horses and cows, and a little bit about how to hold a microphone."

"You've got a voice that makes men steam, and you're good with animals and people. Right now, I need space for warehousing the catalog stock and shipping, and an office to do business. The Club wants me out of town, so they're not going to help."

Cloe wanted her mother safely away from any trouble that might arise. She needed a place big and
sprawling and safe, a nest in which to make her
plans—sketch them out, mull the potentials, and
grasp them.

Josy turned slowly to Cloe. "Exactly how do you
know The Club wants you out of town?"

"The hang-up calls and heavy breathing are a real
clue. They're trying to kill my catalog idea by stopping my suppliers. They're pulling that same junk
they used to, intimidating people. Then there's that
little incident of a knife in my BMW tire."

"A knife? Did you tell the police?"

Cloe thought of how Monroe's small, hot eyes had
lingered on her breasts, not bothering to disguise his
interest in her. "David Williams, the police chief? He
muttered, looked as though he would throw up, and
turned it over to Monroe. Monroe just smirked and
said he'd check on it. He didn't even bother to take
the knife for fingerprints."

Josy took Cloe's hand, holding it as she had for
years. "He got away with everything when his dad
was sheriff. Dad decided he'd testify at your dad's
trial and Monroe's dad turned up with Mr. Gilchrist.
The next thing I know Dad was drinking, and there's
a fire loose, taking the cash crops and endangering
the whole town of Lolo. He didn't have much to say
after that. Dad just seemed to fade away, losing himself into the bottle."

"I remember how awful that was for you."

"The way kids called me 'The Fire-man's Daughter'? If it hadn't been for your mother feeding me, I
don't know what would have happened to me. Dad

loved me, but he couldn't leave drinking long enough to see that I was fed or clean or dressed. Your mother even saw to it that I got my shots and dental work. She and Angelica forged Dad's name when they had to and your mother paid the bills."

"We love you, Josy."

"I love you, too, Cloe. But I'm worried. That knife was a real warning."

"I just love being popular," Cloe singsonged. "I'm going to take this catalog idea and wipe it in their faces, and they know it."

"This is no game, Cloe. You're like a thunderstorm, reckless and wild when you're mad and stirred up. You could get hurt."

"I intend to win this game. I need success now almost as much as I need breathing. Don't worry about me."

Tears spiked Josy's long straight lashes, her big brown eyes shimmering damply. "I can't help it. Friends like you and Angelica don't turn up in the turnip patch, you know."

Josy was too sweet, too easily hurt. Edward would cut her into pieces, using Cody. But not while she was here, Cloe thought, searching desperately for something to shift Josy's mood. "Oh, Jeez, remember when we waited all night out there in the turnip patch, waiting for babies? My dad sat right beside us all night."

Josy swiped at her eyes. "He ran off Dan and Gabe and Michael, when they tried to tell us ghost stories."

Her big black labrador ambled to the door and barked softly. "That's Angelica. Max knows the sound of her car."

Angelica plowed through the door, tossed a doggie

treat to Max, and sprawled gracefully into Josy's battered arm chair. "Like my get-up?"

"Very chic," Cloe answered, taking in Angelica's Armani silk shirt and bib overalls with cigars tucked into the chest pocket. The diamond brooch added panache. "I like the red silk stiletto heels."

Angelica stuck a plastic-wrapped fat cigar into her mouth and sucked it slowly, sensually. "I'm going to blow their little-boy minds. You should come along. It will be fun, puffing away on those big cigars. Can't imagine what they'll be thinking of."

Josy nudged Cloe. "It's all those vitamins and herbs. She's got enough energy for three women."

"Hey, listen. I pay plenty to have that stuff shipped in. If we had a decent—"

Cloe yawned and deliberately slipped her budding idea to Angelica, testing it. The idea had lurked in her mind, tucked behind the hurried packaging of the catalog. "I know . . . if we had a decent spa here, a health and beauty club, you wouldn't be so inconvenienced."

She'd served the idea gently, too massive to be examined thoroughly just yet—an exclusive health and beauty spa, near picturesque Lolo, bordered by mountains—a place where people could come to refresh—and all that lovely money. But Angelica was hunting tonight and not interested in making money for once. "Come with me. Michael will be there. Liam, too."

Cloe lifted an eyebrow. "And Quinn?"

Angelica frowned. "Do you know what that jerk did today? I merely stopped in at The Long Horn for an early afternoon drink—you know, to relax. Quinn handed me a candy bar, a cone of crushed ice with berry juice, and told me to go on home. He didn't want me stirring up the customers with slow dancing. He said he had enough of the Gilchrists for the weekend because he had to toss Jeffrey out on Friday night. Ann probably paid for that. My brother's wife is too sweet, and she won't admit he's beating her."

"Turd," Cloe said flatly, the term jerked from the Wild Willows' youthful conversations.

"Double turd," Josy added.

"I'll have you know that my brother has always been Super Turd." Angelica leaned forward, pinning Cloe and Josy with her frown. "Quinn likes that, you know. He likes swaggering around The Long Horn like a king, pushing people around."

"And you're not pushing him?" Josy petted Max, who had come to her side, nuzzling her hand.

"It's my cause in life. To make him pay for swaggering, for tossing me out more than once—"

Cloe lifted her lemonade glass in a toast. "For making you hot."

"Did not!" Angelica threw back, her chin lifting, green eyes blazing.

"Did too," Josy murmured, grinning.

Angelica looked at the ceiling, studiously ignoring the other women, then she leveled a stare at Cloe. "That catalog venture of yours must need an artist, or a photographer and a high-class printer, to say nothing of buying mailing lists and postage. I'll spot you, on a silent partner basis. Think about it. You can buy me out at any time. I not only like you, fireball, I appreciate your talent, and I'd consider it an insult if you didn't let me in on the ground floor."

Cloe forced herself to be calm. "I've got the photographer—Sergei Cheslav. Strictly a city boy from a New York Russian ghetto, he's been waiting for a chance to do the West. He'd take this assignment in a minute if Josy would let him play cowboy, here on her ranch."

Josy stared at Cloe blankly. "Sometimes I don't know who you are. How can you be so cool when this is so exciting? I can't offer money, but I can show a dude how to ride a horse. He can stay in the old bunk house, but I'm not paying any city boy's medical bills."

Cloe nodded at Angelica's low, appreciative whistle. Angelica's offer, slapped down step by step, was no surprise. All Cloe had to do was to make it look challenging, and Angelica would walk into anything. Because they were sisters of the heart and loved each other. "Angelica, this is chancy. I've got my list of contacts and they are interested—one or two country boutiques want to showcase The Pinto Bean products—and it's going to be a slow project, putting every drop of profits back into packaging, shipping, and marketing."

"Yeah, well, what else is new? I'd like to be in on the fun."

Josy leaned forward, her expression concerned. "Angelica, are you certain you want to take a stand against your family?"

"Hey. What's money for?" Angelica's smooth face darkened and she swept her hand through her hair; the diamond ring on her right hand speared light into the room. "I do more good inside the bank than out of it, so if you decide it's a go, it's our secret, okay? Oh, and there's just one little thing you should know

up front. I have silent partners, too—two of them, and
they've both expressed interest in seeing your business get off the ground—"

Angelica stopped in mid-sentence, lifted her
diamond-laden hand to the light, and studied her
slender, well-kept fingers. "How disgusting . . . another hangnail from working with paper. Is either one
of you interested in opening a beauty and health
spa?" she asked in a distracted tone. "I'm aging here,
falling apart at the seams, and not one of my good
friends has taken up Swedish massage."

Josy glowered at her. "You make me play tennis
with you and that is all I am doing. I am not waxing
your legs or anything personal for you, and do not
buy me another how-to book on beauty because I
never read them."

"Quinn is into that Native American herbs and
sweat lodge. You could go get sweaty with him—"
Cloe ducked the pillow Angelica threw at her. One
thing at a time, she told herself, bucking her usual
stormy eagerness to lay a great project in front of investors. The Pinto Bean catalog business was one
thing, the health spa was several years commitment.

"Ross, I will not give you those disks. If you call here
again, I'll call your . . . your wife. Don't. It won't work
. . . just get off the line." Cloe had no time or energy
to prowl around her past life, dissecting her mistakes.
It was the last week of April now. Sergei Cheslav
would arrive any day. A good fast photographer, Sergei didn't like to waste time, and she expected to
wrap up the catalog for the printers quickly. She'd
taken long hours swaying her suppliers, the crafts-

people still feared The Club, and everything was locked in place for the catalog.

Cloe stared at the lightning outside the kitchen window, running across the rugged mountains in the distance, shielded by the gray curtain of pounding rain. Michael Jedidiah Bearclaw, educated, world traveler, and haunted—by what? What did he want? Why was he still in Lolo?

Why did Cloe want to leap upon him every time she saw him? Why did that slow, knowing grin cause her heart to leap as though she were still a teenager and wondering what sex with Michael Bearclaw would be like, determined to experience him? That kiss had sizzled with promises she didn't understand. . . .

Rain pounded on the kitchen windows and thunder rattled the panes as the health spa idea burned, ideas nagging at her. It had begun with Angelica's complaints, a need to be filled, and now the potential for a profitable business bloomed in Cloe. She wasn't ready to open herself to Angelica, who would dive for the project like a hungry dog after a bone.

Alone in the apartment, the markup of a catalog spread before her on the kitchen table and several bulletin boards propped nearby. Cloe scanned her work. If not a glossy, high-priced catalog, this first effort had country heart and boutique punch. She ran her hand down her Pinto Bean T-shirt. Successes started small and grew, layering ideas on ideas.

Sergei Cheslav couldn't wait to "wallow in the West" and was now battling a temperamental model; his arrival was later than expected. Delays hurt, and Cloe rubbed the slow thud at her temples . . . or was it the fear of failure?

Sergei had lied; he was doing a favor for Cloe. The passionate Russian-American photographer and Josy would be an odd mix, but Sergei's talents would lend the quality Cloe wanted—sheer West, clean air, scented pines, sunflower meadows, and blue sage—she jotted down a note to ask Linda Marshal to create muslin bags for the sage incense.

The muscles in Cloe's neck protested the four hours she had just spent, making use of the quiet apartment. A rubberband held a stack of business letters addressed to radio and television stations. Cloe tapped her pen on her new label design for Emma Luna's natural jams and clover honey. Each supplier would have its own name splashed across The Pinto Bean's logo. The campaign was solid.

Lightning lit the night sky a moment before thunder boomed, rattling the windowpanes. She lifted her arms high and rotated her head. The blue clay and buttermilk face mask she'd applied while taking a breather had hardened and cracked. Used to pushing, working when she was exhausted, Cloe knew how to use tea bags to refresh her eyes, cold herbal water sprays, alternating them with cold showers and mud masks to keep awake on long, hard stretches. She knew how to prop herself up and do the job.

Angelica's silent investors would get their money's worth; the signed contract listed parties one and two, and Angelica wasn't budging on the names. The investors were probably frightened and wanted their secret kept.

Over The Pinto Bean, the apartment was quiet, the kitchen clock ticking, the rain falling gently now. The pencil broke in her hands, and Cloe stared at the two pieces, then pushed them away. They looked like her life; she'd crafted the past to suit her—her future was unpredictable.

Michael Bearclaw had no right to kiss her.

He had no right to enter her life, to disturb her nights.

Cloe picked up the pencil pieces and fitted them together. She'd survive, rescue her mother, and forget Michael Bearclaw.

Chapter 10

❧

FOOTSTEPS RISING UP the apartment's back stairs drew Cloe to the kitchen door. She peered out into the rain-drenched alley to see a powerful, lithe tall man in a western hat surging up the stairs; he looked as untamed as the storm lashing the valley, lightning outlining his harsh, fierce expression. There was no mistaking the lock of his jaw—Michael's mood matched the furious storm whipping his clothing against his rangy body.

Fine. The hardened mud mask on her face cracked as she frowned. Riding on coffee nerves, no sleep, and The Pinto Bean's accounts waiting for her, all she needed was Michael Bearclaw. He looked like the dark avenger, prowling through the storm and looking for trouble, arriving on her back doorstep.

She folded her arms and leaned back against the counter, frowning as he rapped on the door. It wasn't a courteous, please-let-me-in knock, but rather a demand from a man who took what he wanted.

Thunder boomed after another lightning bolt forked down from the black rolling clouds. Metal rattled lightly in the door lock, the knob turned and Michael stepped into the room, rain dripping from the wide brim of his western hat. He whipped off the hat, shook it outside, and hung it on the rack near the door.

Meeting her glare, he wiped his boots on the braided rug. His movements were powerful, determined, calculated, and impatient as his expression lashed at her. His damp hair clung to his cheek and throat, rain streaming onto his dark skin. His black T-shirt clung to his shoulders and chest; he slid from it and too carefully draped it over a chair. A muscle contracted and released in his jaw, as if he were concentrating on something else, forcing himself to act calmly.

His damp shoulders gleamed in the bright light; he ran a kitchen towel over his shoulders and chest and leveled a dark look at Cloe as he ran it over his head, drying his hair. He ran the cloth over his chest, drying the glistening wedge of hair covering his dark skin. "It isn't nice not to answer the door, Cloe. Your mother wouldn't like your poor manners."

"You . . . picked . . . that . . . lock," Cloe managed between her teeth, as he tucked a small plastic kit into his shirt pocket.

"Call the sheriff." There wasn't anything sweet in his tone, his mouth grim. He hurled the towel onto the chair as his brooding, shielded eyes still locked on her. Michael sat, tugged off his muddy boots, placed them neatly by the door, and stood lithely, filling the small kitchen, his tanned shoulders rippling powerfully as he glanced at her. She'd seen a mountain puma once when her father had taken her to the high country; tonight Michael reminded her of the cat's movements, rippling, powerful, predatory. His gaze rode down her bare legs and pinned her toes. Whatever hot and impatient ripped through him, as violent as the growing summer storm, his tone was smoothly intimate. "You've still got the prettiest feet I ever saw, but your facial complexion is a little rough."

"*You picked that lock*," she repeated, still stunned. Her hand wrapped around Jenny Moore's ceramic pot.

Michael's eyes narrowed, pinning her. "You throw that and I'll have the excuse I want to whale the tar out of your spoiled but cute butt."

Eyes narrowed, he watched Cloe struggle for control, and when she jerked her hand from the pot, he nodded. "Anyone could pick that lock with a common hairpin or a credit card. Tell Stella that she needs a solid metal door and frame and deadbolts on any entry points to The Pinto Bean. She'll need sensors in every room. I'll install them and a burglar system with a hookup to my place with a backup system to Liam's."

This wasn't the boy who had cherished her; this was a man taut with anger. Michael looked at her, the fury behind his lashes stunning her. "Where's your mother?"

Violence poured off Michael. Whatever drove him tonight had torn away civilization and replaced it with fury and something else. "My mother is in Cheyenne at a pasta and bread maker food show with Liam," she managed. "I think you should leave."

Michael's level stare told her that he wasn't going until he was ready. He folded his arms across his chest and leaned against the counter. His narrowed gaze studied the floor tiles, then shot out into the night's rain. Lines slashed his face, his expression grim as his throat worked, as though he were swallowing pain. "Damn it! I just found Roy Meadowlark in his barn. He's dead, killed by the bull."

Cloe gripped the back of the kitchen chair. She'd known Roy forever. "Roy? Poor old Roy Meadowlark who worked for your dad all those years?"

Michael scanned the cupboards, padded to one, and opened the door. After a crash of thunder, spring lightning lit the room, outlining his anger—he stood there, tall, shoulders a silvery expanse. Michael's live anger startled her, snapping, heating the room. She'd seen him coolly take apart Ross, she'd seen him brawl when they were younger, but this was darker, more frightening. "I am sorry about Roy."

He took out a bourbon bottle, splashed two fingers into a small glass jar and downed it. He ran his hands through his rumpled, shaggy hair and stalked back and forth across the kitchen. "He's not a pretty corpse, and I should have been more careful. Damn it, Cloe. It's my fault he's dead."

Michael rubbed his hand along his jaw, the sound of his day's beard rough in the sudden silence of the storm. "I usually work the other side, the expert called in to examine evidence . . . people I don't know. It's the kids . . . the helpless women who—"

"Oh, Michael. . . ." Cloe forced back the hand that had reached toward him to comfort a boy who had kissed her bruises, who'd always been fair and good . . . to comfort a man who grieved deeply.

His hands rose to rub his eyes as if erasing the

memories of what he had seen. "I want Stella to help me with Roy . . . clean him up before they touch him. He . . . he needs a woman's touch."

Michael splashed another two fingers of bourbon into the glass, studied the amber liquid, and placed the drink aside. The bourbon looked inviting; he'd used it before to dull the bloody images of victims. A country girl, Cloe knew what a bull could do to a cornered man—her eyes rounded in shock. He should have told her more gently, setting aside his own grief and frustration. She was pale now, knuckles white and fingers locked to the back of the chair. She was shivering—

He wanted to take her into his arms, to soothe her, to soothe himself, just holding her, cutting all those years away . . . letting the softness of her hair, the scent of it soothe him, the warmth of her body giving him something else. Cloe shuddered once, then wrapped her arms around herself as if for warmth.

Oh, hell, Michael thought, even as he moved to ease her into his arms, I shouldn't be doing this. Maybe he needed to hold her more than she needed the warmth he could give her.

Maybe Michael was reacting to the bloody mess that was Roy's body. Cloe huddled against him, and Michael held her tight and rocked her. He closed his eyes, reeling with the thought that this was how he should have been holding her for years—he was pushing The Club now and Cloe could be hurt. For an instant he saw other women who had been innocent victims—rage and fear caused him to hold her tighter, burying his face in her hair. *Cloe. . . .*

She stood too still, breathing lightly, and then she

pushed him away, her eyes wary, shimmering with tears. "Mom and Liam could have trouble getting back tonight, if there is flooding on the roads. I want to help you, Michael. I'll be just a minute."

Michael clasped Cloe's upper arm, jerking her to him. "This isn't pretty, Cloe. Your mother has done things like this before. I thought about Josy, but she's so . . . tender. There's blood—" Michael flung her arm away to scrub his hands over his face. He couldn't touch Cloe now, the violent scene jabbing at him. "I wouldn't think a stringy little cowpoke like Roy could have that much blood in him."

Cloe's hand hovered near his shoulder. Then her fingers touched him lightly, before sliding away. "I've managed blood before, my own, and so much that it— you'll have to tell me what to do, and I'll do it. Get whatever you think we'll need and I'll put on some clothes. Leave a note for Mom."

Michael glanced at her, something intimate and soft flickered in his eyes, and then he leaned over to brush his lips against hers. Startled by the damp, warm contact, Cloe edged back. Michael's hands locked to the counter at her hips, his body too close to hers as he leaned closer, inspecting her eyes. "You look tired, what I can see of you in that mud mask. So this is what you do on a Saturday night. Hole up here and work. No wonder you never laugh."

"We'll have to hurry, for Roy—"

"Roy isn't going anywhere." For a heartbeat, his savage expression softened, as though he were pulling the memories into him for comfort, another happier time. "You used to laugh. I liked the sound of it. It was worth whatever you and the Wild Willows did to me, including tying me to that tree when I slept."

He flicked the hardened mud on her cheek, rubbed the crust between his fingers. Cloe shivered, the hair rising on her nape. "I was researching—testing a natural clay mask, a recipe handed down to Maizie Meadows from her grandmother. I'll just be a minute. . . ."

Michael slashed a hot look at her mouth, as if he desperately needed it fused to his. His gaze darkened, honey-brown eyes gleaming beneath his lashes, and he swore under his breath. "Don't count on me being your friend or a gentleman."

"How like you to assume I wanted you as a friend. Now, stand back and let me—"

His thumbs slowly, sensuously stroked her hips and Cloe's big "dangerous male" warning signs started flashing. She reeled with the thought that only Michael could cause her nerves to leap and quiver, as if she could meet any challenge he tossed at her. He stood back and she hurried down the hallway, away from Michael . . . always away from Michael. She was just putting herself back together, running on too little sleep and stunned by Roy's death. That was why the shadows haunting Michael bothered her, why she wanted to tug his head down to hers and kiss that scar she'd given him years ago.

She wanted to comfort him, hold him tight, and make Roy's death go away, make Michael's guilt go away—

She ran water in the bathroom sink, splashing it onto her face with shaking hands and wiping it dry. When she took away the washcloth, Michael was leaning against the bathroom wall.

He took one step toward her, and Cloe pivoted, facing him.

"When you were a little girl, your cheeks shone like that." He scanned her complexion and lightly ran his fingertip over her nose. "The freckles are back, too. Little ones. . . ."

Michael leaned down to nuzzle her cheek with his rough one. His face was damp, cool, and he smelled like spring rain. She sensed the violence and anger and frustration in him, and saw that frightening heat running beneath his lashes. He glanced down at her bare legs, inhaled sharply, and then slowly traced her body upward until he studied her breasts, her nipples thrusting at the thin cotton.

Michael's deep, slow tone said more than words, and his gaze rose to meet hers. "Are you just going to stand there with your hands feeling up my chest?"

The husky, uneven drawl shielded another emotion, too near and hot, pressing against her. Michael's big hand smoothed the small of her back, the caress possessive yet gentle, as if she could move away from him at any time. Could she?

He needed her on another level, a man needing more than a friend, a man needing her to momentarily wipe away blood and violence and death. She sensed she could give him what he sought—if only for a moment.

Cloe stared at her fingers, locked to his chest, the dark, damp whorls tangling against her fairer skin. His heartbeat pounded at her palms, too strong, too alive—and with enough power to send erotic images into her, his body pounding into hers, hers tossing him back—she snatched her hands back, locking them to the counter, and found them clasped to Michael's. She gripped his wrists, and cords and muscles leaped to her touch. The violence that had been in Michael when he'd arrived was still there, lurking, but now he had it in control, tuned to her, testing her strength for the job before them.

He studied her mouth, tracing it lazily from corner to corner and then circling the perimeter. His fingertip eased into the exact center of her lips, pushed just enough to enter her mouth, and then slowly ran across her bottom teeth. "Why didn't you come over with Angelica on Saturday night to play poker and suck cigars? Afraid?"

Cloe pushed him away and instantly his gaze fastened to her quivering breasts, the nipples peaking against the cloth. She crossed her arms and glared up at him. So much for the independent home worker, comfortable without a bra. The tenderness she'd felt for Michael a moment ago had teetered into something else, live and hot. "Now isn't the time for this, Michael, and if I decided to suck something, it wouldn't be around you."

He laughed abruptly, harshly, coldly, then his golden eyes ripped down to her, tearing at her. "It's going to be rough, Cloe. Damned ugly. Maybe we should wait for your mother."

She pushed her chin up, meeting his gaze. When she was young, Michael had protected her. But now she was a woman who had been tempered by pain. "I'll do what I have to do. I am sorry about Roy. I know what he meant to you, but he was my friend, too, and I want to help. You won't have to pick me up out of the rain . . . I won't pass out at the sight of blood."

He nodded abruptly. "Good enough. I'll wait in the kitchen and write that note for your mother."

Michael leaned back in his father's chair and studied the six frames on the paneled wall. Two days after Roy's funeral and wake, the ragged edges still weren't coming together. Michael's instincts told him that someone had forced Roy to drink alcohol until he was in a stupor, but the electric cattle prod lying nearby didn't have fingerprints. An autopsy and alcohol levels in Roy's blood wouldn't prove anything—

Wade's police scanner crackled: Cloe Matthew's BMW was parked beside Angelica's house. "B.R. on the hill is quiet."

" 'On the hill . . .' " Michael leaned forward, intent upon the scanner. "B.R. . . . Bearclaw Ranch."

Michael propped his feet up on the desk and toyed with the knife that Cloe had given him. At his death, Roy's tooled sheath had been empty, and Michael easily recognized the knife as Roy's. The absence of fingerprints wasn't surprising, and driving that knife into the tread of the BMW's tire had taken a big, powerful man. The sidewalls of the tire would have been much easier—someone had been very angry and very threatened. Whoever had plunged that knife into the tire had taken it from Roy days before.

Holding Cloe in his arms after she had had helped with Roy hadn't helped; she'd lost her stomach, outside in the slashing storm, her face white, silvery with tears and rain as she had turned to him, battered his chest with her fists. "Why? Roy smells like a brewery,

Michael. Why would Roy get into that stall with that bull?" she had asked desperately, her fists gripping his shirt.

Michael stared at the six pictures over the desk. "That's a good question—why. I intend to find out." He rubbed the knuckles of one hand, then in an expert movement threw the knife into the board on the log wall; it struck, point deep, quivering—

He lifted the top to his laptop computer and clicked it on. He brought up the newspaper files of Sam Matthews's case, studying them once more.

"I've managed blood before . . . my own." Cloe's harsh words haunted Michael.

"You're drooling, Sergei," Cloe murmured with a smile as the photographer stared at Josy, his long, elegant hands locked on the corral board, his rangy body taut. Max leaned heavily against Cloe, angling his head for her to scratch his ears. The first week of June spread around them, green fields in the valley, horses and cattle grazing peacefully. The catalog could be late to press, but experienced with tight deadlines, Sergei was prepared to make up lost time.

The summer wind tangled in Sergei's mop of black curls, lifting them out and away from his face, his almond-shaped black eyes focused on the woman inside the corral. Josy was swearing, sweat gleaming on her bare arms and dampening her T-shirt, her long, lean body taut, both hands locked to the lead halter around the colt's head. She was covered in dust and manure, and spitting mad.

"She is beautiful, this Josy. See how the sun lays gold on her skin?" Sergei stated roughly, his gaze pinned on the woman who had just slapped her western hat against her tight dirty jeans and cursed.

"She's sweating, Sergei. Tell her that she's beautiful and you'll find yourself on your expensive silk backside," Cloe murmured, before calling to Josy.

Josy's short, glossy black hair clung to her sweaty face; frustrated by the colt, she snarled at Cloe with all the warmth of a yard dog, ripped off her leather gloves, tucked them in her belt, and scowled at Sergei through the corral boards, looking him up and down. Clearly Josy's sweet temperament had fled as she glared at the colt. "Who's this?"

"This is Sergei—" Cloe began.

Sergei gracefully hiked up to the top board and leaped down beside Josy. Josy slowly studied his loose, stylish city clothes, silk shirt and dress slacks, the mop of black, spiraling curls blowing in the dry Wyoming wind. "The photographer who wants to experience the West? Soft hands, wearing perfume, and about as useful as a tit on a boar."

Sergei swept her hand into his and lifted the back to his lips, kissing it in a courtly style. "At your service, my beautiful lily, my dove."

He drew her hand to his chest. "This expression, 'tit on a boar,' makes erotic image in my brain. This for a man, a woman's mouth upon him, is very good."

For a moment Josy gaped; in the next, she jerked back her hand. "I am not your anything, got it? Cloe, he's wearing an earring. How's that going to look to the old timers around here—Small Bird Ranch with a gypsy?"

"I could tell your fortune," Sergei murmured in a

sexy drawl and toyed with a spiking strand of Josy's sleek black hair.

She stared at Sergei, who was openly appraising her lean curves. Josy narrowed her eyes, glaring at him. "What are you looking at?"

"I am thinking about sex with you and how good it will be," Sergei said softly, firmly, seriously as he considered her mouth, and his gaze slid down to study her chest. "Will you give milk to my children with your lovely breasts?"

Josy's mouth dropped open. She looked blankly at Cloe for half a second, and then her flush rose to meet her temper. "I'm not up to dealing with a ranch, a job, a son, *and* a half-blind idiot with baby-soft hands. I don't have time to play nursemaid, guide, or teacher to a city boy. Make sure he's not here when I get back." With that she ducked under the corral fence, slapped her hat on her head, and stalked toward a saddled horse.

Cloe laughed as Sergei's eyes narrowed on Josy's narrow, swaying hips. "She means it. Kissing her hand wasn't the way to her heart."

"I intend to kiss more than her hands—you see how beautiful they are? A strong woman's hands—strong inside, where the heart is," Sergei murmured softly, as he rubbed Max's ears. The dog almost grinned.

"Leave my dog alone." Josy swung up onto the chestnut's saddle, glared at Cloe, and rode off, dust from the horse's hooves spraying out behind them.

"Such passion, she has. I have waited for a woman like her all my life. I will cook her a dinner that will

win her heart and then I will make her my woman,"
Sergei promised.

Cloe laughed outright. "Where should I send your
body?"

"This Josy is magnificent. Did you see her eyes,
how black as the night, and that body—" Sergei
placed his hands on his waist and surveyed the Small
Bird Ranch from weathered buildings to ramshackle
house to the horses in the small pasture. He inhaled
the fresh air, scented of manure, and nodded thoughtfully. "She does this by herself? Raises her boy and
has a job and does all this work? She should have me
by her side. I am home, my friend Cloe. I thank you
for giving me this."

Cloe escaped from Sergei's big bear hug as soon as
she could, grinning. "She'll make it rough on you."

"The taste of her will be all the more sweeter." Sergei dramatically placed one hand over his heart and
bowed, his other hand sweeping in front of him in an
elegant bow. "I will do your work quickly, so that I
may have more time to love my Josy."

On the drive back to Lolo, Cloe relaxed slightly. In
the passionate Russian-American, Josy had a protector, who valued honor. Angelica had her claws and
Cloe had hers, but Josy needed to be protected and
Sergei was tough behind his artsy exterior.

Josy stared at her hand, branded by Sergei's kiss.
She'd been frustrated with the colt, frustrated with
Edward, who would be coming after Cody. The old
well pump, held together with bailing wire and spit,
wasn't making life easy, and Josy was in no mood for
a soft city man with mocking almond-shaped eyes

and a kiss on his full, almost erotically curved lips. "A man's mouth ought to be a straight line and hard," Josy muttered.

She strode into the chicken house, rubbing her palm against her thigh, scrubbing off the Russian's lingering kiss before gathering eggs into her hat. The banty rooster ran at her, gleaming chestnut in the sun, ready to fight, and when Josy stopped and glared at him, he pranced away. "I'm in a mood to tangle with you, chicken soup, that's for sure," she muttered.

She'd have to clean the chickenhouse soon, noting the layered droppings, and shook her head. She was tired, that bone-dragging tired that had worn out other small ranchers who had failed.

She rubbed the place on her thigh where the colt had kicked her. She wouldn't fail; she couldn't. She had to save Small Bird Ranch for Cody, his homesteader's inheritance, not built on swindling farmers and ranchers. She just had time to start supper before Cody came home from his friend's.

Josy sighed wearily. The huge laundry she'd been putting off was waiting, and she had enough anger left from the gypsy kissing her to kick the failing washer.

She stopped in midstep, fear icing her body despite the warm day. The ranchyard was too quiet. Michael had said that Nimo was missing.... "Max?"

She swallowed, turned the house's old brass doorknob, and pushed. If Edward had been in the house again ... leaving just enough trace to know that he could come get Cody anytime he wanted and she couldn't do a thing about it—if he hurt Max, poisoned him—

Max leaped at her playfully, knocked her back against the wall, and Josy struggled to keep the egg-filled hat in her hand from tumbling to the floor. "Max! My big, pretty boy," she exclaimed, too relieved to chastise him.

She placed the hat on the kitchen counter, roughed Max the way he liked, pushing and playing with him, and stopped, sniffing at the delicious scent. "Holy . . ."

Just then Sergei strolled out of her bathroom wearing a towel around his shoulders, and after that, nothing but gleaming, damp tanned skin—tanned all over, not a white patch anywhere. Stunned, Josy gaped at him.

Max dashed to Sergei, tongue dangling, clearly adoring the man who firmly issued a "Stay" command. Max's tail beat a steady, happy tempo against the floor.

"There is not a shower in the bunkhouse, my dove," Sergei explained, as he whipped a towel around his hips and anchored it. "You are rosy . . . shy of me. I adore you."

Josy blinked and stared at the cords and muscles running the length of Sergei's body. Every piece of male equipment was thoroughly in place, and without his silk clothing, there wasn't a soft ounce on him. She swallowed, a tight unpredictable fist of desire clenching low in her body.

"Ah!" Sergei exclaimed, delighted as he crossed to look at her hat, filled with eggs. "Fresh eggs. Good cow's milk in the refrigerator—you buy that, no? Tonight we have borscht—" He stopped to slosh red wine into the simmering pot. "But tomorrow, I make such linguine—"

He stopped and frowned, crossing his arms in front of him and leaning back against the counter, perfectly at home. "Tomorrow I go shopping. Your cupboards are bare, my darling."

While Josy tried to come back into reality—she'd surely dropped into another woman's life—Sergei frowned thoughtfully. "You know, I think tomorrow when the good light is gone, I start a garden. The soil is good, black . . . rich. Yes, a garden to feed my family. I would have a milk cow, too. I would like to make cheese, good cheese to enjoy when the winter keeps us in bed—"

"Your family! You are out of your mind—" While she glared at him, Josy pushed herself together and with shaking hands jabbed the telephone buttons. Sounding distracted, Cloe answered and Josy ignited. "Cloe, come get this guy. I agreed that a city slicker could play cowboy at the ranch, but this guy is something else— *What? He's paying how much for the experience?*"

Josy slammed down the receiver. After Cloe's fast accounting of how much Sergei could add to her income, Josy decided she could manage—somehow.

Sergei's sensual appraisal of her mouth started her blush, and Josy hated the shiver that ran through her. In the background, the washer and dryer hummed, and the house had been cleaned, the dinner table set.

"When does your son come, this fine boy, Cody?" Sergei asked softly, before he placed his long hands gently beside her face, as if he were feeling her bones, her essence, and slowly took her mouth.

"You've got to go . . . outside . . . somewhere else . . . the bunkhouse . . . New York," she managed unevenly, her heart racing.

His thumbs gently circled her skin, his breath sweeping across her cheek. "I was an orphan, my Josy. I had no home, living on the streets. I was alone."

"An orphan?" Josy felt her resistance crumble.

"You would not turn me away, would you, my dove? I have never had a home, or a family."

"Never?" Josy asked, falling into the black mirrors of Sergei's eyes.

While Mancini's music spread over Angelica's exotic room-to-room sound system, Cloe sprawled back on the long, low modern couch, her newly pedicured and polished toes separated by cotton balls. She critically studied the dark burgundy color, waiting for Angelica to return to the room. Candles of all colors and sizes lit the room, their scents blending. On the massive coffee table, a tray of oils and lotions waited amid the elegant champagne flutes and opened chip sacks. In her kitchen, Angelica was happily whipping up another mud pack, moaning about slave labor and the absence of a good spa in Lolo. With her hands oiled, wrapped in plastic and cloth and heating on electric pads, Cloe's mind wasn't on Angelica's cure-all beauty spa or her need to "fix" Quinn Lightfeather for tossing her out of the poker game.

Josy had been battling Sergei for three days, laying out rules, and was probably backed into a corner. Within the week, Sergei's world-class photography would put the finishing touches on The Pinto Bean's catalog; the project was only running two weeks behind schedule.

The lights of Lolo spread out in front of Angelica's floor-to-ceiling windows. In a corner, Angelica's computer screen scrolled through information she had marked for retrieval.

The small wake that Stella had held at The Pinto Bean for Roy was somber, the tapes playing Mewdowlark's favorite Roy Rogers and Gene Autry tunes. A colorful character blended with the lives of Lolo's pioneer families, Roy Meadowlark had once gone to Hollywood with dreams of starring in movies, and getting him an "aviatrix-woman" like Tom Mix and others.

When the wake had finished, Michael, Liam, Quinn, and the . . . Cloe smiled briefly, the "Wild Willows" helped clean The Pinto Bean. She'd found Michael in the tiny office with her mother, and Stella was crying on his shoulder. Cloe had stiffened, emotions tumbling around her. "What are you doing with my mother?" she had demanded.

She'd flushed then, ashamed of the outraged schoolgirl ring to her voice as Stella turned to her. "Cloe, Michael was just—"

"I know what he was doing. He's just full of games."

"Stella, why don't you see to your guests? I'll take care of Cloe." Then Michael had gently pushed Stella out of the office cubbyhole and without missing a heartbeat had wrapped his arm around Cloe. He half-lifted her into the small office and closed the door. He had leaned back against it and closed his arms across his chest. "You've got an evil mind, Cloe-honey."

She had been rigid with anger, her hands curling into fists. "Let me out of here."

"Not until I'm done. If you had any sense beyond your own needs, you'd see that your mother needed more than words. I was comforting her, and maybe myself, too."

He tilted his head, watching her with humored interest. "You're not going to get violent again, are you?" Michael had reached slowly up to the string dangling from the lightbulb. He tugged, and the room went dark. "This won't hurt at all, but you're acting as if you want to tangle, and tonight, I'm up for just that."

"If *you're* wanting to tangle," she'd tossed back at him, not letting him intimidate her. "You picked the right person."

"I was waiting for that," Michael had murmured, as he'd pinned her wrists behind her with one hand and splayed his fingers through her hair with his other hand. He had tugged gently, stretching her neck back, and then fitted his lips to hers, fusing them in heat and desire. There was anger and punishment in the kiss, as if Michael had finally released his contempt of her, the edge of his teeth bruising her mouth.

She had stood absolutely still, unresponsive, and then the kiss had changed, seduced and intrigued and warmed—Cloe had arched against him, diving into the hunger, taking greedily, and Michael had hitched her higher, cupping her bottom with his hands, caressing her—Heat and hunger drove her. Her fists lashed in his hair, holding his mouth upon hers, until Michael, breathing unevenly, had jerked his head away, his eyes biting at her. "Why, damn you, why did you—"

His mouth snapped closed, and in that heartbeat, he'd withdrawn, almost tossing her away. In his dark, flashing look she'd read condemning hatred and anger, her heart pounding with a savage beat she hadn't known.

He'd smiled coldly then, jerking the overhead light string. The bald light lancing between them exposed her to his slashing eyes. "You'd better work this out, lady, because I don't intend to make it easy."

Now, waiting for Angelica's newest avocado mask concoction, munching on chips, and restless with her emotions, Cloe rose to her feet. Taking care not to lose the cotton balls between her toes, she padded to the computer, which had just sprung into life. Messages for Angelica scrolled down the computer screen, automatically programmed to retrieve at a certain hour. "Michael's investment in The Pinto Bean's catalog business comes to an equal one-third of the investment. He's willing to do more; if need be, so am I," Liam had written.

"Michael is an investor in *my* creation, in The Pinto Bean's catalog?" Cloe ripped off the plastic bags covering her hands. She wiped her hands on the lush, heated towels Angelica had stacked nearby and punched the keys, retrieving earlier messages involving Angelica's silent partner, Michael Bearclaw.

Moments later, Angelica cruised into her living room carrying a blender filled with her new avocado-and-mayonnaise facial recipe. "You're looking good, brat. You've got the long legs for those worn tight jeans, and with that man's big shirt tied at your waist, it gives just an interesting view of your navel. By the way, The Club was really frosted when they weren't invited to the wake at The Pinto Bean—"

She stopped in mid-stride, glanced at the cotton balls leading to her opened front door, and then out into the night, where Cloe's BMW headlamps were cutting toward Bearclaw Ridge. Angelica glanced at the computer screen— "Oh-oh. Big trouble."

Chapter 11

❧

"THE B.R. ON the hill is about to have a visitor," the deputy noted on the police scanner. "Cloe Matthew's BMW is tearing up the road . . . must be doing eighty."

"Don't do anything to get that woman revved up. She's pure trouble and so is Gilchrist's daughter," Michael heard the dispatcher respond to the deputy before he clicked off the radio and concealed it. He tapped out the code to disarm the burglar alarm and settled back to wait for Cloe.

Cloe, furious with Michael, slammed the BMW's door and winced as her bare sole hit a rock. She hopped a few steps and stubbed her toe on the Bearclaw ranch house steps. She glanced at Lopez, who was rearing and racing around the corral. Michael's black heart suited the evil stud. She leaped up the steps, hit the roughly hewn, thick boards with both open hands, intending the sound to serve as his warning—and the door swung open.

Off balance, she plunged into the lighted room, staggered, and surveyed the length of the room, from the old stone fireplace, across the windows that over-looked Lolo and the valley, to the kitchen. She'd find him, and when she did—at the other end of the room, Michael sat at the old desk, his bare legs propped up on it, arms folded across his chest. The towel around his hips slid back to reveal the smooth muscled curve of his buttock. He lifted an eyebrow, waiting for her to speak.

She opened her mouth and closed it. She was panting too hard to speak, and it was his fault. While she was eyeing Michael, the telephone rang. He reached leisurely to pick up the receiver, his eyes locked with Cloe's. "Yes, Angelica, she's here—safe—and breathing fire . . . I know, mad as a wet hen, sparks are flying around her like a firecracker. That red in her hair is really showing up, and I know it's all my fault. I'm lucky she's not toting a gun. . . . Yes, I'll take very good care of her. I'll let her kiss the living day-lights out of me if it will help her cool down. It'll be a sacrifice, though, pure torture, and I'd do it just be-cause I like her mother's soups."

His grin was quick, tender, one tossed to Angelica, as he studied Cloe's toes. "Ruined an evening's work on her toes, did she? Keep your toe-sucking remarks to yourself."

The grin deepened, lines radiating from his eyes, warmth from his eyes as he studied Cloe's frown. He chuckled as he spoke to Angelica. "I know, life is crude and rude here in the sticks, and a really good spa is miles away. Why don't the Wild Willows build a spa like you want? That's right, put up or shut up."

Cloe inhaled sharply. Trust Michael Bearclaw to leap into her plans and spread them out before she was ready for delivery, before she had decided to take on the project, before she was ready to stay in Lolo and commit to a long-term development.

He held the telephone away from his ear as Angelica started screaming. "Give me that," Cloe ordered, as Michael chuckled again.

"Lay off," Cloe ordered. "And don't call back. Michael's murder needs my complete concentration. I want to enjoy every bloody detail."

Angelica was still talking when Cloe replaced the receiver. Then, in an afterthought, she placed it on the desk and eyed her rangy, dark-skinned, and powerfully muscled victim.

Michael replaced the receiver, picked it up when the telephone rang again, and said mildly, "Angelica, this could take all night if you keep calling."

He laughed softly, a sexy, low rumbling that set Cloe's temper raging higher, and then he replaced the receiver. "She's clucking over her little lamb. If you need her, she'll be down at Quinn's, driving him out of his Native American mind. Call her in the morning and try not to include her in your murder. She wanted to help . . . she did."

The next second, the telephone rang again, and Michael didn't wait for the caller's identification. "Josy, she's okay."

Michael was silent a moment, his mouth curving in a soft, knowing smile. "I know. The Wild Willows will murder me if anything happens to Cloe. You told me that same thing when you were six and a few times after that. I hear you have a gypsy living at your ranch. How's that going?"

Josy's voice rose angrily as Michael smiled. "I'll

make certain Cloe doesn't drive while she's revved up. She'll call you tomorrow."

Cloe glared at him as he replaced the receiver again. "You invested in my business. You waited until you could get into the act, and then you did. I once took a competitor out of business for messing with my ad work. I can ruin you, Bearclaw. You set me up."

He lifted a leisurely black eyebrow, obviously terrified, from the humor curving around his lips. "Do you always wear cotton balls between your toes?" he drawled.

Cloe reached down to pluck the remaining cotton from between her toes. "Get out of my business, Michael. Leave my mother alone, leave me alone, and while you're at it, don't come to The Pinto Bean, or any vicinity where I might happen to be. And you can take that distributor cap and shove—"

"Leaving you alone and keeping out of your vicinity would be damned hard, since you and I are going to be lovers." He watched her for a moment and the tense air shifted as he stood slowly and walked to the door, slamming it closed with enough power to rattle the windows. The click of the lock shot through the silence like a rifle bullet at showdown time. He punched a code into his alarm system and turned to her. Sinews and cords rippled tensely in his body; Michael was packed with enough violence to terrorize her. He didn't.

Cloe blinked as the towel slipped a notch on his taut backside; muscles on the backs of his thighs surged, the towel clinging damply.

He turned to her slowly, broad shoulders smooth and powerful, eyes raking her. She should be ripping him apart, she thought distantly, as her gaze dropped to the tanned expanse of his chest, that wedge of black hair gleaming, light skimming across the rounded bulge of tense muscle.

"That night when I found Roy Meadowlark, you said that you'd seen lots of blood—your own—and you'd taken care of it. Why? What happened?"

She refused to yield to the terror pounding at her, to the need that went back to her childhood to have Michael hold her close. This wasn't the laughing boy who had teased her, pulled her braids, and tickled her. This wasn't the boy who had gently explained why a bull had leaped upon a cow in the pasture, and then had placed a newborn kitten in her hand, explaining the beautiful wonder, the result of the creation.

This was a powerful man, moving into her life, and a man who desired her. He was pinning her down, pushing her as no one ever had, wanting more than she could give—

Cloe pushed away the fear that she'd say too much. She'd always been in control—of herself and of the moment—she could manage—*Lovers.* . . . The word echoed in the silence, driving into her.

In one movement Michael reached out to grab a fistful of the man's shirt she wore, tugging her close to him. Off balance, Cloe gripped his waist and stayed, fingers digging into the smooth, warm flesh of his waist, muscles lying beneath his skin, tensing at her touch. His thumb swept slowly, gently across her cheek, his hand cradling her hot cheek. "You've kept your secrets, and this one not even your mother knows. Don't worry, I didn't upset her with questions. How did he hurt you, Cloe? Did he beat you?"

In the following roar of silence, the fury in his voice shook the room. What did Ross do? What didn't he do? There in the burning depths of Michael's eyes she found the passion, the emotions she'd wanted from Ross—

Cloe saw the blood again, running down her legs, the pain slamming into her womb, tearing the baby— She began to shake. She'd kept her pain too long, and now it tore at her. "Michael, I—"

Michael's callused hands framed her face, his thumbs tracing her cheekbones. She leaned against him, feeling as if he held her up, as if her knees would give way if he released her. His eyes held her, dark rims around the gold, filled with concern, sincere as when, years ago, he'd held her as she'd cried for a favorite kitten. The Michael she had trusted all her life gently murmured, "You trusted me once. On this, you can trust me again."

Trust. How long had it been since she'd trusted? She'd left that in Lolo years ago. Cloe breathed deeply, giving herself to the slow caress of his thumbs along her cheeks. She'd been skimming along life for years, surviving, bent on succeeding, and somewhere she'd dropped trust. She placed her hands upon his wrists, the beat of his blood familiar somehow as her own. "Michael, I. . . ."

"I know, Cloe-honey. You're all tangled up inside, and God help me, I know." Michael picked her up in his arms and carried her to the big roughly hewn rocker by the flickering fire. He settled her into his lap as he had long ago, when his mother lay dying in her bed by the window. As a girl, she'd sensed that he'd needed her to face that pain.

His fingers slid between her own, his palm hard with calluses, and familiar as the men she'd adored in another lifetime—her father, Wade, and the others—the fit comfortable.

"I was only a few weeks pregnant—" she told him then, with the fire crackling and warming the room, Michael's body hard and safe beneath her, mooring her away from the pain. The story she'd held for so long tumbled out—a gush of words held too long. The towel, she remembered, had been cream colored and lush, pushed between her legs and ripe with her baby's blood. She'd fought her way to the bed, dialed for the ambulance, and concentrated, praying to keep the baby within her.

She was shaking now, chilled by the nightmare she had never shared with anyone. Michael's large, roughly callused hand turned her face up to his, his thumb drying the tears. "Cloe . . . Cloe. He came at you then, didn't he? Went right for the jugular, found the weak spot, and twisted you apart."

"We were already separated, but—" She noted his harsh tone, the simmering anger in it. "How did you know?"

"A man like that likes to kick people when they're down," Michael stated flatly. "What did he say? Something unimaginative that made you doubt you were a woman?"

The firelight flickered upon his hard, blunt cheekbones, his black, gleaming hair, as she stared at him, shocked by his insight. The pulse running across his jaw was hard, unrelenting, burning gold fury in his eyes. "How did you know?"

"You were drained, when I saw you that first night you came back to Lolo, and a big part of you was missing—that sweet, fiery woman part. You looked as if someone had just vacuumed the life out of you. I've seen that look before . . . I should have known." Michael gripped a wooden horse paperweight on the table beside him, then hurled it into the fire, his face grim. "You wanted that baby, didn't you, Cloe?"

"Old dreams, made of cobwebs. They're gone now," she murmured, suddenly icy and shaking, fighting to pull herself together, to put distance between this powerful man and herself.

"That won't work," Michael whispered, turning her chin up with the tip of his finger.

His lips brushed hers lightly, tempting a response, and Cloe realized she had curled into his body; his large hand was caressing her bottom and the backs of her thighs.

She pushed her head back, resting on his upper arm, and held her breath as his hand covered her breast. His thumb ran across the crest, peaking the softness.

Michael grinned that slow, devilish devastating charm that had captured her as a teenager. "Your heart is thumping like a trapped rabbit and you're all juicy and hot and primed to jump me."

"I'm not interested," she lied, and stared into the flames in his eyes, unable to move, to look away. His skin burned hers, rough and corded, a contrast to the softness within her. Her heart raced as Michael's thumb caressed the taut peak of her breast, his hand cradling the weight, massaging it warmly, safely.

"I am plenty interested." He moved in swiftly, not giving her a choice, taking possession. His kiss was savage, open mouthed, hot, breath sweeping across her cheek, no less demanding than her own, her hands locking in his hair, keeping him close to her until she was finished feeding upon him.

"Open for me, Cloe. Open your mouth and let me have you," he said roughly, nibbling on her bottom lip. She bit him back, matching him, and then admitted him into her mouth. Michael's hand cupped the back of her head as he fed upon her, taking hungrily, his breath hot upon her cheek.

She broke the kiss and realized that his hand rested between her legs, a gentle firm caress, the layers of cloth damp with her desire. "Michael. . . ." she whispered unevenly, her heart pounding, threatening to leap from her keeping.

He placed his hot face within the cove of her throat and shoulder, his pulse slamming into hers as if skin did not separate them. "If you don't stop looking at me like that, I may have to brawl with your brothers in the morning because I will have had their little princess. You can kiss my bruises."

"I wouldn't, not if you begged me," she whispered, as he stood with her in his arms. He cradled her as he had when she was a child with skinned knees, but there was something else now raging between them, an unfinished passion that needing serving before it could die. She needed it to die; she needed it to live and burn her free. Michael held her against him as though she belonged to him, had always belonged to him, and all the years between were only a minute.

His black brows drew together; his wasn't a tender lover's expression, but somehow she hadn't expected that of Michael, nor his deep voice raw with tension: "Tell me to put you down and I will and you can walk out that door. Tell me to take you to bed and I'll do that, too, and all I need to know is if you want your breakfast eggs scrambled or not."

For just a heartbeat, Michael's arrogance was gone, the tenderness in his expression blended with a vulnerability that she had known years ago. "Toast," she whispered, using the word for the "yes" she could not say.

Michael's tense body quivered against her, his arms tightening around her, fingers splayed to brand her flesh. "Good. Still like a layer of jam on it so thick it drips?"

They were moving from the past into the present, cautiously, and each knew there would be no returning from this moment.

"What kind have you got?" It didn't matter, and Cloe couldn't take her eyes from Michael's dark, sultry ones.

"Blackberry . . . strawberry . . . honey. . . ." He punctuated the words with tender light sweeps of his lips across hers, asking—she could leave . . . or she could reach out and take the heat, snaring it in her fist for one night—

He shook, muscles tensing hard against her body, as if nothing could take her away. As if he would take her to his lair and satisfy them both, wildly, passionately. She wanted that storm, freeing herself, she wanted to dive into him and forget everything but the hard mating of their bodies. While Cloe's fear warred with temptation, he carried her swiftly into the shadowy bedroom, his expression grim, determined. He tossed her into the bed where their parents had loved, came down on her with his full weight, already aroused, and tearing away her clothes in a flurry of heat and caresses.

The time was now. She'd have Michael, take everything, and fill herself with him.

She whipped the towel from his hips, lifted her own for him to strip away her jeans and tear away her briefs. He paused, eyes narrowed, as he watched his hand splay wide, dark skin branding pale, skimming over her stomach, and lower to the curls nestled there, and over her quivering thighs. He met her eyes then, his expression harsh, tense, narrowed golden eyes demanding. She dug her fingers into his smooth, hot skin and shivered. Was passion really like this? Fierce and shaking and hot? Dark and damp and stripped of pretense? Raw in the night, quivering and hot and aching—

There in the shadows, Michael's shoulders gleamed, bunched, as he lifted himself over her, powerful legs fitting slowly, carefully, gently within the cradle of her own soft ones. Heavy muscles flexed along her thighs, and as he settled himself firmly upon her, Michael's blunt rigid shaft came to rest at the pulsing, damp entrance of her body. The intimacy left no doubts, nor did his savage expression, a vein throbbing along his temple.

His heart pounded upon hers, his body heating, throbbing, rough skin against softer, chest pressing her breasts, flat stomach meeting hers, sex against sex, and thighs poised to test each other. . . .

"Michael. . . ." she whispered, and knew that time had not dimmed her need of him.

The intruder in the *Lolo Star* smiled coldly. The leather gloves were stained with the dead parakeets' blood, while the old woman slept upstairs, over the newspaper office.

The old woman had never understood what he was capable of doing, and she had broken the rules, helping Michael research Sam Matthews's old case. Muriel Perkins would get the point—she shouldn't help outsiders. The past should be left with the dead and The Club would go on as it had since the cowboys settled and began its rule.

He turned to survey his work and the single parakeet still alive, safe in his cage. The intruder would give Muriel that, one last bird to protect, a reminder that she had better keep out of The Club's affairs.

At the Long Horn, Quinn let himself drift in the sweetgrass smoke which circled his sweat-covered nude body. The baby had awakened him once more, crying softly, steadily.

The firewoman was out in the night, feeding on her storms, tearing into them.

The wolves were howling, the youngest of the pack becoming stronger.

The sunflower was blooming, opening, roots sinking into the earth, curling around a rock that had waited since time began for just that purpose.

"Any little sweet things you want to tell me?" Michael whispered roughly against Cloe's flushed cheek, his hands holding her wrists loosely beside her head.

The bed creaked with their weight as Michael gently rested his sex against the soft, damp opening of hers. She held her breath, pushed her heels upon the bed, and refused to make anything easy for him.

The nip at her throat startled her, sharp, poignant, the stallion after the mare. The elemental savagery— not enough to last, but enough to send her arching against him—destroyed her reeling search for control.

She forced her quivering muscles to relax, and Michael's fierce scowl pinned her. His deep voice was raw and deadly quiet in the moonlit room. "There's two of us in this, Cloe."

Cloe could have pushed him away at any time, his face hard above hers, testing her, giving her nothing of the tenderness she hadn't expected. He lifted his head, waiting. The moonlight from the window laid a savage strip of silver across his face, from his cheekbone across his nose and into the shadows. Above the strip his eyes gleamed, the hunter who had staked his prey, toying with her.

Heat slammed through her again as Michael's blunt body pressed against hers, his shudder telling her that he could force himself away, to end what she wanted desperately.

He was giving her nothing, making her admit her needs. In the roaring silence, the sound of her heartbeat echoed in her ears, the depth of her need quaked within her bones, too primitive, too frightening. . . .

She couldn't give him everything, let him see too much. "This doesn't change anything. I don't want you to have a stake in my life, in my business—"

"Don't count on me to follow the rules where you're concerned." He nipped the other side of her throat, startling her again, and ran his open mouth across the mark. "It's too late, Cloe . . . much too late. Tell me now if you want me to stop."

He moved his hips down on her and tantalizing heat slid along the moist opening of her, causing her to catch her breath.

Michael's eyes cut down their bodies, then up to her breasts, pale and quivering in the moonlight with each heartbeat, and up to her mouth, her bottom lip caught in her teeth. The savagery of his expression, the taut shiver that ran the length of his body told her that he was waiting—

"Yes," she whispered, and closed her eyes, only to have her chin captured in Michael's hard hand, her head shaken gently.

"Open your eyes, damn you. I want you to know who I am—"

The tip of him entered her, stretching those first taut, damp muscles too snugly, and yet Michael didn't move, his breathing harsh in the room. Or was it hers?

She lay perfectly still, focusing on the heat leaping within her, the hunger, the point of where she ended and he began—

"Is this what happened? You lay beneath him, pulled yourself deep inside, and let him have you?" He shook her, the bed creaking beneath them. "Don't try that with me, sweetheart."

The rage in his voice didn't terrify her, it made her angry because he was right—she had withdrawn from sex, and now she was with Michael, every heartbeat, every breath, every touch and ache.

Her instinct to test him, his strength, his possession

of her shocked her. She shook him, returning the favor, digging her nails into his upper arms, more to lock him to her than away from her. The bed creaked with the violence, the passion circling them.

"What do you want?" she managed, looking up at him, shaking with the heat burning her skin, the need to lock him close and claim him.

"This—truth between us." Michael's body slid into hers, startling her, his mouth coming down to claim her mouth, tongue sliding into her mouth, taking, destroying, tantalizing. One hand slid under her hips, hiking her up to him, completing the lock, fingers digging into her skin, demanding.

She retreated, hissing with surprise, filling with him as he pushed deep, stretching her. Music, she thought. Poetry . . . beautiful living poetry. His entry did not hurt, gliding hard and strong to the very depths of her, buried so deep that he was a part of her—too elemental, primitive. Hers, she thought wildly, tightening hard upon him. Michael gave her nothing, stripping her defenses, his features taut, skin gleaming in the dim light.

Not that she wasn't demanding herself, her arms gripping him, her legs wound around him. This was what she had waited for, the primitive base heat, the pounding storm, the reality of Michael, above her, in her, kissing her, his body dragging slowly, erotically against hers, hair roughened chest against her softer contours, nipples etching taut and erect against his dark skin, her heartbeat lodged heavy and low in her belly.

Heat pounded at her as he came at her and she tossed him back again and again. She bit his shoulder to keep from crying out as the pleasure deepened, circled, and dived in, pounding at her.

His hands tangled in her hair; his breath, ragged against her damp cheek, sucked rawly at air as she held him tighter, deeper, past the layers of civilization and into the essence of who and what she was—the power that was hers on this savage plane, stripped of defenses—

At the first sharp tug, she stiffened, thrown back by surprise, her body contracting upon Michael, who had stopped moving, braced once more above her, watching. She could feel his pulse as though it were her own, the tense restraint of his muscles shaking so hard the bed creaked. "Cloe," he soothed in a sigh, brushing his lips against her breast, the sensations deep inside her pushing, driving, taking.

She gulped for air, concentrating on her body now, the unexpected contractions easing. Above her, Michael's tender, knowing smile came after the first sharp, surprised frown. "Now that was something, sweetheart. So is the expression on your face."

She ran her hands over his hot, pounding chest, smoothing it, testing his racing heartbeat, his flesh hard and damp and alive—so alive— Slowly he lowered his mouth to tug at her nipple, gentle movements of teeth and tongue, and the circles tightened within her and she cried out, lifted even higher.

She cradled his cheeks, felt his pulse as though it were her own, the skin hot and flushed and alive beneath her touch . . . so alive, desperately alive, his eyes glowing, molten beneath his lashes.

"Oh, honey," Michael murmured tenderly, nuzzling her cheek. She'd have killed him for the rich delight in his tone, except she was too busy dealing with the touch of his hand between them. One perfect, isolated touch sent her arching off the bed, flinging into sunlight and gold and red, quivering at the height. Again it came, tossing her higher, and she gripped Michael's hair, rolling with the new tide, even as a new storm began.

There was no time now, her cry echoing in the shadows, Michael grasping her tighter, his body locking with hers, heat pouring out of him. Where did he begin? Where did she begin?

She had to claim him, to make him give her what he had taken, and she pitted herself against him, finding that harsh rhythm, matching him, hands open on his back, driving up—

This time the pulsing wave slammed into her, and she hadn't time to recover, as it rose higher. She pitted herself against that fierce flame— "Michael!"

His body tensed, clasped as tightly to her as she could, for she would have everything of Michael Bearclaw, taking everything. And then, high on that burst of sunlight, soaring higher, he cried out roughly, as if his soul had been ripped from his body. His face settled into the curve of her throat and shoulder, the angular bones and flesh pressed close and familiar, leaving no air between them, as if he couldn't take his lips from her skin.

Wasted, drained, yet filled and glowing, Cloe managed to flop her hand from his back. She would lie there, his weight heavy and pleasant upon her, and then she would rise, free of Michael Bearclaw.

Her mind plotted on while her body enjoyed the slow caress of his, the almost friendly lock of his body within hers, a gentle sharing after the fire. She would rise, take her shower, lay out the rules for Michael, and forget him. Sex was simply a dance they hadn't finished, and now all her questions were answered.

The distraction of his lips roaming her throat and jaw, his hands upon her breasts, made thinking difficult at the moment, but once her bones hardened enough, she'd leave him. As soon as her brain returned to her, she'd find just the perfect seething—

"What are you doing?" she managed huskily as Michael smoothly filled her again.

He grinned down at her and her heart leaped, her body tightening upon him instinctively. "Trying for your fourth orgasm. You looked so surprised."

"You're keeping score?" She floundered as Michael turned and pulled her over him. She rubbed her thighs against his rougher ones and bit his shoulder. "That isn't nice."

"You didn't want nice just then, honey. Neither did I," he said with a devastating grin, and brought her mouth down to his.

Later, with Michael curled against her back, his arm across her, and his breath flowing along her cheek, Cloe swam her way back to consciousness and muttered, "So you're an athlete. So you've got more experience."

He chuckled, smoothing her breast and running his thumb across the peaked crest. There was no mistaking the purpose of his big hand, gently opening on her stomach and easing lower to cup her.

The smile inside Cloe slid upward to her lips. Michael wasn't worried about morning gym classes, or circles under his eyes during a presentation, his mouth burning the side of her throat, his heat pressed between her thighs, seeking her. . . .

She lifted her arm, eased it back to leisurely stroke his hair, threading her fingers through it as Michael's hard body flowed, undulated behind her. She lay, spooned into his lap, her bottom cradled close to him. She closed her eyes and sighed, drowsily riding the gentle crest of his lovemaking.

Michael chuckled and flipped her over, his mouth seeking hers hungrily, taking everything, giving everything. In the next heartbeat she found the fire, stepping into it, crying out—

She bit his lip, the scar that crossed it, for he was hers, all raw, passionate and . . . *Michael* . . . *Michael.* . . .

Chapter 12

❧

STILL JOINED TO Cloe, poleaxed by the release of his coiled body into hers, Michael lay his cheek close to her damp, flushed one. His lips rested on the pulse racing beneath her throat. He listened to her breathing slow, her uneven, dreamy sigh brushing his skin, his shoulder, her heartbeat ease as his own, the boneless melt of their bodies flowing into each other like warm water drifting pleasantly on sunlight.

At first he'd thought that once was enough, one loving would erase his passion for her. *He was wrong.* He stroked her breast, warm and quivering and leaping with her heartbeat, from the sex they'd just had, then bent to leisurely taste her skin, the hard, jutting nipple.

"I can't, Michael . . . I can't," she sighed, as he began to fill her again.

But he was too greedy for her to be nice and caring. He nipped her throat and slid to gently bite her other nipple, smiling as her hips undulated just once against him. "You can."

Her eyes were drowsy in the night, soft and laugh-

ing upon him. "Michael," she whispered in an uneven, dreamy sigh. . . .

At two o'clock in the morning, Cloe tapped her pen
on the yellow legal pad. Michael, sprawled across the
rumpled bed in the next room, a sheet flowing low
on his hips, wasn't helping her thinking. She'd leave
him a note, a cool dismissal of necessary adult sex.
She adjusted her body to the desk chair, sore in muscles she hadn't used until Michael. She rolled his shirt
up at the sleeves; the faded cotton bore his scent.

She knew herself—riding high in emotions, unable
to relax, tension clawing at her. She cursed Michael
Bearclaw aloud and in her mind, even now, her body
wanted his. She'd always been complete somehow, in
herself, in directing . . . measuring her needs, and now
she wasn't. He'd left her nothing, demanding everything, and she'd pushed back, fighting to get her
share, hungry for him . . . so hungry, as if some buried
flame inside her had waited for his touch. He'd made
a mockery of her marriage, her adult sensuality, pushing her and taking what he wanted, giving it back to
her until her bones melted, her flesh became his.

Their lovemaking had been savage, surprising, the
barriers down, the war passionate between them, riding on senses. He'd allowed no walls. The searing intensity shot past her experience with Ross, entered a
new dimension, and frightened her.

She was bitter, of course, furious with Michael for
showing her the difference between scheduled, cool,
almost businesslike sex, and the tropical storm of passion they'd hurled through four times.

It was more than sex. It was need of another deeper,

more primitive bond where tenderness and familiarity merged with another fiery element.

Fine. So her experience with long, utterly devastating orgasms was limited. Her experience with men had proved to be an illusion compared to Michael's raw, hungry devastation. How could she know that a light, perfect touch could release pleasure almost to the point of pain? That pleasure could hold her at the peak, reeling from it through endless tides, as his hand cupped her.

Fine. So it was true about orgasms. They did exist. The hoopla was true, and she'd missed it for years. Now, that made her really angry with Michael Jedidiah Bearclaw. She'd flung herself through married life without a glimpse of what Michael had just shown her.

Michael had demanded everything, flowing into her, retreating enough to make her desperate, filling her again. His hands worked magic, his scent, his heartbeat becoming hers.

Damn him more for his tenderness, for the rocking of her body against his while she cried, for the gentle kisses, the sweet whispers. "Baby," he'd called her tenderly, holding her close and warm and safe.

She hated him most of all for that . . . the sweet tenderness that reminded her of a boy, caring for her, a brother and yet not a brother, always with a gleam in his eye that challenged her—

He'd damn well challenged her on that bed, pushing too far, too raw and primitive where she couldn't conceal that she was just as savage in her need, stunned when it came tearing out of her.

Cloe tapped her fingers. They'd had a moment.

Simply that, a meeting of needs and tempers flying, and damn. Why did he have to hold her as if nothing could tear her away?

Cloe frowned at the six pictures lined over the desk, her family's lives blended with the Bearclaws'.

Michael, raw-boned and grinning as a boy, was nothing like the man who had just taken something from her, who made her furious that she had never known, even in her marriage, the passion that could take her out of herself and never give her totally back to her keeping.

Michael had taken away her control and she wanted it back.

She'd survived on control for years, protecting herself, and for a time in his arms, his mouth hot and demanding on hers, she'd given him more than she'd given anyone.

Cloe reached to straighten a picture and it slid slightly, coming free from the nail. The photo was Michael, grinning, a high school football warrior, swaggering and ripe with victory. She placed the picture against a stack of books and ran her hand across his lips. The scar wasn't there then.

She had touched her sensitive lips with her tongue, tasting him and his face, raw with passion, skin taut over bones, a flush riding his dark cheeks and his eyes glittering, sweeping down the pale length of her body, locked with his. He'd torn away the edge of a sheet as if he wanted nothing between them—

Energy poured through her, tightened on her skin. Her body wanted to feed upon him again and something buried inside her needed, desperately needed, the tenderness she hadn't expected.

Cloe shivered; she'd made a mistake with Ross, and she could be making one with Michael. He'd felt only too right, but sex and the repercussions could be disastrous. Michael wasn't born of easy men. He came from a line of males who lived their lives with promises of honor. She didn't want honor, or commitment, or the power he had just shown her.

Michael, once set on his course, would battle for what he wanted. She couldn't give him cause to believe in her, to want a relationship between them.

Michael deserved a woman who could give him a child. . . .

She pushed the thought away. Michael would take what he wanted—and she had to survive. Years of training leaped into her now, slashed at her, pushed her, and she wrote, "Wild Willows," adding "Health Spa" across the top. She paused, then inserted a mark, adding a word. "Wild Willows Health and Beauty Spa," she whispered, tasting the idea, the words, in her mind and on her lips. The concept snagged her, in the predawn hours when she was used to prowling, dealing with life's rotten blows and—

Habit, she thought, as she began methodically outlining a concept as she had hundreds of times before. No more than habit.

Then there was no time for thinking, just the yellow pad, pen flying over it, images dancing in her mind . . . another sheet, more ideas.

Michael lay alone, awake since Cloe had slid from his arms. He'd strained not to reach out, dragging her back close and safe against him. A glance at the bedside clock told him it was now four o'clock. She'd been at the desk for two hours, rising to stalk back and forth across the room, allowing him glimpses of her taut body, those long legs striding past the doorway. The ripping, crumbling sound of paper echoed in the night, punctuated by her dark muttering. He'd been cursed before by women he scorned, and by judges and criminals, but never for making love.

He distrusted that nagging edge of fear that she would leave him, hate him. Fear was new to Michael, and only this woman had the power to make him afraid. He feared that he'd had a taste of heaven and a second taste wouldn't come again. That Cloe would look at him and fear him, his need of her, his body too rough—

The years stood between them. Or did they? He cursed silently. Two hours of scratching pen on paper, of paper whipping against paper, should have been enough to say what she needed—to blast him. The old Cloe would have just—he smiled grimly—plowed him with a softball, temper burning her.

Michael ran a shaking hand over his jaw, the sound of his stubble raw in the silence of predawn. The bastard hadn't loved her, and Michael could have killed Ross for that—for taking the sweet, tender heart of her and stripping it bare. She'd fought to keep a part of herself away from their loving, and he hadn't allowed it. What man would?

She hadn't been loved, not held and soothed and devoured the way he had.

Yeah, right. Michael had sunk into her with all the finesse of a bull in the field, hungry for her. They'd gone at each other, careless of the lamp that had been knocked away as Cloe threw out her hands, finally gripping the bedpost, hips bucking against him, her mouth lifting, taking his— Her hunger had matched his, eager, untutored, just the dig of her nails in his back, her breath catching, releasing. . . . She'd be wearing his bruises and his back—Michael closed his eyes, hauling back the memory of her nails digging in, her hipbones thrusting up, meeting his, those sweet little purrs, like hunger trapped inside a rose curling around him. And she'd taken him inside her, the sweet clenching of her body had devastated him, humbled him.

Michael inhaled sharply. His body should be satisfied. He wasn't; he wanted Cloe in bed with him, lying close and whispering and kissing and cuddling. His fist crushed the sheet. What was he doing? Asking for another shot through the heart, a shattering that had almost killed him?

Any minute she'd be finished with her perfect kiss-off note and walk out the door and he'd— Michael listened closely. The chair wasn't creaking—

He slid from the bed and entered the main room to find Cloe asleep, her head in her arms, her hand on a framed picture beside her. Michael lifted her hand gently from the frame and it slid across the desk. As he caught it, the glass separated at one corner, old tape coming free, a white border peeking out.

Michael lifted the picture, eased the photographs from behind his high school football picture and studied the bloody, dead body of Gus Ballas. Shot at different angles, his father's amateur photography had caught every detail—footprints in the earth, circling the body.

The sight had the effect of a heavyweight boxer's

fist slamming into Michael's midsection. He focused on the pictures, alive with details. The footprints—boots worn at the heel, not western boots—had circled the body in a path, like an artist studying his work. The boot had a trademark in the center of the sole.

Sam Matthews had always worn western boots and fussed about putting on his Sunday dress shoes for church. He even complained his legs ached if he wore anything else.

Michael placed the pictures on another table, tucked beneath magazines. Cloe hadn't seen the photographs, or she wouldn't be sleeping peacefully, her head nestled on her arms, her bare legs gleaming beneath his borrowed shirt.

Michael stroked the soft warmth of her cheek with the back of his finger and noted the swollen contours of her lips. They'd come together hungrily, and Michael had been unprepared for his need of her and she had met him, straining wildly, crying out for him—her cries echoed in his mind, seduced him, addicted him. . . .

Cloe. Soft, sweet, feminine, her bleached hair sliding over her flushed cheek, curling around her jaw. He stroked the dark margin of reddish brown at her temple, smiled at the light spray of freckles across her face. Michael ran his fingertip across the small chafed marks on that smooth cheek, the sweep of her lashes, and eased her into his arms. "Come to bed, honey," he whispered, as she cuddled nearer and he carried her back to bed.

This is how it should have been all those years—

"Lie with me, Michael," she murmured sleepily,

her hand caressing his hair as he covered her with the quilt.

He smiled softly, mocking himself. There was no way he could ever resist Cloe. He eased down onto the bed, curling around her, holding her, listening to her until her breathing was deep and easy in the night. There, holding her safe against him, Michael's professional mind dissected the photographs. There would be more behind the other pictures, and they were what his father had wanted to show him.

This was the missing link in the evidence in Sam Matthews's trial.

"Name, please?" Liam's harsh voice cut through the alarm system, causing Stella to jump and flatten against the wall.

She glared at the blinking alarm installed in Cloe's room. She wanted to check on her daughter before going downstairs to begin breakfast biscuits and the lunch menu's split pea soup. Cloe's bed was empty and Liam's voice had startled her. "Liam, I am in my own house. Why should I have to answer to you?"

His voice came, metallic, relentless, through the intercom. "Punch in the code, disarming the current room."

Stella jabbed at the buttons, the secret code disarming Cloe's bedroom alarm. "I do not like this, Liam."

"You need protection."

"It's an invasion of privacy. I feel like I'm in a goldfish bowl."

"Mmm. What are you wearing, Stella?" Liam's voice took on a soothing, sexy drawl.

She gripped her battered robe closer over her nude

body. "I'm not used to a man's voice in my apartment at four o'clock in the morning. You should be sleeping." She tried for a maternal tone and failed.

"Cloe is at Michael's. He called earlier when he disarmed his system. It's back up and running now."

Stella wrapped her arms around herself. Cloe at Michael's was how it should be, should have been for years. After her bloodless marriage, Cloe needed Michael, what he brought to her—that fine fiery temper, that slashing creative need raised on edge—challenges running through her, lighting her. . . .

"Do you miss me?" Liam's sexy intercom voice intruded.

Startled, Stella glared at the blinking light on the sensor. "Miss you?"

"I miss *you*," Liam noted huskily. "I'd like to come over now and show you how much."

There was no misinterpreting his tone. Stella forced herself to breathe steadily, her heart pounding. "You've got big ideas, Liam."

"Yes, I do," he answered easily. "Would you like a ceremony at the church, or at The Pinto Bean, or in—"

"Liam! You are forgetting—"

His impatient snort carried over the intercom. "Oh, hell, Stella. Are you going to bring up our ages again? What do you think we've been doing these last two months, if not dating?"

Stella flattened against the wall, stunned. *"Dating?"*

"I'm courting you, Stella. I don't bring bouquets of flowers to other women." Liam's voice was rough with impatience. "I don't hold their hands every damn chance I can. I don't look into their sky blue eyes and start floating off the ground at the sound of their voices. It's not your pie that I want to devour, darling," he said too sweetly. Then, with a sharper tone, "Yes, damn it, I have the damnable dreams every night about your succulent anatomy. . . . Go to sleep, Stella-dear, and chew on that," Liam grumbled.

Other men had desired her. With that experience, Stella moved to set up her walls. "I am—"

Liam's bored tone interrupted. "I know. An older woman. Seasoned. Considerate. Loving. Ripe. Juicy. Sweet and more woman than I've ever known in my life. I've waited for you all my life, my dear, and you're not making this easy. In fact you haven't had a clue—do you know exactly what that does to a man, not to recognize his attempts at courting his love?"

"Liam!"

A child whimpered sleepily in the background, and Liam murmured softly, "Tracey, come to Daddy. I chased away the bears from under your bed last night, remember?"

Stella listened to the sound of clothing scraping, a child drawn onto Liam's lap, the steady sound of a creaking rocker. "I'll see you today, Stella. Reset the motion sensor."

Click. Stella was left alone. "For goodness' sake, he's got a six-year-old girl. I passed that years ago. I have sons a little younger than he is . . . I married once and loved Sam deeply. Wade was—"

Stunned, she walked out of the room and set off a series of new alarms, cursing them.

"Don't worry about it, Stella," Liam's calm voice curled around her from the alarm's intercom system. "Your husband and Wade were a part of your life. I expect you to remember them, have a place in your heart for them. . . . By the way, don't skimp on the wedding plans, and I'd like to see my bride in white. I like those little nosegay things, too. And a garter. With those legs, a garter is a must."

"What's a garter, Daddy?" Tracey asked sleepily.

The image of herself as Liam's bride sent Stella flattening to the wall again. Tracey's delicate yawn stopped her from telling Liam McKensie just where he could go—

Cloe awoke to the strip of sunlight blinding her, the rip of the curtains opening, and Michael grinning down at her, a tray held in his hand. She had a glimpse of broad tanned chest, a flat, corded stomach, of jeans unsnapped at the waist, before she flattened to the bed, placed her hands over her eyes, and cursed him. "Jerk."

"Strong word for a woman lying in my bed."

"Do I smell coffee?" She fought to the surface, hating the blush that Michael had just stroked as he sat on the bed, his weight causing her to lean against him.

Naked. She was naked in the morning for the first time in her life and her body ached from lovemaking, a deep very satisfactory ache that only made her more wary of Michael Bearclaw.

He settled his open hand on her hip, squeezed gently. "Breakfast is ready, then it's time to go home, little girl. Unless you want to spend the next few days in bed."

She inhaled the scent of soap and male and groaned, pulling the sheet up to her chin. "Michael, I—"

"I never saw a woman blush like you," he murmured, delight in his deep tone as he stroked her hot cheek. Suddenly she was nineteen again and thrilled with Michael Bearclaw's grin. The years spun away as she grinned back, suddenly shy.

Cloe blinked. Why should she be shy of Michael Bearclaw? The thought mortified her—she was a seasoned, tough businesswoman, a divorced woman, a woman whose body was now melting beneath Michael's hard one. "I do not blush."

"You've probably got a real nice shade of pink beneath this sheet. You're burning hot enough, from the way it feels. Very hot." That boyish grin devastated her as he eased over her body, full length, covering her and rubbing his bare chest against her softness beneath the cloth.

"You're crushing me." She studied him warily. Michael had certainly taken last night, and so had she. Rumpled in the morning, shaggy hair damp from his shower, his skin dark against hers, Michael toyed with her hair, the blond strands curling around his fingers.

He stroked the reddish brown roots at her temple with his thumbs, his expression serious now. "Cloe, you're talented. The spa concept might just work. If that trail ride idea works, Josy could have a good income, and the guide and fishing trips, too."

Michael had seen her work, her notations about Josy's employment, and she didn't care. She studied his broad tanned face, his Sioux heritage gleaming in his shaggy blue-black hair. On this level, she could trust Michael, the old Michael, a part of her desperation, her painful childhood. "I'd like to push it right smack in their faces. With Angelica and Josy, we could do it. We'd need capital, but we've got the talent. Michael . . . if you laugh at me, I'll kill you."

He nibbled on her lips, teeth sharp enough to distract her from her revenge. "Go for it."

She eyed him, rumpled and sexy. "You're laughing at me. Don't you dare challenge me. Listen, you piece of—"

He lifted an eyebrow and without warning, without a dram of tenderness, took her mouth as if it were his. When he lifted his head, Cloe stared at him, breathless, shaking, ready to devour him. "I do not want to get into this," she stated carefully. "I've just gone through a divorce and—"

"That's your choice," he returned, giving her nothing. She could almost hear the old western phrase "Call it," the go-ahead for a shootout. He rolled to his feet and walked out of the room, leaving her hungry, with the sight of his powerful back—the long dark red marks of her nails—and worn jeans that cupped his taut butt and ran into powerful long legs.

Cloe groaned silently, her nails digging into the sheets. Her aching, frustrated body told her that she hadn't had enough of him, that little kept her from running him down and having him. He knew exactly how to arouse her. If Michael Bearclaw was anything, it was sheerly maddening.

Bradley Gilchrist frowned at Cloe's BMW cruising into town at eight o'clock in the morning. "That little she-cat—out fornicating with Wade Bearclaw's boy. Like mother, like daughter."

He looked at Jeffrey, pale and untalented beside Angelica, who was already battling her way through the work on her desk. Jeffrey reminded Bradley of his wife: ineffective, spoiled—

Bradley met his daughter's unflinching stare. She was Gilchrist steel, battling for what she wanted. The girl had stayed because she had his blood, his need to rule.

His eyes swung out to The Pinto Bean and old Judge Lang striding by as if it didn't matter that he wasn't welcome there. The fool had been afraid of public sentiment when he'd sentenced Sam Matthews, but more afraid of what Bradley could do to him— ruining him—and so he had sentenced Matthews. It had been so easy, setting up Sam Matthews, the troublemaker. With a brain the size of a pea, Gus had been easily convinced by Stan Collins, the deputy then, that Stella had wanted him. Gus had raped her brutally and Sam had fallen for the trap that had led to his undoing.

Maggie Ten Feather had been enough for Orson. While his wife slipped into illness and the shadows of death, Orson barely noticed, fornicating with his black-eyed, willowy Indian princess.

In the end, Bradley thought, when the challenge came, Angelica would choose blood over those Wild Willow whores she'd known as children; over her infatuation with Mike Lightfeather, Angelica would see the sense of a useful alliance. For the family. For The Club.

After serving the lunch crowd, Cloe left her mother to work on the catalog, which lay spread across the kitchen table. She was taking a gamble, going ahead with her plans when her suppliers were threatened and hesitant. She'd come this far and she didn't intend to back down, not when the catalog idea was dead-center, surefire, gut-right. "If I have to make buffalo jerky and pick leaves for Indian tea myself— if I have to weave every placemat and sew every apron, I will not let The Club back me down."

The spa was another matter, the idea was too new to share, though Michael had discovered her first drafts. She hoarded the concept of the spa, nudging it, shaping it, subtracting, adding, defining. The Pinto Bean was holding its own, with enough profit for a new large refrigerator. The logo cups were a huge success, and Cloe had designed small ones for children's hands. Going to The Pinto Bean for a special treat on Saturday had become a town occasion, for everyone except The Club.

She glanced at Sergei, bent over the catalog mark-ups, studying them, his gleaming untamed curls shaking each time he jabbed at her sketches and muttered about a photographer's detail. Overnight Sergei had produced a wealth of photographs of the products— and of Josy and Cody. His three sleepless nights had paid off; he'd developed the pictures himself. The pictures of Josy were steamy, unique, brooding, and intimate, the camera revealing a sensual heat.

Cloe placed the yellow pad on her lap and sat back against her mother's couch. She hadn't erased Michael's kiss, the feel his hands moving over her, his body lodged deeply in hers, pushing her, always pushing, taking, giving—She ached, not painfully, just enough to remind her that she was still hungry for him.

She scrubbed her hands through her hair. Oh, she

could trust Michael, all right, to point out the imperfections in her life. She hadn't known lovemaking could be so violent . . . or so tender, riding the edge of fiery explosion with one touch, one brush, one look—

She'd cried in his arms, first for her miscarriage and a bit for herself, and then because of the beauty, the purity of their lovemaking. Michael had been a tender companion, and when their hunger had been briefly sated, he'd been incredibly gentle as a lover. She couldn't afford tenderness. She hadn't wanted it in years and she didn't want it from Michael—not from him.

How dared Michael have absolute, unwavering confidence in her idea, listening to her, stuffing bites of jam-laden toast into her mouth and following it with a kiss as she passed him, working through her ideas as she paced?

She'd buy out his investment in The Pinto Bean's catalog, just as soon as she could, and she'd murder Angelica very slowly.

How dared he pat her on the bottom as she was leaving, the idea moving inside her, the images growing? How dared Michael grin, hand her a cup of coffee for the road, and tell her to "go for it, wildfire"?

Cloe let out a long, frustrated groan. She would show him; she would tear him apart, run him into the ground—build the damn Wild Willows Health and Beauty Spa just to show him she could.

Well. There was that little money-thing, she admitted ruefully, tapping her pencil. Without a hefty investor, the project would take years to develop.

Sergei's dark almond-shaped eyes studied her. "My friend, you are dancing between worlds. This is not

like you. Go get us food. Unless you wish to return
to Michael. Love makes such a soft, drowsy light in
your eyes and a rose upon your cheeks."

A professional model's photographer, Sergei had
missed nothing. Cloe eyed him. "Lay off. He's been
all over the world. Why can't he find somewhere else
to live?"

"Because nowhere else has what his heart needs.
He is seeking something, the same as you. I know this,
the seeking of the heart for a home. Michael is
haunted, Cloe. He has in his eyes too much pain, too
much for him to bear."

Chapter 13

❧

"WHAT IS IT our women, the Wild Willows, do to-night, my friend?" Sergei asked, as he hung the en-larged photographs in the bunk house's makeshift darkroom. In the dim infrared light, the brutalized body of Gus Ballas eased from a blurred shape into magnified, bloody reality.

The June moon lifted high and round overhead, a hunter's moon, and in the main room, Cody had curled up with Max to new comics which Sergei had ordered for him.

Michael studied a black-and-white three-inch rip in Ballas's bloated cheek, probably caused by a big ring; Sam Matthews wore only his wedding ring, a simple gold band, and Gus's face was peppered with dis-tinctive circles, probably from an emblem ring. He glanced at Sergei, who was tracing Josy's lips in an enlarged photograph. "The Wild Willows are proba-bly having a powwow, chewing us over, and doing plenty of thinking."

"If my Josy is doing the chewing, I would like that." Sergei expertly eased another photo from the shallow pan and clipped it beside the others. "My methods are of the old style, but effective in these conditions."

He studied the photographs. "Josy wasn't invited to the Gilchrist soiree on Saturday. This woman, Susan Gilchrist, read the story about me in the newspaper, and alas, I am to be put on display for only the best, she says. I think my Josy is the best. She will come with me."

Michael hoped Sergei was up to dragging Josy to the Gilchrists'. She'd be harder to handle than the colts she trained.

"Today's paper," Bradley Gilchrist said, flopping the *Lolo Star* onto his desk at the bank. He leveled a stare around the room, lingered on Angelica's smooth, stylish suit, her cool perfect expression, and studied Jeffrey and Edward Livingston. "Some jackass murdered Muriel's parakeets last night. The headline reads 'Parakeet Murderer at Large.' If anyone wants to stir up the community's sympathy, it would be to kill that old woman's birds."

Angelica focused on the two younger men in the room. "You'll go down to Muriel's today, won't you, Edward, and make a donation to the capture of the parakeet murderer?"

Edward blinked and paled, but nodded. Bradley smoothed his hands on his desktop. If only Jeffrey had Angelica's instincts—

At eight o'clock that evening, Josy, Angelica, and Cloe lay in the back of Josy's old pickup truck, looking up at the Wyoming stars. The rush of the creek near their old clubhouse seemed to stretch from one decade to another. It was a sound as pure as the frogs' croaking along its waters. Ned Blackburn's newly cut hayfield offered a familiar perfume; the big round bales stood like monuments in the moonlight.

"Okay. I'll wear the damned pigtails. Just brush and braid and I'll calm down," Angelica muttered. She had been tense, furious with her father for reclaiming a young couple's small vegetable truck farm. The murder of the parakeets stretched silently across the Wild Willows.

Josy had settled her back against her knees and brushed Angelica's hair, while she studied the sparkle of her single-carat diamond ring in the moonlight. "Something is cooking in our little Cloe's brain and she's not ready to let go. Must be big—either that, or she's still floating after Michael's big—ouch!"

Angelica glared at Josy. "I let you braid my hair, didn't I? Pinching hurts."

"If you tease Cloe, I will never play mud packs with you again. I will never play masseuse. I will never play tennis." Josy quit her task, turned to pilfer through the wine and cheese banquet above their heads, and stuffed a handful of olives in her mouth. Around them, she mumbled, "Remember when we made those lumpy ashtrays in third grade? I like to bash one of them—maybe all three—over Sergei's head. I didn't agree to be his model. He must have shot a thousand pictures of me today. He cooks—stews with wine in them—and throws herbs into food with an artistic flair. Too bad I lost good old Liam to Stella. He's dependable, and another thing—Sergei is moody. I'm certain he's cussing at me in Russian sometimes. Like today, when Marge Field's pretty little filly took a kick at me. Sergei leaped over the corral and started crooning to the filly in Russian. I can't train a horse if a man is sweet-talking and fondling her," Josy muttered, and added darkly, "He does like to fondle. Most fondling man I ever knew. And he's passionate about everything. I don't think I like passionate."

"Darn, a passionate man. He picked her a bouquet of wildflowers, cooks supper, cleans, does her laundry, and on top of that he's passionate. Don't you hate him?" Angelica teased, and lifted her eyebrows innocently when Josy glared at her.

Cloe wiggled her bare toes; from the way Sergei looked at Josy, he preferred to fondle her long, lithe body, not the filly's. "How's it going with Edward? I wouldn't like Sergei's presence on Small Bird Ranch to be a tool Edward could use against you."

Josy was quiet, then she spoke carefully. "Yes, I know there could be a problem with Edward. He tried to kiss me the other day—rather grabbed at me in the radio station . . . right there in the sound room. I had to knee him, but I apologized."

"*Apologized?* Only you would do that to that creep." Angelica laughed outright, a bawdy, rich sound in the quiet night. "That's Edward. Thinks if a woman is in his vicinity, she's available." Her tone dropped into ice and steel. "I'll take care of Edward."

Cloe flipped a tiny cheese cracker into the air and caught it in her mouth. "Mom thinks Liam's got Gary Cooper eyes. It didn't dawn on her that he had something else going there . . . romance with her. She's sitting at the house now, staring into space."

Angelica lifted her bottle in a toast. "I like Michael. Now, are you going to tell me how good he was in bed, or not?"

"Not."

"Blast. If I can't live by vicarious lovemaking, I might as well rent a porn movie. The whole place is practically frothing in sex foam and I'm an outcast, just a lonely little innocent virgin lamb among the orgy."

Cloe raised up to peer over Josy to Angelica. "Or you could jump Quinn Lightfeather."

"Take that back. That was low. There isn't a thing about Quinn that interests me," Angelica stated too harshly.

"I need a place to work," Cloe said quietly, changing the subject, settling down beside Josy. "I'm planning something other than the catalog business—"

"Sure. I knew something else was brewing. When you're ready, you'll tell us, and not before you've got all the pieces in place." Angelica's answer came fast and easy, born of years of deep friendship. "Move in with me, kid."

"You can stay at my place, if you don't mind Cody and me."

"You're staying, aren't you?" Angelica hooted, and kicked the pickup bed with her boots. "I'm glad. You'll stay with me, of course."

"What? And be subjected to be your beautician, masseuse, and pedicurist? No, Angelica, you've got enough problems with your family. I'm not adding to them." Cloe was silent for a moment, thinking of the birds in the tiny casket lined with scented geraniums. "They left Muriel one parakeet, Clark Gable."

Josy and Angelica were silent, recognizing The Club's handiwork. "What did she do with Clark?" Josy asked.

"Stowed him. Muriel will miss him, but Clark is safe."

"I should have known that would happen," Angelica muttered darkly. "It's just like them to leave her one, as a reminder."

Josy spoke quietly, "We had a beautiful little Appaloosa filly once, when Dad was trying to leave the bottle alone . . . just about the time your dad was sentenced. Bradley Gilchrist came to the house, checking on the mortgage, I guess, and she was dead the next morning. I saw Dad cry, just like he did before the fire. After the fire, he was drunk and said he'd made The Club mad. When he looked at the dead filly, he had that same sad, helpless look. And then he began to drink again. He had me do something important for him and made me promise never to say what."

"What?" Cloe and Angelica asked in unison.

"I promised Dad not to tell," Josy murmured firmly.

"We should get her drunk," Angelica noted, frowning at Cloe when she tugged away Angelica's new glass of wine and threw it over the side of the pickup.

"Or tickle her until she wets her pants," Cloe added, and then they lunged upon Josy, tickling her.

Later that night at the Bearclaw Ranch, Michael again studied the photographs Sergei had enlarged. Michael had seen enough corpses to know that Gus Ballas had been old-fashioned, western-style pistol whipped. The marks on Gus's wrists said the raw trails were caused by a smooth, regular surface, like handcuffs. The corner's report showed there was blood and tissue beneath his fingernails as if he had scratched someone, and there were no marks on Sam Matthews when he was arrested, but for the grazing on two knuckles, right hand. The pictures had already been scanned at Muriel's for use in Michael's computer.

The bastards had left Muriel one parakeet, tears in the old woman's voice as she described the ritualistic placement of her pets. She'd hurried to clean away the nightmare, and Cloe had come in just then, to work at the *Star*'s computer. Cloe had urged Muriel to have a proper funeral and had gotten a tiny sample casket from the undertaker; the ceremony had eased Muriel's pain, and raised her anger.

Michael stared at the copy of a note, folded and yellowed with age, found with the framed photographs. The orginal note to Wade, a composite of threatening words pasted together, had been sent with the original photographs for safekeeping. Michael intended to see justice done. "I'll take care of it, Dad."

He folded away a newer note from his father, one admitting to his son that he had been forced to lie about the photographs; his family and sick wife had been threatened. Wade had testified that the film was bad and produced film he had damaged for evidence; he'd tampered with murder evidence and it had tormented him.

Michael scanned the pictures, an expert at the bloody horror he'd seen too many times. But this time was personal, and he pushed away the other images, the children bloody and ruined, women, young boys.

The Club had won—years ago. Michael couldn't let that happen again; he couldn't let anything happen to Stella or Cloe. *Cloe....* On an impulse, he opened the desk drawer and pulled out a small, aged envelope, extracting the worn folded paper within. Cloe's childish scrawl lay within a color crayon heart—"Cloe + Michael."

Michael inhaled sharply and ran his fingertips over the heart. Tangling with Cloe after all these years was sheer madness and he couldn't afford the pain a second time.

Pleasing Cloe, listening to her soft, purring hungry sounds could be an addiction Michael could not afford.

In the Long Horn, Orson bent over the counter, clutching his drink. "Maggie Ten Feather rode like wind, best trick rider ever ... practically danced on that big Appaloosa—all over it, bareback, you know, no saddle. Black hair gleaming like a raven's wing—coal black silk, rippling in the wind, and scented like sweetgrass. Long it was ... reached past her knees when it wasn't braided," Orson Smith rambled as he sprawled on the Long Horn's bar stool, alone and speaking more to himself than to Quinn behind the bar. "She stood on that horse's back, the wind pulling at her clothes, those buckskin fringes like a part of her—and she was smart—smart as a whip. Prettiest maiden in the whole Nation by the time she was sixteen.... Pretty Maggie ... pretty, pretty Maggie." Orson wept.

Quinn wiped the last of his stemmed glasses, sliding them into the overhead racks. The old man was a faded remnant of himself, taking too many bribes, bending too many laws for The Club. Suddenly Orson's dim blue eyes focused on Quinn. "You've got her same look—there around the eyes, sort of a lilt at the edges and maybe that black hair."

"We're cousins. She took care of me sometimes when my folks were gone to powwows across the country. Or when they were too drunk to send me off to reservation school."

"Cousins. . . ." Orson echoed hollowly, then focused and smiled shrewdly. "That's why you look alike. I always liked you, boy. Fine boy, that's what you are. Grew up to be just fine. I held you when you were born. No more than a cap of black hair and a hungry squawl, you were. Maggie was proud of you. She kept a book, always writing in it—what you did, your first tooth, how you had something Indian in you that saw things."

Quinn took the old man's glass, plunging it into the dishwater. "Keeping my Indian blood wasn't hard to do on a reservation."

"Fine boy. Grew up just fine. Proud of you," Orson muttered drunkenly. "You think Maggie remembers you? Thinks of you?"

"Maybe. Maybe not. I visit her sometimes and she's pretty well vacant." Quinn thought of how Maggie had taught him to mix paint from plants and earth, to step into the different worlds, to let himself drift on the smoke, seeing, opening. . . .

A look of pain swept over the old man's face, his bald head gleaming beneath the sparse, concealing strands of hair pulled across it. In comic contrast to Orson's misery, one long strand flopped over his ear as he placed his head in his hands, bony fingers digging into his skull as if to push away memories. "I saw her today. Sitting there in the sanatorium, all shrunken and white, eyes blank. She would have fought—"

"Yes," Quinn agreed grimly, thinking back when Maggie was vibrant, her mind and laughter quick. He remembered her touch, sometimes along his cheek. She'd married an abusive man, and Orson had run him out of town; and soon after, high on drugs, Maggie had tried to kill herself.

"I'm alone now," Orson whined, looking at Quinn as he dimmed the lights.

"I left a message on Angelica's tape machine. She'll come for you." Why did Angelica faithfully collect the old man when he drank? Quinn wondered.

Secrets whispered around Angelica, Quinn thought, like how she had given her body to him, all those years ago . . . how she had pledged to run away with him, marry him. . . .

Bitterness rose up in Quinn throat as Orson looked at him hopefully. "You wouldn't come to my house sometime, be my friend, would you, Quinn, boy?"

"Maybe." *No, I will not have you in my life.*

Orson's bony fingers reached out and grabbed Quinn's hand. "Don't forget Maggie, boy. If something happens to me, you watch out for her."

Quinn nodded as Angelica stepped into The Long Horn, dressed in a wrinkled black silk shirt, skin-tight black jeans, boots, and braids. The large diamonds in her earlobes catching, sending off the dim light like multicolored spears. She crossed the barroom, weaving around the tables, the chairs already placed on top, and slid onto a bar stool beside Orson. She snubbed Quinn as he had expected and nudged the old man. "Hello, Orson. Having a bad night?"

Orson's hand reached out to snare her forearm, a man who had based his life on greed and power, now alone and seeking friendship. "I always liked you, Angelica. And Quinn. Maggie did a good job with him."

Quinn tossed the bar towel over his shoulder and slid the cup of coffee and the ice water in front of Angelica. She scooped ice from the water and dropped it into the coffee. "So, Orson. What's the problem tonight?"

Orson's eyes were owlish as he whispered fearfully, "Someone killed Muriel's parakeets. I like Muriel. Didn't always see eye-to-eye with her, but she liked Maggie and that was important. Maggie and Quinn. They were important."

"The braids add another dimension to your Fifth Avenue look." Quinn tugged one dark red braid and Angelica glared at him.

"Hands off," she snapped.

"Why do you do this for him?" Quinn asked Angelica, as she steadied the cup for the old man, urging him to drink.

"Going to wet my pants . . . 's embarrassing," the old man muttered, as Quinn moved around the bar and supported Orson, leading him into the men's room.

"Thanks," Angelica muttered begrudgingly, when Quinn returned with Orson and settled him on the bar stool. "Orson, drink this. Quinn, he needs broth of some kind. Sometimes he forgets to eat."

Quinn slid a bowl of Stella's reheated chicken noodle soup in front of Angelica and she began to feed spoonsful to Orson, wiping his chin. Quinn couldn't resist the taunt, "You're all heart, Angelica."

Angelica's green eyes flicked at him like a cat's, about to strike. "Look, I can leave him here just as easy as not—Orson, you open up and eat." She pinched the old man's nose so that his mouth popped open and she spooned in the soup. "Swallow."

"They'll put me away like they did Maggie," Orson whined.

"Nobody is putting you away like Maggie," Angelica stated harshly. She glared at Quinn. "He did something for me when I was little, okay?"

"Did I?" Orson asked in his drunken mumble.

"You did," Angelica said firmly. "I won't forget."

"Did I do something good for you, Angelica?" Orson asked desperately.

"You did something good." Angelica's expression closed into bitterness and for a moment Quinn wanted to take her into his arms, to hold her. Angelica carried her wounds quietly, a warrior woman, and she would have hated him for the sympathy.

"I'll help you get him home," Quinn offered, and expected her to refuse.

She searched his face, her expression wary and drained, too tired for the task ahead of her. "No wisecracks? No questions?"

He ignored her and moved to pick up Orson in his arms, the old man's frail body nothing but bones and flesh and fear.

Later, inside Orson's cluttered shadowy musty mansion, Angelica tucked the old man into his bed.

She straightened, rubbing her hands on her thighs. She scrubbed her face, looking too weary, dark red hair gleaming in the dim light. She looked like a woman who needed holding and the tenderness in Quinn's heart lurched. She looked as though she was nineteen again, before the world came between them. "Will you come to me when you need me, Angelica?" Quinn asked quietly, the answer more important than his heartbeat.

There with the old man snoring deeply in the shadows, there was honesty between them, undiluted by the past, as Angelica spoke, "Orson protected me when I needed him and he didn't back down. He never backed down when it came to . . . to that . . . to my father . . . to me. I went to him sometimes and he was always there for me. I survived and I won't forget him. He's not like the rest . . . he's just weak."

Tears shimmered in her eyes and she dashed them away. "I've got to go. Call me if this happens again."

Quinn caught her arm as she passed, furious suddenly with her like the wind that springs from the storm, whipping at him. "You ran away to Europe. You ran away from your redskin lover. You were ashamed."

The accusation sunk between them like a war spear, buried in him for so many years—centuries, it seemed. Her eyes were dark and old, shadowy with secrets, and inside him the ache to hold her rose again.

"Maybe," she said, using his noncommittal word to seal him away, giving him nothing and leaving him in the shadows.

After she'd hurried away, tires squawling on the

front driveway as if racing away from her demons,
Quinn sat beside the old man. The bedside photograph wasn't of his wife, but it was Maggie, holding
a black-haired infant and beaming into the camera.
Was that the baby who cried in Quinn's dreams?

When Quinn finally slept in his room, scented of
sweetgrass and sage, he dreamed of the firewoman
walking through old paths, burning the ground,
sparks coming off her like sun, her eyes clear as blue
mountain lakes, fire catching in her hair—and the
baby cried.

At five o'clock in the morning, Cloe sat cross-legged
on the apartment floor, arranging the catalog se-
quence. Sergei, in the space of a week, had finished
his work, eager to spend his time with Josy, who was
totally flustered by having someone to care for her,
for the ranch, and for Cody, sharing duties. The paycheck Sergei provided left her no choice but to let "the
dude" remain.

In return, Josy tried to make life miserable for Sergei, taking him on a horseback ride into the mountains that would make an experienced horseman
hesitate. Sergei had manfully ridden into town on
horseback, muttered to Cloe in the deli as he'd passed,
and had painfully inched his way up the stairs to
Stella's apartment to soak, drink vodka, and curse.

Cloe glanced at the telephone, which had not rung.
She slammed a couch pillow against her, hugging it.
Fine. She'd had a night with Michael Bearclaw. He'd
made her breakfast, patted her backside, kissed her
cheek, and sent her off to play. "Go for it, champ."

"Go for it," Cloe muttered, and closed her eyes,

only to remember Michael above her, fierce, demanding, taking her higher. She groaned. He hadn't used her; he'd pushed and taken, and he'd given. Damn him for showing her the difference. He'd made her feel . . . really feel, taken her into the fire and then raised the ante, and she'd been with him for every inexperienced untutored heartbeat.

She glared at the silent telephone and then her mother passed, dressed for .work and looking stunned. "Mom?"

"Oh, 'morning, honey. Did I remember to order garbanzos?" Stella asked blankly. "They really are good marinated in salads, don't you think? Or was it feta cheese?"

That afternoon, Cloe bent closer to Jeffrey Gilchrist's wife. "Ann?"

Ann's smooth cheek was swollen, the bruise around one eye carefully touched with cosmetic concealer. Because Ann shrank deeper into the shadows of the grocery store, attempting a smile, Cloe did not come closer. She pretended to study the virgin olive oil. Ann smiled again at her shyly, a shadow of the vivacious girl Cloe remembered. "Hi, Cloe. I . . . I'm glad you're back."

"How about lunch on me, at The Pinto Bean, Ann?" Cloe asked, wanting to give Ann a place to rest, to get strong again.

Ann's good eye widened, emphasizing the swollen contour of the other. "Oh, I couldn't. Jeffrey wants his favorite dinner tonight, and beef wellington takes hours to prepare. Jeffrey needs me to run errands for him—"

Ann stopped the gush of words and touched her swollen cheek, a shadow crossing her face and she suddenly wilted, a tired old woman before she was thirty. "Maybe some other time. Jeffrey needs some figures calculated before tonight. We don't have children, you know," she said suddenly. "Oh, it's my fault, of course. Jeffrey is too much of a man, and it isn't his fault."

Cloe reached out her hand and closed it over Ann's, locked to the grocery cart handle. Cloe had lost an amount of pride, too, Ross more subtly wearing her down, making her feel insecure. There in the shadows of the grocery aisles, anger stormed out of her. Had she been so little?

"Ann," she began unevenly in a hushed whisper. "Will you be my friend?"

"Jeffrey says I don't have time for friends, Cloe, and you're one of the Wild Willows. They always get into trouble somehow, and really, you should have a man help make your decisions; that way, you won't make mistakes," Ann said, as if she'd been programmed, and hurried away from Cloe.

Monroe Tibbs, Jr., moved the toothpick to the other side of his mouth as he spoke into the telephone. "Mr. Gilchrist, that Bearclaw guy is stirring up trouble. If we don't put the fear into him pretty soon, he could bring a bunch of outsiders in here and ruin things."

"He won't bring outsiders into our valley. I've told you, he's pure Bearclaw, and they like to handle things themselves the same way we do." Bradley's voice came smoothly across the lines, giving Monroe

what he wanted to hear. Monroe smiled at the
shielded language, because Gilchrist was too smart to
out-and-out say, "Beat the living hell out of Bearclaw." But Monroe knew what to do.

❦

Chapter 14

STELLA BLINKED AT the huge soup pot, smoke churned as Joe Issaks dumped water into it. He hitched up his sagging jeans as he hurried back and forth from the sink. "Damn near burned the bottom of the pot clear through."

"I have never burned a pot of beans in my life," Stella muttered dazedly, and sank onto a stool.

Cloe tried not to grin at her mother's stunned expression; Liam McKensie had stepped up the pace and had kissed Stella passionately in front of the customers. "Why don't you go lie down, and Joe and I will clean up for today?"

The fire alarm, disturbed by smoke, went off, and Stella blinked. "I have never burned beans or anything else."

At her ranch, Josy glared at Sergei, who was expertly spiking her hair with mousse. "If I hadn't promised Angelica and Cloe that I would be there, I'd—"

He tipped her head in a better position and artistically tugged at her hair. The practiced movements

252

reminded her that he'd had his hands on many models. The man knew women, and Josy felt as restless and nervous around him as she had when she was just twelve and discovering that boys weren't so bad. The black silk shirt and flowing slacks he had arrived in needed only a black jacket to be formal. She glared at him, this beautiful, expensive, exotic creature from another world, and fought the unique feeling that she was sweet, feminine, and desirable.

"You are adorable. Hold still." Sergei touched too much, warm hands strong and gentle, as though he were getting a filly accustomed to his touch.

She pushed his hands away. "Cloe and Angelica used to get me into trouble all the time. It appears that they still do. I'm not going. I should never have let Angelica talk me into it. She said I had to do it for Cloe. She knows how to get to me."

"Of course." In a lithe movement that startled her, Sergei sprawled on the couch, rumpled Cody's hair, and began a playful tussle with him.

"I mean it," Josy said, digging in. Someone had to take her seriously. "I'm not going."

Sergei's black almond-shaped eyes solemnly studied her. "You are frightened."

"I am not. I just don't. . . ." Josy scrambled for a reason not to go to the dinner. She couldn't face all the women who knew her background. "I . . . I don't have the right earrings."

"So then this is a fashion matter, and you do not have the right accessories for your beautiful dress?"

"Angelica got it for me years ago. I look all gangly and—"

Cody looked up at her, his young face serious.

There was no doubt in his words. "You look like my Mom and you look pretty."

Sergei came to his feet in that surprising lithe movement. He left the house, and in a few moments he returned with a large, blood-red merino shawl across his arm. "I would be honored if you would wear these."

In his palm were two simple gold earrings. His earlobe was empty, and the match to that earring lay in his hand. In his eyes was a question. . . .

She shivered and looked up into Sergei's eyes to find a gentle understanding she had not expected. "I would be honored if you would wear these as my gift to you."

Josy swallowed, her heart leaping. She stared at the earrings and knew that no one had ever given her anything so lovely or expensive. "I can't take them."

"This is your choice." There was arrogance and pride in Sergei's tone.

"Mommm. . . ." Cody pleaded. "Put the earrings on and let's go. I want to go to Timmy's house."

"You don't know these people, Sergei," Josy began quietly, fighting the painful memories.

Sergei's beautiful long fingers framed her face, bringing it up to him. "I know that you will be with me and that Angelica and Cloe will also be with you. Is that not enough?"

"This is important to Angelica. She wants to protect Cloe, who is determined to put herself right in the middle of trouble."

"You would go for your friends. You have the heart of a warrior and an angel. Never have I known such a woman."

"Mush," Cody surmised flatly. "Pure yuck."

* * *

At Gilchrist House, Susan hissed to Angelica, seated beside her, "Josy Livingston wasn't invited. She's Edward's ex-wife. His new one is a member of The Women's Team and she's here tonight. You've got to get rid of Josy and you've got to get Cloe Matthews to be more agreeable. She's mocking me with all the events The Pinto Bean is planning. I cannot have myself barred from a wake in a deli, and she's up to something . . . you know what your father says, 'Get them into The Club, that way you know what they are doing.' "

Angelica smothered her smile. "Mother, that will be hard to do since your honored guest, Sergei Cheslav, is practically wearing Josy."

"Do something," Susan hissed again. "Her father was the town drunk and he set a fire that almost wiped out everyone."

Elegant, continental and enough beautiful male to make the women at the table swoon, Sergei lifted his glass. "A toast."

Susan straightened, beaming, certain that the famed photographer would toast his hostess.

"A toast to Josy, my friend. Without her kindness, I would not have insight to the West. To her, I say, you give my pictures life, you give me happiness." Sergei lifted his glass and waited. There was nothing sweet about his narrowed, challenging expression as it shot down the table, leveling at The Women's Team.

Angelica and Cloe lifted their glasses while Josy glared at Sergei; the rest of the women lining the ornately set table stared at Susan. Pale and rigid with fury, Susan smiled tightly, then lifted her glass. The women followed her lead.

An expert in appearances, Susan summoned her serving woman and sent her to Josy. "Tell her there is a telephone call for her in the study."

Moments later, Josy, worried about Cody, entered the study to find Susan. "I . . . I had a call."

"No, dear. I wanted to chat with you privately. You know that you weren't really invited tonight, don't you?"

Josy inhaled, the bitterness in Susan's voice slapping her, throwing her back into the reality of who she really was. "I didn't want to come. . . ."

"Of course, that's why you're here, isn't it? You didn't want to come?" Susan's soft saccharine tone lashed at Josy. "I will make your excuses . . . a headache, or something, and they won't miss you at all. I'll even order a car to take you home. Get out and Sergei will take the remainder of his stay at Gilchrist House."

Josy fought tears . . . it was wrong of her to believe that she would be welcome, wrong of her to let Sergei make a fool of her. She tore out of the house, the daughter of the town drunk.

Half an hour later, Cloe skidded her BMW into the curve without braking. One glimpse at Josy's tear-stained face as she fled the Gilchrist mansion, and Cloe had left the party, not caring how The Women's Team had looked at her. Angelica, experienced with the Gilchrists' vicious games, had asked coldly, "Where is Josy, Mother?"

"She had a headache and gives her excuses," Susan had murmured, smiling at Sergei. "I wonder, dear

Sergei, if you would consider taking my portrait?"

Cloe rounded another turn, the BMW's tires squawling in the night while Angelica's furious expression locked in her mind.

Sergei had raged at Susan in Russian and in English, and had hurried after Josy. It happened so quickly—in the space of the time that Cloe had risen to her feet and walked from the grand dining room. Angelica had been calm, precise, cold as iced steel, cutting at her mother brutally, and Susan had shattered.

Cloe fought for control of the car on the next winding curve. She should have prevented Sergei from showing off his lady love. Josy had come to support Cloe; she had been determined to make a statement, and Josy had paid. Cloe's fingers tightened on the steering wheel and she sailed into a low flat stretch, pushing the BMW to one hundred through the pine- and fir-lined farm road.

She braked for the next curve, and in the headlights she saw a horse and rider, too close to the road. She veered around the horse, braking hard; the BMW slid sideways on the dirt road and into the bushes. Pushing out of the car, Cloe ran back to see if the horse and rider—

Lopez surged out of the darkness, and Michael Bearclaw leaped from the saddle to grip her wrist. "Michael!"

Through the blur of her tears, Cloe stared at his familiar scowling face—eyebrows black and eyes flashing fiercely, the moonlight catching the hard lock of his jaw, his mouth set tight in anger. In that instant, Cloe saw him as a man she knew—a man who loved

Josy, who had protected her, who would understand—She threw her arms around him, needing to
know that he was safe, that a part of the past, of Wade
Bearclaw and of her father, remained safe and strong
and standing. His legs were braced apart as if he
would stand forever with the rugged mountains behind him.

Furious with herself, with Susan, with Michael,
Cloe held him tightly. He stood very still, his arms
going around her to tug her closer, his face close to
hers. "Cloe?"

She shoved back from him and swiped at her tears.
Her need to be held by Michael frightened her; Cloe
fought her crumbling walls. "What are you doing out
here in the dark, riding a horse—"

"Why wasn't I wearing taillights?" he prompted,
stroking Lopez's neck.

She hit him in the chest with the flat of her hand.
"I could have killed you, you jerk."

"It's a lonely road, honey. I didn't expect a BMW
to come barreling down a dirt road at a hundred
miles an hour."

"I slowed for the curve."

Michael reached to run his fingertip across the
neckline of her dress. "Barely. What are you revved
up about? Me?"

She pushed his hand away. "You? What do you
have to do with anything?"

Michael grinned, the wind tossing his shaggy hair,
the moonlight glinting upon his teeth. He slowly took
in her short tight black dress and lingered on her long
bare legs. "Plenty, where you're concerned."

"Now, that is just what I expected from you—pure

arrogance. You're not the light of my life anymore, you know. Susan Gilchrist hurt Josy tonight and I didn't stop it. I failed her, Michael. We pledged to take care of each other and I let Susan have Josy on a platter, hurting her."

Michael's broad grin died. This time, he drew her slowly into his arms and rocked her. She held onto the safety, wrapping her arms around his waist, her frustration lashing at her. She nuzzled the hair on his chest; he smelled so familiar, his body warm and strong and his words soft, caressing her skin. "Josy will be fine. You'll take care of her and so will Angelica. She'll take care of you. That's how the Wild Willows work, remember?"

She sniffed and wiped her eyes on his cotton shirt collar. "Mascara stains, you know. This reminds me of when that old barn cat died and you told me how her kittens were a part of her and that she would always be with me. I cried then, too."

His hands smoothed her back, humor in his tone. "You're a lot more to hold now. You used to be all elbows and knees."

The past tangled with the present and Cloe pulled herself back. "I'm not ready for an affair, Michael."

He shrugged lightly and that set her off. "You don't care, do you? Last night was just a one-night stand. You didn't bother to call today, or to send flowers, or to come see me."

"Did you send me flowers? Did you call?" Michael tilted his head and looked down at her, his expression unreadable. "I'm not playing games. When I get ready to, I'll let you know."

They stood there in the moonlit road, dappled by

the shadows of the trees lining it. Curse him, he made her ask, "Why didn't you call me, Michael?"

"I was giving you time to cool off and sort it out. I thought it was real nice of me." He tipped back his hat and braced his legs wide, grinning at her. "Why didn't you call me?"

She eyed him. "There's no reason for us to take it further than it already is, is there?"

She waited while Michael nodded. "There's one or two reasons I can think of."

"You're not giving me a thing, are you?"

"Nope. Not a thing, but a moonlight ride up the mountain." Then he swung up onto Lopez and looked down at her, as unyielding as the rugged mountains behind him. He held out his hand to her.

"I can take this town, Michael. I can make The Club pay for every—" Cloe jerked up the hem of her short tight cocktail dress, took his hand, placed her foot on his boot, and allowed herself to be swung up behind him as she had ridden years ago.

She wrapped her arms around him as the horse moved to the press of Michael's long legs. "You know, that spa idea would work."

He nodded, scanning the night, and looking as stoic as his mountainman ancestors as Cloe rushed on. "All we need is land, some backers not involved with The Club, untouchable backers. I need an office, a big place where I can keep working on the catalog—I'd be placing it and The Pinto Bean in danger, you know." Cloe inhaled the sweet night air, filled with the scent of pine, junipers, and newly cut alfalfa in the field. She eased back against the warm safety of the hand Michael had just reached to caress her back.

She held him tighter as she pushed through the reasons why she shouldn't leap into the spa idea. . . . *She'd be endangering her mother's dream.* She'd be putting her new project on the line; her blood was invested in the catalog now, the profit from the mugs and T-shirts. Other people were depending on her and they had taken a stance against The Club's wishes.

She could fail and lose everything.

"Are you going to stew about this, or are you going to do it?" Michael asked, pressing her against his back.

She pinched him. "Lay off. I'm thinking."

Michael caught her hand and brought it to his lips. "Rest against me, Cloe, and think a little kinder, okay? Out loud?"

Too busy with the ideas flooding her mind, Cloe placed her cheek against Michael's hard, safe back. "I'd have to stay longer than I planned. I hate this town and I can't wait to leave."

Michael was silent, then he said slowly, "You could use that old milk barn for an office and storage. You're welcome to lease Bearclaw Ridge to build a spa. All your ideas were solid. There's enough grazing in that meadow to keep a small herd of horses. Josy could take care of them, teach people how to ride. If you let me in on the investment, I'll sell it to the Wild Willows corporation. That's what the spa should be called, you know . . . The Wild Willows."

"We could fail, and then there would go land that's been in your family for generations—The Club could get it." She looked up at him, this man she'd always known and yet did not know. She caught his hair, sleek and cool in her fingers, tethering him to her. "Michael, they hurt Josy tonight."

"You take care of that, won't you?" he asked quietly, as he took her hand and placed it beneath his shirt, over his heart.

"What do you think?" She smoothed his chest, comforted by the warm, solid strength.

"I think you're going to have to call it."

"I'm glad you're not hairy, Michael." She closed her mouth, surprised that she had spoken the thought aloud.

Michael caressed her thigh. "That's something. I'm glad you're not hairy, either. You can do this, Cloe."

Near the old site of the Wild Willows' rickety old clubhouse, Angelica scrubbed her face; tears that she had hidden for years dampened her shaking palms. The Wild Willows weren't here for her now, out by the rippling moonlit stream and the winds whispering in the cottonwood boughs, flipping the leaves like memories.

Angry with her mother, she knew the emotional ties to her mother remained. There was no reason for love, for Angelica to have a love-hate war raging inside her. A desperate part of her was missing, plaguing her. Whatever had happened had to do with Quinn Lightfeather and her parents. Memories tormented her, shadowed and dim and never enough to grasp.

She inhaled the wild rose fragrance of the June night. Tonight Josy would be safe with Sergei, and somehow Cloe would manage to pit herself against The Club and win. Angelica fought whatever stalked her, the unknown, and closed her eyes . . .

When she opened them, it was to the stark, ghost-white face of Maggie Ten Feather.

The wind lifted Maggie's long white hair, taking it up and out from her face. Her clothing was torn, shredded, as though she had come across the mountains; her bare feet were bloody and she clutched a battered bag in her arms. Maggie spoke in halting yet clear words. "Orson . . . has killed himself tonight. He called me."

"Orson?" Angelica placed her hand across her chest to stop the icy chill tearing at her. Orson had defended her, going against her father. She could always count on him; he'd always been there for her in those early years, not as a father, but as a protector of a child. "Maggie, are you certain? And how, how did you *get* here?"

Maggie shuddered, hugging a parcel close to her. "Sometimes my mind is good, like tonight. Clear as the stars in the night, the round moon that sees everything. I did not take the drug they gave me to sleep this morning, spitting it aside. I have a friend there, a nurse who is part Indian, and she gave me the call from Orson, as she has before. When I heard his voice this morning, I knew . . . he had decided to end it, this long journey he began long ago. The sadness in his voice came from one who has already decided to enter the earth."

"I cared for Orson very much. He was a kind man. There were times when he defied my father, when he kept me at his house, or took me for car rides, anything to keep me safe. I owe him so much. Maggie, you could be mistaken—" Angelica swallowed, emotion wadding her throat. Orson had more than once taken her to the Matthews, protecting her—

"No," the other woman said gently. "I was not. For you, Orson was good, and you already weep for him. In your heart, you know it is so. When I heard the dark spirits move in his voice, I knew it was time for him to go and my mind suddenly became clear as the mountain streams. I knew what I must do . . . with Orson gone, it was time to run to the mountains and get my book. Now it can't hurt him, my book, those words I wrote of what they did."

"But how did you—?"

Maggie's head lifted, a portion of her old pride and beauty outlined in the moonlight. "My friend got me outside the grounds. Once I was in the timber, the trees, and the brush, I knew my way to the book, hidden there in that mountain cave. Once free, I tried to run like I did as a girl, running to Orson . . . but my body is unused and weak."

She reached out a dirty, scratched hand to touch Angelica's bowed head. "You are weeping now, but Orson is at peace at last. You took care of him well in his last years. You became his defender, and because of you, he kept some small part of his pride."

Angelica heard a distant anguished sob and knew it had come from her.

Michael braced his boot on a fallen log and studied Cloe, silhouetted in moonlight at the edge of the forest. She stood, arms across her chest, studying Lolo's valley, the town twinkling in the distance. The short, tight cocktail dress did little to soothe his need to make love to her.

He traced the heart he'd carved long ago with his thumb, locking their initials together. He'd fed her the offer of the barn and Bearclaw Ridge, challenging her. Cloe wasn't thinking about him now; her mind was locked on to weighing the dangers of staying in Lolo—the dangers to her family and friends.

Michael forced his body to relax, muscle by muscle. They'd moved into a new level, and there, out on the plain of lovers and adults, she didn't trust him.

That grated. Yet he hadn't given her romance— flowers, candlelit dinners, soft words. But they were in him for Cloe, like secrets coming from the past, dreams rustling at his feet. And that grated, too.

Cloe turned, moonlight outlining her profile as she studied the spot where her father rested, overlooking the valley. "This can't be about revenge. This has to be new and clean, a dream to last."

Michael gave her this time, the tears silvery in the moonlight, sliding down her cheek, pride warring with fear, love warring with the past. She wasn't any more frightened than he. He couldn't fail in what he was about to do, rake up Sam Matthews's trial, rake up all the pain that went with it. He had to have all the pieces in a tight case, and valuable chunks were missing. *To bring down The Club, he needed more.*

Roy Meadowlark's torn body leaped in front of Michael, followed by a ghostly parade of haunting images—women, children, young boys, and so much blood, so much evidence. He broke the twig in his hand, discarding it. Muriel had remembered a design stamped in the bloody footprint, and to every crime the perpetrator brought something—a carpet thread, fingerprints, DNA, soil particles—and he took something away.

Michael watched a big mule deer glide through the forest, going down into the valley to water. Cloe looked at Michael over her shoulder. "You could lose everything, too. Isn't that high rocky spot and the warm water lake where old Xavier Bear Claw stood and surveyed the valley?"

"I think old Xavier would like to think about women getting pretty up on those rocks. Maybe taking a skinny dip in that warm water."

She turned to him fully, her face shadowed. Her fists were at her side, the moonlight shooting through the wide brace of her long legs. "I don't want to owe you anything, Michael. This is a business arrangement, and it's new and clean, without revenge."

That statement snagged his anger, his pride, his honor. "Exactly what do you mean?"

Her arms went around herself protectively. She walked slowly to him, picking her way over the rocks and leafy rubble until she stood in front of him. "I think I just may want to do this more than anything I've ever wanted."

Michael locked his hands to his back pockets, fearing that he would reach for her. Old habits died hard when you practically raised the girl to the woman, who had left him with a hunger that still raged. Cloe needed success for herself, built by herself, for her pride.

Her eyes were pale in the night, gazing up into his. "I could fail and we'd lose everything. If Angelica comes in, and we fail, she couldn't stay here; neither could Josy. It would be rough on Dan and Gabe and

Mom. . . . I couldn't bear to have her evicted again, an auction to sell her things. Part of her grandmother's estate went in that auction."

She looked to the area of her father's grave and placed her hand on Lopez's neck, stroking him. "This could get rough."

"That it could." It would be hell, and he'd back Cloe all the way, let her make the calls.

Cloe looked at Michael, her eyes fierce, her head high. "Now, why are *you* staying?"

Michael's head went up, the beard darkening his jaw lending to his hard look. "Getting personal, aren't you? Well, I'm not answering that right now."

She laughed outright, enjoying the edge she could strike on this new Michael. "Did you know that the Wild Willows went skinny-dipping in that warm-water pond when we were teenagers?"

"Nope," Michael lied, not wanting her to know that he'd hungered desperately for her when she was nineteen and yet successfully fought looking at her through the hunter's binoculars he always kept close at hand. Back then, he'd had some fool notion that the first time he saw her without her clothes would be their wedding night. There would be candlelight and innocence and love in her blue eyes, rose petals on the bed. Dreams and years would be spread out before them.

She studied him, blue eyes now a flickering, wary steel. Cloe reached for his shirt, fisted the cloth, grabbed his hair, and jerked his head down to hers. Her mouth was open, a furnace burning his, her tongue agile against his. She tasted ripe, hot, and filled with power, the excitement of her ideas riding her. Michael forced his hands to remain in his pockets, because more than air, he wanted the lush, silky feel of her skin against his.

There was nothing tender in her demand, just the raw power of sex raging between them. Maybe he wanted just that, nothing more, to get Cloe forever out of his system, to push out those haunting young romantic dreams and be free. Maybe he wanted to claim her forever.

Michael gave himself to answering her kiss, the soft nibbles of her lips, the edge of her teeth skimming his lips, the sweep of her skin fragrant against his cheek. His body was steel hard now, rising against his jeans. She was playing, experimenting, hips rotating against his, and Michael breathed sharply before jerking his head higher. "Cut it out."

"Gotcha," she said, watching him closely, her voice husky, sexy. "You're breathing hard, Michael Bearclaw. You're hard all over and you're steaming."

Michael pushed air into his lungs, fighting his desire for her. Cloe was halfway between girl and woman now, tormenting him just as she had that day in the barn. "You haven't learned much," he said slowly, as she stood back from him.

She turned, walked a few steps, looked over her shoulder to him, and walked back. "I want to make this perfectly clear—"

Michael held his breath. This was the part where she told him that he'd taken advantage of her. Maybe he had. Maybe he was too greedy now to care.

"Number one," Cloe stated. "You're not much, but you're the only one I have at the moment to celebrate my decision with. Number two, this isn't really personal, Michael, but I would like to make love with you right now, right here."

Michael almost smiled, for across the shadows, Cloe's cheeks had just flushed. He walked to her and stroked the smooth warm surface of her cheeks, cradling them in his hands. "I'd call that personal. Are you saying you want me?"

She shifted restlessly, easing away from him. "Well . . . yes." Her look challenged him. "I don't go around asking men to make love to me every day, Michael."

"Then, you want me, right? You liked what we had and you want that again," he pushed, tugging her hair. His heartbeat slammed into overdrive and then suddenly paused, waiting for her answer to kickstart it again. She wasn't asking for his heart, but that she wanted him in any sense was enough.

She scowled up at him. "It's just like you, Michael, to make things difficult. Ah . . . I think we should be going. If I'm going to get this project off the ground, I've got to—"

"Not a chance," Michael murmured, and drew her close to him, where she belonged. She jerked away slightly, her chin up, her eyes like the steel edge of a moonlit sword. She'd been pushed into corners, and now the decision was hers. Michael forced himself to wait, until slowly the tension eased from her and her lips lifted to his—

At one o'clock, Michael drew Cloe from the saddle into his arms and carried her into his house. In his bedroom, he tugged her dress away. She poured into his sheets with a luxurious sigh. Michael kissed her bare shoulder before covering her. Another sigh and she settled into sleep. He sat beside her, one hand resting open on her jutting hip, caressing the softness and studying her.

He eased a leaf from her hair—in the forest, they'd made love hungrily, his shirt serving as their pallet. He smiled briefly; he'd been steamrollered, Cloe eager for him, leaving tenderness behind. She was riding an edge of her fears—fearing she would lose her mother's dream, lose the catalog business that had not yet begun, endanger her family, Angelica, and Josy. Tension had sprung from her pale skin like electricity. Her lovemaking was raw, sweaty, still humming inside Michael, who needed a second time to cool the first. He'd needed her tenderness and she'd given it to him.

Would a third, a fourth lovemaking be enough for him?

Much, much later he rose, studying the woman in his bed, and stripped his shirt away, leaving the house to unsaddle Lopez and free him to the field.

Michael paused and stared out over Lolo Valley. Cloe would fight; she'd stand by her family. Dan and Gabe should be living on the Matthews' spread, raising their families. Sam Matthews's name should be cleared. The Club's grasp on the valley should be torn free.

With a few calls, Michael could get a top forensics team. An attorney friend could go over the transcripts, and Michael could raise all hell to clear Sam Matthews. Gus Ballas's body would have to be exhumed.

Michael hefted a saddle onto a waiting rack and crouched to sit on his heels, grasping a handful of soil.

He held it out to the night breeze; the rich, fertile grains slid like a shimmering thread, returning to the ground that his ancestors had kept free of renegades and poachers, and The Club. He could sell the land, but he wouldn't. He'd dreamed of his children playing in that old tree, swinging in the tire cut to hold a small body. He'd dreamed of taking them to the fair, of helping them learn how to feel the weather change on their skin, of raising calves and horses.

The night rode warm and fragrant upon his bare chest. His hair lifted away from his face. All the scents he'd ever known came into him, sage and pine, fields newly cut and waiting for baling, the fresh, snow-fed stream Sam Matthews had fought to protect, wandering like a silver ribbon through the valley. Crops came from it, cattle drank, and families fished and swam in it.

Michael stood slowly. He wasn't an outsider; this was his land, and he had a job to do. Letting others do his work didn't sit right with him.

Fresh from her shower and dressed in Michael's T-shirt, Cloe stood outside. Michael, legs braced, shoulders square, hair brushing his throat, looked like a man from any century, surveying his land.

Michael turned to the house, surveying the additions that had been made to the original cabin, the way each generation had surrounded the log cabin with their lives. He turned to the empty milk barn looming in the night.

Cloe rubbed her hands over her face. She could cause him to lose Bearclaw Ridge. Whatever ran hot and urgent between Michael and herself, she didn't want him to lose the family land he loved. So many people could pay for her failure.

She slid back into bed and curled onto her side. For just an hour or two, she wanted the safety that he made her feel when they weren't fighting the storms.

Michael came back inside; his shower was brief. He returned to the bed to curl around her back, drawing her close. "You'll be fine," he murmured tiredly, and nuzzled her hair. "Call it."

At three o'clock that morning, Cloe slid from bed and Michael muttered drowsily, "Don't you ever sleep?"

Michael's offer of the old milk barn nagged at her, supported with new images of what she could do with all that lovely space. Cloe slid into a pair of Michael's cotton boxer shorts and stepped into his boots, and he reached out to curl a warm hand around the back of her knee, stroking it with his thumb. "I suppose you're revved up now."

She stopped his hand from moving upward. "I want to see the barn."

His hand pushed an inch higher on her thigh. "Honey, it's dark outside now."

Cloe couldn't resist; she bent quickly, kissed his cheek, and stepped back before he could grab her. "I know. Where's a flashlight?"

"There's spiders out there as big as a plate . . . could be a few snakes, lizards, toads, maybe a rat as big as a cougar. Bats, too," he drawled, sprawling on his back, putting his arms behind his head.

Michael, lying before her, obviously aroused from the shape of the sheet over his hips, was a sight that could be packaged on any calendar—especially that dark, molten gleam of his eyes as they strolled down her body. Cloe braced herself against her instant reaction—the tug of her breasts, tightening, suddenly heavy, her skin almost dancing with heat. "Scaring me with spider stories won't work anymore, Michael. Where is that flashlight?"

"Come back to bed and I'll tell you better stories. Maybe I'll tell you about how I feel when I'm inside you." Michael's inviting sexy drawl curled around her, and he tugged her borrowed boxer shorts and strolled a fingertip beneath them.

Cloe sucked in her breath, shivering. She wasn't ready to exchange that intimacy, to give him how she felt, and that was complete—just complete, as if nothing else mattered but making love to Michael. "Just how do you feel then, Michael?"

His hand tightened on her thigh, his lashes gleaming as he lowered them over the leaping flames in his eyes. "If you want to know, come here—"

Chapter 15

❦

"You always were single-minded. Get a notion into your head, and all you can think of is doing it." Keeping up with Cloe hadn't ever been easy, Michael brooded, as he unlocked the old barn. Cloe's hand rested on his back and he eased slightly into her touch. In her excitement, she had already kissed his neck, and he treasured the tiny spot. Cloe was shy of him, uneasy trusting him with her emotions. What had he expected? For her to hand him hearts and flowers and commitment on a silver platter? At times she seemed just nineteen, experiencing lovemaking as a new toy, and then, as a woman, she had the ability to knock his senses straight into heaven. Either way, she still fascinated him, and right now he wanted to yowl at the moon in frustration. "I could use a little pillow talk, Cloe," he grumbled, nettled that she'd exposed that weakness in him.

"I've never done that," she said in a distant tone. He glanced at her, poised upon what she wanted, distracted by her plans. He shouldered the double door open and the musty smell of the old milk barn came

274

out into the night. Concrete block walls spread into the shadows. The flashlight Cloe held lasered into the gloom. "I love it."

"You've never told a man how you felt?" Michael asked carefully, his heart missing a beat.

Cloe leaned forward, scanning the shadows. "No time. I didn't think it was needed, and I've never been exceptionally sexually hungry . . . until now."

Michael's heart slammed into running leaps. "What do you mean, 'now'?"

Cloe pointed the flashlight at the rafters, scanning them. "I haven't seen what all the excitement was about until recently. Several big skylights would do wonders for the place. How's the roof?"

"Good." Michael eased back into the shadows and his thoughts about Cloe, trying to catch his wind. "So you like making love with me?" he prodded, as she moved into the barn. "Watch that sawhorse."

Locked in her plans, Cloe answered distractedly as the flashlight speared into the dark. "We need lots of shelving. Brochures, a mail center—You scare me. You're too intense, and then I find myself the same way . . . and you make me too emotional, and *that* scares me, too. I'm not an emotional person, Michael . . . I just do the job. I performed in my marriage, and somehow kept myself apart. . . . This barn is magnificient."

Michael held perfectly still, absorbing her words. If she focused on him with the same intensity she concentrated on what she wanted, she just could frighten him. He looked at the baggy shorts covering Cloe's curved backside and desire skidded over his flesh, hardening him instantly. She turned to him, a brilliant smile on her face that made his heart leap. He stared at her, wanting to hold her, to protect her, to make the past right for her. Desire took his eyes lower, to her breasts, no more than a soft quiver beneath the thin fabric. He shot a look down her long legs, her feet wearing his too large boots.

"Why do you want me, Michael?" she asked too quietly, coming near him, the question roaring, echoing off the cold blocks and slamming into him.

"I want what is right," he said carefully, after circling the words; she'd just handed him more than he expected.

" 'What is right,' " she repeated flatly, and that bitter expression came over her again as she closed herself in, away from him. "I lost 'right' a long time ago."

"You'll have to get it back, won't you?" Michael fought the wave of anger, hitting him with fresh intensity.

Her eyes glittered in the dim light, wet with tears, and Michael's stomach tightened painfully. "I don't think I can have children, Michael. Inside me, I feel empty that way. I know I can function, I know I'm good at what I do, but inside—"

Cloe's soft words slid into the shadows and Michael inhaled sharply. Fine, tough adult male *he* was, scarred by Cloe and waiting for a second helping. She turned to him. "Haven't you ever thought of what it would be like to hold your own baby, Michael? That warm, tiny living piece of what was and what would be, a piece of your parents and of you."

Michael lifted his head to study the huge, looming shadows of the milk barn. Maybe he was afraid to bring another life into the world; he'd seen too much of what monsters could do to children.

He locked himself against the pain, and Cloe frowned, misreading his expression. "When you get that look, I could murder you. You stop and stare off somewhere and look as if you couldn't care less. You look like Dan and Gabe and Dad, when you don't want to discuss emotions."

Emotions. A man couldn't lay his heart out for her to tromp over again. Or could he?

"Let's think about this instead." Michael did what he felt, placing his hands around Cloe's smooth jaw, and carefully angled Cloe's lips for a long, slow kiss that spoke not of desire, but of his need for her to be in his life.

Dawn came pink and new and frightening, filtering into the window where Michael's mother had lain waiting for death. Cloe listened to him toss on the bed they'd shared, muttering darkly, cursing as he slept, his soul restless, nightmares stalking him.

She sat near the old spinning wheel, the wood gleaming, smooth. Michael's mother had spun for hours, humming, putting the world and her sickness aside. Cloe had lifted away the plastic from the other woman's sewing basket, finding cotton quilt pieces cut and started and a piece of Michael's tan cotton shirt, and Rose's blue blouse. The handstitching was perfect, tiny, and waiting for completion in the star pattern that Mrs. Bearclaw had begun.

Pieces, she thought, as Michael tossed in the other room, pieces of lives that had to be put right, sewn together by dreams . . . making something new from the old. Cloe had then eased into the old rocker, and she began to finish the star pattern that had begun long ago. Her needle flashed in the dim light, morning birds began to sing, and she listened to Michael cry out—a protest of sheer pain, frustration, rage.

She began to rock again. *Michael . . . we can make something new and lasting. Thank you for what you have given me, the hunger that tells me I am still alive, still feminine. . . .*

"Cloe?" he called from the bedroom, as if not believing she was near.

She made him wait before answering and began stitching again as she smiled.

There was silence, then Michael spoke softly. "You're really here, then. I meant my offer of Bearclaw Ridge, Cloe Matthews. Think about it, and don't leave until—"

"Until what, Michael?" She wanted to torment him just a bit, because nothing should come easy to Michael Bearclaw.

"I like the sound of you rocking. Don't go anywhere until I make your toast and jam. If I'm going to catch hell from Dan and Gabe, and look your mother in the eye, at least let me tell them that I fed you breakfast."

Cloe smiled again. That was all she would get from him for the moment, and it was enough. Later, she stood over him, the filled bottle resting on the nightstand. Michael had fought his demons and maybe he needed this new start as much as she.

His eyes flickered open, gold and savage in the strip of morning sunlight, and his hand lashed out, capturing her wrist, jerking her down. He flipped over her, his expression furious, his body hard and heavy. "Why did you marry him, Cloe? Damn you, why did you have to marry him?"

"Let me up." She wasn't ready to let Michael into her pain, to let him see what she had become.

He gripped her wrists, pushing down hard on her body when she bucked against him. Their eyes met and clashed, and his jaw tightened, cords running taut across his broad, gleaming shoulders. "You run from me again before we're finished, and I'll come after you."

She sucked in her breath. Why did Michael think she had run from him all those years ago? "Threats? How typical. Don't push me, Michael. We're not involved. You have no hold over me."

"The *hell* I don't," he said, low and deep and fierce. "You're mine until I say we're finished. Whatever else happens, this—here in this bedroom, or wherever else—is between you and me." And then, just as quickly, he eased from her, his eyes locked with hers. Then he firmly turned his back to her.

"Okay, here I am, and I'm not happy," Angelica said, as she tugged her designer handbag from her shoulder. The leopard print negligee and peignoir she wore were elegant and long and sexy. Cloe stared at Angelica's pale face, the circles under her reddened and swollen eyes. "It's been a long night, I've had exactly one hour's sleep, and you call me at six o'clock in the morning to get my butt to Bearclaw Ranch. Here's the shocking news. Maggie Ten Feather is back. She's at your mother's and sleeping like the dead. She actually hiked across the mountains from the sanatorium, as the crow flies, and that must be a good thirty miles of rough land. She dug a bag out of a cave and now she won't let go of it. Where's the coffee, and where is Michael?"

"Maggie Ten Feather is back? Angelica, that means she must have escaped. They'll be looking for her. Is she all right?"

"She won't be all right for some time. Orson is dead." Angelica's voice was too flat, her expression unreadable. "I loved that old man. Damn him for killing himself. At one time, he was all I had besides your mother. But there were times when the Matthews ranch was too far to go, and there was Orson. He understood, somehow, and he was always there. He called Maggie, said his good-byes, and downed three bottles of pills with a bottle of whiskey. Damn him!"

Angelica stared at her shaking hands. "I could really use a cup of coffee."

Cloe reached to hold Angelica's hand. "You know this for certain?"

"I have his key. There he was . . . dead . . . holding that picture of Maggie and that little boy. Orson was the one man I could always trust, and now he's gone."

Cloe listened to the motor stop outside. "Josy has just pulled up outside."

Dressed in a faded cotton shirt and long tight jeans, Josy walked through the door Cloe opened for her. Angelica and Cloe waited, watched for signs of last night's pain. Josy met their looks blandly. "I've walked into a discussion about me. I can feel the tension in this room. . . . Don't worry about me," Josy said. "I knew what I was walking into last night. I've got worse problems."

Angelica's face tightened. "My mother has always been as sensitive as barbed wire."

"Is Sergei the problem?" Cloe asked.

Josy leveled a look at her. "You have no idea what you've done, darn you. Have you ever had a guy serenade you in Russian love songs from outside your bedroom window? Then he broke the door down, scooped me up, and held me in his arms like I was a baby. I cried, blast him! I'm a grown woman, and I cried all over his silk shirt. Silk spots, you know. I can't afford silk, or the Romeo wearing them."

Josy swallowed rapidly, blinked, and shivered. "He wants babies with me. *Me.* You can't believe the things he said. He's emotional and overprotective, and how can *any* man say the things he did? He wants to marry me right away. Now, that would be one fine mess, wouldn't it?"

"Sergei knows his mind," Angelica stated thoughtfully. "Did you make love with him last night? I want details."

Cloe glanced at Angelica; she noted that the smooth protective shield had been replaced and she wondered when Angelica would finally have too much.

"Mind your own business," Josy ordered. "Well . . . for your information, no, I didn't make love with him. I can't lean on someone else to protect me, to make my living for me. It's enough that I'm taking his money now, when he's actually cooking and cleaning, and fixing fence. He wants to raise grapes and make wine, and milk cows and make cheese, and—he's scaring me." She stroked the coffee cup and glanced at Michael, who had just strolled from the bedroom into the kitchen as though finding the three of them in his mother's corner was an everyday experience.

His worn cotton shirt hung unbuttoned and loose, his long legs were encased in jeans, and his bare feet padded against the wood planks of the old Bearclaw cabin. " 'Morning," he murmured with a nod, and his lazy smile sent Cloe's heart tumbling. There was that fierce claiming as he looked at her, that stark, primitive sweep of his golden eyes that caused her heart to leap: *You're mine.*

"Orson killed himself last night, Michael," Cloe said quietly. "He called Maggie and she's come back. She's at my mother's."

Josy held Angelica's hand. "All this time I was blathering about my life and you've lost Orson, Angelica. I know how much he meant to you."

"Not anymore," Angelica said flatly, as she stared out the window.

"Take it easy, Angelica," Michael urged softly.

She turned on him, furious, hurt, raging. "Easy? You don't know what that old man did for me. None of you do."

"You took care of him," Josy murmured softly, smoothing Angelica's hair.

"I did do that much, at least . . . when I could. I should have known he would—he could have called me, couldn't he? Couldn't he?"

"You know he loved Maggie very much, and she loved him," Josy murmured.

Cloe placed her hand on Angelica's taut, white-knuckled fist. "We're here."

Angelica seemed to draw herself back into control.

She smiled tightly. "Yeah. You and Josy, like always. You're here."

The smile became warmer. "You're here, and you're useless. I still don't have my coffee. Feed me."

Minutes later, Angelica stared at the jam-laden toast Michael had placed beside her. "I want some. Josy, too. And more coffee, while you're at it."

"What am I, the maid?" Michael rubbed Cloe's tumbled hair as he had when she was little. The slow caress of his thumb across her cheek spoke of another adult and sensual memory.

"No, but I think *you've* been made, and blush is definitely our girl's color this morning," Angelica purred, smirking. "Jeez, when I grow up, I want one of what Cloe and Josy have prowling around their houses at dawn. A male, tall and lethal and sexy."

"Fireball doesn't sleep." Michael's hand moved to massage the tense muscles at the back of Cloe's neck, and his look down at her said he knew she'd heard his torment, and he wasn't ready to share himself with her yet.

There in the morning shadows, amid her friends, his words wound around her, binding and frightening: *You're mine. . . .*

Cloe looked at Michael, remembering the shadows haunting him. "No one knows about Maggie, where she is."

Michael's rumpled, sexy morning look slid into a grim one. "I'll call Quinn Lightfeather. He'll want to know."

Quinn reached for the telephone before it rang, sweat cold and damp on his body, the dreams still quivering in him, troubling him. In his dreams, the fire-woman was stalking the earth, summoning her powers, getting stronger, thunder in her heart and lightning in her eyes. She was a warrior, and she called to the others, also warriors, and a man stepped in behind them—Michael, wearing a bear claw necklace. Then there was the baby crying. . . .

Quinn held very still as Michael told him of Maggie Ten Feather, the woman who had cared for him when his parents had not. Why had Maggie fought her way back to Lolo? Why was the fire-woman stalking Lolo? Why was the baby crying? And why did Quinn still want to hold Angelica Gilchrist in his arms when the night was soft and sweet?

Angelica stared at the quilting piece Cloe had just placed in her hand. "You jerked me out of bed to sew?" Angelica demanded. "I'd ruin my manicure."

"Hush, Angel. Cloe is doing this her own way," Josy said softly, and began to sew the cotton pieces into the star.

"This is what old women do," Angelica grumbled, but picked up a piece, studied it as though it were an intricate contract. She picked up the needle and thread with a determination that made the other two women smile, and began to sew. "The things I go through for you."

Cloe grinned at Josy. "The Wild Willows always stand together."

"This is beyond the call of duty," Angelica answered darkly.

Cloe inhaled slowly and began rocking and sewing. "This is among us. I need you here."

"Torture," Angelica muttered, as she determinedly picked up another cut piece of fabric.

"This is Mrs. Bearclaw's quilt," Josy murmured.

"I think there's something we should do," Cloe said softly, there amid another woman's living and dying place. The tone of her voice brought the other women's heads up. "It's time."

Cloe quietly explained her concept of the Wild Willows Spa, laying out the dangers of failure. She brushed aside the tears sliding down her cheeks, pushing, welding the idea that was so strong inside her that it was a part of her life now. She laid out her plans, building on Bearclaw Ridge, the exclusive clientele that Josy could teach to ride, and campouts and guide trips. Josy and Angelica watched her intently, tears glittering in their eyes. Josy placed her hand on Cloe's shoulder and kissed her cheek, and Angelica's emotions were in her brilliant green eyes. "We can do this," Cloe said softly.

She watched Josy, who was very still. Josy would be gambling her family's ranch, the Small Bird homestead . . . and eventually her son.

Angelica leaned back, looking weary and drained. She placed the quilt block in her lap and curled her fingers tightly on the arms of the old chair. In the dim morning light, with the mist curling outside the window, she seemed as if all the brittle act she'd used to protect herself for years had suddenly drained from her. "I knew this would happen. I knew you'd find a way to do this as it should be done, and—"

Cloe held her breath; if her friends were afraid, she could understand and she would do what she could.

Angelica gripped the napkin that Michael had

placed before her. "You're right. We *can* do this." She placed her quilt pieces aside and hefted her designer purse onto her lap, jerked out a checkbook, and wrote a check. "Here, don't try to cash that in Lolo. They can't handle it. Take it to Liam. He knows how to manage discreetly. Tell him to run a check on my assets—I'm invested enough for another two million at least, and then there are my diamonds. I'd be willing to toss a few carats into the pot."

"Angelica, this is one million dollars!" Cloe showed the check to Josy and they both stared at Angelica blankly.

"Hey, what's money for? We're good, we're the Wild Willows—I like that, the Wild Willows Health and Beauty Spa. I don't see the point in quibbling about a few worthless dollars that the stock market dumped in my lap," Angelica said lightly. "Now, don't bother me . . . I'll look at the milk barn later, but right now I'm just getting the hang of this quilting thing."

Cloe looked at the paper quivering in her hand. "There's more," she whispered unevenly. "Not one brick of the spa, not one plan, should be built on revenge. It should be clean and new. There's been enough pain in the past. Agreed?"

"Agreed," the Wild Willows returned firmly, and shared a look deeper, more binding than any they had shared before. Too much was at stake if they failed.

Angelica held up the star block she had fashioned from the pieces. It was lopsided, poorly stitched, but it was hers. She beamed at Josy and Cloe, oblivious to the broken nail on her middle finger and the tear stains on her cheek. "There is nothing to this pioneer woman business," she exclaimed with delight. "Give me another piece."

At Gilchrist House the next morning, Susan raged, "Orson willed everything to that Quinn Lightfeather . . . just because that bartender listened to his sob stories. Orson's heir is an Indian. I wanted those lovely antiques his wife purchased in France. Get them for me, Bradley."

Bradley ignored Susan and turned his mind to Angelica. She was out there, made of steel, his blood, his darling daughter. Bradley glanced at Jeffrey, who was reading the stock news at the breakfast table. Jeffrey was weak; he didn't have Angelica's power. Bradley leaned back in his chair, sipped his coffee, and slid Jeffrey a level look. "You're not going to be able to manage Cloe Matthews, are you?"

His son folded the stock report into his briefcase. "I know about that catalog business she's got under way. It seems she has investors apart from our control—"

"Liam McKensie, for one. He would stand to gain from taking business away from us, and he wants Stella Matthews. She's a powerful woman who draws men and women to her like a magnet." Bradley glanced at Susan and hated her for her whining, her lack of power. If Stella Matthews had wanted to woo a world-famed photographer into taking her portrait, she would have succeeded.

Jeffrey forked a browned link sausage from the platter onto his plate. "I'd think he'd see that an older woman does not make a good image for a businessman, and he is respectible. This photographer, Sergei

Cheslav, has brought his own problems. The man is charming the entire valley, but the novelty will wear off when Cheslav leaves. After that, we'll crush that little catalog, which will, of course, ruin the Matthews women."

"You have to find out who the other investors are, Jeffrey," Bradley pointed out carefully.

Jeffrey spoke around a mouthful of toast. "By the way, Dan Matthews's garage had a little fire last night. Nothing too bad, because he is the best body man in the valley, but enough to make a point."

Bradley frowned and scanned the morning paper. "I wish Muriel Perkins would stop running the obituaries of those damn birds. She's running a full-length front-page article on each one. If I knew who murdered those parakeets, I'd kill him myself for making me suffer through daily parakeet sagas. But I don't see anything about a fire."

"It hasn't had time to make the news. Monroe called this morning. Insurance won't pay for it, because it was neglect. The Matthews family should be more careful."

Dusk settled over the valley as Michael sat outside watching the smoke from his fire rise, twisting into the shadows.

The Wild Willows had been quiet through the day, busy and concerned about Maggie Ten Feather and the news of Orson's death.

The mattress had taken longer to burn than the wooden bed frame Michael had dismantled that morning.

Michael held and smoothed the large bear claw

with his hands. It suited what he had to do, reclaim the valley. *Cloe. . . .*

Leaving clouds of dust behind them, Dan and Gabe's battered pickups were sailing down the ribbon of road leading to Bearclaw Ranch. Michael smiled grimly. He'd expected Cloe's brothers, and when they emerged from their pickups, slapping western hats on their thighs and with murder in their eyes, Michael braced himself.

"Boys," he said, nodding to them as dusk skimmed through the pine trees behind him, leaving finger shadows on the rich land his family had claimed long ago. "Nice night, isn't it?"

"No," Dan returned flatly.

"*Hell,* no," Gabe snapped. "You're sleeping with our baby sister and there isn't a marriage certificate hanging over the bed."

"I burned the bed," Michael said, just before Dan's fist shot into his jaw. The starburst behind his lids was no surprise. Even as Michael staggered backward, he welcomed the hell-of-it, friendly-brawl feeling inside him and wiped the trickle of blood from his split lip. He eyed Gabe, who always thought his sister Rose was a "pretty little thing," and understood perfectly.

"Save some Bearclaw for me," Gabe ordered, his expression cold as Michael sidestepped Dan's next punch. "What are your intentions?" Gabe demanded, looking like Sam Matthews had, years ago, when he'd asked the same thing.

The punch Gabe threw was familiar, something remembered from their schooldays' brawling. But now, with a man's weight behind it, the punch landed solidly in Michael's stomach, whooshing the air out of him. Michael panted and grinned, the scene familiar, and the three of them had brawled equally, fists flying, blood damning them as their parents made them move woodpiles and pushed them to repent. "Oh, hell, boys. Let's do this right," Michael said, and ran at them, arms outstretched, to take them all into a rolling fight.

"Bearclaw, you'll eat dirt for this," Dan gasped, as Gabe hauled him back to get at Michael, who ducked. Michael swung a light punch at Dan and a second at Gabe, spreading the favors around, and they all went down in the dust, cursing, panting, snorting.

Liam and Stella arrived in his new navy blue pickup and he hurried around to her side to open the door. They walked toward the brawling men.

"Some things never change," Stella said with a fond smile as she watched the three men roll in the dust, the fire smoldering behind them. "They once did that over the last piece of my pie."

"That looks good," Liam said thoughtfully at her side, measuring himself against the brothers and Michael. "It's been awhile since I've had that fun."

"Boys." She shot him an eloquent look that said he was years younger, after all, if he could appreciate the dirt and the pain and the curses.

There was nothing boyish in the look Liam shot down at her. "You know, there is one way we could settle quite effectively this age problem you have. But I'd prefer to do that within the bounds of matrimony, thus avoiding what Michael Bearclaw is currently experiencing."

While Stella blushed and floundered, Josy and Sergei and Cody and Angelica arrived separately, laden with brooms and buckets and soap to clean the milk barn. Within minutes, Cloe, after a stop at the grocer's to pick up more cleaning supplies, arrived and stood, hands braced on her waist. "I've got an architect. He'll design a simple building with potential for expanding the spa. He needs a survey of the land dimensions and he'll take the job, in exchange for me doing work for his clients on the side. . . . Angelica, here's his computer e-mail address, and he's going to work with you on contracts for the builder."

Cloe handed Angelica a fat file, studied the brawling men, and asked, "What are they doing?"

Angelica whistled, hefting the file. "You've been busy."

Stella studied her daughter's expression; it was the look of a woman experienced with male antics, and knowing that a large percentage of boy remains in the adult male. "Dan and Gabe have been muttering about your honor for the past two days. Evidently they decided to do something about it."

"My honor? Is this the last century?" Cloe exploded as she stalked toward them. She grabbed the first hair that came into her fist and lifted Gabe's bloody, too innocent grin. She reached out another fist and came up with Dan's face, his grin equally innocent, the effect ruined by the bruises and the blood.

She glared down at Michael, who was at the bottom of the tangle of legs and arms. "What do you have to say for yourself, Michael Jedidiah Bearclaw?"

Michael stared thoughtfully up at the darkening sky, then to the two men whose hair Cloe held in her fists. Then he grinned cheerfully, his lip swollen, and said, "Hi, honey. What's for supper?"

"I will kill you," she said, meaning it, when she could finally speak.

Michael's hand shot out to capture her ankle. He pursed his swollen lips in a kiss that waited for hers. As her brothers began to guffaw, Cloe shot them a deadly look. "I'll kill you, too, while I'm at it," she muttered, and pleasantly bumped their heads together.

Chapter 16

∾

MICHAEL SAT BACK in Lopez's saddle and studied Lolo. The June morning, fresh with the tang of sagebrush, was only days away from the Fourth of July. While the Mexican horned cattle bawled and milled, gleaming blue-black and rangy in the valley in front of him, Michael brooded over the challenge he was about to make to The Club. Driving the cattle through town would make a definite statement—Michael wanted the focus of The Club on him, and not on the Matthews or on Cloe's plans. She'd start hiring workers today, hurrying to prepare the building site on Bearclaw Ridge, and Michael wanted to distract The Club, to define his allegiance and make clear that he was ready to go to war.

He stretched in the saddle, unused to riding all night, to herding the cattle. Typically used for rodeo stock, the tough *Corriente* breed was suited to the native gama grass and buffalo grass on Bearclaw Ranch. "Dog," the shaggy, mean black dog that came with the *Corriente*, knew his business, working the cattle on command. Bred for short bursts of speed, Lopez had glided through the long midnight ride as if it were his destiny.

These tough, raw-boned cattle had been Wade's dream. Michael briefly placed his gloved hand over the big bear claw beneath his shirt. Old Mac Simmons had understood and had taken Michael's offer.

Michael lifted his hat, wiped the sweatband with his bandanna and eyed the big black bull. "Nothing But Trouble" hadn't been ridden yet, and he didn't like being pushed all night.

With the Fourth of July only days away and the Wild Willows on the prowl, the time was perfect to make the statement that Michael Bearclaw was staying. The Club would understand the cattle drive straight for Bearclaw land.

His saddle creaked beneath him as he stretched. "Calling it" western style had its advantages.

Calling it with Cloe was another matter, he thought grimly. Telling her that she was his was just like waving a flag in front of that contrary bull eyeing him. She was contrary, a whole lot of trouble and—and his, damn it. She always had been.

He inhaled the morning air and watched a red fox move through the sagebrush, quail soaring into the clear blue sky. A red-tailed hawk sailed over Michael while a meadowlark trilled. Mist rose from the stream meandering through the valley, and rectangular bales layered Mel Johnson's emerald green field. Up on the mountain, the rocks of Bearclaw Ridge caught the morning sun, a bolt of sheer vermilion rising out of the pine- and juniper-studded mountain.

Cloe. . . . He'd left her last night, curled up on his couch, looking little more than nineteen, circles of exhaustion beneath the thick fringes of her lashes. "Michael...." she had sighed before falling back into sleep. The drowsy whisper had stirred those dreams again, making him want . . . making him want more than the memories of bloody murders and stalking sickness. . . .

Michael traced Lolo's 1880s buildings, the old posts layered with paint, the chipped cobblestones of the main street almost gold in the sunlight.

The kitten mewing in his saddlebags needed comforting, and he reached to lift it free, cuddling it close. He placed his western hat on the back of his head and smiled as a big buck leaped over the sagebrush, heading for water in the valley, and antelope lifted their heads, staring at him.

Riding behind a herd of cattle on a moonlit night gave him plenty of time to think about Cloe's soft skin, the way she arched to him hungrily.

Michael tugged up his leather glove and tightened his body. He placed the kitten back into the flannel-lined saddlebag and watched her head poke free to watch him. He nudged Lopez with his knees and began moving the herd down the hill. He hoped Joe Issaks had done his work, keeping bystanders off the streets in the morning and children safe.

Monroe Tibbs cursed and hurriedly threw his four-wheeler into reverse, backing away from the black, horned herd milling down Lolo's main street. Joe Issaks hurried down the street, shoving bystanders into buildings and grinning ear to ear. Children were pulled inside, and old-timers were crawling out onto the porch rooftops.

While the black gleaming herd moved slowly through Lolo, Michael tipped his hat to Bradley Gilchrist, who stood scowling through the safety of the bank window. The challenge was out now.

Josy came out to greet Michael with a grin. "Your dad would have been proud, but Cloe's good and mad. She's hunting you."

Michael smiled briefly, warming to the idea of Cloe hunting him. "I appreciate the notice. How's Maggie Ten Feather?"

"Quinn spent yesterday treating her with the old herbs, the ceremonies she remembers, and when she was well enough to travel last night, he took her to a friend, a trauma nurse, for safekeeping. He's going to the sanatorium to claim that he's her next of kin and to have her released to his care. He's got the income now to protect and care for her."

Michael nodded and moved on. Maggie needed Quinn's Native American medicine, his spirituality, and his insights—not needles and drugs. Further down the street, Stella handed Michael a mug of coffee and grinned up at him. "You look tired, cowboy."

He sipped the hot brew, waiting in front of the deli for Cloe to come out onto the street. He tipped his hat to Ann Gilchrist, who shot him a timid, hopeful smile.

" 'Morning, Mr. Bearclaw," Angelica crooned, toasting him with her cup of morning cappuccino. Dressed in designer shorts and a sweater studded with real pearls, she winked at him. "I'm unemployed. I just quit the bank. Know where I can get a job?"

"Try The Long Horn and Quinn," Michael returned

with a grin, and watched Angelica steam. She'd turned on Bradley; Angelica was in for trouble and desperately alone, except for the other Wild Willows.

Dan and Gabe and their families sat in the beds of their pickups; the Matthews brothers nodded solemnly, acknowledging Michael's statement to The Club.

Monroe Tibbs, Jr., waddled up to Michael, huffing with the effort. "You're creating a public disturbance. I should arrest you—"

Michael took his time in answering, saddle leather creaking as Lopez drank from the bucket of water Joe Issaks held to him. "Check the town's statutes. There's nothing in it about herding cattle down Main Street. There is a stipulation that any damage must be paid by the owner. I agree to pay damages."

Monroe glared at him. "You're wearing a sidearm."

Michael rested his hand on the butt of his father's Colt .45. "Lolo's laws say that any cowboy riding night herd needs protection. We can do this two ways, Monroe, and you know it. I lifted two good prints off Roy Meadowlark's knife—the one you shoved into Cloe's tire. The question is, what were you doing with a dead man's knife in your possession?"

Instincts and bluffs were always good to use in a pinch, Michael thought, as Monroe's small eyes widened and he paled. His jowls trembled before he recovered. "You're threatening to bring in your high-powered fancy buddies and muck up Lolo."

"I'm not threatening, Monroe. You stay off my land, and the next time you step on it, you'd better be wearing legal papers."

Monroe struggled to defend himself, and failing,

launched an attack. "Those goddamn women are stirring up enough trouble, and since they're doing it on your land, you probably started the whole mess. They'll be trouble, big trouble, if they don't settle down and mind their places. Lolo is a peaceful town. We don't want all those outsiders—"

"Doing what? Bringing in new jobs? Bringing money and life to Lolo?" Michael asked.

"A worthless beauty spa ... perverts running everywhere ... men in tight pants, women wearing little or nothing—" Monroe glanced at the laughing crowd and stormed off. Michael knew that this only set the trench deeper, that Monroe's ego would force him to make a dangerous move, and someone could get hurt.

Then Cloe, hair cropped into reddish brown curls, dressed in a stylish gray suit, skirt, and heels, came out onto the sidewalk and Michael's heart stopped.

Michael looked too tired, stubble darkening his jaw, and circles beneath the hard eyes that stared at her, giving her nothing. "Did you miss me?" he asked, so softly that the excited children's calls almost swept the words away.

"Not much." Liar. The sight of him set her heart churning, softening, her pulse leaping. She'd ached for him last night, holding his shirt against her—

"Same here." Then the slow, sexy smile belied his words and took her heart, tangling, quivering around her.

Silence. Cloe's chest tightened until she couldn't breathe. "I've hired a local construction crew. Everyone is willing to work nights and weekends. Anyone who can pitch in can work at any time. We'll work around crops and harvest time. Angelica is hunting for masseuse and exercise people."

She glanced down at the clipboard in her hand, her knuckles white with tension. She couldn't meet what was in Michael's eyes, the heat and the passion; she jumped into the safety of her plans. "We won't have a dietician at first, but—"

"Come with me to that warm-water pond on the Ridge," Michael stated slowly, and the hunger in his gaze caused her heart to kick into overdrive. "The mist rises over it this time of morning."

I need to hold you, Michael. I need to know that you are safe.... Then anger caught her broadside. He made everything so simple—as though the years between had never happened, as though she'd never married and lost her dreams. Life wasn't simple, not with Michael Bearclaw pushing her. He'd left her asleep... didn't tell her his plans, and he knew everything about her. "How dare you take off like that, Michael?"

Cloe stared at the soft, mewing ball of fur he'd placed in her hands and tried to catch her heart as it went sliding into warm mush. The kitten was the image of Topaz, Cloe's favorite cat.

Michael removed his hat, propped it on his saddlehorn, and pushed his big hands through his long, black hair. He stood in the saddle and stretched, looking all tough and western and lean male, and then pinned her with those golden eyes. They skimmed the hair she had chopped off this morning, furious with him, and dropped to her lips, caressing them—visually eating them. The bolt of white-hot hunger shot through her, and Cloe took a deep steadying breath, which jerked Michael's gaze down to her chest.

The raw primitive emotions flinging out of her into the clear morning sky were enough to take away her breath. A civilized man wouldn't stare at her as if he wanted to devour her until she begged—begged? For Michael Bearclaw? Civilized? Michael?

"Are you coming or not?" he asked roughly.

Her mind skidded to a stop. Right now, with her breasts peaked and taut and her body wet, throbbing for Michael's touch, she wasn't exactly civilized—the cool executive, powerwoman, meticulous, unaffected by her emotions, had a definite breathing problem in the vicinity of Michael. She hated him for the way he sat on his saddle, loose limbed, tough, unaffected as she fought her way through her tangled emotions.

"See you, sweetheart," he said finally, and with a click to Lopez and a nod to her, he rode out of town— straight backed, easy in the saddle, a man who knew exactly how to stir up trouble . . . and her heart.

Cloe shivered and cuddled the kitten to her. If there was one thing Michael Bearclaw could do, it was to set her off. He hadn't done anything but look at her and hand her a kitten, which she loved already. He hadn't asked how she felt and he'd made her feel like a schoolgirl hankering after a good-looking cowboy who looked as if he'd just ridden out of a *True West* magazine, complete with Colt .45. She'd already drooled over him years ago— *"Did you miss me?"*

Michael had tossed away his degrees, and he'd made a statement that The Club could easily interpret—"calling it."

"You're mine. . . ." Panic and fear churned within

Cloe, her body taut. She wouldn't be forced into a relationship—yet the need to capture Michael Bearclaw and claim him was almost painful, pushing her to run after him and drag him down from the saddle. But she wouldn't.

"You're all flushed, and Michael Bearclaw is the reason. He's gotten to you again," Angelica singsonged in a whisper. "You didn't expect him to ask you to the Fourth of July dance in three days, did you?"

Cloe turned to look at her blandly. "Why don't you just go stick your head in a mop bucket?"

"Darling, that would ruin my last facial."

Josy wrapped her arm around Cloe's waist, while she fought tears, the tawny kitten nuzzling her. "That rat. He remembered Topaz."

"You're right. He is a rat," Angelica agreed with a smirk. "He's a definite button pusher where you're concerned."

"Why are you dressed up, Cloe?" Josy asked. "I haven't seen you in a business suit and heels until today."

"She's going to war. It's her armor . . . she's been summoned to my father," Angelica stated grimly. "I'm going out to the milk barn, excuse me, the Wild Willows executive business center, to see what the architect has faxed me."

Images of Michael's naked, tanned, and muscled body gleaming in that warm-water pond didn't help Cloe's concentration as she sat across from Bradley Gilchrist's desk. The eleven o'clock appointment in his office was a showdown—a time for threats. She remembered coming here when her father needed a loan; she remembered his look, a proud man, coming to beg—

Bradley smiled coolly and angled his desk picture of Angelica slightly toward Cloe. "Thank you for coming to see me. You've always been ... very astute."

In contrast to the tension humming through her, Cloe returned the smile easily. "I was glad you called and asked to see me."

"I thought we could work together. . . . You and Angelica have been friends for a long time, and I'm concerned about my daughter."

Cloe smoothed her gray designer business suit. Bradley was heading for her weakness, her friendship with Angelica.

"Lately Angelica has been acting erratically. She's left the bank." Bradley's voice vibrated with bitterness.

"I'm certain you'll miss her." Platitudes, thought Cloe, she'd served enough of them in managing Ross's career.

"Yes." Bradley's answer was curt. He steepled his fingers and stared at her over the tips. "I'm worried about my daughter, Cloe. She's quit a profitable, long-term family business, and she's apparently invested in a chancy operation. She's put her house on the market. She's working with you and Josy, isn't she? I hear you are interviewing construction workers, gearing up for a big building project on Bearclaw Ridge."

Cloe also knew how to avoid obvious questions, "stonewalling." "News travels fast in Lolo."

Bradley shifted impatiently. "You're hiring construction crews, setting up a full-scale operation out there on Bearclaw Ridge. . . . The Pinto Bean catalog project was one thing, but I'm afraid my daughter won't be able to play your little game."

Cloe smiled coolly even as she braced herself. "Really?"

"She's broken the law—helped Maggie Ten Feather escape the sanatorium. Then there's your mother, who sheltered Maggie and didn't call authorities, and then Quinn—oh, yes, Quinn. You know that the bank holds his mortgage, don't you?" Bradley slapped a file in front of Cloe. "Read this."

The file contained incidents of Angelica's forging, maneuvering accounts, shifting funds from her account to those of people needing help, specifically those of Josy Livingston. Angelica had padded the bank's expenses and diverted the money into other accounts. Cloe tried to keep her hand steady as she replaced the file on the desk. "Thank you for the information, but I have a business to run—"

"She's broken the law, and if pushed, I'll have to protect Lolo First Bank. That catalog business, a little simple female-thing to keep you busy . . . I could tolerate that, but not this—"

"Major business enterprise?" she provided, and watched Bradley's thin cheeks flush with anger.

"As Angelica's next of kin, I could see that she be examined for mental frailty. I wouldn't want to, of course, but she has broken the law and I am responsible for seeing that she doesn't hurt herself. I'm certain mental incompetence would be a better alternative than jail."

Cloe shielded her fear and her anger—Angelica was the pawn in this struggle for power and survival. An expert at sensing his victims' weaknesses, Bradley leaned back in his chair and sank home another veiled threat. "Then there is the matter of the old Matthews ranch. The purchasers are letting it go back to the bank. That ranch should logically be broken into ranchettes, the two thousand acres placed into five-acre lots."

Cloe forced her fingers to relax on the arms of the chair. She couldn't let Bradley see how vulnerable she was to her brothers' dream. "That land isn't my business."

"Really? I would think you'd want the land for your family. I'm prepared to co-sign for a loan to you. I'm certain we could negotiate."

At the Bearclaw ranch, Michael rammed the handsaw back and forth across the tarred end of the lodgepole pine, stripped of its bark. The wood was good, stored in the high rafters of the dry barn and properly aged for crafting the bed. He was bonetired and angry with himself—what had he expected? For Cloe to greet him with a kiss?

The seasoned wood ran smoothly beneath his hand, waiting. . . . When he was twenty-two and lusting after sixteen-year-old Cloe, Michael had gone into the high country and searched out the tall straight Bearclaw timber to make his wedding bed. Back then, slamming an ax into the tall pine, he'd sweated, worked himself into exhaustion, and fought the need for sex. He dreamed of lives twined together and a lifetime sharing the bed.

With a vengeance, he'd dragged the logs back to the ranch; his father had understood as he'd handed Michael the draw knife to strip away the bark. Then, the logs bare, Wade had helped Michael raise the narrow pine logs to the high rafters of the barn to cure.

Suffering from lack of sleep and riding a raw temper, Michael worked in the barn, fashioning the pieces of the pioneer-style bed. He made holes in the four basic posts, whittled the ends of others to fit inside, and mocked himself for showing off this morning in front of Cloe . . . a real ritualistic Bearclaw male, setting up the woman he wanted to claim. If he had any sense, he'd leave her alone and make a life without her.

The vicious tearing of the saw across the seasoned wood didn't help relieve Michael's churning frustration. What had he expected? For Cloe to ride off into the sunset with him?

Michael grimly carried the last of the sections into the master bedroom and fitted them together, without the use of nails or glue. He shouldered the new box springs and mattress onto the bed, a delivery made by Gabe that morning. The simple framework of bed was old-fashioned, standing firm and empty, mocking his dreams.

Chapter 17

ᐧᐧᐧ

Aɴɢᴇʟɪᴄᴀ ᴘᴏᴜɴᴅᴇᴅ ᴛʜᴇ nail into the old weathered wood. She'd dragged the wood from the scrap pile behind her house, tearing at it. It was dark now, her body aching and scratched as she hauled the old weathered boards to the brush, thick enough to hide the tiny, poorly constructed hovel. She'd been safe in the old clubhouse and nothing could touch her with Cloe and Josy. But they weren't here now—she hurried to open the bottles of fingernail polish, writing, in pinks and reds, "Wild Willows" on the old wood. Then she hurried inside, dragging an old blanket that Cloe's mother had made for her, inside in the shadows where no one could find her and she'd be safe. Orson would keep her safe, but . . . Angelica swiped away the tears. "Gilchrists do not cry," her father had said. Then Angelica clenched her lids shut and willed tears to spill from them. For Orson.

She tore open the package of pudding-filled chocolate cupcakes, jamming them hurriedly into her mouth. "Gilchrists never eat like pigs," her mother had said. Angelica didn't want to be a Gilchrist anymore, not since she'd opened Maggie's book—

She began to retch violently, dragging herself outside so as not to foul her safety. She wished she could tear the ugliness out of her bones, her blood, as easily.

Cloe closed the new door to the milk barn and locked it, setting the security system that Liam and Michael had installed. With photographs and measurements, the architect had begun creating the first of three stages of the resort, a huge hunting lodge–style building, a main great room with rooms bordering it on the lower and top levels. The design for the first stage was simplistic, allowing room for addition of phases two and three. The exercise room and kitchen completed the basic plan, and by September the first building would stand, ready for guests.

She hugged her briefcase, laden with lists and details and dreams, and looked out into the night, damp with the approaching storms, mist curling around her.

She had to destroy Gilchrist's file on Angelica. . . .

Cloe inhaled the summer night, fragrant with the scent of new lumber in the barn, of wild raspberries that would soon ripen, of wild roses, mountain columbines, gold flowers, and pine. Lightning had begun to glow, outlining the rugged peaks of the Rocky Mountains behind Bearclaw Ridge. She would build the spa and she would protect Angelica.

Cloe stepped out of her shoes and turned to see Michael looming beside her, a shaggy black dog at his side. She'd never leaned on another person's strength, but Michael's broad shoulders looked too inviting. "I'm tired, Michael," she said simply, too drained to care about raising her walls.

"I know." He lifted her in his arms and carried her toward the ranchhouse.

"This is ridiculous," she muttered, and wondered how easy it was to give herself to his keeping, to share her problems with him on another, more intimate level. She lifted her hand to touch his hair lightly, the cool clean crisp locks sliding beneath her fingers. He tensed when she touched his jaw, exploring it. "You're worried. What is it?"

How easy it was to answer, to talk with him. "Something is wrong with Angelica. Quinn gave her Maggie Ten Feather's book this afternoon, and after one look, she just walked away from all the business calls, the architect needs—she turned pale, Michael, and she left without a word. She won't answer my calls, or Josy's. . . ." Michael held her, his strides taking her closer to the Bearclaw house. He carried her as if he had a purpose, as if nothing could stop him. "Put me down."

He looked haunted, as if he were driven by ghosts and by needs he'd reined in for too long. "I like bringing you home, carrying you, and I like those freckles across your nose."

She blinked, trying to dislodge the sweet tremor he'd left—his kiss brief and upon her nose. "What makes you think I'm staying? You ran off in the night, leaving me. I could have killed you."

She grabbed his hair, fisted it, fighting the terror that she had felt when she'd awakened and he was gone. "Don't you ever leave me again, Michael, not unless I know. I know Roy wouldn't have stepped into the bull's pen on his own, and someone wrung Muriel's parakeets' necks just for the fun of it—you could be lying out there in the woods somewhere needing help . . . or worse. On top of that, you stirred The Club deliberately this morning . . . riding into town, dusty and tired, strapping on a gunfighter's six-shooter, and looking like a drover from the 1880s, driving that devil herd through town. What was the point, anyway?"

"I want to let them see me coming, and I wanted to—" The porch light caught the dark red color of his cheeks as he carried her up the steps and into the house.

"You're embarrassed, Michael. Were you trying to impress me?" she pushed, excited by this new aspect of her relationship with Michael.

He snorted poignantly, dismissing her idea; his scowl delighted Cloe. "You were, weren't you? You were showing off?" Michael held her aloft, close against him for a moment, his expression taut as he glanced at the bedroom, as though he had a destiny to keep—then the look was gone, shielded.

"Why?" asked Cloe, when he stood her upright and walked into the kitchen.

In the lighted kitchen, Michael ladled soup into bowls and placed them on the table. Then he turned and walked to her. "Stop pushing me. You know what I want."

His hand wrapped around her wrist and he slowly drew it to his lips. "Your temperature just hiked up a few degrees, sweetheart. You'll take care of Angelica . . . you'll do fine," he whispered upon her skin.

"Will I, Michael?" she asked, as he slid the first button of her blouse free, running his finger slowly across the length of her chest, just where the lace of her bra stopped and her skin began. The intimate gesture branded her, claimed her, and then the second button and the rest slid free.

Her skirt slid to the floor as he watched her, her hands coming to smooth his cheeks, this Michael who looked as though he'd come from another century, a drover riding into town.

There, in the first Bearclaw cabin, log walls gleaming with layers of varnish and time, he undressed her slowly, concentrating on each garment as it came away, until silk and lace pooled at her feet and she stood in front of him, the dim light skimming her bare flesh.

He brushed her cheek with his fingertip, ran it down her throat, then up along her shoulder and down her arm. His inspection saw too much, devoured her inch by inch, as though he were seeing her for the first time. His intensity frightened her, she who had protected herself for years, as though he was seeing to her bones, into her future. He traced her collarbone, following his fingertip with his lips. Along her throat, his mouth burned, open and hot, devouring her, tempting, never staying but a heartbeat before moving on—

She found his waist, the solid shape of him, anchored her hands to him as still he sought more, tasted her shoulder and then the other. His breath curled in her ear, skimmed along her flesh, jolted her senses, slammed into her body, low and hot and hungry. . . . "Michael. . . ."

His hands cradled her face, thumbs stroking her cheekbones, those golden eyes burning beneath his black, glossy lashes. "Come with me."

Thunder rolled nearer as Cloe walked into the bedroom with Michael, their fingers laced as intimately as she knew their bodies would be, for her hunger rode her, and something more tender. The room smelled of the bouquet by the bed—larkspur, columbine, wild roses, and sunflowers, tucked in a fruit jar. The bed was new, made of stripped pine logs, fitted together without nails or glue, just the raw plain look of solid wood. Michael eased her upon the new bed, covered by an old quilt and plain cotton sheets, and she watched as his clothes slid away, his body hard and aroused as he came to her. He levered down upon her gently, as though he were fitting them together to last an eternity, melding skin upon skin, masculine scent against feminine, steel against velvet. His fingers slid between hers, blunt, strong, dark against her pale skin, calluses hard against her smaller palm. He flexed his hand, studied the contrast, slender fingers against his own masculine hand. He closed his eyes and eased away, drawing her to rest upon him. "Talk to me."

The challenge was there, curling around his soft voice, the steel slashing at her, frightening her. She braced her arms on his chest, his body solid and aroused beneath her. "What do you want from me?"

"Stay here with me." His hands moved in her hair, winnowed through it, testing the new short length. "This is some crop job—you must have been mad."

He frightened her, wanting more than sex, the hard fast mating that left her emotions free. "I don't want to talk, Michael," she whispered, and her heart went sliding, skidding into overdrive when she caught his flickering, shielded vulnerability, quickly concealed.

She gave him what she could and feared giving more. "I sent the disks back to Ross."

He stiffened, searched her face; his thumb ran across her eyebrow, tracing it, as she stepped into the silence beating, pounding at her, frightening her. "That must have cost you."

"I can't be caught up in this . . . here with you, Michael. I'm just discovering myself. I'm focused on what I need now. I have to make this work, not only for Mom and Josy and Angelica, but for myself. . . . I have to reclaim a part of myself . . . I gave too much and I can't afford that again."

"All that doesn't change the fact that you're here in my bed now, does it? That this is important to you?" Was that pain flickering in his expression? Why did he seem vulnerable?

"I'm in your bed and it is important to me. I know what I'm doing."

"What are you doing? Here, with me?"

"Let me show you. . . ." Cloe smoothed the weathered skin over his blunt cheekbones, the black feathery circles of his lashes, and Michael held very still, his hands opening upon her waist. She kissed his throat, flicked her tongue over the soap- and male-scented surface, and Michael went taut, his hands moving to her hips, digging in possessively, yet not hurting. Cloe lay upon him, the challenge too much as the taut muscles beneath her did not begin to love her, did not take her mouth or her body as she had wanted.

"Games, Michael?" she asked, leaping into the challenge, and caught the scar she had given him long ago between her teeth. His teeth instantly claimed her upper lip and released her with a kiss.

"What would you know about games, sweetheart?" he whispered, and sucked in his breath as Cloe found him with her hand, circled him, and he arced suddenly, his breath harsh. It was the first time she'd touched him, filled her hands with him, wondrous velvet shielding living, throbbing steel, and Michael shuddered. "I'd rather you didn't—"

She touched the softness lower and Michael groaned, capturing her hand and dragging it up to his chest, where his heart pounded heavily. "That's enough. Slow down."

"Why are you wearing this?" she whispered, finding the bear claw lying, gleaming and savage, upon his chest and grasping it. She tugged, drawing the leather thong tight as her lips sank into his, demanding. Then Michael's hands were cupping her breasts, molding them until they ached heavily, his mouth opened to hers—

In the last sane bit of her mind, Cloe knew that she'd been untouched, that passion had not ruled her, that no man had ever wanted her like this— He'd handled her carefully that first night, but this was a claiming; and looking down at Michael, the need burning in his eyes and the heat of his body, she knew that Michael had come to the barn to bring her to his bed. She knew that the wildflowers were for her and that the quilt had been given to him by his mother.

She lowered her mouth to his, touched the tip of her tongue to his, pushed her hips down, capturing him slowly, fully, taking him deeper, higher into her. Michael suckled her tongue, his hands urging her knees higher until she knelt over him. His fingers locked to her quivering thighs, caught her bottom, teaching her gently to rock upon him.

Michael fought bursting, fought the savage burgeoning of his body as she enclosed him, slid upon him tightly. She moved slowly, experimentally and he knew that she'd never dominated another man . . . loved him like this. The tiny contractions caught her unawares, her stunned expression over him sliding into pleasure as she folded beautifully, limply upon him.

She awoke moments later, cuddled against Michael's chest, her leg draped over his. "Tired?" he asked, a raw tone rimming his question.

You're mine. He'd come to the barn to claim her— Cloe leaped off the bed and hurried to shower. She was just getting all the pieces back—Michael stepped into the shower, the intrusion another first in her sexual life, the intimate sharing of soap and hands, sliding smooth and warm and big around her.

"You're shivering," he whispered against her throat.

"What do you want?"

"This," he answered simply, and with the water sluicing streams down his face, black gleaming hair webbing across darkly tanned skin, drops clinging to his lashes, spiking them, he cleansed her intimately. He bent to take her lips, then lower to gently suckle her breasts, one, then the other—pushing her higher, always gently, seeking, hands flowing around her, over her. . . .

Cloe drifted on the soft caresses, the toweling of her body and his easing her into bed. Then he lay beside her, hand resting on her breast, studying it in the flashing lightning. "Michael," she whispered, protesting as his lips moved on her body, teasing, brushing, tasting, and lower, the intimacy frightening her—

She caught his hair in her fists, released the strands as the first burst of pleasure went through her—the intimate kiss rocketing through her and snapping that last hold. . . . Then Michael surged over her—the rain shadows from the windows coursing lines down his rawly savage expression in the sudden flash of lightning.

The rain patterns caught them, wove them together, her pale body undulating beneath Michael's powerful, angular, tanned one. She dived into passion, unrestrained—heat . . . storms . . . fire . . . pulses running, fitted tightly together—

She was sweating now, bones and flesh driving her, pushing, pulling, giving, taking, and Michael's mouth opened upon hers, demanding even more, his hands cupping her bottom, lifting her higher, the rhythm old and filled with magic and racing to a beat that finally enveloped her in waves, in heat, blinding her—

Even as she fell, warmly, softly, Michael's body poured into hers, savagely, as though this moment was where time began and ended, as though this was the heart of his universe, her world, and everything would begin anew from this heartbeat, this millennium of swirling tropical storms and the pounding of their hearts. His sigh against her throat lasted endlessly as the waves passed on, crested, and she held him tight, mooring him and herself in that moment.

He eased into her keeping, her arms, a warrior spent and tender as his damp face rested upon hers, his body heavy and lax on hers, and the storm thundered on outside, rain slashing at the windows.

Michael Bearclaw thought he'd won, driving that herd through Lolo like the old drovers, playing macho cowboy in front of the women, and that slut, Cloe Matthews, went wet when she saw him. Bearclaw would pay if he stayed, the intruder thought, leaning his cheek against the rifle stock. Bearclaw would soon learn that The Club was still powerful. The intruder closed one eye, sighted on Lopez, grazing on wild grass, and waited for the next blast of thunder . . . it would cover the sound of the high-powered rifle. Bearclaw's forensic skills couldn't track footprints destroyed by heavy rain. The intruder's father had taught him how to use storms.

Quinn straightened in his chair, the night shadows of his room quivering, the gentle rain preceding the thunderstorm that would soon sweep into the valley. Maggie had wanted Angelica to have the book she'd gone into the mountains to retrieve from its hiding place. Why?

The book was in Angelica's hands now and she'd disappeared into her mountain lair, that stark, angular redwood box, that coffin fitting into the mountain and giving away nothing of the warm woman she shielded.

With the flat of his hand, Quinn hit the scarred table that served his spartan needs, the violence surprising himself. He still wanted her after all these years. . . .

In the night wind, the old shadows stirred. . . .

* * *

Michael flattened to the bed as the thunder rolled outside the house, rain slashed the windows, and a cold sheaf of papers slapped him across the face. He pushed himself into consciousness and met Cloe's furious glare next to his face. "Hi, sweetheart," he whispered, trying to place this furious Cloe with the sweetly innocent women he'd just loved—he glanced at the bedside clock—an hour or a lifetime ago. He inhaled her scent, the freshly showered fragrance of his woman, the sexual perfume of their lovemaking still clinging to his bed, their bed.

He ran his hand up her thigh. At eleven o'clock at night, in the middle of a thunderstorm, he wanted Cloe again—one look at her scowl told him loving wasn't on her mind. He settled back, eyeing her, fascinated as always by the lift of her chin, the blue fire in her eyes.

"Don't look at me like that." She hit him with a pillow, slamming it down on him. "I went down easy, didn't I? Fell for the macho cowboy image, the wildflowers, your mother's quilt—all that sweet malarky . . . you kissed me as if—kissing like that should be illegal . . . and now I am really mad . . . all this time, you—"

He lay perfectly still, trying to focus, to bring the loving, sweet woman into the one who looked as though she could scalp him. He jerked the pillow away from her. "Is this how I can expect to be awakened every night?"

"Every night?" Her tone said Michael had better not pursue a commitment at the moment. He could wait; he'd waited for years. She straightened, braced her legs apart, and the large T-shirt she wore tightened on her breasts as she sank her fists into her waist. "You made this bed . . . *you made this bed with your own hands*—I know why Bearclaw men make beds. They make them for the women they intend to claim, to marry. You wasted a perfectly good bed, Michael Bearclaw, and a romantic legend, and romance is a terrible thing to waste."

"I don't intend to waste anything, not with you." He eyed her warily and hitched up a pillow, drawing himself up to watch her. He picked up one of the papers scattered on the bed and replaced it carefully over his suddenly aroused manhood. The paper quaked, mocking him.

Cloe battered him with another pillow, which Michael ripped away. "I'm feeling delicate, Cloe. Take it easy."

"Delicate, you? Hah. Those pictures . . . I found them on your computer when I started working. You had them, and not a word to me? They're all blown up and portions of the injuries circled and magnified. How dare you! We've been . . . intimate . . . terribly intimate, and I've allowed you to . . . become intimate. And you're keeping *this* from me."

Fascinated by Cloe struggling with her temper, Michael struggled with his desire to reach out and nab her.

"You." The word was tight, condemning, and not at all loverlike. She grabbed the bouquet of wildflowers from the jar of water and hit his face with them. Then Cloe stalked out of the room, leaving Michael drooling over the quivering sight of her well-shaped backside and blowing wildflower petals from his mouth.

After drawing on his jeans, he found her in the kitchen, slashing at a loaf of French bread with a butcher knife and crying. He handed her a stalk of mountain larkspur, and without missing a beat, Cloe reached out and ripped it away. She dashed the tears from her cheek and slammed the reheated bowls of soup onto the table, slapping down the mauled slices of bread. "Don't try a peace offering with me. Eat. You came out there when I was tired, took me—carried me in here like a captured bride or—Michael, your family has a tradition, and someday you may want to . . . to save yourself for a woman who—"

She pivoted to him, body taut. "You . . . that bed . . . the way you held me . . . I took you, too, and I've never, never taken like that. I opened myself to you, let you . . . took you—Michael, if you have bite marks on your shoulder, it's your own fault . . . you took me too long, held me there—" Cloe groaned in frustration and gripped the bear claw necklace in her fist and demanded, "All that time, you had these awful pictures. How could you?"

Michael took the knife she had just reclaimed, slashing at the bread. He leaned back against the counter and folded his arms over his chest.

"I'd like us to go back to bed," he said carefully. Awakening to Cloe's scowl when he wanted to cuddle and talk about dreams in the bed he'd just made didn't do much for his sweet temperament.

She stared at him. "What are you talking about?"

Now, that hurt. He'd just bonded with Cloe, taken his time in making certain that she knew exactly who she was meant for, how they would spend the rest of their lives, and she looked at him blankly.

"You're not an easy ride, and I've got things on my mind other than sex—Michael, it is not normal to be so . . . non-stop or have so many . . . to feel so much," she managed after a moment.

Michael caught the feminine fist that was plowing toward his midsection, and brought it and the other up to his lips, kissing the fine inner skin of her wrists, one at a time.

"You're no gentleman and you're giving me a headache," Cloe whispered after a moment, war in her flashing blue eyes. "I want to know about those pictures."

"I wasn't ready to tell you. You're a fireball, Cloe, and I'd prefer to hold any evidence until I have enough to clear your father. Evidence always turns up. You just have to know where and how to look. When it does, I'll be there." Michael eased his fingers between hers, studying the contrast of their hands. "Those pictures. I found them behind Dad's photographs over the desk. He sent me the bear claw necklace before he died. Those pictures were evidence, Cloe. Dad must have known that your father did not murder Gus. Dad was threatened—our family would be harmed—if he helped Sam. It was a secret he kept, probably one that ate at him and shortened his life."

Cloe trembled, eyes wide, as he continued, "I've reviewed those photos. Someone wearing a big ring and using a pistol butt like a club killed Gus, and someone wearing flat-soled workboots—"

"Dad always wore western style . . . he never wore a big ring, only the wedding band—"

"The ground was sandy, leaving good impressions. No rocks or hard objects to cause the final blow to

Gus's head. His hands had been handcuffed—I've seen the marks before."

Michael closed his eyes, fighting the image of a dead woman's delicate wrists, torn and bloody as she tried to escape her tormentor.

"Dad thought he killed Gus. Mom never believed he did, not for a moment."

"He didn't. He was probably visited in prison . . . your family threatened, and he—"

"Oh, Michael! I know he didn't do it. He couldn't have—" Cloe's wild, raw cry of pain tore the heart from him before she crumpled into his arms.

She clutched at his shirt, drawing herself up, her eyes desperate with fear. "Michael . . . Bradley Gilchrist has a file on Angelica . . . enough evidence to damage her. He's made me an offer—"

Michael stroked her taut back, ran his fingers beneath the hair at her nape and massaged the cords there. "That's good."

Cloe stepped back, frowning at him. "Good? No way. If I don't play ball, Angelica is headed into disaster and the ranch will be divided into five-acre ranchettes—*ranchettes*, Michael. There would be no way to put the ranch back into one piece then."

Even better; The Club was frightened enough to make a move and Bradley had spread his threatening hand to Cloe. She was thinking now, circling who could get hurt if the game went bad. "How do you feel about it?"

Cloe slapped her hands flat on the table and glared at him, her eyes like blue fire. "I want to fight, Michael and you know it, but other people are at stake here."

Michael swept his hands through her soft curls, turning the reddish strands around his fingers. "I think we should eat."

Cloe turned to slather butter on a slice of murdered bread. She thrust it at him. "You eat."

"Okay," he said, sitting down to the hot bowl of soup.

After a moment, Cloe sat down in the chair opposite him. "That was too easy."

Michael eased a spoonful of soup to her lips. She eyed him, but ate the soup. "What are you up to?"

"A logical schedule. Making love to you, for one thing. Listening to your soft cries as we make love, tasting you." He looked out into the crashing thunderstorm and prayed that every move he made would be the right one. "When they make a mistake, I'll be there. Now eat."

Michael, you're in this too deeply for your own good, Cloe thought later, as Michael cried out, fighting his nightmares, damning the serial killer of little girls. She drew him into her arms, cradling his head upon her breast, smoothing his hair. His forehead was damp with sweat.

Michael cried out suddenly, raising up over her, fierce and shaking, still locked in his nightmares. "Cloe?"

"I'm here, Michael."

His hands were trembling upon her face, searching out her bones, smoothing her hair back, fisting it tightly. Tears glistened on his black lashes, hell in his eyes. "They were only little girls, Cloe . . . maybe five or six. The bastard thought ten-year-olds were too old for his tastes. He smiled when they sentenced him . . . smiled, Cloe."

He shook with the violence riding him, and Cloe raised to kiss his chin, his tight lips, the lines bracketing his mouth, stroking his hair. "Shh. Come here."

She eased upon him, gave him her heat, the solid feminine curves and her strength, taking him gently, until Michael gave himself into her keeping.

Chapter 18

◌

"STOP DROOLING, SON," Michael murmured, after a glance at Sergei, standing next to him.

In the Fourth of July heat, Josy's long taut body leaned forward in the saddle, her horse weaving around the barrels in the rodeo's racing competition. Her western hat low on her head, the wind pasted her blouse against her breasts. The poetry of woman and the horse flowed together, determined and strong.

Nostrils flared, body taut, and a red shawl around his shoulders, Sergei looked like a cross between a gypsy rogue and a camera-ready cowboy, his pocketed vest filled with extra film and lenses. He inhaled sharply, as though he had been holding his breath. "My dove defies my wishes . . . she ropes those calves, and frightens me into gray hair. Yet I love her, idiot that I am. She would not let me duel with that Edward, that sniveling poop of a wasted male organ."

He jerked up the forgotten camera around his neck and began clicking at Josy, muttering as he moved around the arena to get better shots, stalking her.

Michael's enjoyment of the other man's plight skidded to a stop when Cloe hit his chest with both open hands. "They've just announced that you're riding that killer bull," she stated, as Michael slowly took in her red satin blouse and long tight jeans. The sight of her stopped his heart.

"Stop looking at me as though—as though you want to toss me over your shoulder and head for the nearest barn," Cloe ordered tightly. "We've spent the last six nights in that bed and you never mentioned riding that bull."

"If you'll remember, I was too busy to say much, sweetheart," he said, wanting to see her eyes flame.

"Nothing But Trouble hasn't ever been ridden. You're out of shape . . . you're too old to get on that bull . . . and right now, you're all I have—"

He grabbed the finger jabbing his chest and brought it to his lips. She glared up at him and jerked her hand away. "You know how much I'm worried about the project, about failing. You think I'd let the others know exactly how scared I am? I've never opened myself to anyone like you. I saw what that bull did to Roy Meadowlark. If the clowns in the barrels don't distract that bull, there won't be enough of you to—"

He stroked her hot cheek. "There will always be enough of me for you, Cloe," he stated with a grin.

"Meathead. I can't believe that you're the same man who explained Gus's injuries in such infinite detail, almost making it sound like a story that needing reading. And here you are, without a lick of sense. Just because—" She glanced uneasily at the crowd cheering Josy as her horse high-stepped into the arena, the winner of the barrel racing competition. Cloe clapped automatically and continued in a low voice. "I'm worried enough about Angelica. Now I have to worry about you—"

Michael couldn't resist. He wrapped his arms around her waist and lifted her up to his lips. "Give me a kiss for good luck, then."

"Everyone is watching! Michael, put me down."

"You kissed me enough last night. I'd think you'd have the hang of it by now." Michael gave himself to the pure joy of watching Cloe blush. She was still shy of him, entrancing him as she tried to wiggle free. "Think of it this way, sweetheart . . . how would you feel if that bull tore me into ribbons, broke every rib, and tossed me good, and you had denied a dying man's last wish? When I'm lying out there, making friends with that monster's horns, I'll be thinking of you, wishing I'd had that last kiss."

Cloe inhaled, glared at him, and fisted his hair, jamming her mouth to his. She pushed her tongue into his mouth, slanted her mouth, and devoured him.

When the kiss was finished, Michael slowly lowered her. The heat in his eyes, the flush rising beneath his dark skin, said that she'd gotten to him. "That wasn't exactly a sweetheart kiss. Riding a bull in this condition is going to be damned difficult." He slapped a cloth square into her hands and turned his back. He wanted her touch on him, waiting for it, holding his breath. "Pin that number on me, will you?"

Cloe stared at Michael's strong, wide back. Public displays of affection weren't in her experience, and— she ran her hand across her eyes and realized she was close to tears. Because Michael's back was closest and looked like a safe harbor in her emotional storm, she wrapped her arms around him and held him tight. She rubbed her tears against his shirt and admitted shakily, "I can't take care of everyone. Please don't ride that bull. I saw the bullet grazes on Lopez's rump. You'll be out there and an easy shot. I need you, Michael. Don't do this."

"Why do you need me, Cloe?" he asked, his shoulders tightening until his back looked like a wall.

She hit his back with her fist and he didn't turn. He just stood there and let her hit him again and she hated him for forcing the words from her. "You're safe, Michael. I haven't trusted men—not even Dad— he left me—I know that's childish, but it stuck. I don't think I ever trusted Ross . . . I know I didn't, not like you. I know when you say you'll do something, you'll do it—but this bull is something else, Michael—"

"You're right. I will do what I say . . . and what I've promised myself. Whoever took those shots at Lopez is a coward and a bad shot. He won't try anything with a crowd around." Michael turned slowly and lifted her chin. "Believe in you, Cloe. Believe in you and what you can do. Believe in me. Trust me. Pin that number on my back and let's do what we have to do."

"I'm scared and I'm going to cry, damn you." She hurried to pin the number on his back. "I used to be in control of myself. There, be stubborn. Go kill yourself. Topaz and I need more room in the bed anyway. You take up too much room."

"You can count on me not taking much tonight, because I'll be directly over or under you, sweetheart, and Topaz is sleeping in her box," Michael whispered against her ear, biting it.

"Men! Idiots! Pride up to their ears and not a bit of sense between." Minutes later, Cloe stood beside Josy, fingers locked to the arena's boards. In the chutes, Michael was trying to ease down onto Nothing But Trouble's broad back and the bull was heaving against the boards, fighting the rider.

"I'm going to kill Michael the minute that bull does," Cloe sobbed unevenly, and dashed the tears from her cheeks.

"A man's gotta do—"

"Don't. I don't want to hear it. I thought I could trust him. Then he goes and does a thing like this. He's supposed to be an educated, intelligent man, and he's reverted to a show-off cowboy."

Sergei came beside Josy, wrapping his arm around her. He took off her dusty western hat, placed a kiss upon her hair, and replaced the hat.

"He just does that. I don't know why. I think it's a custom or something," Josy explained sheepishly to Cloe. She closed her eyes luxuriously as Sergei's lips pressed against her throat.

Sergei laughed, delighted as Josy tried to look distant and interested in Michael easing down onto the bull, his gloved hand wrapped in the bull rope. Men hauled the chute door open and Nothing But Trouble hurled into the dusty arena, a gleaming black devil, furious with the man on his back.

Cloe knew instantly that Michael was fighting his demons, the bloody terror that pursued him. He had to win some part of himself back, reclaim something he'd lost, bit by bit as he tracked murderers. Pitting himself against the bull was easier.

Josy wrapped her arm around Cloe. "He was good—"

"*Was* ... the operative word," Cloe heard herself say. Michael, free arm swinging for balance, long-muscled body finding the bull's rhythm, spun and slammed against the corral boards. Leather chaps flying, whipped by the wind, hot July sun gleaming on his sweaty face, Michael's grim expression did not change; he'd locked onto the fight, declared himself the bull's enemy, and wasn't letting go—the bull threw him up, air between the beast and the man, before Michael locked on the bull again, and the time-whistle sounded.

Cloe heard herself cry out as the horseman nearest Michael leaned close and Michael grabbed him, swinging down to the ground. Nothing But Trouble sighted him and ran, horns lowered toward him; Michael ran, grabbed the corral boards, and hefted himself high and over in one leap.

Through the distance and the crowd's roar, Michael found Cloe's eyes and locked onto her. There wasn't anything sweet about his expression, just a man who knew what he wanted and how to get it. He started around the arena toward Cloe, and she knew that he wanted too much ... everything—

Edward came near Josy, jerked her arm so that she faced him. "I won't have that foreigner putting ideas into my son's head. You're not a fit mother—"

"Not now, Edward."

Josy tried to twist away, and Edward jerked her back. "I want full custody—"

"Josy?" Cloe glanced at Josy, then back to the woman in the center of the arena. Angelica, looking dazed, her chestnut hair gleaming long and free in the sun, and clad in red satin pajamas, had walked into the ring. She pushed away from the horseman who would have lifted her onto the saddle.

"I'm tired of being nice, Edward," Josy noted flatly. She sank a hard punch in Edward's soft midsection. When he grunted and began to sink, she clipped him on the jaw and sank her knee into his crouch. He fell, face first, into a perfect, fresh batch of horse dung. Josy pivoted and glanced at Cloe. "Let's get Angelica. She'll listen to us."

Sheer terror pinned Cloe for a heartbeat and then she whispered to Josy, "Go!"

Both women slid through the space between the boards, separated and ran a distance apart, arms waving, shouting, trying to distract the bull. The bull tossed the barrel into which the clown had scampered; the force broke the barrel, injuring the clown, who slid outside the arena.

"Oh, hell," Michael cursed, as fear speared him. He ripped a coiled bullwhip off the shoulder of Jeremiah France and put it on his own as he climbed up on the corral boards.

"Angelica. Get out of the ring. Let the horseman take you out, now," Cloe ordered, as the bull stopped circling the ring and focused on Angelica.

"I don't care anymore," Angelica chanted dully.

"Get my daughter out of there," Bradley Gilchrist shouted wildly, though the rest of the crowd was silent, trapped in the drama and fear of the scene in the arena.

Sergei leaped over the corral boards, Josy's red merino shawl around his throat, and landed by Michael. "Our women. . . ." he muttered unevenly as Angelica pushed Josy away.

"They love each other. They'll go down together." Michael's curse hit the silent air, terror clawed at him as the bull made a pass at Cloe, then circled the ring. The horsemen tried to distract the bull, charging at him, and a horse squealed in pain as a sharp horn tore into him.

Michael would never forget the sight of the three women standing together, Josy and Cloe flanking Angelica, determined to protect her.

Wild with rage now and scenting blood, the bull charged again, hurting another horse.

"I love you, Angelica. You'll do this for me, won't you? Come with me?" Cloe couldn't bear how Angelica turned from her and from Josy, avoiding looking at them, her shoulders hunched.

"I don't care anymore. . . ." Angelica repeated dully.

Josy smoothed Angelica's wild, tangled hair, and she jerked away, huddling within herself. Josy spoke quietly, soothingly. "Angel, I need you. What would I do without you?"

"I'm like *them*. I know it. Go away."

Michael slowly walked toward the bull, the long black whip gleaming and deadly as he swung it in an arc. It cracked, the sound echoing in the hot dry day, the crowd silent.

"Oh, no," Josy muttered, as Sergei whipped her red merino shawl around himself, in a matador pose. "Get . . . out . . . of here."

"You are my woman. I will not leave you. Tell me you love me and then you leave."

"You've never been near a bull in your life," Josy countered without looking away from the bull, pawing the arena dust.

"Have I not?" Sergei swung the shawl expertly, his body taut and curved. "Toledo, Spain . . . last year. I wore a suit of lights with very tight pants. I was beautiful," he explained with a rakish grin as the bull charged him; only a handspan separated the horns from the man.

Michael cracked the whip around the bull's ears and the bull swayed, torn between charging him or the man swirling the shawl. Panting, black and deadly, the bull stopped; he swayed and alternately eyed both men.

Quinn had entered the arena, walking casually as though the drama was not taking place, straight to Angelica. He spoke softly to her. "Come with me now, Angelica. I know where you can be safe."

"I can't bear it!" With a broken cry, Angelica folded into his arms and he hurried, carrying her to the gate, which had just been opened.

Michael took one look at Sergei, who was intent upon the bull, not moving as the bull charged again. "Let's get out of here."

"If that bull doesn't kill him, I will," Josy muttered.

"You women are savages, out for blood. You're frightening me. Look at him." Michael pushed Josy and Cloe toward the side of the arena. "Sergei knows what he's doing."

Josy wouldn't move, studying the man who taunted the bull with the cape, moving expertly in a matador's grace. "This is just like him to upset me. He's ruined my life and I will not wear that lace wedding gown, not if he dies out there, making a fool out of himself."

"He looks like a man who's enjoying himself. . . . come here." Michael placed his arm around Cloe's waist as she hurried away and jerked her hard against him. "Don't ever do anything like that again."

"I've got to find Angelica."

"Quinn will take care of her. You're staying put."

Cloe eyed him. "Orders?"

"Stay back. I want to go with Quinn," Angelica ordered, as Bradley Gilchrist reached toward her. Monroe stood huffing behind her father.

"You're obviously sick. You need care—" Bradley began, the smell of alcohol curling around Angelica. She hated the scent that had been frighteningly familiar in her childhood.

"I will tell everything . . . *everything*," she threatened too quietly as Quinn started his battered pickup. As fear widened Bradley's eyes, she concentrated on moving into the pickup, moving on her own strength, forcing herself to be calm. Quinn had said he was taking her to a safe place; she had to believe in him, in Cloe, in goodness and families and love.

She felt too unclean to be with Cloe and Josy, both their lives ruined by her father. Her stomach turned, soured. She knew Jeffrey was biding his time, and he would destroy Bradley. She'd been bred of hatred and discreet, and yet she wanted to be clean. "Leave me alone. Quinn, take me away from here."

*   *   *

Hours later, Josy followed Cloe up the old iron fire escape. "Cody will have a jailbird for a mother," she muttered.

"Shh. Because you love Angelica, just like I do, and I need you. Now is the perfect time. Gilchrists are throwing their usual Fourth of July party. The Club is there, even Monroe, who is never going to really be a part of them. Michael and Sergei are returning the cattle to the pasture—and we've got all this lovely time to get Angelica's file."

"What's wrong with her? Did you see how she avoided looking at us?"

"Watch that old chimney. She's going to be fine. Everyone is going to be fine, Josy. We'll get the spa running, make tons of money, and you won't have to listen to Angelica moan about not having a good facial. We just have to tidy up a few loose ends." Cloe shivered and glanced at rockets shooting into the night sky, firecrackers popping in the distance. She'd pushed Angelica too hard, laying out an idea that she knew Angelica would grab with both fists. *Angelica . . . I'm sorry. . . .*

"You make it all sound so easy." Josy almost giggled. "Only you would think that robbing a bank was tidying up."

Cloe glared at her as she gripped Josy's hand and hauled her up to the roof. "It's only a little blackmail file."

She crossed a rooftop and anchored the rope she carried onto an brick abutment, dropped it into the iron bar enclosure behind the bank, and began to climb down it. Midway to the ground, Michael's raspy, silky voice curled around her. "Why, Cloe, fancy meeting you here."

While she was considering Michael's powerful body on the brick enclosure beneath her, he called up to Josy. "You'd better leave. Sergei took Cody at the dance. They're waiting for you."

"I can't leave Cloe," Josy whispered after a moment.

Michael's hushed, rough tone condemned Cloe. "Josy has a son, Cloe, but you didn't think of that, did you? You just dragged her into it. Damn you, why the hell didn't you ask me to help you? Now, get her back to safety, and tell me why we're here."

"You're a forensics expert, Michael, and you have connections with the law. I wanted to leave you out of it." Cloe dropped to the ground. "I'll be fine, Josy. Go on."

"We'll be at the dance later, Josy," Michael added, and glanced darkly at Cloe. "Alibis for everyone. You're going to that damned dance with me and you're going to look like you enjoy it."

"I think I can manage that," Cloe said, looking up at Josy, who hesitated for a moment, then was gone.

"Why are we here?" Michael repeated too softly, and eased the iron gate at the back of the enclosure closed. It clicked, locked once more.

He'd made her tell him more than she wanted; he'd torn out her heart today. "You're not happy, are you? Well, neither am I. You rode that bull, deliberately endangered yourself—"

"Don't hold anything back, Cloe. Just let it all out, right here, behind the bank you're planning to rob." He glared at her, ran his fingers through his hair, and stared up at the stars as if waiting for his patience to return. "Let's get this over and talk later. Hold still while I disable the outside alarms."

"You don't have to do this," she whispered. "There goes the old forensics career. Michael, you're counting under your breath, aren't you?"

He snorted, a disgusted sound, jerked open a box on the old brick wall, studied the wires, and unhooked them. "You can move now."

Inside the bank, Cloe hurried to Gilchrist's office and pointed to the locked drawer. Michael opened it with a paperclip left lying on the desk. When she snatched the file folder, flipped through it, and nodded, he asked, "Is that it?"

"Just this." Cloe plucked up the picture of Angelica and stuffed it in the shoulder bag with the file.

In the old milk barn, Cloe stood in a pool of moonlight coming through the skylight, her arms around herself. She looked at the shelves of goods for the catalog, at the architect's plans for the Wild Willows, and at Michael as he came into the barn. "You're very angry, aren't you? Not the hot, seething, out-in-the-open kind, but the cold, last-forever. . . . Michael, Angelica couldn't bear to look at me. I've pushed her too hard . . . I've pushed everyone too hard. You're right. I focus on what I want and go for it. . . ."

She dashed her hand across her cheek, damp with tears. "Whatever Angelica says, she loves her family, just as I love mine. This is costing her too much. She's out there now, in pieces—"

"Quinn is with her." Michael's seething anger eased, cooled. Cloe was hurting deeply, blaming herself—

Cloe laughed wildly. "She's turned to him. Why not to me and to Josy? She couldn't look at us today." She faced him, tears running down her cheeks. "I wanted this so much, Michael—but it isn't worth Angelica."

She grabbed his shirt. "You know where they're at, don't you? All that time we were at the dance, faking a good time, you knew where Quinn would take her, didn't you? I'm going to her. You're not my big brother, Michael. You don't have to come with me."

"I'm the man in your bed, and that's something." Michael cursed silently. So much for romance, he thought, as Cloe paled. "Damn it, Cloe. A man could do with a little romance," he finally stated as the silence raged on.

"Romance, at a time like this," she scoffed after a blank look. "Michael, don't you see? They'd all have been better off if I hadn't—"

"Bull. Did you love him?" Michael shot at her, freeing his thoughts.

"No, I know that now, but—"

"That's good enough." And then he reached for her, and she met him with equal hunger.

Sergei lay on the bunk, his arms crossed behind him. The boards on the porch creaked. After noting the fresh bullet wounds skidding across Lopez's rump, and Josy's punch to Edward, Sergei expected trouble. He slid out of bed and eased behind the old board door, just as it opened slowly.

Josy stepped into the moonlit square. "Sergei?"

He closed the door behind her. "You are frightened? Is Cody—"

"Cody is asleep, filled with ideas of being a matador, no thanks to you. Max is with him." Josy shivered beneath her tattered robe and glanced nervously at his narrow bed. Then, closing her eyes, she lowered the robe away from her nude body, dropping it.

"What is this?" Sergei asked carefully, as Josy walked to the bunk and eased into it, pulling the sheet up close to her chin.

"It's time," Josy whispered. "I'd like to make love with you."

"You are worried about Angelica?" Sergei's fingertip toyed with her short hair and circled the earrings he'd given her. "Am I your distraction for the moment?"

"No. I am worried about Angelica, but this is apart from everything else."

"You know I hunger for you, of course." The statement was arrogant, flatly shielding what Josy knew to be deep emotion. Then, softer, "Why do you come to me, my heart?"

She left her pride in the darkness and gave him the truth. "Because I need you."

Tears . . . he's a loving man. Josy stroked the warm dampness gleaming on Sergei's lashes as he rose over her, shoulders tense and quivering in the moonlight. His glance down at their bodies, the mating about to begin, caused her to shiver. This man had known the most beautiful intelligent women, while Josy had little experience to bring to him.

A rush of foreign words, spoken with reverence, tumbled out of Sergei as he stroked her shoulder, kissed with his open lips. "You humble me, my dove . . . to give me this gift."

She closed her eyes, giving herself to the sturdy weight of his body over hers, the rigid desire pressing against her softness. "I'm . . . fertile, Sergei. I'll try not to—"

He stopped her admission with a fingertip. "To have my child within you would be a blessing, a dream. I have not been with another woman in years . . . I would have you know this." Then, more shyly, he gave her a secret. "I am not so romantic with other women . . . in bed. I am more interested in angles and cameras than women's bodies—but with you, I forget everything."

He shuddered and stared at her small, up-tilted breasts hungrily. "But with you, my Josy, I walk in constant pain, so hard am I for you. Even without the body, my heart would still beat for you."

Josy closed her eyes; she held a man who cherished life and love. She'd placed stallions within the keeping of mares, and yet to actually touch Sergei, to bring him within herself—

Sergei lay his cheek close to hers, his tears blending with hers as he whispered, "This night we are married, in my heart. I will never take another woman to my bed, to my body. I would live all my life with this one rose in my memory, my bride, my woman. Cody will be like my son, and forever I will be yours."

He kissed her reverently as he moved to complete them and Josy slowly enveloped him with her arms, stroking his back as he came to lie gently over her, in her. "This, to me, is my marriage vow, heart of my heart, breath of my life . . ." he whispered.

Josy couldn't find the words, and instead she gave

her body in the most beautiful symphony of pleasure, surprise, and gentle taking.

"My beautiful silent bride," Sergei whispered against her throat as he caressed her body. "You will give me the words when your heart tells you."

My heart tells me this is what love should be, Josy thought, as she plummeted into a sweet, short sleep.

The whirring sound of the spinning wheel ate at the silence. Michael had made love to Cloe quickly, thoroughly, leaving her in bed as he dressed at midnight. "Whatever Angelica might need, pack it," he'd said. "I'm riding out."

Pleading, arguing didn't help, as he grimly saddled Lopez. In the end, Cloe had shoved a bag filled with clothing, soap and towels, and food at him. The smaller bag was filled with quilting scraps and needle and thread. "Give her this. It soothes her."

Now Cloe was alone, dawn creeping pink and fragile into the day, her hands smoothing bits of wool into thread, the continuous creation at odds with the lives she had torn apart. Angelica's file was no more than ashes in the fireplace.

Cloe had come back only to hurt them all, to ruin them all. But she wasn't leaving now until they were all safe and Michael came back to her in the morning. She clung to that thought—Michael coming back to her with news of Angelica.

When Michael rode into the ranchyard hours later, she was spinning, careless of her aching fingers, her restless body. She tore from the house into the barn. He moved slowly, wearily, lines etched deep in his face, and shadowed by a new beard. "Michael?"

His gaze ripped down her body, covered by his shirt, heat leaping in his golden eyes. "She's fine and resting. She's worried that she's let you down when you needed her for Wild Willows. Give her a few days and she'll be fine."

"I've decided I'm stopping it all now. The Wild Willows project is dead. The catalog will be good for Mom's business. The Club will give her that. I can't do any more damage, building worthless dreams."

Michael stared at her, the new day settling upon his rigid jaw, his shoulders. "Backing off? That doesn't sound like you."

"I'm hurting the people I love, Michael."

"I saw three women in that arena yesterday, standing side by side, helping each other. When the time comes, you and Josy will be there for her . . . your mother and Dan and Gabe, and all the rest." *Cloe, don't give up. Don't run . . . I'll be there, too.*

Michael ripped his gloves away and rubbed his jaw. He needed more evidence to clear Sam Matthews, and he needed Cloe. "Angelica will be fine," he repeated. "You just hold steady and don't drop any dreams without talking to the people who believe in you."

"Easy for you to say," she shot at him, tears shimmering in her eyes.

"Why don't you come lie over upon me, and tell me how much you enjoy my company?" he asked.

"You want to make love? Now?"

Michael bent to sweep Cloe up into his arms. "Sure do. After that, everything should settle down into place."

Chapter 19

&

HE'D BROUGHT THIS chestnut-haired woman who haunted his dreams to a place where she'd once laughed, open and free, too seductively husky to be sweet and innocent. Quinn broke twigs, feeding them to the late morning cooking fire. The flames leaped and he fought the terror that had enclosed him when he saw Angelica in the arena, the bull ready to kill, and the women standing beside her. He'd forced himself now to move slowly toward Angelica, the woman who always seemed to be in his mind, perhaps in his destiny. Her green eyes were shadowed, dull, slow to recognize him, and filled with agony. What had happened to her?

Angelica lay upon the pallet she'd shared with Quinn on the mountain clearing, bordered by pine trees. Her bones were limp within her cold flesh. The old trapper's cabin had been their shelter in rain, when they were lovers, long ago. She narrowed her eyes against the bright sunlight, feeling as old as the earth. Quinn had bathed her in the warm water at Bearclaw Ridge and dressed her in his shirt, because she could not bear to have the clothing of her past against her flesh. He'd treated her like a sick child, his touch impersonal, his voice soothing. His fingers stroked her nape, her scalp, finding her nerves and easing them.

Over her head, birds soared through the sky, laced by pine boughs, and the scent of the morning cook fire curled around her. A wide-eyed doe stopped at the edge of the clearing, studying her, and then slid into the brush. Quinn was right. She was safe here . . . free of the shadows and the book's haunting truths.

He crouched by the fire, feeding it slowly, bringing it to life. She'd needed his warmth last night, his strength, and Quinn had held her without questions, lying beside her beneath the stars. He smelled of the fragrant woods, the herbs he had gathered, of freshly bathed male and of a clean heart.

She'd never been clean, never would be.

A chipmunk scurried across the clearing and Angelica closed her eyes, scratchy from crying. She turned away from the beauty of Quinn's naked body, gleaming bronze in the morning, haunches hollowed with muscle, back graceful and long. She sensed he'd lain with her long past his usual rising time, giving her comfort, smoothing her hair.

His hand weighted her shoulder, turned her. "Drink."

Her instincts told her to flip words at him, taunting him, but she couldn't. There was no judgment in his black eyes, no condemnation. The laughing taunts were gone. He handed her the cup of herbal tea, tiny bits of leaves and bark swimming in it like lives gone past. He cradled her hands to the cup's warmth and

Angelica shuddered. She was weak, she knew that now, her defenses stripped by Maggie Ten Feather's journal. Quinn looked into her eyes, smoothed his big hand gently across her brow, her eyebrows, the gesture from long ago calming her. "Rest."

Angelica sipped the tea, let it flow through her, and gave herself to the sleep she badly needed. When she awoke, Quinn wore jeans and nothing else as he turned the rabbit roasting on the spit. A hair brush rested near her pallet. Grateful for the lack of a mirror, Angelica eased into sitting and with a massive effort lifted her hand to draw the brush through her hair.

Quinn turned, rose, and went to her, kneeling as he took the brush, slowly drawing it through the tangled strands. He ran his fingertips through her hair and looked deep into her eyes. "Better," he murmured.

Oh, Quinn . . . you don't know. I can't bear for you to know. . . . She closed her lids, shutting him away, keeping the pain inside her, where it couldn't harm others. She knew too much . . . terrible things—Startled by the sound of her voice, she realized she'd been speaking.

"When you are ready, I will listen."

"The bastard savage" her father had called him, and yet Quinn had been the gentlest man she'd known—except Sam Matthews, a man her family had desperately wronged. Oh, Cloe. I'm sorry . . . I'm sorry. . . . Josy . . . I'm sorry.

Just when she thought her eyes were drained of tears, more spilled over his hand, falling through the brilliant sunlight like sins. She grabbed his hand, holding it tight against her chest, where the darkness threatened to envelop her. "Sing to me, Quinn, like you did then . . . those lovely words about life . . .

about birds and flowers, and about . . . life."

The traditional warrior's courting song came slowly out of him, curling around her, soothing. He settled her in front of him, wrapped his arms around her, and swayed as he sang, giving her more than she deserved.

She hadn't wanted to be touched long ago, not by a man, but Quinn had gently enfolded her as he did now. She leaned back against him, tucked her face into the shelter of his throat, and whispered, "They took our baby, Quinn—"

His heart leaped, pounding fiercely against her cheek. Angelica waited for him to throw her away, to curse her, but instead he folded her closer, holding her fists in his hands. "Tell me."

She shuddered, fighting the wad of emotion clogging her throat. The truth-time was here. "Maggie knew everything. Orson told her. She wrote and dated everything. . . . Most of it was about you, and somehow she knew I was pregnant with our baby, unaware of it, but my father knew because Mother always kept track of me. Quinn—they drugged me, had the baby aborted, and sent me to Europe, all without me knowing that I—I remember the fog, the drugs, but then you were married and I had no reason—For years something has been missing in me . . . *my baby . . . our baby.*"

Angelica released the cry that came boiling out of her womb, her heart, her soul, gave herself to it until it seemed to quiver in the treetops, flowing into the sky. When the birds began to sing again, Quinn was rocking her, humming gently.

His child had cried out to him . . . the dreams true. The

fire-woman was Cloe, stirring the storms, and the young wolf tearing at the old, would come prowling for Angelica, for power.

Quinn listened to his heart and knew that the child would not cry again, and then Angelica turned his face to hers. "I wanted to marry you. I didn't care about your family . . . I just wanted you. Now I know Orson was your father, Quinn, and Maggie was your mother. You are his heir . . . he is the one who arranged the loan for The Long Horn. He loved you, named you after his father . . . but he was terrified for you and for Maggie. She knew too much, and you. . . ."

Quinn forced himself to breathe, trying to place the old man within him, to see Orson's likeness in himself. "They used her—my mother—to control him," he said quietly.

Angelica's meadow green eyes turned sadly to him, her skin pale and glowing in the shadows, her hair like stripes of darkened blood along her cheek. "I'm a part of all this . . . it's in my blood. My father arranged Sam Matthews's guilt."

"This is what burdens your heart," Quinn noted softly. He noted his speech changed, returning to the old phrasing when he spoke to Angelica, his treasure. "You must tell your friends."

Angelica shuddered. "I can't. I can't bear to tell them."

"You will find a way. They need you. I will help you."

Angelica sobbed, placing her hands in front of her face. She rocked herself. "I love them—my parents.

Isn't that a laugh? This shouldn't be that hard, but it is."

Quinn smoothed the gleaming dark red strands. "You will do what your heart tells you to do."

She turned to him, eyes bright with tears. "You don't despise me?"

Quinn gave her the truth, coming from his heart in the phrasing used long ago. "You are the woman of my heart. You have lit the shadows which trouble me. How could I do less than cherish you?"

Cloe sensed someone moving behind her in the old barn, even before she turned to see Jeffrey Gilchrist walk into the lighted, airy office.

The new shelving, the desks made of sawhorses and planks, were cluttered with vendors' samples, catalogs of products for the spa, chains of tile samples, and thick books of carpeting. He picked up a mock brochure to study it. "Very nice. My sister has been gone for three days. She wasn't really disturbed until you stirred her up. We'll retrieve Angelica from her romp with Quinn Lightfeather and then we can talk business. Since she's obviously unbalanced. Her mental state is fragile. Until she's better, I'll manage her share."

Cloe smiled coldly. She had experience holding the rage inside her. She could paste a smile on her face and tear Jeffrey apart. "Angelica is fine, but tired."

"You need a man to run things—cool, logical thinking. We can work together."

"*We* have the ability—Angelica, Josy, and myself."

Jeffrey's hand slashed out, dismissing her. "Don't tell me that Michael Bearclaw isn't in this somewhere, ramrodding the show. But without my sister's financial backing, you can't make it."

Years ago, the Wild Willows had put itching powder in Jeffrey's shorts. Now, Cloe wanted to dump a gallon of paint over His Royal Full of Himself's head.

He flicked a dried bunch of lavender with his fingers. "My sister is unwell. I have to protect her investment. I want approval of anything you do."

Jeffrey did not choose a good day to make his claim. Cloe studied him; she was bone tired from working twenty-hour days, and worried about Angelica. Josy was working just as hard, though *she* was blooming. Cloe was pushing, putting her blood into building Wild Willows. Once Angelica returned, the three of them would decide on their future. "Get out, Jeffrey. From this moment, you are persona non grata on this land."

She knew how to bluff; she'd perfected that skill in the years married to Ross. "But first, I want to clear up any misunderstanding about what happened at the rodeo—"

She punched Josy's number at the radio station, and Josy's voice purred at the speakerphone. "Josy Livingston at Coffee Time."

"Josy, Jeffrey Gilchrist is here. He seems to think that Angelica is having a mental problem and that he's planning on taking over her share. What exactly happened at the rodeo? Was that planned or not?" Cloe prayed desperately that Josy would pick up her cue, and through the brief pause before Josy answered, Cloe forced herself to smile at Jeffrey.

Josy's smooth voice echoed through the barn. "We had the whole thing planned, a staged gimmick to put the Wild Willows Spa out in front of Lolo. You don't just come up with an expert matador at the snap of your fingers, Jeffrey."

Perfect. Josy, I love you.

Jeffrey smirked, meeting Cloe's bland smile. "Then why did Quinn have to walk Angelica out of the arena?"

Josy sighed and spoke slowly, as if explaining an important detail to a small child. "Quinn and Angelica are getting married. We got so busy setting up the ad gimmick that we forgot to tell Quinn about it. He was worried and then was no time to explain anything. Think about it, Jeffrey. She was even wearing red. Cloe is an advertising expert . . . red . . . bull . . . matador."

That's enough, Josy. Make it believable. Not too much—

Jeffrey clicked off the intercom, his expression vivid with rage. "My sister is marrying Quinn? That Indian?"

"Do I have to lay that out for you, too? Now they want time alone, and Angelica deserved the rest."

Jeffrey ran his hands through his hair and it stuck out in peaks. "They're not getting married right now, are they?"

"You could be Quinn Lightfeather's brother-in-law already," Cloe lied. She eased her lips into a mocking smile and handed him a perfect humiliation for The Club. "Think of it . . . a Native American in the Gilchrists."

She almost admired Jeffrey's forced composure, despite the rage in his eyes. Almost. He smiled coolly. "You'll be moving on. Bearclaw is only settling his father's estate, and then he'll be gone, too. I can wait."

*   *   *

He had to hurt something . . . someone. The women were witches, brewing plans to overthrow The Club. If they weren't stopped, the valley would be impure, taken over by strangers, and years of work would be ruined——the natural order of the fittest would be ruined.

"That's a sight you don't see every day," Michael murmured, as he unstrapped the old Colt from his thigh and wrapped the gunbelt around the holster. He braced his boot on a log as Sergei leaned against a tree. Stirred by the afternoon breeze, lush grass moved around them, gleaming green waves where the horses grazed. Cloe and Josy, dressed in western shirts and jeans, sat with crossed legs, trying not to look at Angelica. In Quinn's shirt, with her hair in thick twin braids, Angelica could not bear to look at her lifelong friends.

His mother's old quilting basket sat between them. Each took a piece of cloth, fashioning it into a quilt block. Periodically, Angelica glanced at Quinn. Without cosmetics and a tough attitude, Angelica looked like a wounded child.

The Wild Willows talked about the pattern that grew, block by block, small pieces into larger, as they worked, needles flashing in the afternoon sun. With a look, Angelica summoned Quinn, and he sat behind her, his hand upon her shoulder. She spoke quietly, her gaze pinned to the basket, tears flowing down her cheeks, shining trails in the sunlight, glittering as they dripped to her opened palms.

Then Josy began to cry softly and Sergei instantly crouched by her side; Michael placed his open hand on Cloe's back and she leaned against him, her face pale.

Angelica's expression was agonized, fearful, as she whispered, "I have Maggie Ten Feather's journal. She wrote everything, even how Sam Matthews was framed . . . so was Josy's father. They threatened him, promised to hurt Josy, and when he found the evidence—the gun that had beaten Gus Ballas to death—he hid it, because he knew they would keep him alive—and Josy—until they found it."

Josy looked down at her folded hands. "I know where the gun is. My father asked me to hide it."

Chapter 20

❧

"WE HAVE OUR case to clear Sam's name. But what do *you* want, Stella?" Michael asked the next morning. He placed his notes and Maggie's journal to one side, and took Stella's trembling hand; he hated the fresh agony in the older woman's expression. This family had been through rivers of pain, and yet there was beauty, pride, and grace in the woman who had loved Sam Matthews, who still kept him in her heart. Liam had another part of her now, and the past had come back to tear her apart.

Michael wanted justice. He wanted to cut Lolo free of The Club. He wanted all their lives—Cloe's, Stella's, Angelica's, Josy's and all the rest—clean and new. That couldn't happen, but he could make The Club pay. A glance at Cloe's bent head and hunched shoulders told him that she was the one paying now—the memories were tearing at her.

She'd gone to her mother immediately after learning the truth, and Michael had worked throughout the night, verifying the identification number of Stan Collins's revolver, his shoe type, and evidence of

352

scratches on his arms after the murder. Stan Collins had murdered Gus Ballas after Sam Matthews had returned to his wife; dates from news clippings matched Maggie's diary, an endless story of black-mail, of wielding power.

Maggie Ten Feather's dated journal was explicit, written at a time before the drugs had been admin-istered to her—Michael had checked the hospital rec-ords, lined them up, and suspected Orson had acted to save her life. He'd placed her in a sanatorium, his signature on the legal papers.

In The Pinto Bean, Stella's monument on Lolo's Main Street, the decision of retribution was left to the woman who had been used as a pawn. The baking heat of mid-July sank into the scrolled gold lettering as Stella looked out onto the Sunday morning, stared across the street to the bank, and lifted her chin. She remembered the years of shame and hardship, and yet her family had survived. Sam would have been proud of his children. She rubbed her arms, chilled to the bone, and knew what Sam would want. He wouldn't want a fuss, just "the right of it." "I want Sam cleared . . . right here in Lolo Valley, where it would have mattered to him. I want everyone to know that he was innocent and how fine he was."

"Mom . . ." Cloe placed her arm around Stella, hugged her close. "Muriel will run the story. What Michael needs to know is how far you want to take this."

"How far? How far has it gone already? Too far, too much. It has to stop somewhere." A tear slid down Stella's cheek as she folded her arms around herself. She turned to Michael and lifted her chin, tears brimming over her lids. "I want the land to go back to his children. That meant everything to Sam . . . his children inheriting the Matthews homestead. Is that possible?"

"They'll get it and more," Michael said firmly, meaning it. He wanted to plow The Club, hold them accountable in court, make them suffer as Sam Matthews had, with shame and loss of everything they loved. And still it wasn't enough. "Anything else?"

Stella studied Michael, a man she understood, who would protect those he loved. Shadows haunted him still, and he was possessed with a grim, bitter determination that frightened her. The violence within Michael could rip him away from their lives. "I loved Wade, too, Michael. In a different way. Neither Sam nor Wade would have wanted a fuss over this. And there's Angelica. She can't turn off the love she feels, regardless of whether her parents deserve it. Whatever has to be done, it should be done quietly."

Michael's open hand slammed down onto the counter as he fought his anger. He cursed, then spoke too softly. "Stella, these men are murderers . . . criminals. They've ruined lives—yours, specifically. What you're saying could let them slink away without real damage. A good attorney will take them for everything they have and lay their lives open to the press, ruining them."

"Michael—" Cloe stood in front of Michael. His body taut, throbbing with the need for revenge, a vein pounding in his temple, he could go too far . . . he could be harmed. His gold eyes slashed down at her; he was deadly now, locked onto persecuting The

Club, bringing them down into nothing, punishing them. He'd worked without rest, fighting her, fighting himself and the images that rode him. He fought his guilt for not returning to Lolo sooner. His revenge could destroy, could devour Michael as surely as The Club.

Her fingers touched his lips and framed his unshaven jaw, and the violence in Michael's expression shimmered uncertainly and eased. His gaze locked with Cloe's and slowly he came back to her, the man who she'd known forever, who shared her body and had her heart. His rage and frustration could take him away from her.

Her heart started beating again, when he said curtly, "If that's how you want it."

Then he nodded to Cloe and Stella and walked out of the door, his back rigid.

"You've just asked the man to give up a measure of his pride," Liam said quietly.

"What do you mean?" Cloe asked.

"He's got the skills, the tools to do what he says. It's like asking a gladiator to sit back and watch the fight. He wants to protect you, to make everything right. He can't. But he wants to try."

In the shadows of the barn, Michael tore away an old board and hurled it into the pile of others. He glanced at Cloe, standing in the open doorway and continued working. She walked to him, wishing that all those years hadn't slid by . . . wishing that he'd taken her that day—

"Michael?"

"Stay away from me, Cloe. I'm not in the mood to

hear more about saving The Club from ruin."

She lifted an eyebrow, familiar with Michael's need to brood, his silence. He eyed her, a warning to keep her distance. "Don't push me."

"Oh, you know I'm going to," she replied, using his own words to taunt him. She had to tear him away from the past, from the nightmares that punished him. "Talk to me. Get it out."

A man used to choosing his time, and keeping his heart concealed, Michael straightened, his bare shoulders glistening in the dim light as he ripped off his gloves. "They should go to jail, Cloe. Not be let off the hook . . . buying their way clear."

The shadows under his eyes told of bloody, haunting images, and Cloe wished she could give him what he needed—revenge. But she couldn't, because that would only feed the darkness within him. The pain had to stop. "Too many people could get hurt, Michael. I can't let that happen. I couldn't stop all those things years ago, neither could you, but we can now."

"Just let them get away with everything? That's not finishing anything. If we don't move fast and hard, someone could get hurt. The Club has too much tied up here to leave easily. Muriel's parakeets and Roy's death were threats, Cloe. Take them seriously."

"I do, but I think that working together, we can take care of The Club. Taking everything they have, uprooting them, keeping Angelica's family away from her—and protecting Josy and her son. We can structure their downfall, make it all happen. Look what we're doing now—building the Wild Willows. It's all possible, Michael. We can do this together. You and me. I'm depending on you, Michael. You're all I have.

Angelica and Josy and Mom can't take this now—
we've got to do for them." Cloe scanned Michael's
hard expression, his grim mouth, and the pulse throbbing in his temple. His demons were eating at him,
waiting to destroy him. Cloe moved close to him.
"You like closure? I'd like to finish one thing today,
Michael. . . ."

Tethered from what he wanted to do, needing to
satisfy his revenge, Michael's look at her was savage,
dark, impatient, cutting at her. "What's that?"

She touched his chest, his skin quivering to her
touch. "I'd like to finish that day in the barn—"

He stood very still, heart racing beneath her palms,
eyes wary as he slid his hand into his pocket and
withdrew a locket. Amid its coiled chain, the locket
gleamed in his dark, callused palm. "Only if you wear
this. I was going to give it to my sweetheart that day,
before you blindsided me. I wanted to give it to you.
I had big ideas back then, before you hurled that ball
at me."

In the dim light, the gold shimmered in his hand
and Cloe hesitated before running a fingertip over the
worn surface. "This was your mother's."

When he placed the necklace on her throat and fastened the clasp, she looked up into Michael's eyes and
through her tears caught the same tenderness all those
years ago, when she'd come prowling, hunting him.

"The wood for that bed was harvested when you
were sixteen, Cloe," Michael whispered huskily, as he
drew her close to him. She rested her cheek against
his, her hands pressing the locket close to her throat,
emotions skittering through her like gold dust. "I
missed you last night," he said, nuzzling her hair.

"I think we may have a problem," Cloe managed carefully, after images of years ago hurled through her mind. She eased away from him, shaking with emotion. *Michael had wanted her all those years ago* . . . "Let me get this straight," she said, pacing back and forth in the barn. "Years ago, I came after you—"

Michael leaned his shoulder against a stall. "You wanted me to take your troublesome virginity, as I remember. I had other plans that involved a church, vows, and a wedding night that gave me dreams no righteous man should have."

Cloe turned, stalked back to him, and planted her hands on her waist. "You. You had a master plan, right? And you didn't let me know—"

She snagged a whorl of hair on his chest and tugged. "You never said anything. You never asked me for a date . . . you never gave me flowers—" The image of the wildflowers by the bed slapped at her. *"Michael Jedidiah Bearclaw. You had your wedding night the other night and you did not inform me."*

He rubbed his jaw, suddenly aware that understanding Cloe was not always simple. "I thought you had the idea."

She threw out her hands. "What? What idea? When was I supposed to have gotten this marvelous idea?"

"Now that hurts. Sometime during our lovemaking—now, Cloe. . . . Take it easy. You're getting all worked up. You've got that look—" Michael warned, as Cloe's hands shot out to push him back into a haystack. He grabbed her wrists, taking her with him, laughing as he pinned her beneath him.

"Let me up. I want to murder you. Mmmft—" Cloe

twisted away from Michael's lips, bucking her hips against his.

Suddenly, Michael flipped over to his back, arms at his side. He grinned at her. "Go ahead. Murder me. It won't change anything. I had my wedding night. So far as I'm concerned, I'm a married man—"

"Married!" Cloe sat up, swatted the hay from her hair, and struggled to find logic.

Michael brushed a stalk across her cheek and down her throat to the locket. "Nothing has changed for me, Cloe. Not really," he said quietly. "You call it how you want."

A shadow crossed the sunlight skimming into the barn, and a woman's soft southern voice curled into the silence. "Why, Michael. How delightful."

"Howdy, Miz Magnolia," he drawled silkily, sensually.

Cloe took in the suit-clad, briefcase carrying beautiful woman standing near them. Long, smooth legs led up to a slender, fit body and a wealth of midnight black hair topped a perfect face. The unfamiliar emotion zinging through Cloe wasn't pleasant, and she recognized it as jealousy.

"Hello, Mary Lou." Michael stood up, hauling Cloe to her feet. "Mary Lou Beauregard, meet Cloe Matthews. Mary Lou is going to be staying with me—us." He glanced warily at Cloe before continuing, "She's a top attorney, an expert at settlements like these. We've worked together before."

"It's nice meeting you, Mary Lou," Cloe said, fighting to stay composed. Michael had just told her he'd waited for years for her, that he'd had his wedding night; she'd wanted to explore every word—"I'm not staying here tonight, Michael. Sorry. I'll just be going—"

"You can't. We need you to put this deal together. It could take all night. Mary Lou doesn't sleep well at night and she's highly creative then . . . just like you." He smiled innocently at Cloe's scowl, then Michael's tone changed, softened, warmed to intimacy. "You look good, Magnolia Blossom."

She laughed huskily. "And you look like you're feeling good. She's good for you, you handsome devil." Mary Lou kissed Cloe's cheek. "Michael and I go way back."

"That we do, darlin'," Michael agreed, hooking an arm around Cloe's waist and dragging her near to him. He glanced at her face, grinned, and hauled her up and over his shoulder, smacking her bottom lightly. "Why don't we go into the house and see just what we've got for this little party?"

"Write down everything you want to occur, Cloe. Make a real good list. We've got one time to do this right, and Michael tells me that you are up to what we need. Mark down the smallest whim and we'll make it happen. We'll get the bastards. We'll make them pay." Dressed in shorts and a T-shirt from The Pinto Bean, her hair in a ponytail, and her feet bare, Mary Lou did not look like a power attorney. She didn't look beautiful or polished; she had the hard look of a hunter, matching Michael's as they itemized Maggie Ten Feather's journal against the dates and facts Michael had compiled.

More than once, Michael and Mary Lou shared a long look, emotions passing between them, as Michael took her hand and she smiled weakly before pushing herself back into harness. During a break on the front porch, Mary Lou rocked and held Cloe's hand, as she scanned Lolo Valley. "It's beautiful here, just as Michael said. He's in love with you. That's such a precious gift from a man like him. I miss him. You're good for him. That cold, dark steel inside him eases when he looks at you. He didn't give up when the others did . . . when my babies were . . ."

Mary Lou's soft voice hardened. "When my babies were slaughtered. My little girls, only five and six—" She dashed the tears from her eyes and stared out into the night. "It was Michael who brought that fiend to justice and kept me from going to pieces. He needed me to track times, dates, the people I knew—Michael kept me together . . . he slept with me those first nights, holding me, rocking me. I don't know what I'd have done just then—yes, I do, and it wouldn't have been nice. I'd do anything for that man. You're a very lucky woman, Cloe, honey, because he's madly in love with you."

Cloe touched the locket he'd given her. Michael had waited all her growing-up years and she'd ruined both their lives. "I'm not ready for what Michael wants—"

Mary Lou rose to her feet, ready to go back to war. "Don't waste precious time, darlin'. Take what you can."

Grueling hours later, at one o'clock in the morning, Michael tugged Mary Lou to her feet and she leaned against him.

Cloe looked away, the sight too painful, as Michael rocked the other woman. She clung to him, her voice soft with tears. "I miss my babies, Michael. I can't sleep yet for the sight of them. I see those bloody footprints leading away from their poor little torn bodies—"

Michael looked at Cloe, his eyes haunted. "I know. Cloe will be sleeping in the bed next to you."

Those were the images that stirred Michael every night, and now Cloe understood his pain. . . .

In the Justice of the Peace's office, Sergei adjusted the bridal veil over Josy's face; the French peau de soie and lace did not soften her scowl. "I said I'd marry you tonight. I didn't agree to this designer gown shipped in from New York that cost more than my whole ranch. Stop fussing."

"Damn the florist for being closed. I should have broken a window and taken that bouquet—no dancing, no celebration . . . but I have you now and you are not getting away. If we make a child tonight, at least we will be married. How could I be a papa to a child and not marry the mother? It is not for the children we will have that I want to marry you, my heart, but for you alone. Are you wearing the garter?" Sergei asked.

Josy grabbed the yards of long skirt on the wedding gown and hitched it high to reveal a blue satin garter, long legs, and worn western boots. She dropped the gown. "Stuck my mother's favorite lace handkerchief in there for good luck."

"I have dreams of undressing my bride, slowly and with many kisses. I will kiss your legs and you will make love to me as my wife wearing the garter. As my wife, my heart, my life." Sergei, dressed in a tuxedo, straightened. He ran his hands through his curls, pushing them back. "I am nervous. I do not like it. You marry me because it is in your heart, yes?"

Josy realized that Sergei was as vulnerable now as she, fearing that she would not commit to a second marriage. If they could just get through the Justice of the Peace ceremony, she'd be more comfortable. She didn't want to remind Sergei that she'd been married before, in a hurried service, dressed in a cheap dress, and it had all been a mistake. Sergei wanted her to remember this ceremony, though it was hurried, the aftermath of his seduction. She'd been driven to the Justice of the Peace instantly and fully prepared, except for her shoes, which Sergei had carried in a large box from the truck. "I know how to rope a steer, flip him and tie him so he can't run away. You just try to run away now and I'll show you how good I really am."

He smiled that beautiful, devastating smile, looking elegant and foreign and as frightening as he was familiar. An hour ago, he'd been a fierce lover, demanding everything—Josy smiled softly up at him, suddenly shy. This gentle man wrapped in artistic and Russian temperament loved her. It shown in his black eyes, in the reverent way he touched her, loved her, as though she was a gift he hadn't expected in his life.

The Justice of the Peace, a short round man, hurried into the office. "Everything is in order. Paperwork complete. Ready?"

Sergei turned slowly from Josy, drawing himself to his full imposing height, scowling at the Justice of the

Peace, who blinked. "You want to get married, right?"

"You will marry us. You will do it now," Sergei said firmly, and then he turned to take Josy's hand in his. When the brief ceremony was complete, Sergei took Josy in his arms and lifted the veil from her face. He studied her intently, then with formal dedication, placed his lips lightly on hers. But she had seen the tears glittering on his lashes, the promise of heaven in his eyes.

He insisted on taking pictures of them with his self-timing camera, and forty-five minutes later, lying in the back seat of Sergei's car, amid yards of bridal satin and lace, his hand slid up Josy's thigh to find the garter. He smoothed her short black hair, his eyes glowing with tenderness. "You may keep the boots on. I cannot wait longer for my wife. I wanted to undress you slowly, but I am weak," he admitted ruefully, shuddering. "I cannot wait—you are my wife, my heart," he repeated as though tasting the words, stunned by them.

Josy ran her fingers over his face, loving him, this man who had tormented and torn her from pain, giving her joy. "I love you, Sergei."

"Of course. You would not marry me if you did not. What I see in your eyes humbles me. And I love you—" Sergei stopped, shuddering, the sensual heat pouring off him. "You remember that I promised to be a papa to your son, do you not? There are other things that I would tell you."

"Tell me now in that dark beautiful voice, while you're loving me. . . ."

*   *   *

Mary Lou slid into the bed beside Cloe. "I feel silly, but grateful. The alternative is sleeping pills, and medication ruins me the next day. We can't afford that time gap."

"You're more than welcome. You need your sleep. We all do. This seems sensible to me." Cloe glanced at Michael, who had just shot her a scowl.

On the other side of Cloe, Michael inhaled sharply when Cloe jabbed his ribs with her elbow. Taking her cue, he said, "You need your sleep. Uh!"

Topaz Jr. had just leaped onto the bed, landing firmly on Michael's manhood and prancing across Cloe to find the newcomer. Cooing with delight, Mary Lou was soon asleep, the kitten in her arms. Michael turned on his side, away from Cloe, and she curled to his back, looping her arm around him. Michael took her hand and drew it to his lips. She lifted slightly, eased over his shoulder to kiss him. "You're really a nice man," she whispered, before settling down, spooned to his back and tumbling into sleep.

In the morning, Cloe awoke slowly to Michael propped against the headboard, sipping his coffee. "I could get used to this service," he said.

Josy and Sergei sat on chairs near the bed, their stocking feet resting on it; Josy's rested comfortably on Sergei's larger ones. Cody watched the television in the next room.

Mary Lou slowly, beautifully awoke, a tangled raven haired confection, lying next to Cloe. "Are we havin' a party?" she asked in her soft drawl, as Sergei handed her a mug of coffee and Michael introduced them.

"Sergei cooked breakfast for all of us, and you're right, it is a party. We got married last night," Josy said, beaming at Cloe and extending Sergei's hand, where a wedding band gleamed. An intricate, feminine, and pricey wedding ring circled her finger.

Cloe's bottom lip began to tremble, tears shimmering in her eyes. "I wanted to be there. I wanted to—"

"You will be," Sergei noted sternly. "When it is time, there will be a proper ceremony, and pictures to remember, for our children. I want Josy to have a bridal shower, as is fitting. I want a church with vows for my woman. She should have this, not some—" he grumbled, before Josy took his head in her hands and kissed him thoroughly. Then Sergei grinned boyishly. "It is good enough for now. She is happy. I am happy."

"She's going to have everything, Sergei. So are you," Cloe promised, as tears streamed down her cheeks. "Everything. The full tamale."

"We should have candles and flowers and dancing and wine, and children should be there, too. My friends and my family will come."

Josy's eyes rounded. "Oh, no. I'm not going through that. I'd love to meet your friends and your family, but no one is stuffing me into that designer gown Sergei ordered again."

Sergei scowled at her. "You may wear your boots. I find I have a fondness for them and they are you. But—"

Josy scowled back at him, preparing to argue, and Cloe stepped in to prevent a full-scale war. "We'll see. There's Angelica to make happy, too. Do you think

she'd want to miss shoving us around? I just love you
guys!"

"Cloe, don't—" Michael held his mug of coffee
aloft and away from the bed as Cloe scampered across
him to hug Josy.

Michael scrubbed his face and shared a doomed
look with Sergei as Mary Lou softly informed them,
"I'm gonna cry."

"You're making me cry, gentlemen." Mary Lou's
crisp tone held no sympathy as she addressed Bradley
and Jeffrey Gilchrist in the bank's conference room.
"You have two choices. Comply with our list, meet
every obligation, cut yourself free of any connection
with Angelica. If she makes contact with you, that is
another matter. You will inform the rest of your ...
accomplices of the exact details of this agreement. The
alternative is not pretty, and you will—I promise
you—spend considerable time in the hoosegow. And
in the end, the Matthews family will get everything
that is coming to them and more, anyway. I do not
intend to fail, so help me God. You are leaving this
land, one way or another."

Cloe barely recognized the woman who slept like a
child beside her as Mary Lou listed the settlements,
the land that would be deeded to Dan and Gabe, the
Gilchrist fortunes sliced into bits, and the bank managed by Angelica.

"This is blackmail," Jeffrey began heatedly when
Bradley reached for the bottle in his desk drawer. Jeffrey removed his glasses and placed his glass of water
on a coaster.

"Blackmail? Shall I give you blackmail? Josy Small

Bird Cheslav's father knew about blackmail, didn't he?" Mary Lou battered Jeffrey. "Michael's expert word won't be questioned, if this comes to trial, and you make one wrong move, gentlemen, or any of your associates, and I will damn sure see that it does," Mary Lou continued.

"We'll . . . consider the package," Bradley muttered, after downing his bourbon. Jeffrey sat, crossed his legs, and glared at his father, hatred filling his expression. Michael stiffened slightly at Cloe's side, then smiled at Jeffrey coldly.

"Consider it? Yes, I would advise that." Mary Lou clicked her briefcase closed. "You have two hours. I will be at The Pinto Bean, helping with the luncheon menu. One call to anyone but Michael, Cloe, or me, and I will take that as a challenge, gentlemen. Do you understand me? Discussion closed."

Quinn stiffened, listened to the rhythms of the night, of Angelica's heart beating softly within his palm. The shadows had come to the trees, circling them, and the bear claw glistened, poised to strike. The fire-woman called forth her power—

The witches had ruined everything and another one had joined their coven, all servicing Michael Bearclaw. That hot-mouthed southern lawyer woman would pay slowly for threatening The Club, demanding that they leave Lolo and reside in another state with barely enough funds to keep them out of bankruptcy. Bradley Gilchrist was too weak, and now it was time to take control of The Club. He positioned his body on the ground, finding Michael Bearclaw in his rifle's scope. Minus one forensic expert and the witches, all in one night, and The Club—he squeezed slightly on the trigger as Michael strolled through the pasture at dusk, surveying his land. "Gloating over your little victory, are you? Gloat over this—"

The shot hit the ground ten feet away from Michael. "Perfect," he said. He turned and began running straight toward the shooter as the shots peppered the ground on his left side. He ran to the edge of the pasture, stepped behind a tree, and let the shadows envelope him.

"Michael!" Cloe's frightened cry stopped him, and then, as she hurled herself toward the rocky ground above the ranchhouse, Michael pushed himself harder, fearing for her. He ran through the striplings, hunting, seeking the man who ran from him, footprints in the forest rubble, crashing wildly through the brush as he turned to use his handgun.

The intruder backed against a tree, throwing his empty gun at Michael, who slowly crossed the clearing. He smiled coldly at the man cowering before him. "Why, Jeffrey. How nice of you to visit."

Cursing, Jeffrey swung at Michael, who blocked the blow. "Is that how you hit Ann, Jeffrey?" Michael asked, and tapped Jeffrey lightly with a right punch. And again. "You know, I like the feel of this—"

Cloe sailed into Michael's back, holding his arms. "Don't, Michael."

Violence coiled through Michael's tall hard body. "He murdered Roy—didn't you, Jeffrey?"

Jeffrey was babbling now, blood running down his chin as Michael slapped him hard.

"Michael, don't—oh, please don't. I love you, Michael. I always have," Cloe cried, digging her fingers into his arm.

She stroked his cheek, smoothed his hair, and slowly Michael pulled himself back. "You picked a fine time to tell me," he said huskily.

She slapped his back. "He could have hit you."

"Nope. He's off on the right. I've noticed that when he wasn't wearing his glasses, he couldn't set a drink glass down on a coaster . . . missed it to the right. The scars on his ankle are from Nimo. The dog didn't die easy."

He glanced down at her torn clothing and shook his head. "Cloe, your knees and hands are scraped. You look like you did when you fell off that bike and I bandaged you."

Cloe peered closer to the tree behind Jeffrey's head. "Michael, someone has carved a heart and our initials on that tree."

"I had to do something while I was waiting all those years, honey."

Gilchrist House blazed against the cold September night, flames escaping through the windows. Angelica stood, legs braced, outlined in the firelight. With orders to let the house burn to the ground, the fire department stood ready. When the house crumbled, Angelica finally turned away, tears streaking her face. Her shoulders were straight, her head high, and her eyes soft upon the man she loved. "Take me home, Quinn."

She slid into Quinn's pickup without a backward glance at the burning house. Shortly after Jeffrey had been sentenced to prison, Ann had filed for divorce.

Ann, a timid woman, had taken courage from Cloe and would be the Wild Willows Health and Beauty Spa's new accountant.

Angelica leaned her head on Quinn's shoulder, anxious to be in his arms in the small mountain home he had purchased. There, with Quinn's heart beating against her own, she could cry openly, shedding yesterday's fears and revenge. With Quinn, she was clean and new and loved, and tonight he would sing his courting songs and she would hold him forever.

Under Michael's cold, relentless pursuit, the bank had been turned over to her—until new officers took charge. Before moving to Florida, the Gilchrists had provided Dan and Gabe with the title to the old Matthews ranch, the mortgage paid.

Angelica rolled down the pickup window, letting the icy wind cleanse her. She was drained emotionally. Only the tremendous effort of getting the Wild Willows Spa up and running at the last of the month had kept her going. Josy and Cloe needed her, just as she needed them. Up on Bearclaw Ridge, the first level of the spa was almost complete.

Her parents were gone now, with Judge Lang and the rest, in only a heartbeat, and all of the change was silent, guided by Michael. Uprooted from the land they ruled, The Club would not be back. "It was all so wrong," she whispered to Quinn.

"It's done. The Wild Willows have built something new and good. Cloe was right to separate it from revenge. You are free."

She turned to him. "How do you know?"

"Because tonight we are going to have a ceremony, putting the past behind us."

Angelica scanned the moonlit scenery. "We're not going to the house."

"No. I have horses waiting. Open the package behind you."

Angelica eased the package from behind the seat and opened it slowly. The doeskin shift was new and soft beneath her fingers. "It's lovely."

Quinn placed his hand over hers. "For our marriage ceremony . . . tonight . . . in the old place . . . if you will have me. I would take you tonight as my wife, the woman of my heart."

Angelica held his hand tightly, for when Quinn spoke in the old-fashioned way, his emotions ran deep. She caressed his cheek and whispered, "Sweetheart," just to watch the endearing blush rise beneath his dark complexion.

Epilogue

&

"INTRODUCING THE WILD Willows Health and Beauty Spa," Cloe whispered in awe. Angelica, Cloe, and Josy stood, looking up at Bearclaw Ridge and the new, unfinished structure jutting from it. Sundown shone gold in the huge windows that overlooked Lolo Valley and the clear-water stream that Sam Matthews had fought to protect.

In the dusk, after a hard day of preparing for the first ten guests, they'd come to view what they had created. They held hands, women who had been friends since childhood, who had met tragedies and sorrow and who had survived and found happiness.

"All new," Angelica said, as if disbelieving the past had been torn away.

"We did it. Cloe did it," Josy murmured, Sergei's red merino shawl wrapped snugly around her.

"*We* did this. All of us."

"People are actually paying money to come here. To walk on the trails, to ride horses, to—"

"To find peace," Cloe finished for Josy, who had borne so much pain and was now thriving.

Angelica tipped her head, studying the first phase critically. "Beats the rickety clubhouse down by the cottonwoods, but it's a little late. Quinn is really good at massages and he's working on pedicures, but if you say anything I'll kill you. He gets embarrassed—it's that man-thing."

"Sergei thinks we should all three get married at Wild Willows. He's still grumping about the civil ceremony."

"I'm game," Angelica said. "It's up to Cloe, but it better be quick. Josy's got a little Russian on the way."

"November. We'll be on schedule this time. Angelica, keep us under budget. Keep in mind that I'll be using the weddings as promotion for a wedding chapel idea later on. We'll send out flyers right away. I want lace, greenery, lots of catalog products stashed around, happy guests, and Josy, you'll have wear that long lace gown . . . Sergei will need to shoot—"

"Doesn't she ever stop?" Angelica asked with a grin. "Let's bask in our success before we have to start work tomorrow morning, and find out about reality, okay?"

They looped their arms around each other, marveling at their creation. Then Josy turned to Cloe. "We made it, but is this enough for you?"

Her friends wanted her happy, if she stayed or left them. "I've found my challenge. Michael has been too patient and understanding, too perfect while we worked ourselves to the bone on this project. He stayed right with us, so did Sergei and Quinn. I've sorted my feelings about myself and none of it was easily, and I know who I am and what I want. He terrified me when he caught Jeffrey, and he was a man I didn't know. I think I know him now, but I truly hate patient and understanding. Do you know that I told him I loved him, and he hasn't said anything about that, except 'You picked a fine time'?"

"You may have to spend some time on this project, Cloe," Angelica singsonged. "You know, product development and marketing? Er . . . packaging? Michael hasn't seen you in anything but jeans and sweatshirts for months. You order him—us—around like a general massing troops."

Josy patted Angelica's shoulder. "Angelica got a little miffed at times, but—"

" 'Miffed'? Where were you when we were yelling at each other an hour ago? Who needs a peacemaker now?" Angelica shot back easily. "You know, if we have kids, we'll be the Godmothers, not the Wild Willows."

"You two like to teethe on each other, sharpening your claws. I've never understood it, but it works. Neither one of you holds grudges—"

Cloe looked at Josy and at Angelica, each absolutely happy. They made her happy just looking at them, eyes glowing, a new softness enveloping them. They were hers and they were happy. "I love you guys."

Cloe leaned into the shadows of the barn, watching Michael pour grain into the trough for the horses in the corral. On impulse, she'd hurried to the florist and purchased a rose bouquet, and now the scent mixed with the animals and hay. He turned, found her, and took off his gloves.

He'd been working on a new case, the shadows sometimes curling around him. Michael's talent ran to hunting and to details, and whomever he was seeking, he'd find. His silence at times said his moods ran deep, to regret that he hadn't returned sooner, that he hadn't done more.

He stood there waiting for her, the same every night, waiting, as if he feared she wouldn't come to him. Cloe placed her fingertips on the locket, and prayed Michael would understand as she walked toward him, shedding her clothes, until she stood before him, wearing only the locket. She cradled his angular face in her hand, feeling the bones beneath his weathered skin, watching the fire in his gold eyes begin to glow as his hands settled upon her waist. He trembled, she realized, his fingers too light upon her. This man was her heart, her life, her air, and her temptation.

Michael Jedidiah Bearclaw. He'd built her a marriage bed . . . he'd never stray . . . he'd torment and love her with all his heart, and all the tomorrows would be theirs. She would be his comfort and his strength, and they would grow old together.

"This is the first time I've ever given a bouquet to a man, Michael Bearclaw."

He lowered his face to nuzzle the roses. "This is the first time a woman has ever given me flowers."

"You're a very special man who deserves lots of them. I think we could save a florist's bill by planting roses by the front porch. Because if this is how you're going to look at me, I'm doing this again. . . ."

She moved against him, let his arms tenderly enfold

her as Michael asked, "Have you come for me, sweet-heart?"

She stood on tiptoe to gently bite the scar she'd given him long ago. "We're in the same barn as all those years ago—"